There was only one way out of the Legion...and if she couldn't pull this off, she was dead.

Joan sensed the hesitation in Duncan. "Is there something I should know?"

"What do you mean?"

"Something isn't right. You're up to something. I can feel it."

Duncan stood up to get closer to her. He put one arm on the back of her stool the other on the bar. "I told you I would never lie to you." He nodded to the bartender for two more shots. "I'm getting the same feeling about you. Something's going on with you, too. We need to put everything out on the table. We have to clear this up tonight." He accented the word "tonight" by tapping his index finger on the bar.

Joan wanted to tell Duncan everything, but she knew she could tell him absolutely nothing. "I'm sorry, Duncan, if I've caused everyone grief. I guess my relationship with the Legion is like my relationships with men—push/pull. When I feel like circumstances are closing in on me I push away. When I feel like I have too much space, I start pulling everything back. It's just the way I am." She hoped her explanation was believable.

Duncan moved his hand from the bar to her thigh. He was distracted. The tequila and the wine at dinner were making it hard to focus on the task at hand. "That's how you are with men, huh?"

"I pushed you away for months, then when I thought you were pulling away, I pulled you in."

"Yes, you did." He thought back to the first time they were together. "And you think you can push me away now that we're...we've..."

"Think? I know I can. It's what I do."

He was distracted. Good. She just might get out of this evening alive.

Following a worldwide economic collapse, a tyrannical administration has taken control of the United States government and nullified the Constitution. Joan Bowman, a highly skilled veteran and patriot, joins an underground resistance group to restore America's beloved freedoms. Too late, she realizes that the group she so idealistically joined is just as corrupt as the administration in Washington. However, since she knows too much to ever leave the group alive, she turns State's evidence. But when the task force demands she go back to the group to obtain one last piece of crucial information, Joan knows she faces certain death. Dispirited, exhausted, and paranoid, she's hardly on top of her game—and she needs to be or, this time, she'll pay with her life.

ACKNOWLEDGEMENTS

I want to thank the members, past and present, of the Critique Group North—you know who you are. Although this book was not submitted to my critique group, I took what I learned from them and made the edits and revisions as my craft improved. I have no reservations in saying that the writer I am today is a direct result of their lovingly harsh corrections and suggestions. But I especially thank my beta readers: Jan, Nancy and Susan.

Like most writers, I have very little knowledge of the basics of interrogation and police procedures. I would have been far outside the realm of reality without the direction of Kim & Kevin, who are accomplished interrogators in their own right (as well as family members.) David and Kathy were instrumental in showing me certain police procedures.

Mr. Bradley J. Steiner took time out of his busy schedule of teaching martial arts and writing to look over one of the fight scenes. His confirmation that I got it right was invaluable in affirming my knowledge of counter-attacks and fighting in general.

I have to mention my boss at my bread-and-butter job, Canon Jim, who gave me time off to attend the meeting with my critique group, fully confident that I wasn't blowing off work to screw around. And more importantly, he patiently pretended to listen as I babbled on about scenes of which I was particularly proud. God bless you. Your support was instrumental in the journey to publication.

Of course, I must thank Black Opal Books for giving me an opportunity to tell Joan Bowman's story. Those thanks include Faith, my editor, who edited the crap out of my manuscript. She kept my story on track and my characters in line. Thank you for all your kind words, moral support, and the commas. You know what I'm talking about.

WORST OF ALL EVILS

JANET MCCLINTOCK

A Black Opal Books Publication

Black Opal Books

BECAUSE SOME STORIES JUST HAVE TO BE TOLD

GENRE: THRILLER/SUSPENSE

This is a work of fiction. Names, places, characters and incidents are either the product of the author's imagination or are used fictitiously, and any resemblance to any actual persons, living or dead, businesses, organizations, events or locales is entirely coincidental. All trademarks, service marks, registered trademarks, and registered service marks are the property of their respective owners and are used herein for identification purposes only. The publisher does not have any control over or assume any responsibility for author or third-party websites or their contents.

I dedicate this book to my twelfth-grade English teacher, Mr. Paul Paparella, who planted the seed to be a writer. I never forgot your words, Mr. Pap. It may have taken a few decades to germinate, but when it did, Worst of All Evils was born. Thank you for believing in me all those years ago.

INTRODUCTION

When I enlisted in the US Army, I took an oath to defend the Constitution from all enemies foreign and domestic. The question at first was: is the oath for the term of service or forever? Once I decided it was forever, I asked myself what I would do if a tyrannical administration in Washington, D.C. voided the Constitution. What came forth was Joan Bowman's story.

Joan's story is a metaphor for the lives of all of us. We all have to make decisions, depending on what has a grip on our lives. Hopefully, we will never have to make *her* decisions.

"Live free..."

What's interfering with your freedom? For Joan Bowman it is the new political system in Washington, D.C. But it doesn't have to be something as wide-sweeping as a political system, culture norms or economic policies. It can be an abusive relationship, addiction to drugs, a gambling habit or mental illness that is treatable with medication. It can be as individual as overspending or hoarding or being trapped in a job you hate. Only you know what it is.

"...or die."

The lifestyle that is causing stress for you and those around you will be the death of you—not necessarily physical death. It can be emotional, psychological or professional death, as well. It can tear apart your family or alienate your friends. For Joan, it is death to her sense of honor. She believes the oath she took was forever, not limited to her time serving her country. When a tyrannical administration comes to power, it ignores the US Constitution and Bill of Rights. Joan feels obligated to do something, or her honor will be tarnished, her dignity assaulted. She joins an underground resistance group called the Constitution Defense Legion, believing it is the honorable thing to do.

"Death is not the worst of all evils."

What can be worse than death? Fearing an abusive spouse. Needing the next fix. The disappointment in a loved one's eyes after a gambling binge. Mental illness before the welcome relief of medication. For Joan Bowman joining the Constitution Defense Legion turns out to be a mistake that is worse than all evils, including, but not limited to, torture at the hands of fellow members of the Legion. And it just gets worse from there.

CHAPTER 1

The woods went silent.

It felt like her heart was pounding against the moss under her belly as Joan squeezed and released the grip on her M-16 semi-automatic rifle. She scanned the surrounding undergrowth.

Jason tapped her shoulder and pointed to her right. "Seventy-five yards at our two," he whispered. "The oak with two notches. The notch on the left."

"How did they get so close without us seeing them?" she said as she zeroed in on the double-notched tree.

"They're shape-shifters, man."

Joan pressed the rifle butt against her shoulder and snuggled her cheek against the stock so she could see down the barrel. In a measured movement, she raised the rifle until the notch of the tree was centered in her sights. "I'll shift their shapes for 'em," she said.

Jason reached with his tattooed hand and pressed down on the barrel of her M-16. "Let's go down the other side of this hill and slip away. No sense getting shot when the exercise is almost over."

"We can take them."

"Ever get hit with a round of simu-nition? It hurts like a mother—"

A twig snapped to their right.

Jason snatched the back of Joan's shirt and jerked her upright. "Let's go. Now."

Joan planted her feet, tightened the band on her brunette

ponytail, and glanced over her shoulder toward the sound. "I'm a fighter. Fighters stand their ground," she said, but Jason had disappeared through the nearby stand of mountain laurel. "*Shit!*" she whispered through clenched teeth.

She took a quick glance in the direction of the OPFOR—or opposing forces—who were shouting to each other in the woods behind her—and took off down the game trail. In less than twenty yards, she stumbled when her toe snagged a tree root, throwing her forward. A dull *thunk* filled her head as her temple slammed into a rock.

Pain clamped around her head like a vise. On her knees, holding her head with both hands, Joan squinted through the pain, trying to locate her rifle. Her thoughts slogged along as if through hair gel and the muffled yells of the OPFOR searching for her and Jason filtered through. The sounds of the ongoing pursuit tripped a switch, kicking in her survival instincts.

Joan struggled to her feet. The ground under her boots felt wonky, as if it were fluid. On her feet and reeling, Joan shook her head to widen her field of vision. Pain shot down the side of her face. Through the haze, she spied her rifle and leaned forward to grab it. The earth rolled and tilted away from her. She lurched past her rifle as her feet tried to keep up. Then she felt it—the burning sting of a bullet. She grabbed her right butt cheek and fell to her knees.

Dammit! She dropped to her left hip.

It wasn't a real bullet. Joan knew that. But being hit by a Simu-nition round was as close to being hit by a real bullet as possible without damage to the body.

"That'll leave a mark," she grumbled under her breath.

Trained to the point of perfection, she wasn't sure which hurt more, her buttocks or her pride. She got to her knees and snatched the sling on her rifle. Before she could get to her feet, a strong hand grabbed the back of her shirt and propelled her down the trail. One look over her right shoulder and all the anxiety, aggression, and fear of the previous several hours drained from her system and congealed in her stomach. It was Duncan.

"The first time I met you, I knew you were trouble and I'd have to save your ass," he said.

Joan looked up into Duncan's direct, unflinching eyes

framed by battle-hardened lines. "If I'm too much trouble, put me down. I can make it on my own."

The throaty response might have meant disbelief, but she didn't have time to think about it. Something changed. At first, Joan couldn't put her finger on it. Everything beyond her breathing was still muffled. She exhaled—the shooting had stopped. No more yelling. The exercise was over.

Thank God.

Duncan half-carried her the last thirty yards to the spot in the game trail where Jason was retracing his steps to find her.

"Isn't she supposed to be with you?" Duncan asked as he released his hold on Joan with a slight push in Jason's direction.

"She was right behind me," Jason replied, "but when I looked back..." His voice trailed off when he realized Duncan had vanished.

Jason then took a good look at Joan. "Holy, shi—i—moley."

Joan's field of vision was clearing and widening, but her head was pounding. She pulled the camouflage-colored kerchief from around her neck, patted the side of her head. She looked at her kerchief. "Damn. I'm bleeding. Is it bad?"

"Nah, a little make-up and you'll be fine," Jason lied.

Silently wishing for the pounding to stop, she eyed the pinhole scars from piercings, the rings long gone. A tattoo peeked at her from the edge of his collar. She was told he was former Marine Recon.

Wondering what happened for him to pierce and ink himself up, she watched as he took his khaki-colored scarf from around his neck and folded it to form a makeshift bandage.

"So, what are you bringing to the Legion?" he asked.

"What do you mean?"

"You're ex-military, for sure. Army? Marines?"

Before Joan could answer, a voice penetrated the forest. Murphy, their team leader, shouted for everyone to move out.

"We're moving to the rendezvous point for our ride." Jason ducked his head a little so they were eye-to-eye. "You gonna be okay?" Without waiting for an answer, he grabbed her kerchief from her hand and used it to secure his makeshift bandage to the side of her face. "There. You look better already."

Her eyes narrowed from the splitting headache, Joan glared at him. "Funny. I don't feel better already." She shifted the sling on her shoulder. "Let's go. It'll take more than a rock to the head to keep me down."

With the jarring from every step sending lightning bolts of pain to her temple, she followed Jason down the trail to the rendezvous point. The sky spit snowflakes into their faces. The wind kicked up and the autumn leaves, mixed with the icy flakes, slapped into them.

"This has ceased to be fun," she said.

"Roger that."

CHAPTER 2

Joan hesitated with her hand on the doorknob of the clap-board cabin used as the field office of the Constitution De-fense Legion. The leadership had asked her to meet with them before she headed back to Pittsburgh. As she took a deep breath of the raw November air, she braced herself for disappointment.

All her training in martial arts, the hours at the gym, her military background all led her to this weekend with the CDL. She was more than good enough for this group, but she had made a mistake...or three. She had managed to take a bullet, fall and hit her head, and get separated from her battle buddy. She pressed her eyelids together. A simple "We regret to inform you..." note would have been better. That way she wouldn't have to face her shortcomings around strangers.

With one last breath to clear her head, Joan straightened her posture, turned the knob, and entered the makeshift office.

The only sounds were the squeak of her hiking boots on the rough-hewn wooden floor and the crackle of the fire in the fire-place. As she crossed the floor with graceful, leonine confidence, she tried to read the faces of the four camouflage-clad men as she approached them. They all stared at her swollen, half-shut eye. She knew three of the four men. It was the man she did not know who spoke first.

"How's your head?" The man pointed to the empty chair closest to the fire. His blue eyes and sharp features hinted at German heritage. But the long, dark-brown hair tucked behind his ears indicated something else. Joan guessed Native American. His smile was relaxed and comforting.

"It looks worse than it feels," she lied as she slid gently into the chair, avoiding the purple bruise on her right butt cheek.

Duncan started the ball rolling. "This is Pallaton," he said pointing to the man who had just spoken. "He's the captain of the area that includes Pittsburgh. You know Travis and Murphy."

Travis was the recruiter for the group, and the one who brought her to the attention of the CDL leadership. Murphy had been her team leader the day before.

Well, the gang's all here. Let's get this over with.

"We've discussed your performance this weekend, and we all agree that we like what we've seen," Duncan continued. "I know you were recruited just to provide a house for a base of operations, but we think you have what it takes to do more."

Reality trumped her expectations. It took a while to sink in.

"Maybe you're not interested in doing more," Duncan said.

Joan found her voice. "What do you mean by 'do more'?"

"Be an operative. You have skills the Legion can use," Duncan said. He was not the leader of the CDL, but as the Operations and Security Officer, he had the power to hire and fire.

"But I got shot."

Blank stares greeted her statement.

She pointed to the side of her face. "I got injured."

"That was an accident. I'd say it could happen to any of us." Duncan looked around at the men in the room then continued with a slight upturn to the corner of his mouth. "But in reality, it probably wouldn't."

Joan controlled the urge to fidget, unsure of what to say, unnerved by this unexpected affirmation of her abilities.

With no response from Joan, Duncan continued, "We see promise in you. Your part won't be anything big at first. You have to walk before you can run...no pun intended." After scrutiny of her bruised face, he added, "Did you put the ice on that?"

"All night."

"Make sure you see a doctor tomorrow."

"I plan to."

"What are you going to tell the doctor?" Travis asked. He

had the typical slender but muscular build of a personal trainer. His sandy-colored, curly hair was cut short to keep it under control. Joan had met him at the gym, and they quickly became friends. The rest was history.

"I'll tell him I was at The Woods training with the CDL."

The Woods was the training site for the Constitution Defense Legion, a group dedicated to restoring the Constitution. After the economic collapse two years earlier, the current tyrannical regime came to power. Elected by people desperate for help, the government promised economic recovery, but their intent was power. Power for the few at the expense of the struggling citizens. Newly elected administration disregarded the Constitution and the Bill of Rights. Actions not acceptable to veterans, police officers, and patriots.

"If you think this is a joking matter, maybe this is not for you." Duncan shot her a searing glare. "This is serious business. We have to trust that we are all equally resolute about our mission."

Joan had been warned about Duncan and his menacing disposition that seemed to intimidate everyone she met. *Give it your best shot, buster. I've been to Iraq and back. It's gonna take more than a glaring look from some man I've met once to make me tremble.*

She leaned forward in her chair and rested her elbows on her thighs. "I'll tell my doctor I tripped while extreme running in Raccoon State Park."

"Extreme running, what's that?" he asked.

"It's when you leave the trail and dead reckon through the woods to get to another point. It's like land navigation, except you do it on the run."

"We did that in Special Forces, except we didn't have a fancy name for it." Duncan's eyes narrowed. "I've never heard of doing it for fun."

Joan sat still and confident under his stare, knowing he was waiting for her response. Her silence dismissed his comment. She smiled inwardly when he mirrored her body language and put his elbows on his thighs.

"And your doctor will buy your story?" Murphy asked.

Without taking her eyes off Duncan's, Joan nodded. "I've

been to my doctor before for other injuries from extreme running. He'll buy it."

"Other injuries," Duncan mused. "Then you're clumsy..."

She leaned back, crossed her arms, and answered him with a quiet calm. "No, I just train hard."

Duncan leaned back in his chair. Joan could feel him studying every detail—her face, her build, her body language.

Travis leaned toward Duncan. She heard him whisper, "I told you. She is a primo recruit."

Duncan scowled at Travis, who sat back in his chair and cleared his throat. She looked from Travis to Duncan. If this meet and greet wasn't so important, it would be amusing.

"Tell us why you joined the Legion," Duncan said.

She shifted slightly to relieve the pressure on her bruised butt. "When I joined the Army I took an oath to defend the Constitution, and I believe an oath is forever. The tyrants in Washington have trashed the Constitution and the Bill of Rights. My oath obligates me to not only defend it, but to restore it. It's my duty."

Certain Duncan was about to jump in, she changed the direction of her answer. "They control energy, banking, most manufacturing, and the media. When they passed Proposition 510, they seized control of food production and transportation. I knew then what would happen, and sure enough, it's happening right before our eyes. The states that supported President King and were instrumental in getting him elected get the lion's share of the food. The other states be damned."

The men were listening, but Joan couldn't tell if they were interested. She decided to wrap up her response. "When those bastards instituted what is basically Martial Law, it was the last straw. I knew I had to do something. As Edmund Burk once said, 'The only thing necessary for the triumph of evil is for good men to do nothing.' I knew I couldn't do nothing. Travis recruited me, and here I am."

"Is that all?" The corners of Duncan's eyes crinkled slightly. Joan watched the expressions on the faces of the other men at the unexpected joke.

Duncan continued his questioning. "So what do you see as your role in the Legion?"

"Whatever you want me to do—I'm in."

"Spoken like a true soldier, and I can appreciate that, but I want to get an idea of what *you* see as your role here," he said.

"I can drive anything with two wheels to eighteen wheels. My bomb making and handling skills are zero, so that's out. Years of martial arts training has given me the ability to recognize strengths and weaknesses in an enemy, so I guess, I could do surveillance and provide security for the operatives."

"You guess? Are you hesitant or humble?"

Joan locked eyes with him. The offer to be an operative had renewed her self-confidence, and she was ready for a war of wits—even with Duncan. "I'm talking off the top of my head here. With some thought I'm sure I could come up with a better answer." She took in his reddish-brown curly hair, his blue eyes, his muscularity.

If Duncan was feared because of political clout he held over others, twenty years in the Army had trained her well in the art of political infighting. If it was a physical threat he posed, with twenty-five years of training in three martial arts, she felt confident she could take him down. He was well-built and had a quick agility unusual for such a muscular man. But she was muscular, too...and even more agile. He would be a formidable opponent, but he would go down.

Pallaton was uneasy with the power play between Joan and Duncan. "So, how about it? Do you think you have what it takes to do more?"

Joan broke her gaze from Duncan and looked first at Pallaton then each of the others. "I do."

"We do, too." Murphy hesitated a few seconds then added, "C'mon, you can't tell me you didn't think about being an operative before now."

"Actually, yesterday I was enjoying the exercise and was actually wondering about the possibility, until—" Joan waved to indicate the side of her face. "The feel of the M-16 in my hands, training in the woods, it brought back memories. I thought I blew it when I had to be rescued."

Her eyes flicked to Duncan then quickly turned to Murphy when he started to speak.

"We all make mistakes at some time or another. It's what

you do afterward that makes the difference. You recovered quickly and without so much as a whimper, drove on. I'll bet you never thought of quitting. Am I right?"

"No—I mean, yes, you're right, and no, I didn't think of quitting."

Duncan squinted at Joan for a long minute that would have made anyone else uneasy. There was silence except for the crackling and popping of the fire. Joan looked from one to the other not showing the discomfort they expected. Without taking his eyes off her, Duncan pulled a folded sheet of paper from the front pocket of his shirt and handed it to her.

On it was a graphic of a bleeding heart wrapped in thorns. Above the heart was a banner that said, "Live Free or Die."

"You'll need this when you go to the tattoo shop on Neville Island," he said. "Every member gets that tattoo. It's used as a way for operatives to recognize each other as well as a way to recognize imposters."

"Great! I always wanted to get a tattoo," she replied without hesitation.

"But you already have a tattoo." Duncan said.

"No, I don't." She was sure he had no way of knowing there was a tattoo of a heart with wings and a banner that said "Psalm 119:11" on her left calf. If Duncan wanted to play at bluffing, she was determined to go him one better.

They all stood up.

Murphy offered his hand first. "Welcome aboard."

Travis shook her hand, then Pallaton.

Duncan stepped forward into Joan's personal space in one last act of intimidation. "You'll have to learn to take care of yourself. I won't always be there if you trip up." He was stone-faced when he shook her hand with a firm almost bone-crushing grip. Joan firmly shook his hand back and tried to sense if he was joking.

As she turned to leave the room Duncan added, "I want to check out your eye and face before you leave. Wait in the bunk-house."

Joan waved in acknowledgement without turning around and walked out of the room with no visible emotion. She was in shock and the emotions ranging from elation to dread had not broken through yet. She used her good eye to carefully navigate the steps and stopped at the bottom to take in a long breath of cool fresh air and look around this place the Legion called The Woods. She was wondering how much time she would be spending here in the future.

 especo

When the door closed, Duncan said to Travis, "I'm impressed. Her bluff about not having a tattoo was convincing. I would have believed her if I hadn't seen it when I was at the gym talking to you. She wasn't overly aggressive, she was unruffled, she didn't blush, she didn't hesitate. With proper grooming, she could become a true revolutionary. Good job, Travis."

Travis smiled. "As strange as it sounds, I noticed her precisely because she is a relatively unnoticeable brunette. Not too tall, not too short, not too skinny, not too fat, not too pretty, not too plain. She's strong, fit, and smart. *And* she's a church secretary—who would ever suspect a church secretary of belonging to an underground resistance group?"

"So, she's a church secretary that can rip a phone book in half then shove it up your ass?" Pallaton piped in.

"Yep," Travis replied.

"And she's going to be on your team, Murphy," Pallaton added. "Think you'll be able to handle her?"

Murphy rubbed the stubble on his chin with the back of his fingers. "I'll handle her."

Duncan sat down and propped his feet on the chair Joan had just vacated. "I'm glad I didn't have to kill her that night when I checked out the viability of her house being a safe house. Remember, Travis?"

"Yeah, you started checking her house and she started to express doubts about her decision to join the CDL. I heard you pull your gun out of our holster and I knew I had to do something."

"She had passed the point of no return. If you hadn't talked her back from the ledge, we wouldn't have this great addition to our movement." Duncan shook his head. "Damn, what a waste that would have been, right guys?"

Everyone nodded.

They all watched the fire as it whirred and popped, lost in their own thoughts. After several minutes, Duncan stood up.

"Well, I'm sure Joan wants to be on her way home," he said, "so if we're done here, I want to go check out her head and eye."

"You never took an interest in anyone else who got injured on one of our training weekends." Murphy said.

"It's her first weekend with us. We don't want her to leave here thinking we're cold and uncaring, do we?"

℮⁊℮⁊

Everyone except Joan scattered when Duncan entered the bunkhouse.

"Why is everyone so afraid of you?" she asked, looking over her shoulder to see where everybody went.

He sat on the bunk beside her and moved her head to get a better look at her injury. "You aren't afraid of me." It was more a statement than a question.

She liked his style. "Should I be?"

Without comment, he cleaned her wound with alcohol. Joan didn't wince. She was not going to give him the satisfaction.

"I know this has to hurt," he said.

"You know what they say—no pain, no brain," she quipped.

Duncan gave an almost inaudible *hmph* and, without even a shadow of a smile, he disinfected and bandaged her bruise. "Here's an ice pack." He turned his attention to the rest of her face, and she flinched as he pressed on the puffy tissue. "So you do feel pain." He handed her a second ice pack. "Really, Joan, why did you join the Legion?"

"The America today is not the same America I joined the Army to defend. I want to bring that America back."

Her left eye was so swollen there was only a slit. He pried apart the eyelids and shined a light in her eyes to check her pupils.

"You have some broken blood vessels." As if satisfied with

what he saw, he continued the conversation. "You must have some ulterior motive. Everyone does."

"I'm not 'everyone' and, besides, what ulterior motives could there be? This is a straight-forward group, with a straight-forward mission, and I'm a straight-forward person."

"I'm used to women who join the Legion either because their man is a member, or they want to shoot guns and meet a man. Some want to have a rough and tumble activity entirely different from their everyday life. But you aren't like that. I can't figure out your angle."

"You vetted me, so you know I go to the target range at least twice a month and I'm trained in Krav Maga, American Combato, and Jun Fan Gung Fu, so I get enough—" She emphasized the next three words. "—*rough and tumble*. And did you find a man in my life?"

"No, but maybe that's it. Maybe you're lonely."

"I don't have time to be lonely, and I don't have time for a man. I work, workout at the gym and train. That's my life. That's the way I like it."

"That's about to change. You're okay with that?"

"Yeah, I'm okay with that."

Duncan finished his initial evaluation of her injuries and started putting away his medical supplies. "So then your real reason is, what?"

"To serve my country—the country I grew up in. The America I swore to defend."

"That's it?"

"Should there be more?"

"Not necessarily."

"Can I ask you a question?" Duncan just looked at her. "That night at my house, were you really going to shoot me if I backed out?"

He paused for a split second. She squinted at him trying to read his face. When Duncan came to her house to check it out to be a safe house, he had been intense, gruff, and bristling with weapons. She still wasn't sure what had made her question her decision, but when she heard him pull his Glock from his holster, the reality sunk into her consciousness. She decided to go ahead with the plan, not because her life was on the line, but because of the adrenaline dump. The exhilaration of coming within inches of death, and surviving. It was a high she hadn't experienced since her return from Iraq. A high she hadn't realized she missed.

Duncan tried to change the subject. "Any pain in your neck or shoulders?"

"No." Joan was not going to let him off the hook. "I mean you had your gun out of your holster. Would you have shot me if I backed out?"

Duncan exhaled slightly. "Yes."

Joan was really liking his style—few words, and all business and not afraid to tell the truth even if it might…what?…scare her?

She pushed forward. "You didn't answer my question."

"Yes, I did." He stood up and put his medic bag over his shoulder.

"No the other one: should I be afraid of you?"

Duncan stopped in the open doorway. Without turning around, he said in a hoarse whisper, "Yes."

ↁↁↁ

"Hey, Kiddo, I just saw Duncan leave. Ready to go?" Travis was standing in the doorway of the bunkhouse that Duncan had just vacated. "You are in, Kiddo. I knew you'd make the grade. And I'm not at all surprised that it was so quick. So, how does it feel?"

"So I'm really one of you guys now," Joan mused.

"You're one of *them*. I'm not an operative. I just recruit."

"I'll remember that. You're the guy who got me into this."

CHAPTER 3

Two weeks after her acceptance into the Constitution Defense Legion, Joan looked into her bathroom mirror and gingerly touched the new tattoo on her chest over her heart. She turned off the light and went into the living room. The anticipation of two operatives moving into her house was making her a little edgy and she kept reminding herself this was real. *Just like this tattoo.* She paced for a while and finally sat down to wait.

At 8:32 a knock sounded at the front door. She looked through the sheer curtain that covered the window in the door. A man and a woman stood on the porch. With a sigh of relief, she recognized Jason's five-foot-nine build and black hair slicked back into a ponytail. He gave a chin nod. Joan unlocked the door and opened it to let them in.

After a handshake and elbow bump, Jason said, "This is Vaida, our electronics tech. She's the best in the Legion."

The corners of Vaida's mouth tightened as if unaccustomed to praise. She was about five-foot-two and skinny to a fault. The dark circles under her eyes and downturned mouth made it hard to guess her age. She looked like the quintessential female revolutionary: black, straight, shoulder-length hair; camouflage clothes with requisite beret; hard, angular facial features. She held a large, lumpy duffle bag in her left hand.

"Can I pull the car in the garage?" Jason asked. He removed his windbreaker revealing the head of a snake tattoo on his neck and arms covered with sleeves of tattoos.

Joan pushed the button to remotely open the garage door, and Jason skipped down the stairs to the garage leaving her alone with this strange woman she had just met.

Before it became uncomfortable Vaida asked, "Where can we set up?"

Joan led the way. "You'll have the back bedroom."

Vaida asked about coffee. "…black," she stated, answering the inevitable question before it was asked.

Not sure what to think about these cell members taking up residence in her house, Joan rubbed the tattoo again. While she was scooping the coffee into the filter, Jason appeared at the top of the stairs with a large suitcase.

"Can you give me a hand? We have a lot of equipment," he said as he squeezed past Joan in her narrow kitchen.

Joan helped bring a couple monitors and a box of computer paraphernalia upstairs, each time placing them in the room with Vaida before heading back for another trip. When everything was upstairs, Jason and Vaida got to work, hooking up everything.

A little uneasy in her own house, Joan decided to stay out of their way and waited in the kitchen while the coffee finished brewing. When the coffee pot stopped gurgling and the house smelled of fresh coffee, she filled three mismatched mugs and took them to the back bedroom. When she got to the doorway, she was stunned at the array of technical equipment.

Jason was lying on his side on the floor, plugging things in, while Vaida was feeding him wires. He looked over his shoulder at Joan. "Coffee? Great. Put it on the dresser. Hand me the surge protector behind you."

Watching them work, Joan realized that Vaida was the tech guru. Her computers were her art, and as hard drives booted up and monitors came on, it was like watching a Zen Master become one with her equipment. Vaida gave Joan a brief explanation of each piece of equipment and its purpose then asked for Jason and Joan to leave so she could concentrate on programming.

Once in the dining room Joan asked Jason, "Her programming is really hacking, right?"

"Murphy said you were sharp."

"Can you tell me what your job, operation, or whatever it's called, is?"

"Not yet." He slid into the chair on the far side of the table, so his back would be toward the wall. Joan chose a seat opposite him. "Not because we don't trust you. Nothing has been finalized yet. When the powers that be decide, we'll start the recon." They each took a sip of coffee, and he continued, "Let's go over code words in case things ever get dicey."

"Do you make them up as you go along?"

"Pretty much. Each operation is different." He spent a few minutes going over the codes and ended with, "Oh, yeah, by the way, you buy the burn phones. We'll need a half dozen to start."

"By burn phones you mean throw-aways—pay as you go cell phones, right?"

"Right. Some cash will be arriving in the next day or so. You'll handle all the cash." He summarized, "So all you have to manage are the phones and the cash so far. Okay?"

"Okay with me."

ぐぁぐぁ

Three days later Joan arrived home from work and Jason and Vaida were counting cash at the dining room table. There was an electricity in the air that Joan couldn't quite put her finger on. Vaida, who until then had been quiet and withdrawn, was beaming and chatting with Jason as if they had an inside joke. Jason looked up. "The cash is here. There's a little over $5,000. Start buying the phones." He slid some of the money across the table toward Joan.

Vaida shot an amused glance at Jason and looked at Joan. "You might want to watch the eleven o'clock news tonight."

"Oh, no, you didn't—"

"This is how we partially fund our operations," Jason explained. "We don't have to make all the money. Most of it we get from the leadership."

"You say 'make' like you earned this money."

"We did earn it. Do you think it's easy to rob a bank and not get caught?" Jason pushed more of the cash toward Joan.

"But it's not right."

"It wasn't right for the government to steal our country and our rights. What goes around comes around."

"But the banks didn't steal anything from us."

"They were part of the collapse that allowed the Marxist bastards to take over our country. They vicariously stole our way of life from us. And we're taking it back anyway we can."

"And *every* way we can," Vaida added with venom.

"Look, we aren't going to go out and buy luxury items with this," Jason said, indicating the money. "This all goes to support the resistance. We're using their own money against them. It's kind of poetic justice. Besides, it buys us time until we can eventually bring their fascist system down around their ears. You want to do that, right?"

Joan nodded, eyeing the money, then glanced at Jason when he continued, "So, don't sweat the small stuff. The end justifies the means. We're all working toward the same end, right?"

Joan thought about the banks' complicity in current monetary situation. She had never bought into the story that the banking industry engineered the collapse of the economy, but they didn't take any steps to soften the blow to the average American.

Though a bit irrational, this reasoning appealed to her.

Joan slid into the nearest chair. "You're right. Who did this hurt anyway? That's why they have insurance."

"That's right! See? Nobody gets hurt here, and we have some operating cash." After a moment he said, "Do you know the Irish folk song, 'Galway Bay'?"

"No."

"Well it has a stanza that goes something like:

"'For the strangers came and tried to teach us their ways.
They scorned us for just bein' what we are.'"

Vaida joined in for the last two lines and they said in unison:

"'But they might as well go chasing after moonbeams, or
light a penny candle with a star.'"

"Cute. What does that mean?"

"It means the new regime in Washington wants everyone to conform to their new ways, but there is no friggin' way they can make *us* comply," Vaida said.

A silence followed while Joan thought about the lyrics of the song Jason and Vaida had just sung. She looked at Vaida. "How does the leadership get their money?"

"We don't ask," Vaida said. "Plausible deniability and all that."

Jason put his fist over the center of the table. "Live free or die."

They did a three-way fist bump and continued together, "Death is not the worst of all evils."

Joan reached for the money. "Let's find someplace to put this where it'll be safe."

CHAPTER 4

"Come in here I need you for something," Vaida called from her room, a.k.a. the Command Center.

Enjoying a rare moment of relaxing in front of the television, Joan reluctantly got up and walked across the hall to Vaida's room. "What do you need?" she said, leaning into the room from the door jamb.

"Come here and check out this monitor. Look at the corner of that building. What do you see?"

"The front bumper of a car." Joan leaned in closer and squinted to make out the image. "Is that Jason's car?"

"Yes. Our audio has gone down and he needs to know that the car can be seen. You need to go down there and tell him to come back. Do you know where this is?"

"I think so. It's East Main Street in the West End."

"That's right. It's that new office building across the street from where that old diner used to be."

"Okay." Joan was excited. She was being asked to get involved. This was only contacting Jason, but it showed they trusted her.

"Don't forget the Zone 2 Police Station is right down the street. No pressure or anything."

Joan grinned. "No pressure. What do I tell them if they stop me?"

"What are the chances of that happening? But if they do, just think of something."

Joan put on her leather jacket and pants and grabbed her helmet. "I'm outta here."

Vaida waved good-bye without taking her eyes off the monitor.

As the rickety garage door rolled up, a wintry blast took Joan's breath away. Rolling her vintage 1976 Triumph Bonneville toward the open door, she addressed her bike as if it were alive, "Sorry, Old Lady, but we have to go into the cold."

While the 650cc engine smoothly puttered and warmed up, she put on her helmet, sat on the bike, and admired the restored chrome. When the engine was warm enough, she headed down the driveway and stopped to adjust her scarf and gloves to plug up where the cold air seeped in. She wasn't even in fourth gear before she realized she should have put on her heated vest.

It was only a five minute ride to the West End and, when she arrived at East Main Street, she headed straight to the office building. Looking forward to getting back home and warmed up, she swerved into the parking lot and headed to the corner of the building to pass the message along to Jason.

"What the *heck*?" she said into the helmet. After a slow circle of the building, she concluded Jason wasn't there. She pulled out of the parking lot to head home, but only went thirty yards before she saw flashing lights behind her.

She pulled over to let the police car go by, but it pulled in behind her.

Shit. I knew this was going to happen. I just knew it. She reached for her wallet to get her license.

"Sir, shut of your bike," the officer said, hand on the butt of his gun.

Joan turned off the bike and removed her helmet.

"Sorry, ma'am. License and registration, please." He shined his flashlight on the license. "You're Joan Bowman?"

"Yes, officer."

"Pretty cold to be riding a bike tonight."

"Gas is too expensive. I can't afford to run a car anymore."

"Where are you coming from?"

"Home."

"Where are you going to?"

"Back home."

"You aren't just driving around in the cold. What are you doing out here?"

Joan replied without hesitation, "My girlfriend said her car broke down here so I came down to get her. But I guess I got the directions wrong. You haven't seen a girl in a broken down Ford anywhere around here, have you?"

"Not tonight."

"I left the house without my cell phone, so I have to go back home and wait for her to call again."

"Wait here." He went back to the car and she waited calmly, knowing that Vaida was watching everything and probably going ballistic.

When everything came back clean, he got out of the car and walked up to Joan. "Here are your license and registration." While she was putting them back in her wallet he said, "Do you know why I stopped you?"

"No idea."

He shined the flashlight in her eyes. "I saw you pull out of the parking lot of the office building back there. What were you doing back there?"

"Just looking for my girlfriend. Her message wasn't very clear about where she was exactly."

He gave Joan a long look. "Drive carefully," he said and headed back to his cruiser.

She started up her Triumph and slowly pulled out into the lane of traffic. The police cruiser followed her. She stayed calm and, after two miles, he turned left, presumably to head back to the station. The ride back to the house seemed to take forever, but when she finally got home and opened the garage door, she stopped in her tracks. Jason's Chevy was there. He was back.

They met her in the kitchen, talking over each other. "What did he want?"

"He just wanted to know what I was doing at the office building."

"What did you tell him?"

"I told him we were doing recon for the Legion and our audio went down and I had to come down to take care of it."

They both frowned.

"No, come on, really, what did you say?" Jason asked.

"I told him my girlfriend called me and said she broke down there and I came down to get her, but I must have gotten the directions wrong."

"Your girlfriend?" Jason and Vaida asked together.

"I figured he would fall into that stereotype crap. You know, girl on bike says she's a Lesbian—sounds right."

"Did he buy it?"

"I think so."

"You *think* so?" Jason was losing his cool. "He followed you down the road. What happened?"

"Nothing. He followed me for about two miles then turned onto Center Street."

"Why would he follow you?"

"It's what they do," Joan said. "I told him I was going home and he probably wanted to make sure I was heading in the right direction. You know, to make sure I didn't lie to him."

Jason rubbed both hands over his eyes and down his face. "Now the police have your name and address on file."

"Relax. It was just a routine traffic stop. They don't know I'm connected with the Legion." Joan wondered why she was the level-headed one when they were the veteran revolutionaries. "Jason, did the police see you there?"

"I don't think so."

"Where did you go?"

"The audio wasn't working. I came back because we didn't have any communication."

"Is that standard procedure?" Joan asked.

"Yes."

"Then why did you send me down there?" Joan snapped at Vaida.

"I thought he didn't realize the audio was out. We have to tell Murphy," Vaida said, trying to turn the conversation away from her.

"Who's going to make the call?" Joan asked.

"You are. You're the one who got stopped by the police." Vaida was adamant that she was not going to make the call.

"Okay, what's his number?"

"You've never called Murphy?" Jason asked.

Joan felt like she was on the outside looking in. "No. I never had a need. Why? Is that unusual?"

"We talk to him at least once a week. He never calls you?" Vaida asked.

"Never. You're making me nervous. What is going on?" Joan asked, looking from one to the other. "Why am I out of the loop?"

"I don't know. You tell us," Jason said. "How do we know what you said to the police tonight?"

"Oh, yeah, like I want to go to jail."

Jason nervously rubbed his goatee and his neck. "Maybe you're one of them. I heard they think there's a mole in the Legion. How do we know it isn't you?"

"I'm the new kid on the block, remember? How could I be the mole?" Joan had to put an end to this. "Let's just call Murphy and straighten this out before we go *Sierra Madre* on each other." Jason and Vaida looked at Joan with blank looks on their faces, so she explained, "You know the movie, *The Treasure of the Sierra Madre*?" Still no response. "Humphrey Bogart? They discover gold and then they start getting paranoid about each other's intentions?"

They still did not understand the movie reference.

"Let's just call Murphy," Jason finally said.

"I'll get my phone," Joan said heading for her bedroom.

"No, I'll dial him on my phone. Maybe there's a reason you don't have his number." He dialed the number. When Murphy answered, Jason said, "Joan has a reason to contact you, but she doesn't have your number. Is there a reason for that?…Oh, okay…yes, I do, but…yes, I can tell you. Joan was stopped by the police tonight." He shoved the phone toward Joan. "He wants to talk to you."

Joan explained everything just as it happened. She couldn't give him the officer's name because it was dark and his flashlight had been in her eyes. The officer gave her a warning. That was it, pure and simple. When the conversation was finished, she gave the phone back to Jason. "He wants to talk to you again."

Jason and Murphy had a brief conversation and then hung up. Jason went to the dining room table, wrote a number on a piece of paper, and gave it to Joan. "Murphy says to call him if anything suspicious happens that you think might be related to this—anything at all."

Joan took the paper with the number on it.

"And don't put his number in your phone," Jason added. "Memorize it."

CHAPTER 5

Jason and Vaida spent two more months checking out three sites. One was the federal building in downtown Pittsburgh, the other was the Fort Pitt Bridge, and the third was the Pittsburgh Consortium Building in the West End. They fell into a comfortable routine, broken up only by Alice spending a few days here and there lending a hand with the surveillance.

Alice was the CDL's bomb expert. His street name was Aloysius, but everyone called him Alice. The nerd in the group with a degree in chemistry, he was quirky and sometimes downright goofy, but his bombs were flawless. He reveled in configuring each bomb specifically for each situation. Rarely were two ever the same.

Joan continued to keep up a front by continuing her routine so no one would be suspicious of her or the house. When the others were out on recon she assumed the responsibility of manning the monitors and the audio. When there was money to do so, she continued to buy throw-away cell phones. The money came in spurts, suspiciously coinciding with a rash of bank robberies in Eastern Ohio. She didn't ask questions.

Mid-February, Murphy made the decision that the next target would be the federal building. Alice moved in full time. Everything was humming along right on target until Vaida came down with the flu. Joan pumped her with fluids and chicken soup, but it became more and more evident, as the date of the attack drew near, that she would be unable to drive for the final few recons.

Vaida would have to stay back and keep her bleary eyes on things at the monitors.

Jason tossed Joan his car keys. "You're driving."

"Me? I don't think I'm ready. They said I'd start out small."

"You have a tat, right?"

"Yes, but—"

"Then you do operations. We're leaving in five minutes."

"I have to check with Murphy first."

"Do what you have to do, but be in the car and ready to go in five minutes." Jason did not look up from checking the magazine in his Sig-Sauer and gathering up his binoculars.

Alice looked up briefly and glanced from Jason to Joan and back, then resumed changing the batteries in the video camera.

Joan punched Murphy's number into her cell phone, but hesitated pressing the Send button. He would want her to do whatever it took to support the mission. She turned off her phone and put it into the front pocket of her leather jacket. She spent a few minutes checking on Vaida and asked if she had any advice for her.

Vaida assured her that all it entailed was going where the guys said to go and keeping an eye out for the cops. The best recommendation was to go to the bathroom before leaving. Joan heeded her advice.

She headed to the garage to warm up the engine. The guys piled into the car right behind her. Jason sat shotgun and Alice settled into the passenger-side rear seat. She backed the car out of the garage and headed downtown.

The first couple miles, Jason and Alice joked around to shake off some nerves.

Jason turned his attention to Joan. "So, I hear you're a martial artist. What style?"

"Some Krav Maga, some American Combato, some Kung Fu. What about you?

"I'm a street fighter—other than hand-to-hand combat I learned in the Marines."

"That's it?"

"All you need is a few basic defense techniques and the will to prevail."

Joan nodded and looked in the rear view mirror. "What about you, Alice, any martial arts?"

"You guys do security, I do explosives," he answered.

Jason continued the ribbing. "He didn't waste his time learning three different styles of self-defense."

"I do it for the art as well as for the self-defense."

"Oh, for the *art*," Jason said, stretching out the word "art." He started to laugh and pointed his finger at her. "Gotcha!"

She pushed his finger away and laughed with him. Then she threw down the gauntlet. "Yeah, well I could beat you anytime."

"Anytime, anywhere," Jason said, jokingly taking up the challenge. "You name the time and place and I'll be there to beat your ass."

"You're too young and stupid to beat me."

"You're too old and slow. What are you fifty, sixty?"

"You shit. I'll show you how old I am when you're begging me to stop beating you."

"The only thing I'll be begging for is for you to stop making me laugh."

Getting bored with the bantering, Alice said, "If you're done playing *Quien es mas macho*, we have to turn around. We just passed the bar where we usually get the six pack."

"Quien es mas what?" Jason asked. Pointing to the left he added, "Turn here, we'll go around the block."

"What six pack?" Joan asked as she turned down the side street. "You didn't drag me out here, in the cold, to go drinking did you?"

"No, it's part of our cover if the cops stop us. It's the details that'll kill ya."

"Ever get stopped by the cops before?"

"No," Jason said. "Well, once, but we had a tail light out. I don't think they were onto us. Here, pull in front of this fire hydrant." He looked to the back seat. "Do your thing, Alice."

Watching Alice crossing the street toward a corner bar called Zombies, Joan asked Jason about their cover story. He explained that she and he were girlfriend and boyfriend and they just gave Alice a ride to get a six pack—hence, the stop at the bar.

If the cops checked with the bar, the story would check out, and they had a six pack for later when they got back home.

"There's one thing that bothers me," Joan said.

"The story's been good enough for Vaida."

"Yeah, with Vaida," Joan said, turning slightly in her seat. "She's closer to your age. What are you? Late twenties?"

"Twenty-four. Don't worry, you can pass for a cougar, you dirty old lady," he said with a wink.

"Great. We get stopped for a tail light, and I go to jail for corrupting the morals of a minor."

"I'm not a minor."

"Well, you act like one."

"Are you two at it again?" Alice asked, sliding into the back seat with a paper bag in the shape of a six pack.

Joan pulled away from the curb and headed south. They cruised downtown for a half hour and, finally, backed into an alley diagonally across from the federal building. Then Jason and Alice got out and disappeared around the corner. After thirty long minutes, Joan wondered if she should go look for them. Before she could come to a decision, they returned and got into the car without a word. As Joan waited for instructions, a man tapped on her window. It was a security guard for the building to their left. Joan rolled down her window.

"What are you guys doing here?" the security guard asked.

"We were just trying to figure out what to do tonight, and we didn't want to waste gas driving around until we decided," Joan explained.

He shined the flashlight in the car, looking for God knows what. "Well, you can't stay here."

Jason put his arm on the back of the seat and leaned across to talk to the security guard. "No problem. We'll move. Have a good evening."

"You, too," the guard said.

Joan started the engine and pulled out of the alley. "You don't think he'll call the police do you?" she asked.

"Nah, he probably wants to go back inside and go to sleep. He doesn't want to spend the night with the cops answering questions." He turned to Alice. "Remind me to change the plates tomorrow, just in case."

In the rearview mirror, Joan saw Alice nod in agreement. As she turned onto Western Avenue, Joan checked the rearview mirror again. "Cop behind us."

When Jason hunched to the side to check the side view mirror, flashing lights lit them up.

As Joan pulled to the side of the street, Jason said, "The name on my ID is Tom McKnight. What's yours, Alice?"

The cop told them over his P.A. system to put their hands where he could see them. While they were raising their hands, Alice replied, "Michael Russo."

"You don't look Italian," Joan said. In the rearview mirror, she saw Alice shrug.

The two police officers split. One approached the passenger side and the other appeared in Joan's side view mirror. Before he tapped on the window, Joan rolled it down.

"License and registration," the officer said. He splashed his flashlight in the front of the car. The light illuminated Jason's Sig-Sauer lying on the front seat.

The cop said, "Gun!" to alert his partner.

The police officers pulled their handguns and ordered several times, in several different ways for Joan, Jason, and Alice to raise their hands.

They immediately complied.

Jason said under his breath, "Don't worry the gun is legal. Everything will be okay once the cops get everything straightened out. Stick to the story and we won't have any trouble."

The officer opened the driver side door and stepped back with his gun still on Joan. "Driver, get out of the car and on the ground."

She got out as quickly as she could, but he shoved her to the ground anyway. After he cuffed her, he picked her up, pushed her face down on the cruiser's hood, and did a quick frisk for weapons and drugs. Then he sat her down on the curb in the headlights of his cruiser.

They followed the same routine with Jason then Alice, and when they were all sitting on the curb, they cleared Jason's gun and put it on the hood of their cruiser.

Backup arrived, and the officer who had pulled Joan out of the car took charge.

"She was the driver. Here's her purse. You get her story. We'll talk to the guys."

The new cop searched her purse then took out the wallet and pulled out her license. "You're Joan Bowman?"

"Yes."

"Aren't you the one I stopped on a bike a while back? You were in the West End picking up your girlfriend or something."

"Yes—" *Shit! Of all the officers to respond as back-up it had to be the one who stopped me a few weeks ago.*

"*Girlfriend!*" Jason jumped in trying to distract the police, "I bet it's that cunt, Carol, right?"

"Who are you?" the cop asked Jason.

"I'm her boyfriend—*was* her boyfriend." Jason glared at Joan. "I let Carol stay at the house because she was down and out and this is how she repays me."

"It's not like that, Tommy," Joan said using Jason's alias.

"Yeah, how is it? I'll bet you can't even remember the last time we had sex."

Fighting a smile, Joan said, "Well, if you weren't so distant and cold, maybe I wouldn't have to go somewhere else for—"

"Knock it off, you two," one of the officers said.

They were quiet for a few seconds, but Jason couldn't stop himself. "I'll bet she's not as good as me."

"Don't flatter yourself."

"You never had any complaints before that bitch moved in."

"I said knock it off," one of the backup officers said. You," he said, grabbing Joan's arm, "come with me." He pulled her to her feet and opened the back door of the cruiser. "Sit here."

Joan shot a look at Jason before she sat down, but he was talking to one of the other officers. Alice had been moved to the front of the other cruiser, where he was being questioned by one of the original officers.

"Those are pretty big arms for a woman," the officer continued, watching her closely. He was trying to see if she might be a cross dresser or a transvestite. He'd seen it all in his eight years on the force.

"Is it a crime to work out?"

"You aren't under arrest. We just cuffed you for our safety

and yours. But if you want to go to the station, I can make that happen."

"No, I'm sorry, officer. I'm just a little shook up." Joan dropped her eyes to her lap. The last thing on the agenda for the evening was a trip to the county jail.

"Now, you want to tell me what you are doing driving around at two in the morning?"

Thanking her lucky stars she had discussed a cover story with Jason, Joan related it using Jason and Alice's aliases. When she was done, he told her to wait and went to check the stories the other officers received from Jason and Alice.

The officers seemed to be satisfied with the story. Jason's gun permit checked out. When the bar confirmed that part of the story, they removed the cuffs and moved Alice and Joan back to the curb where Jason was still sitting.

Jason kicked Joan in the ankle, which started a scuffle.

"Knock it off!" one of the cops said. "Do you want to go to the station?" Jason and Joan stopped. "I'll take that as a 'no.'" He turned to his partner. "What do you want to do?"

"We don't have anything on them," his partner said. "Besides, these three screwballs will tie up our whole evening with paperwork. Let 'em go."

After a stern warning about driving around in early morning hours again, Joan and the guys were released. Jason and Joan were further warned to settle their differences. If the cops received another call that involved them, they both would definitely be going to the station.

CHAPTER 6

It was the day, or early morning to be exact, of the mission.
"Mount up," Jason said at precisely two-thirty. Punctuality was one detail he demanded.

Joan and Alice silently followed him down the stairs to the garage and into the car. Each person mentally reviewed their part of the plan, psyching up for the danger that faced them as adrenaline pumped into their systems. Undertaking a subversive, dangerous, detail-demanding mission was a grave situation, requiring full concentration of everyone involved. There was only one way for the mission to go right, but countless ways for it to go wrong.

Because Vaida was still under the weather, Joan was the driver. Driving on the final few recons, she felt confident in her role, and she could feel Jason's confidence in her growing. She was the driver, Alice was the bomb guy, Jason was boss-slash-security. Recon complete, jobs assigned, everything was ready.

They rode in silence until they were two blocks from the federal building.

Jason broke the silence. "Remember, if something goes wrong the code is 'surprise' and you leave. If for some reason we can't give you the code, and we aren't out in five minutes, you leave. Got it? Let's keep our losses to a minimum."

"Five minutes, roger that," Joan responded.

"Okay, hoods up." He and Alice put the hoods up on their sweatshirts. "Final check on the audio. Ear plugs in—testing, testing." Thumbs up. Audio clear.

"Vaida, can you hear me?" Joan said. "Good."

She nodded and Jason and Alice piled out of the car and headed toward the loading dock twenty yards down a macadam drive at the rear of the building.

Joan was the only one who could communicate with Vaida at the home base. Vaida was hacked into the city's street cams, and she watched the street activity around the federal building. She would alert Joan if it looked like something could compromise the mission. Joan could assess the information and pass it along to the guys inside if, in her assessment, they needed to know. They had their own job to do. The last thing they needed was superfluous information.

She tapped her fingers on the steering wheel and kept her eyes on the swivel for about three minutes. Sitting idle in one spot was making her nervous.

"So, Vaida, how does everyone get a nickname?"

"Kempton decides. He chooses names that mean warrior or fighter."

"Who's Kempton?"

"He heads the whole Ohio Valley Area."

"I haven't met him." Joan checked her mirrors before asking, "What's the story with Duncan?" She wondered why everyone seemed so afraid of Duncan. Certainly, his demeanor and words could be chilling, but such a dangerous persona didn't fit with the man who had gently tended to her wounds at The Woods.

"What do you mean?" Vaida asked.

"Why is everyone so afraid of him?"

"He's unpredictable. One seemingly innocuous word can send him into a rage and, when that happens, someone always gets hurt."

"Why is he like that?"

"The story is that he has severe PTSD from something that happened on mission he was on as a mercenary. I don't know any facts and I don't even know if it's true. He doesn't talk about what happened."

"What could have happened that was so bad?" Joan mused, still checking her mirrors.

"I don't know.

"I'm starting to get a feeling something isn't right. Are all the streets clear?"

"Everything's good—you're good."

"Vaida, it's been four and a half minutes. Heard anything on the police scanner?"

"No. Relax and just wait it out. They'll be there."

"Tell me when you see them leave the building, okay?"

"Roger that."

Joan was startled by static in her earphone. "Jason, Alice, say again." She thought she heard something but static drowned out the words. "Jason, Alice, you're breaking up. Say again." The static stopped.

"Vaida, something's wrong. I thought I heard something through the static, but now even the static is gone."

"Get out of there. Time is up. They're big boys. They can take care of themselves."

"I'm going to go find them." Joan pulled up a bandana to cover the bottom half of her face and adjusted the hood of her hoodie.

"No. Stay with the plan, Joan." She saw Joan get out of the car and head toward the loading dock where Jason and Alice had disappeared just five minutes earlier. "Joan, no, stop!"

But it was too late. She watched helplessly as Joan stealthily moved in the shadows to get to the dock without being spotted.

Joan jumped up onto the loading dock, but a sharp pain stopped her short. She hadn't been as nimble as she would have liked, and she scraped her shin on the metal edge of the dock. She bent over to rub it and saw legs she thought belonged to Jason and Alice then saw another set of legs in blue pants with a stripe down the side. *Damn, they're caught*, she thought as she slowly and quietly walked up behind the security guard.

Alice looked over the guard's shoulder and saw her within a couple yards and closing. "Here's our boss. She'll vouch for us."

The guard turned to his left to see who was coming toward them and a powerful jolt to his left kidney sent a shock wave through his body. Joan then gave him a powerful left hook on the chin which snapped his head back to the right.

The snap of his neck resulted in immediate unconscious-ness and he fell to the ground, slamming his head on the floor as he hit it.

Joan shook her hand and hissed, "Shit that hurts."

Alice stood gaping at the unconscious guard. Jason grabbed him by both shoulders and gave him a gentle shove. "Come on let's get out of here before he wakes up." They started to move toward the loading dock. With their escape door in sight, a few feet from a clean getaway, they came face to face with another guard.

"There were never two guards here before," Jason muttered under his breath.

Joan didn't wait to hear his explanation. She pulled down her bandana and ran right up to the second guard, yelling, "Help me. These guys said they're going to kill me." Then she grabbed both his shoulders and head butted him in the nose. She grasped the back of his neck and, as she brought his head down, brought her knee up to meet his head—twice. A backhand to the temple sent him sideways to the floor, half-conscious and moaning. She executed a low side kick to his head and the moaning stopped.

"That's our cue to get out of here," she said, pulling her bandana back up over her face and jumping off the dock with Jason and Alice right behind her.

They ran to the car and Joan floored the Chevy too hard. It hesitated and sputtered, but finally kicked in and took off.

"Slow down we have—" Jason checked his watch. "—six minutes yet. We'll be on the bridge by that time."

Alice leaned forward with his head between Jason and Joan. "Wow, Dude. You took those guys *out*." He pointed at Joan. "You are *good*. One shot, bam, lights out."

"They were wusses," Joan said, slowing to a stop at the traffic light just east of the West End Bridge.

"No. No, don't do that, dude. Don't get all humble and shit." He flung himself back against the seat. "Jason, did you see that first guy? His head spun and he went down just like in the movies."

"Yeah, I saw it." Jason said, looking over the back of the seat at Alice and giving a fist bump. He remembered Joan shaking her hand after slugging the first guard. He glanced at her hands on the steering wheel. "How's your hand?"

"My knuckles are fractured."

Alice came forward again. "How do you know they're fractured?"

"I've had fractured knuckles before, *dude*," she said, teasing him.

"No way. Was it from hitting some other dude?"

"Nothing as romantic as that."

"Come on, how then?

"I don't want to talk about it."

"Still man, you saved our butts back there." He put his fist over her shoulder. She bumped it with the back of her right fist. "You were *awesome*."

"I shouldn't have had to save your butts if you had done a thorough recon—"

"Oh yeah, the new girl is going to tell us how to do our jobs."

"Well, the new girl had to save your butts, and if you had been thorough, it wouldn't have been necessary."

"We were thorough," Jason answered testily. "They must have changed something since the last inside recon. All I know is there was never a guard there at this time—ever."

A silence fell over the group until they pulled into Joan's driveway. Vaida met them at the top of the stairs in her fuzzy slippers holding a cup of tea. She wanted details. Alice gave her the blow-by-blow playback while opening a beer. Jason put his backpack in his room. Joan got a bag of frozen peas out of the freezer and put it on her knuckles.

Vaida saw her and said, "Maybe you should see a doctor later today."

"There's nothing they can do. As long as I can move my fingers, all he'll do is tape the fingers together. I can do that—without all the questions." She smiled a thank-you at Jason as he handed her a bottle of beer.

Jason lifted his bottle of beer. "Hey, everyone, to Joan, the savior."

Alice raised his bottle and Vaida raised her cup of tea. "To Joan."

They stood in the kitchen drinking their beers, and Vaida made herself another cup of tea. While Alice animatedly retold the evening's events, Joan was deep in thought. Jason could be a hard-ass, but he just gave her credit for her small part. Humble, low-key, gracious—all descriptions she would not have given him before tonight. In the Army there was a saying: "Don't confuse rank with position." It referred to situations such as a sergeant MP giving a speeding ticket to a colonel or a staff sergeant medic quarantining a field site commanded by a captain. In this instance, it morphed into: "Don't confuse age with position." The youngest in the group, Jason was more than qualified to be the leader. Smiling inwardly, Joan finished off her beer and rinsed the bottle before putting it in the recycle bin.

Exhausted and bored with the rehashing of the night's events, Jason clamped a hand on Alice's shoulder. "Dude, act like you've done this before."

A quiet fell over the kitchen. A news flash blared on the television in Vaida's room. They rushed to her room and flipped through the news channels to see the result of their work. The reporters were interviewing witnesses and describing the mayhem and damage they could see. Flashing lights from all the police and fire vehicles formed a backdrop as the reporters described the scene of smoke and scattered debris. Joan made the comment that she was glad to see the loading dock area wasn't destroyed in the blast, so the two guards were spared. Jason stopped stroking his goatee long enough to turn and look at her.

"*What?*" she asked, widening her eyes and turning her palms up.

Jason turned back to the television.

As the adrenaline drained from their systems, they got tired and, one by one, went off to bed. Before leaving Vaida's room Alice shook a finger at Joan. "You are one tough girl."

"She ain't no *girl*," Jason said.

CHAPTER 7

Joan found herself sitting in an interrogation room after being lead through a maze of cubicles. It had been ten days since the bomb explosion at the Federal Building, and she had been brought in for questioning by the CDL Task Force. She couldn't shake the feeling that the two were connected. The man in the rumpled suit had introduced himself as Agent Massa when he had walked into the church office to "ask her some questions."

"Wait here," he said, standing in the open door next to a sign that indicated it was Interrogation Room 3. "Can I get you anything? A soda or coffee?"

Joan shook her head. He disappeared after saying he would be back in a few minutes. She heard the click of the lock on the door.

Agent Massa was a middle-aged man of Hispanic descent with a medium build and short black hair. There was a touch of gray at the temples. He had a kind face, but Joan knew better than to be fooled by it. His partner, Agent Woyzeck, on the other hand, had a more angular face that gave him a mean look which, she surmised, he used to his advantage whenever he could. He was tall and, even through the material of his suit, she could see he paid his dues at the gym.

She spent the time alone looking around the room but there wasn't much to see. There was a table and three chairs. She took a seat in the chair on the side of the table closest to the door. On the wall behind her was a chalkboard. She was tempted to write something on it that would play with the agents' heads, but she thought better of it. Instead, she wondered about the long string of people who had been in there over the years. Were they all suspects or, like her, someone they wanted to pump for information? The room was stuffy, so she took off her blazer and put in on the back of the chair. Under normal circumstances, she would not have bared her arms, not because she was self-conscious about their size. She trained hard to develop them. It was because they always incurred a comment from somebody. She wasn't in the mood for comments.

At one time she had trained to be a power lifter, which had pumped up her arms and thighs beyond what most women would find attractive. During the height of her training, the army had reassigned her, and the activity of moving and adjusting to her new assignment had thrown her off her training regimen. She was now only maintaining the muscle she had. She was powerful enough to get out of a bad situation alive. She hoped by removing her blazer, she would stay cool and avoid perspiring. Sweating would give the agents the impression she was nervous, so she chose to endure the inevitable comments.

When the federal agents had shown up at the church where Joan worked, she had answered their questions as best she could without implicating Jason and Vaida, as well as herself. She must not have answered their questions satisfactorily, or maybe they had intended to bring her down to the station from the beginning. She wasn't sure. All she could think about was the work she was not getting done sitting there—it was Friday and the Sunday Bulletins were yet to be prepared. She made a mental checklist of what she had to get done when she was finally released. She didn't waste her time thinking that she might be in trouble with the feds, because if she was, there was nothing she could do about it now. She would "take one" for the Legion if she had to.

Twenty minutes later, Agent Woyzeck breezed into the interrogation room. He had removed his blazer and looked more informal and approachable. It also revealed the firearm holstered to his belt at his side and his muscular build. Joan wondered at his mixed messages. She made a mental shrug and looked down at brown folder he placed on the desk. Placed in such a way so

Joan could see her name written on it. Meant to pique her curiosity and raise her anxiety level, it failed to do its job. She knew it was a ruse. If they had anything on her, she'd be under arrest.

Agent Woyzeck opened the conversation. "You look like you're in excellent shape. Where do you work out?"

"A gym in Crafton." *So he's going for rapport rather than intimidation.*

"I can appreciate what it takes to get into your level of fitness. What do you do?"

"I lift some weights, do some karate, but I know you didn't bring me down here to discuss my physical fitness program."

"You lift more than *some* weights. You pay your dues at the gym—if you know what I mean." Joan's only response was a shrug. "What style karate do they teach at the Crafton gym? Krav Maga, right?"

Joan did not respond at all to his questions. This whole bit of getting-to know-you was boring.

He noticed her lack of response and moved on. "It seems like a nice place. What are the hours there?"

Joan exhaled loudly. "Monday through Friday 6:00-10:00, Saturday and Sunday 9:00-4:00." She looked straight into his eyes without moving her head to the right or left. She watched reality television and knew exactly what he was doing—checking out her body language. "Maybe if you told me what it is you think Jason and Vaida have done, I'd have a better idea of what you're looking for."

She looked up as Agent Massa entered the room and grabbed the back of the other wooden chair. He dragged it across the floor toward Joan. When it was within arms-length of her, he sat down, casually leaning back, a notebook and pen in his hands.

He got right down to business. "Joan, we brought you down here because, like we said at the church, some information has come to our attention about the two people in your house who you say are boarders. Do you want to tell us anything you didn't tell us at the church?"

"Really, Agent Massa, I've told you all I know."

"We know you want to cooperate with us, okay? And right now our investigation is centered on Jason and Vaida. All we need from you is anything they may have said or done that you think might be of interest to the task force—anything at all."

"While I was waiting I was trying to think of something, but—"

"It may even be something so minor it doesn't mean anything to you, but it could be huge to us."

Joan pretended to think. "No—nothing."

Agent Massa changed tactics. He wanted her to know she was on the task force's radar. Maybe it would shake something loose. "We know you're covering for them. Jason wouldn't cover for you especially after he found out that you cheated on him with that girl. What was her name?"

Joan continued her cool gaze.

"Carol," he said, looking at Woyzeck. "How is that working out, by the way?"

"I'm not covering for them. I'm being—"

"Where were they a week ago today?"

"I don't know."

"Were you with them?"

"No, like I just said, I don't know."

The pucker-factor was setting in. They were going somewhere specific with this. Outwardly she stayed calm, but her mind raced wildly trying to get ahead of the questioning.

"Did they say anything that might have indicated where they had been?"

"No. I don't pry."

Agent Massa picked up the folder with her name on it and pretended to leaf through it. "Jason owns a Chevy Malibu, is that right."

"Yes."

"Have you ever driven his car?"

"Two or three times, why?" Her instincts told her not to lie. *They have me in the car. Where are they going with this?*

"Where did you go?" Agent Massa asked.

"Around…to a store or whatever."

"What store?"

"I don't know…Radio Shack, once, and the grocery store." *Shit, they're going to check this stuff out.* She kept her gaze on Massa, only moving her eyes occasionally to look at Woyzeck.

He tossed the folder back onto the table. "Did you ever drive his car in downtown Pittsburgh?"

"Yes, once," she said, knowing she couldn't lie after that notorious traffic stop.

Agent Woyzeck opened the folder and took out two photos. "These were taken by street cams a week ago. I recognize Tom McKnight, who is also known as Jason, and Mike Russo." Joan nodded. He took another photo out of the folder. "Who's driving in this photo? It looks like you."

The pucker-factor ratcheted up a notch. She wanted to cross her arms across her stomach to keep her hands from shaking, but instead she put her hands on her thighs and leaned forward to pretend to get a better look at the photo.

"That's not me. It looks like me, but it's not me. I wasn't in Jason's car a week ago."

"It's you. Look at it," he said, shoving it closer to her.

"It really does *look* like me. It looks so much like me, even *I* want to think it's me, but it's not me."

Agent Massa leaned forward, placing his elbows on his knees. "You said you *want* to think it's you. How can we help you tell us it's you?" His tone was calm and encouraging.

"It's not me." *Deny, deny, deny.*

"Maybe you drove that night, but don't remember. Sometimes it's hard to remember something a week ago. When was the last time you drove Jason's car?"

"The night of the traffic stop a few weeks ago."

"You didn't drive it after that night."

"No."

Agent Massa stood up and put his hand on the back of Joan's chair, a move that, with another woman, would increase the psychological pressure. He leaned forward with his face about eight inches from hers. "All we have is a photo of you in Jason's car," he said quietly. "That's not illegal, okay, but we can hold you here indefinitely for obstructing an investigation. All you have to do is tell us what you were doing in the car that night."

Joan looked down at the photo then did something neither agent expected. She turned just enough to place her arm on the back of her chair so that her forearm brushed Agent Massa's hand. She was not intimidated. She intruded on his space. Then she lifted her gaze from the photograph. "I wasn't—"

"Joan," he interrupted. He reached forward with his left hand and put it on the edge of the table. Joan recognized the subtle game of one-upsmanship. His intent was to make her feel pinned in. There was no escape. Joan could smell the scent of mint on his breath when he said, "I think you want to tell us, but don't know how to change your story. It's okay, Joan. Like I said, it's Jason and Vaida we want. All we want from you is some information."

She looked back at the photo and slid it closer to Agent Massa. "This is Photoshopped."

Agent Woyzeck stood up and slammed his hand on the desk. Massa stepped back. "Come on, Joan, do you think we're stupid? We have a *photo*!" Agent Woyzeck jabbed his finger at her face in the photo.

"You know how I know it's not me?" She flashed her eyes up at him. "I was not in Jason's car a week ago."

"We'll be right back." Agent Massa motioned for Agent Woyzeck to follow him. When they were in the hallway, he turned to Agent Woyzeck. "Do we have anything to keep her on?"

Agent Woyzeck shook his head. "Not enough."

"What do you think?"

"I think she's going to be a tough one. She's not as girly as you might think at first, and she doesn't intimidate easily."

"I could see that," Agent Massa said.

"We should tag team her and wear her down. She is facing irrefutable evidence, and she'll get tired of sitting here. Then she'll give us what we're looking for."

Over the next six hours, Agents Massa and Woyzeck took turns trying to get Joan to change her story. Another agent on the task force tried his hand at finding the elusive "button" that would get Joan to capitulate. Nothing worked.

Finally Woyzeck said, "If we step up the interrogation a notch or two, if you know what I mean—we might be able to get her to say or do something that we can keep her on."

"Who's going to do it?" Massa asked.

"I will."

"Just don't go too far."

"What's she going to do? Sue us?" Agent Woyzeck said with a smirk. "There's no such thing as police brutality anymore. The beauty of the current administration is that nowadays *getting* information is more important than *how* we get it."

"We don't want to alienate her. She might still be a source of information, if not now then some time in the future."

"She won't be a source of information if we don't get her to soften up and start talking."

"Just don't go too far," Agent Massa warned again, and he plopped into his desk chair to watch on the monitor.

When Agent Woyzeck opened the door to the interrogation room, and Joan saw the look on his face, she knew nothing good was going to come out of this session. She steeled herself for the worst.

"Let me ask you something, Miss Bowman," he said leaning as Massa had done—one hand on the table and one on the back of the chair—putting his face inches from hers. His breath wasn't as minty-fresh as Agent Massa's. It smelled of burnt coffee. "Did anyone read you your rights at any time today?"

"No," she said, meeting his stare.

"Do you know why that is?"

"I'm not under arrest."

"Rrrrr," he said imitating a buzzer. "Wrong answer. You were not read your rights because you don't have any." He moved his face even closer with the final three words.

Joan did not budge. Before she even knew what happened, she was up against the wall pinned by his forearm, the bone of his right arm painfully pressing into her collar bones. She didn't wince.

She did not so much as raise her hand.

"What are you going to do now, Bowman?" She didn't respond. "Do something. Oh, please do anything. I'd like to go a round with you."

"I'm not stupid."

"You're not as smart as you think you are."

"If I so much as raise my hand, in literally seconds there'll be a half dozen agents in here. I won't stand a chance in hell.

And then you'll be able to keep me here for days, maybe even weeks."

"That's right. If you so much as blink, you'll never get out of here. I'll see to it personally."

"It ain't happenin'—" She spit out his name. "—Agent Woyzeck." She had to stay calm and wait this guy out.

"You know what I think, Miss Bowman," he sneered her name and continued, "I think you are a member of the CDL and you're covering for your fucking fellow scumbags. You were driving that car a week ago and—"

"I wasn't."

Agent Woyzeck slid his arm up to Joan's neck cutting off the air just enough so she couldn't speak. She instinctively grabbed his arm with both hands and pulled downward, but couldn't budge it. She was at a severe disadvantage. Not only was this guy stronger, but he was using his weight to apply pressure. All she could do was glare into his eyes and deprive him of the satisfaction of knowing he was hurting her.

"You little bitch, you and your little group are going down—*hard*." With the word "hard" he pressed hard enough to cut off Joan's air, and then just as quickly as he had slammed her to the wall, he released her. He grabbed her by the back of the neck and whispered in her ear, "You are lucky there are cameras in this room or this could have gone a lot worse." He pushed her back down into the chair and let go of her neck.

Joan had her hand on her throat, gasping to re-open her windpipe. She glared at him out of the corner of her eyes through stray strands of hair. *That's right, you snake. If I ever catch you where there aren't any cameras, you are going down. Every man has three weak spots, and I'll hit all of 'em, you bastard.*

Woyzeck pulled back at the look on her face.

Agent Massa entered the room. He stood with a wide stance with his arms crossed. "If there's anything you want to tell us, now is the time."

"I don't have anything else. I've told you all I know."

"Let's go," Agent Woyzeck finally said, stalking out of the room with a glance over his shoulder before shutting the door. He and Agent Massa had a conference in the hallway. "She comes across as this nice, helpful church lady, but she is one scary bitch," he said to Massa. "She didn't miss a beat when I choked her—not a flinch, not even a wince—she just glared at me."

"Why don't we put her in a holding cell for a while? You know, give her a taste of her future if she doesn't cooperate with us."

"Good idea. We'll let her sit there for a while. When the techies upstairs finish bugging her cell phone, we'll let her go, and see who she calls. I can't help but think she is the key to Jason, Vaida, and this Mike guy." He clapped a hand on Massa's shoulder. "You look like you could use a cup of coffee. I'll break the news to her and take her downstairs."

A few minutes later Agent Woyzeck guided Joan down the hallway and through the heavy doors to the holding area. He stopped in front of the men's holding cell and unlocked the door.

"The men's holding cell—really?" She glanced over her shoulder at him. "This is low, even for somebody like you."

"You have no idea." He opened the cell door, unlocked the handcuffs, and locked the door behind her. As he walked away, he said over his shoulder, "You're calm now. We'll see how calm you are in a couple hours."

The next sound was the slam of the heavy steel door out of the holding area.

Joan sized up the men in the cell. There was a drunk snoring on the bench along the far wall. He smelled like urine and vomit. There was a slender, dark-skinned African-American man sitting next to him in shorts and a tee shirt—straight from the B-ball court, she guessed. There were two other men who were openly sizing her up. One of the men had coffee-colored skin that stretched over a muscular physique. He wore tan cargo shorts and a wife-beater shirt with a "Brown Pride" tattoo peeking out of the neckline. The fourth guy looked like a local punk, rather tall, short curly hair, with a spare tire at his waistline—a tough guy wannabe. These two were the bad boys.

The Hispanic man was the closest and moving in on her. She smelled alcohol on his breath. Anything she did with him would have to be sharp and hard—and fast. Drunks could be unpredictable. The punk standing behind him would be easier to take down. The Hispanic was the biggest threat. He would have to go down first.

"Look, Woody," he said to the tough guy wannabe behind him, "a gift from the Pittsburgh PD."

He was so close Joan could feel his breath.

"There are cameras on us," she said, hoping to discourage them.

"That don't matter. We'll make this quick. Right, Woody?"

He put his hand on Joan's shoulder at the base of her neck. Big mistake—Joan had an aversion to being grabbed by men.

"Yeah, real quick," tough-guy wannabe agreed.

"You don't want to do this," Joan said.

She knew it wouldn't dissuade him. She just wanted him to say something—talking reduces reaction time. As soon as he started to respond to her statement, she hit him with an upward chin jab, which knocked him back a couple steps. He regained his balance and flew at her, reaching for her throat. She pinned both his arms with her left one and kneed him in the groin twice, delivered another upward chin jab, and pushed him away. He fell to the floor, moaning and holding his groin. Woody reached for her. She smoothly side-stepped him and executed an upper-cut to the solar plexus. While he stood still, trying to get his breath back, she stepped back and brought her instep up to his groin. He went down like a rock and lay moaning. The Hispanic man was struggling to his knees, still holding his groin. Joan grabbed his head and kneed the bridge of his nose. He fell to the floor grabbing his face. As both men were on the floor moaning, she faced the black man sitting on the bench.

"I'm only in here for unpaid parking tickets," he said, raising his hands in submission.

After a nod of acknowledgement, she sat down next to the drunk on the bench. He had blissfully slept through the fight. She lifted his head, placed it on her lap, and tenderly pushed his hair out of his eyes.

Several minutes later, three Pittsburgh cops, with Woyzeck hot on their heels, came flying through the door to the holding area and opened the cell door. After leaving Joan in the holding cell, Woyzeck had distracted the guard who was watching the monitors as he flipped the switch off. Woyzeck pulled Joan out of the cell and, with a rough push, headed back to the interrogation area. Joan smiled and turned as they passed the jail's on-duty nurse on his way to check on the injured men. Agent Woyzeck pushed her arm to quicken her steps.

When they reached Interrogation Room 3 he asked, "What happened back there?"

"I warned them. I told them they didn't want to attack me. I'll bet they're now wishing they had listened to me."

"They're reviewing the tapes now. You had better not be lying."

"Why would I start something with two punks?"

"I don't know. We'll see." He walked out of the room.

About a half hour later, a uniformed policeman opened the interrogation room door and told Joan she was free to go to the property clerk and pick up her belongings. After asking who was giving her a ride back to work, she was told to find her own way back—too bad she hadn't cooperated with them. She shrugged her shoulders and exited the building.

She dialed CityCabCo, which she used often since she had given up owning a car, and asked for Leo. Over the past year they had gotten to know each other, and she had learned all about the ups and downs of Leo's family. What she didn't know was that when she dialed the cab company the agents were listening in. Leo wasn't on their radar, but they decided to check him out anyway—just in case. They waited for the next call, but it didn't come.

Joan was smart enough to know not to make any incriminating calls on her cell phone after it had been in the possession of the police. After Leo dropped her off at her office, she called Murphy from a burn phone she always kept in her desk.

❧❧❧

When she finally got home at 9:15 that night, the house was quiet and dark. Everything had been wiped clean. No trace of Jason and Vaida remained—reduced to a figment of her imagination.

Too late to go to the gym, she showered and put on the shorts and tee shirt she slept in. The barrenness of the house was depressing, and she felt a loneliness she hadn't felt in a long time. She had become used to having people around. Left alone in the unnerving silence, she lay on her bed, wondering where they had gone and what they were doing, when her cell phone rang. She smiled when she saw the caller ID.

"Hi, kiddo, it's me, are you hungry?"

It was Travis. He always seemed to know when she needed someone to lean on. Most people saw a strong-willed, self-reliant woman and never thought she might need moral support, if they saw her at all. *Well, the cops have seen me. There's no doubt about that.* She was now on their radar and, sadder still, her house was no longer a safe place for a base of operations. Her hand went to the CDL tattoo on the left side of her chest.

"I could eat," she replied. She hadn't really thought about eating anything.

"Meet me at Cho's in ten," was all he said before the line went dead.

'Cho's' was his nickname for the Chinese restaurant on California Avenue. She threw on some jeans and a sweater. Grabbing her helmet and leather jacket, she headed out the door. It was a chilly April evening, and she hoped the leather jacket would be warm enough.

When she pulled up to the curb at 'Cho's,' Travis was leaning on his Harley waiting for her. "Let's go," he said as he pushed the ignition to start the engine.

Joan had no choice but to follow him on her bike. They went down California Avenue toward downtown and, after several sharp turns, they pulled into a parking garage and turned off their bikes. Travis put his fingers to his lips then pointed to his ear, and Joan removed her helmet so she could hear better. It was quiet for a few minutes then they heard a car's tires squealing through the garage. They apprehensively waited as if they were ice sculptures until Travis saw the car and recognized the driver as a tenant in his apartment building.

She flashed a girlie, cutesy wave and continued on to the next level. After thirty minutes, nothing seemed out of place. Travis was satisfied they weren't followed and he motioned for

Joan to follow him. They walked across the Red Level and took a staircase up one flight. Travis unlocked a security door that opened into a long corridor

She followed him down the hall to the third door on the left.

Travis unlocked the door and held it open for her to go through. Joan had never been to his apartment before and her first impression was that it was a typical guy-space. It was relatively neat and clean—"lived in" as Travis described it—but there was sports equipment piled into corners.

There were Harley-Davidson posters on the walls and other Harley-Davidson paraphernalia scattered about. The furniture was comfortable, but chosen without a sense of style. It didn't matter. For the first time that day she could relax.

"I promised you food," Travis said, hanging his jacket on a coatrack. "Talk to me while I cook something up."

Joan slid onto a stool at the breakfast counter and leaned on her elbows. With her chin in her hands, she watched him put a pan on the front burner of his stove and adjust the flame. He grabbed a couple steaks from the refrigerator and seasoned them.

"What happened today?" he asked, checking the temperature of the pan.

"They tried to pump me for information, but I denied everything."

"You were there for seven hours. You didn't give up anything in that length of time?"

"How do you know how long I was there?"

"The Legion is everywhere and knows everything," he said, raising both eyebrows in a pathetic impression of a villain.

"If you know how long I was there, then you should also know I didn't give up anything."

"Touchè," he said as he grabbed a bottle of Dalmore and two glasses from an upper cupboard. He put the two glasses in front of Joan and eyeballed two ounces of scotch into each glass. "Drink."

"I'm driving—"

"Drink," Travis commanded.

Joan took a few sips and Travis turned back to his steaks,

shaking his head. "So what do they know? Did they tip their hand at all?"

Joan told him about the photos and that they knew Jason's nickname and the name on his ID. They didn't seem to know Alice's nickname.

They fell silent while Travis checked the steaks and poured another scotch for himself.

After several minutes, he flipped the steaks and turned to Joan, leaning on the counter across from her. "I hear they can be rough, even on women. Did they get rough with you?"

"The big, dumb cop choked me with his forearm. I wouldn't call it getting rough, though. I've taken worse."

"So now you're a tough guy."

"Girl," she corrected, shooting him a quick smile, then continued, "It seemed to me to be calculated, as opposed to being something personal."

"And now you're a shrink?"

Joan took a big gulp of the scotch and put the glass down on the counter. She smiled, keeping her gaze on the glass as she pushed it to the side with the back of her hand.

"I'll take that as I-don't-give-a-shit-what-you-think," Travis said as he put a big pile of deli coleslaw on each plate.

"They put me in the men's holding cell."

"They did *what*?" He turned from the fridge where he was replacing the container of slaw to face her. "What the fuck, man. Then they wonder why there are people fighting to change things. What happened?"

"Well, there were two punks who thought they were going to have their way with me."

"And…"

"And I had my way with them."

"I'll bet your way was a little more painful than their plans for you."

"Oh, yeah. They won't be having any kiddie punks for a while."

Travis winced. After plating the steaks, they ate in silence for several minutes. The only sound was the clinking of the forks and knives on the ironstone plates.

While pouring another glass of scotch for himself and a

glass of water for Joan, he said, "So you took one to the throat for the Legion. Let me see your neck."

"The bruises are where the clothes hide them."

"Where's that?"

"My collarbones—from the bone in his forearm. He knew how to use pressure points, that's for sure."

"Let me see."

Joan pulled the neck of her sweater to one side so the bruises showed. They were already a bright purple.

"That's all?"

"That's all."

"They probably thought you could be of use to them so they didn't want to alienate you your first time in."

"How do you explain the holding cell incident?"

"Good question. Maybe they wanted to give you a taste of what jail would be like."

"With *men*?"

"Got me there. I can't explain that." He stabbed the last chunk of steak with his fork and put it in his mouth. He chewed for a while and took another sip of scotch. "You're on their radar now. They'll bring you in for questioning every time they get any new info on the Legion, even if it doesn't have anything to do with you."

"So you're saying these two dopes are my new best friends."

"Yep. Try not to think about it." After putting the plates in the dishwasher, Travis motioned for them to move to the living room, which was actually the other end of the same room as the kitchen.

Joan sat cross-legged at one end of the couch with her back resting on the arm. Travis sat at the opposite end half-turned toward her with one leg on the floor and one on the couch.

When they were settled, Joan said, "Travis, you always seem to know when I need someone to lean on. Do you do this with every recruit?"

Travis brought his other leg up to sit cross-legged. Instead of answering her question, he started telling Joan about his background and military experience. Some of it Joan already knew, but he had never brought up the subject of being a mercenary in Central America, and that was how he had met Duncan. With that information, she tried to do the calculations in her head to figure out how old Travis was, but gave up and listened to him open up to her. She guessed it was because he knew so much about her that he felt he should share something about himself. There were holes in his story which raised the question of why he was not involved in operations. But he wasn't obligated to tell her anything, and she felt honored that he trusted her with whatever information he chose to share with her.

Joan yawned and stretched.

"You okay to drive?" Travis asked while he held her leather jacket as she eased her arms into the sleeves.

"I'm fine." Joan grabbed her helmet and headed for the door.

Travis put a hand on her arm to stop her. "You did good today. The depth of your trustworthiness showed itself. The Legion won't forget it."

Joan just looked at him. What do you say to a statement like that?

"You're sticking around, right?" he said. "I mean this didn't change your mind about being a member of the Legion."

She shook her head. "I'm in. I'm good." She opened the door and stepped into the hallway.

He walked her to her bike and gave her a long hug before she took off. She wondered if men actually understood that a simple thing like a hug could transfer strength—in some sort of metaphysical way. Renewed physically as well as emotionally, Joan zipped her bike down the ramp to the city streets.

ⲉ⳿ⲟⲉ⳿ⲟ

She didn't see him watch her drive away and had no idea he was thinking about the first time he had been grilled by the police, and how much he had needed someone to get his mind off it for a few hours. Nor did she see him pick up his cell phone and dial.

CHAPTER 8

"So tell me again why you think this is a good idea." Kempton liked Travis's idea, but wanted him to make the case one more time. "Other inside jobs have been very successful," he continued, "but businesses are getting jittery, and it's getting more difficult to get people inside."

"Up to now," Travis said, "all our inside sources have been male, and although they've done excellent work, employers are getting very cautious of new employees—like you said." He could see Kempton getting impatient so he hurriedly completed his pitch. "Joan has shown an ability to take care of any situation that arises—using her verbal skills when the situation calls for it, but can quickly crush and put an end to any situation that turns physical. No employer will suspect her because she has a quiet, almost passive demeanor about her. She'll go undetected for a long time. She'll be in and out before anyone suspects any-thing—" He looked around the table at the assembled leadership and continued. "—and if they don't suspect her, we can use her again on other jobs."

"What do you think?" Kempton turned to Duncan who had not said anything up to this point. "You vetted her. Is she right for this assignment?"

"She does have a quiet, passive manner. From the moment Travis brought her to my attention, her almost humble attitude had raised doubts. So I delved into her background more than any other recruit. She undoubtedly has abilities and skills the Legion could use. So far, her actions during operations have revealed her ability to think on her feet. She has proven to be strong—psychologically as well as physically. Seven hours of interrogation by the task force and—"

"And they got physical with her." Travis interjected.

Duncan shot Travis a savage glance and finished Travis's thought. "And she gave up nothing. That's impressive for anyone, but she's relatively new to this, and yet she took one for the Legion. Her loyalty and fortitude are above question. She's mission oriented. Given the opportunity to leave an operation that hit a snag, she put herself out there to make it happen. I'm impressed with her. Will she be able to get the intel we need? I don't know for sure, but I think it's worth a try."

Kempton trusted his head of security and operations. "Me, too. Let's give her an easy assignment for the first time out. What do we have?"

"There's the Fusion Center in Cleveland." Pallaton's area had just expanded into Cleveland and he was anxious to hit the Fusion Center. It was a high-profile, but well-guarded target. It would be a feather in his cap to hit it.

"Too important for a beginner. Anything else?"

"What about the National Guard Armory in Columbus?" Duncan had had his eye on that target for a long time. "She's prior military. She knows the lingo and I think she can slide right in there."

"I like it. Anyone have any other ideas or suggestions."

There was general consensus around the table. Kempton gave a long penetrating look at Kearney, who had been uncharacteristically silent. Kearney was the captain who covered the Upstate Pennsylvania area up to Buffalo. Even silent, he was a skin-crawling, sinister ex-CIA interrogator.

With an eye still on Kearney, Kempton ordered, "Travis, break the news to her. Duncan, get it set up and get her up to speed. Kearney, get her a new ID." Each man nodded. "Pallaton, I know this is your geographical area, but I want Duncan to be her handler on this assignment. Let him train her up. She'll report to him. He'll report to you. Questions?" He looked around the table. "Any other items of business?"

Seeing headshakes all around he dismissed the meeting and pulled out a bottle of Scotch.

CHAPTER 9

Joan gritted her teeth. The incessant talking of her undercover boss was like the buzzer on an alarm clock that was just out of reach. Delmar was a decent boss, but he loved the sound of his own voice, or at least he never got tired of it. Pressing her lips together, she concentrated on sorting the mail into the distribution boxes. She made a silent vow to complete her reconnaissance as quickly as possible.

After the interrogation by the feds, Joan's life had spiraled out of control. She resigned from her job rather than be fired. The rector had made it clear that he did not want to let her go, but churches remained open at the whim of the new government. They couldn't risk being closed down from being associated with someone *suspected* of being a part of an underground resistance group. With a written letter of recommendation in hand, he told her they could call him at any time and he would give her a glowing endorsement.

She hadn't planned to be unemployed for very long. However, as weeks turned into a month of no job offers she became edgy and unfocused. Her retirement check from the army allowed her to stay in her house, but money was tight. Not wired to be a homebody, waking each morning with the whole empty day ahead of her eroded her desire to go to the gym and work out every day. The irony baffled her—when she worked every day there was no problem going to the gym every night, but when there was nothing to interfere with her workouts, getting to the gym took a monstrous amount of effort.

Then Travis came to the rescue with this undercover opportunity.

Escaping the surveillance teams sitting on her house was liberating. Evidently she wasn't a big enough priority to follow to Ohio. In Columbus, she could live a normal life. Almost normal.

The idea of checking out the security of a target before an operation appealed to her. Slipshod recon put everyone in danger. This was an opportunity to end the careless reconnaissance and provide thorough, accurate information to the leadership, so the proper decisions could be made.

"Hey, Millie!" Joan was yanked back to reality. Millie Trumbull was the false identity Kearney had given her. It came with a fabricated background and false references. As a temp, she didn't have to go through the long drawn out application process required for a permanent civilian position with a government agency. She was musing that maybe she should have used a false ID to get a job in Pittsburgh when Delmar continued, "Are you listening to me?"

"Frankly, no. You talk too much." She turned to look at her African-American mailroom colleague. Delmar thought he was her supervisor, but Major Lewis had been very specific that he was not.

"Everyone says that." He smiled, showing a gold front tooth. He was a tall, dark skinned man, in his late-thirties, Joan guessed, and very skinny, but likeable in a talkative kind of way.

"Maybe everyone is right. What's up?"

"Time to band up the mail and deliver it to the offices. Think you can do it on your own today?"

He had been helpful at teaching Joan the ins and outs of the mailroom. Never saying a mean word about anyone made him particularly endearing to Joan, and she made a mental note to get Duncan to promise that the operations would not include a mail bomb.

"I guess so," Joan replied. *Could there be any job easier than this?*

"I'm sure you can," Delmar said, attempting to give Joan a vote of confidence. "Do a good job. I don't want anyone to think I didn't train you right."

"I'll do my best. I don't want to make you look bad."

She smiled at him then turned to bundle up the mail. With the bundled mailed stacked in the cart, she headed out to walk the building, delivering incoming mail and picking up mail to be sent out that afternoon. This walk through the entire building gave her an opportunity to see every office, but there were areas she needed to get into. Areas that didn't receive mail.

In the back of the armory, away from the bustling front offices, Staff Sergeant Vincent approached her. Over the past few days he had been flirtatious and sexually suggestive, but with sexual harassment policies being strict and aggressively enforced, he was guarded and vague. If his interest turned out to be more than innocent flirting, she could exploit it. With a little manipulation, he could be instrumental in getting her into a few of the locked areas.

"Sergeant Vincent—"

"Mick."

"Mick, how's your day going?"

"Slow. Most of my section is out doing a community service project today."

"Really?" Joan stepped into his personal space and lowered her voice. "Do you think you'd have time to show me around, you know, where you work?"

"Yes, ma'am, it would be my pleasure. When do you go to lunch?"

"Twelve."

"See you then."

"Don't you do P.T. at noon?"

Most of the soldiers went out at lunchtime to run or go to the weight room.

"Oh, I'll be doing P.T.," he said with a wink, turned, and walked away.

Men are so fucking easy Joan thought as she continued on her mail delivery. Some of the staff members chatted with the new mail girl. They all seemed genuinely interested, but she was not there to make new friends.

At noon she wandered to the Supply Room, now empty of other soldiers. Without hesitation, Mick grabbed her wrist and headed to the room where the protective masks were stored. He unlocked the door and held open it for her. Once inside, he locked the door behind him and immediately made his move.

"Hey, aren't you going to show me around first?" she asked, turning her head to look around the room.

He pulled her close. "That's boring. I have something more interesting to show you."

She looked up at him. "Do I look bored?" Then she coyly added, "Show me around—please?"

He showed her the small room as quickly as he could and Joan noted the windows with the caging over them. She knew exactly where they were in the building. "Now it's your turn to show me something," Mick said, pulling her against him.

She unbuttoned his shirt to expose his well-toned chest and abdominal muscles and unbuckled his pants. "I'll show you something you are going to like a lot."

Voices in the hallway got louder as they neared the storage room. Joan froze. Someone jiggled the knob and, finding the door locked, left. With a silent sigh of relief, she insisted the moment was gone and she had to get back to work. After several impassioned protests, Mick gave in, zipped up his pants, and buckled his belt. She suggested they make a game of it and hook-up in every locked room in the center. He jumped on the idea, and she was on her way to getting the intel the Legion needed. Using sex to gather intelligence was outside her comfort zone, but she was determined to get the information the operatives needed to pull off this operation.

ᥱᢙᥱᢙ

Duncan watched Joan deftly lean her bike as she zipped into the parking lot and parked it at the far end of the diner. She put down the kickstand, removed her helmet, and fluffed up her hair. His eyes followed her as she jogged up the stairs, opened the door, and looked around the diner.

Each Saturday morning for the past four weeks, they met for a debriefing, but it was getting more and more difficult for him to keep it on a professional basis. He wrestled with the thought of her becoming more than an undercover asset to him. He was losing the battle. Her casual wave, her slinky self-confident walk toward him, her freshly scrubbed smell, even the way she pushed her helmet to the far side of the seat and slid into the booth across from him was overwhelmingly intoxicating.

While she placed her breakfast order, he thought of the overly-perfumed stripper he had been with the night before. It was all fake—the playfulness, her enjoyment, his satisfaction. There was a vague, nagging sensation that he had somehow dishonored Joan by the sham of sexual amusement with a prostitute. He gritted his teeth and inhaled to pull himself back into a professional attitude.

Joan must have seen him clench his jaw. "Something wrong?"

"Let's get down to business. Have you found a way to get into the key box?"

"I'll steal Mick's key ring, get a copy of the key made, then get the keys back before he suspects anything."

"Do you think he'll suspect you? Because if he will, it's too shaky."

"He's smitten."

"Smitten?" His mocking tone concealed his imagination going wild, thinking about what she might be doing with this Mick guy to get him...smitten.

"Yes, you know, 'smitten,' thinking with the wrong head."

"I know what smitten means."

"Good. I was worried about you for a minute." She shot him a playful look then reached for the sugar shaker. He watched as she put one teaspoon of sugar and one sugar substitute packet into her coffee and added just the right amount of 2% milk. She looked up to see him watching her and noticed the creases at the corner of his eyes.

"Did you get laid, or something? You look like you're about to break out in a smile. And God forbid *that* should happen."

Duncan pressed his lips into a thin line. When her oatmeal arrived, he watched as she went through a similarly precise routine. Noticing his unusual attention to her, she shrugged. "What? I've gained a couple pounds and I already exercise an hour twice a day, so I'm cutting back on the calories." He put his hands up to indicate he was not judging her. She got back on topic. "Sometimes I almost feel bad, you know, duping Mick this way. It doesn't seem right."

"You're not getting attached to this guy, are you? Because that's the number one rule in undercover work—to stay objective."

"I said, 'almost.'" Keeping her eyes on Duncan, she took a sip of coffee and gave him a half-smile. "I thought the number one rule was to not get caught."

"That, too," he said, wondering when he lost control of the interview. "Enough frivolity. This is serious. We're getting down to the final week. When can you have that key?"

"Monday—Tuesday at the latest."

"Good. Have they changed the passcode to unlock the outside door?"

"No."

"They don't suspect anything?"

"No. Not that I'm aware of."

"You have to be sure. Are you sure?"

She stopped with a spoonful of oatmeal halfway to her mouth. A flashback—the memory of hearing Duncan pull his gun from his holster and Travis asking if she was sure. She had to be sure she wanted to join the CDL. She looked directly into Duncan's eyes. "I'm sure."

While Joan ate her oatmeal, Duncan continued, "Once we have that key, you have to be present for the briefings with the cell. I'll let you know where and when that will be. Anything new I should know about?" Joan shook her head. "Good. Just stay on your toes. This isn't over until we're out of town."

CHAPTER 10

Well, Micky-boy, today is your lucky day. Joan laced up her bustier and winced at the bone stays sticking into her ribs. She hoped her plan to get Mick's key ring would work as she donned a blazer to cover the sexy, red and black undergarment. The lace was scratchy and the boning stabbed into her side, but this wasn't about her. It was about the Legion. After a long look in the mirror, she added a scarf to cover her cleavage, hoping Delmar wouldn't send her home to change.

As usual, Mick crossed paths with her in a secluded part of the armory, and when he approached, she pushed back the scarf and opened her blazer. The look on his face told her that her plan just might work—and work well. She flirtatiously asked if they were still on for noon. His answer was a gentle push to the wall and a hand feeling her chest and breasts. He mumbled something about right then, right there.

Joan pushed him away and buttoned her blazer. She rubbed his thigh and said in a soft, husky voice, "Anticipation is the best foreplay."

Adjusting her scarf, she continued on her rounds of delivering and picking up mail. She contemplated her feelings about the coming rendezvous. Loneliness and boredom enveloped her. The only high spots were the weekly briefings with Duncan. The long five weeks of teasing Mick had increased her need for something more. Well, today was the day for her—as well as for him.

On her way back to the Supply Room at noon, Joan was surprised at how much she was anticipating this afternoon's hook-up. She knew it was merely lust. A desire that had been awakened by a man who obviously lusted after her. But the possibility of getting caught stealing his keys could be a huge factor in the intensity of her feelings. This was a big moment. If she got caught now, it would be a death knell for the mission. The pressure was almost unbearable. Well, she was going to release that pressure.

Mick sat with his feet on his desk, his hands clasped behind his head in a casual posture. Joan wasn't fooled. He got up when she approached, took her hand, and led her to a room they had not yet been in—Major Lewis' office. Joan hesitated. The commanding officer? It seemed sacrilegious.

Mick felt her hesitation. "Don't hesitate now, baby. He's at a conference at Fort Meade. He won't be back until this weekend."

This is wrong, but I want this even more. "You are a wicked man," she said and brushed her body against his as he unlocked the door.

Mick felt the tension in her body and misread it as passion. He held the door for her. "Not nearly as wicked as you." He looked both ways up and down the hallway, stepped into the office, and closed the door.

He eyed her as he crossed the room to her. She was standing, blazer open and scarf on the floor, in front of the green leather couch that faced the commander's over-sized wooden desk. His hands went right for Joan's waist and he started kissing her hard on the lips. Joan assumed that for him kissing hard was passionate kissing. Never mind. She had a job to do before letting go and giving him the ride of his life.

She unbuttoned his shirt with one hand while her left hand reached around his waist. She felt the clasp that held his key ring, released it, and dropped the keys to the floor. He stopped and started to bend over to pick them up, but Joan gently placed her hand on his chin and turned his head to face her. "Hey, I'm up here. They aren't going anywhere."

She saw the fire come into his eyes. He responded even more passionately than ever.

She unbuckled his belt and his pants. Then she knelt in front of him and, while looking up at him, pulled his pants and briefs to the floor in one passion-fueled yank. *Yes, indeed, anticipation is the best foreplay.* She increased his pleasure and, while still watching his eyes, reached for the key ring, and put it in her scarf to quiet any clatter they might make. She shrugged off her blazer and placed it on top of the scarf. But Mick didn't notice a thing. He was on some other level of consciousness.

Before they could go any farther, there was someone in the hallway calling for him. "Shit! I'm sorry, I have to go." He jumped up, pulled on his briefs and pants, frantically tucking in his shirt, and gave Joan one last kiss. "I'm sorry. Duty calls." He became a ball of frenzy as he looked for his key ring.

Joan kissed him gently. "Go. I'll find them and bring them to you. You go ahead. It's probably better if we leave here separately, anyway."

"Yeah, thanks." He gave her a quick kiss on the lips and rushed to the door. "It was fantastic. *You* were fantastic. You…you…we have to talk." And he was out the door.

Joan gave an audible sigh and finished dressing. As she carefully peered out the door to see if the hall was clear she reminded herself, *Don't be too relaxed. This isn't over until you get that key.*

∾≈∾

"What are you doing in here?" It was Mick's supervisor. She was in his office and had just stepped from behind the door where the key box was bolted to the wall. It had been tricky getting the timing right. He had to be out of his office, but Mick couldn't be anywhere close by or he would have asked for his key ring. She had started toward the office a couple times, but either one or the other would be in the area. When she saw her opening, she took it, hoping against all odds that she would have enough time to get in, get the key, and get out. How much had Mick's supervisor seen?

Joan dropped the key to the Communications Room—the intended location for placement of the bomb—into the pocket of her blazer. "I had some mail that looked important, so I brought it to you now instead of waiting until tomorrow."

He moved toward his desk and looked toward where Joan was pointing. He picked up the letter and looked at it. "This doesn't look very special." He gave her a shrewd look. Noticed her uncharacteristically revealing clothes and pinned his eyes on hers for what seemed like a full minute, but was only a few seconds. He gave a cursory look around his office, but didn't see anything out of place, so he dismissed her with a warning, "Don't come in my office again unless I'm here. In the future, pick up the phone and call me if there's something *special* in the mailroom."

Joan noticed the inflection on the word "special." He was on to her. She was sure of it. "Got it. Sorry for invading your personal space." She walked out of his office casually, but her heart was racing. Was it because she almost got caught? Or because she had succeeded? It didn't matter. She had accomplished her mission.

As she walked down the hallway toward the mailroom, Mick approached her. "Not now," she whispered. "I have your key ring. Come to the mailroom in a few minutes." The hair stood up on her neck when she looked over her shoulder and saw Mick's supervisor standing in his doorway watching her.

CHAPTER 11

Joan took in a deep breath of early morning air and smiled. The exhaust from the cars and trucks had long since dissipated and left the air clear and cool. Alice brought her back to reality with a short shove on her right shoulder.

"Move out. The sooner we get in, the sooner we get out," he whispered.

Joan pulled the knit ski cap down over her face and stealthily headed around the corner of the building followed by three men dressed in black. Adrenaline made her senses sharp and she noticed every piece of trash on the ground, every whiff of breeze. They quickly approached the most dangerous part of the mission—getting in the front door—where they would be exposed to the prying eyes of anyone who should pass by on the road only a sidewalk width away. She bounded up the eight steps and entered the four-digit code into the keypad. A click seemed to echo in the quiet of the early morning hours. The lock released, and she motioned to the others to come forward.

They were in.

The hallway was dark, lit only by the exit sign over the door, and the intruders moved along the walls like cats on the prowl. The men stopped at the end of the hallway to wait, heads on the swivel, listening for anything that would compromise the mission. Every mission was perfect until the people factor was added. People were speed bumps with feet.

The key to the Communications Room in hand, Joan passed the man at the head of the group. In a crouch, she moved across the drill hall. The group followed her at a distance. The only sound was that of their soft soles padding cross the floor. She stopped and knelt on one knee beside a desert-cammo Humvee parked in the middle of the cavernous assembly hall. Then her blood went cold. A noise came from one of the offices. *No one should be here.* She motioned the group to stop and pointed to her ear. They all strained to hear what Joan had heard, but only silence filled the drill hall.

The team leader tapped Joan's arm and pointed, indicating for her to move out, but just as she partially rose up to take a step forward, he grabbed her shoulder. He must have heard it, too. He zeroed in on the source, motioned for Joan and Alice to remain by the front tire of the Humvee, and gestured for two of men on the team to follow him. They snaked across the remaining drill floor to the wall on the opposite side. Once there, they continued past two offices and stopped just short of a third. The leader peeked into the office and turned toward his team to gesture that he saw two people. He then counted down with his fingers, starting with three. When the last finger disappeared, he motioned for them to move forward and into the office.

The wait while the team took charge of the interior of the office was excruciating. Then it got quiet. The memory of scolding Jason for sloppy recon at the federal building popped into Joan's head. She made a mental note to apologize—sometimes the unexpected just happened. She looked over at Alice but turned her head back when movement caught her eye. A long exhale escaped when she saw the team leader slinking back toward her.

The leader whispered to Joan, "Some guy was in there doing the bone dance with some skank he picked up at a bar. Let's do what we came to do and get out of here before there are any more surprises."

Joan nodded and headed to the corner of the drill hall and the door to the Communications Room. She hastily unlocked and opened the door. As she stood watch in the doorway, Alice quickly set up the bomb in the designated spot. The other two team members waited outside standing guard, alert for any more kinks in the plan. The bomb planted, Alice rejoined the team. Joan cautiously headed to Mick's desk. With her gloved hand on the drawer handle, she hesitated before putting the key into the top drawer. He had been nothing but nice to her but, if the desk wasn't destroyed in the blast, the key would implicate him, diverting the investigators' attention from her. She dropped the key and exited the office.

Joan tapped the shoulder of the rear member of the team, indicating she was a Go for exiting the building. Crouched and quiet, they made their way to the front door, where they had entered the building less than five minutes previously. They hesitated only a second at the front door just to ensure the whole team was clustered together. The leader peered through the small wire-infused window of the door and, seeing no traffic or people outside, he pressed the slam bar, unlatching and opening the door. They all sped to the back of the building and the exfil vehicle.

Exfiltration could be tricky, but this exfil went off like clockwork.

As the van slowly pulled down the alley, the team members pulled off their black watch caps and took a distinct, collective sigh of relief. They joked about the guy who they surprised in mid-stroke, and gave fist bumps all around. Joan didn't participate. She was not part of their cell and she sat separate from them letting them bond and enjoy their camaraderie.

She rocked gently with the van as it maneuvered through the streets of Columbus. In the darkness, the outside lighting lit the interior with varied intensity, alternately exposing and darkening the faces of the men around her. She sighed and relaxed against the side of the van. This mission was almost over for her and intense fatigue overwhelmed her as it rushed to fill every cell of her body—she no longer pushed off the inevitable adrenaline crash—as if coming off some kind of drug.

Until now she hadn't fully realized the physical cost she had been paying for the constant fear of slipping and saying the wrong thing, doing something out of character for her assumed identity, or simply being discovered. Undercover work, while exhilarating at times, was draining and lonely. She worked in the company of others, but they were just pawns and dupes. She was never working *with* them.

She worked with the cell of operatives, but she wasn't a

part of them. The loneliness and stress weighed heavily on her nerves, locked away in a dark nook of her brain. She had refused to think about it—until now in the shifting darkness in the back of the van. Working undercover also required a mindset capable of working alone—alone on the fringes of the cells. The information she gathered was used by the cells, but only twice before tonight had she had any contact with the operatives. It was lonely on the fringes, but it was where she could best serve the Legion—at the moment.

This undertaking had been harder than she thought it was going to be. Hell, looking back, it was harder than it had seemed when she was in the thick of it. Would every mission be like this? Duncan her only lifeline to the Legion. Stressed. Looking over her shoulder. Alone.

With a rock tune from the 'eighties playing on the radio, Joan rested her head back against the inside wall and stared at the shadowy light dancing across the ceiling. *Make friends with loneliness. This is your new life.*

ℰↄℰↄ

The next morning the local news channel reported that half the armory was reduced to blocks of stone and dust but, most importantly to Joan, no one got hurt.

Later that morning at her apartment, she tossed her suitcase onto the bed and started throwing clothes into it while the news reporter blabbed on. Most of what she said was half-truths or completely untrue. Joan shook her head, picked up her backpack, and headed for the bathroom to clean out the cabinet over the sink.

Her cell rang. It was Major Lewis. She half-listened to him as she continued to empty the medicine cabinet over the sink and haphazardly dropped the items into her backpack. Rather than an impersonal call from the temp agency, he thought she deserved a personal call from him to tell her she was not needed any longer. Once the mailroom was re-established, Delmar would be able to handle it for a while. He continued that he had been happy with her work, and he might call her back in the future for a permanent position, if she wanted to return. With the bathroom cleared out, Joan placed the phone between her shoulder and her ear and folded the last of her tee shirts. She told Major Lewis she was grateful and very much interested in returning when things got back to normal. Zipping up her suitcase and tossing her backpack over her shoulder, she told him how much she had enjoyed working for him. While heading out the door to Duncan's waiting van, she finished her conversation and disconnected the phone. She trotted down the front steps of the apartment building and loaded her bags into Duncan's van.

"All set? Got everything?" Duncan asked.

Joan pulled the seatbelt across her chest. "We're done here."

He pulled the van into traffic and headed back to Pennsylvania, leaving Columbus to pick up the pieces.

CHAPTER 12

Over the next several months, Joan worked as a receptionist in an international company and a dispatcher in a trucking company that had a government contract. Each assignment challenged her a little more. Each mission honed her intelligence collection skills. Her confidence soared. The leadership noticed.

Duncan was not only her mentor, but he was her champion with the inner circle of the leadership. As Duncan's support of Joan increased, Kearney became increasingly sullen. Many years before, during a mercenary operation in Central America, when the other five members of his team were killed, Duncan had come home alone—alone physically—but the painful cries for help from his comrades never left him. He was riddled with PTSD, but Kearney had been there to pick up the pieces. A strong, unbreakable bond formed between them. In spite of this bond, or maybe because of it, Duncan did not grasp the depth of Kearney's antipathy toward Joan.

She was elated when she was assigned the mission of the fusion center in Cleveland. She knew this would be the most difficult assignment so far. She was anxious to show off the skills she had learned. The Legion got her a job in a ma-and-pa deli across the street from Homeland Security Field Office side of the fusion center, gave her fake identification, and let her loose to do what she did best.

It was a relatively quiet few weeks at the corner-store gig, until Chuck, the owner, started prodding Joan about her Social

Security number. It was not checking out. Chuck was a highly decorated former Marine and a Viet Nam veteran. Being the patriot he was, though misguided in Joan's estimation, he took the location of his store seriously.

Joan kept brushing him off, hoping she could get through another couple weeks, complete her mission, and move on before it became a big deal.

She was cleaning up the meat slicer after a busy lunchtime rush when a voice behind her said, "We're looking for Millicent Trumbull. Is she here?"

She turned to see two uniformed policemen standing several feet apart in the open area in the front of the store. Her blood went cold. She regained her composure quickly, but not before the closest officer saw the fleeting look of alarm in her eyes.

Wiping her hands on a towel she said, "I'm Millie Trumbull. How can I help you, officer?"

"Miss Trumbull, may I see some identification?"

"Sure." Joan reached under the counter. "May I ask what this is about?" She pulled out her backpack and dug around for her fake driver's license. She handed it to the officer.

He looked at the license then up at Joan and said, "Miss Trumbull, please step out from behind the counter."

As Joan lifted the counter-door and approached him, the officer keyed the mike on his shoulder and started giving the information off her license to the dispatcher. She looked to her left when she heard Chuck's voice.

Walking down the aisle along the counter Chuck said, "I want these officers to check your ID. I'm sure everything is okay. I just want to be sure."

"You called the *police* on me?"

"I'm sorry, Millie."

"I told you I was working on getting the problem with Social Security ironed out. Couldn't you have waited?"

"If everything checks out you have nothing to worry about, right, officer?"

"That's right." The officer hesitated as he listened to the response from dispatch, then said to Joan, "Miss Trumbull do you know you have an outstanding warrant?"

"A warrant? For what? It has to be some kind of mistake."

Fucking Kearney. Didn't he check and make sure the ID he gave me is clean?

"Ma'am, turn around put your hands behind your back. Clasp your hands." As she felt the officer's hands grasp hers, something snapped in Joan. She was not going to jail. Not today, not for someone else's warrant. Stepping back with her right foot she scraped the officer's shin and stomped his foot. Simultaneously, she spun and elbowed him with her right elbow. Because he pulled back to avoid the elbow, she missed his jaw and grazed his throat. As she continued the spin, she hit him with a left hook. He lunged to grab and control her, but before his arms got all the way around her, she recoiled her spin, brought the left elbow back, and caught him squarely on the jaw. The officer rocked back on his heels. Simultaneously, Joan jabbed his throat with a half-fist and swept his foot to knock him down. She looked down at red laser dots on her chest. His partner had his Taser trained on her. Grabbing two bags of chips from the shelf next to her, she tossed them in quick succession at the cop as a diversion. A shoulder roll got her under the electrodes. Only one of the electrodes caught her and stuck into the back of her thigh. Not enough for a full circuit. Joan kicked up between his legs landing a strong blow to his groin. He fell to his knees and as his head came forward she kicked upward again, this time to his face. It snapped his head back. She jumped to her feet, grabbed the back of his head, and brought it sharply down to meet her knee.

Like a pinball, Joan bounced off the potato chip rack, then the counter. She grabbed her backpack, shrugged the straps over her shoulders, and snatched her fake driver's license off the floor, frantically putting it into her back pocket as she raced toward the back door. She stopped in her tracks. Chuck had a gun pointed at her. *Dammit, I forgot about him.*

"Get on your knees. Hands behind your head."

Joan knelt, hands open and in front of her. The best way to handle this situation was to let him think she was complying. The gun was only a foot from her head. A surprising mistake for a former Marine. Joan grabbed the gun, deflected the barrel, and, using his pull-reflex, got to her feet. By the time she was on her feet, she had his gun in her hands. The butt of the handgun slammed under his jaw sent him stumbling backward, grabbing at shelves as he fell. Candy sprayed over him like sweet pellets of rain. Joan leaped forward. As she dropped to one knee, she smashed the butt of the .45 against the left side of his jaw. The impact sent his head backward with a loud crack as it hit the hardwood floor. As he lay on his back, Joan kicked him in the head with the heel of her boot. Bags of chips and packages of cookies crashed to the floor behind her as one of the cops behind her staggered to his feet.

Dropping Chuck's handgun into a sink full of gray water, she ran through the kitchen to the back door. Her motorcycle was parked there, waiting to whisk her to safety. She jumped on it, raced to the end of the alley, turned right, and sped away.

☙❧

For the first time in her life Joan panicked.

She had seriously hurt two police officers, and if the police caught her, it was going to be a Bad Day in Dodge. She fled down alleys and crossed streets without slowing down to check traffic. Behind her, tires squealed from locking brakes and thuds as cars ran into each other, but she didn't have time to think about that.

She looked desperately for someplace to stop and make a call on her phone. Duncan would know what to do.

A green dumpster in an alley looked like a good spot, and she slid her bike to a stop behind it. She dialed Duncan's number.

Her stomach clenched at his familiar greeting. "Talk to me."

Talk to him. She had wanted to tell him, but now that she had him on the phone, she was afraid to tell him what she had done. *Talk to him.*

"Joan, what's going on?"

"I assaulted two police officers."

"What? You better have a good reason."

"The ID Kearney gave me was dirty. There was a warrant—They were going to arrest me."

"Warrant for what?"

"I don't know, but I'm not going down for something some other bitch did. What do I do?"

"Where are you?"

"On my bike in an alley somewhere."

"Get off your bike and walk to the nearest bus stop and take the first bus to anywhere. Get out of that neighborhood, then call me."

"I'm not leaving my bike."

"Get off the damn bike."

"I can't leave it."

"You called me for advice, right? Here it is: *leave the fucking bike.*"

"I—" She saw a cruiser back up after going past the alley. "—I gotta go."

The cruiser crept up the alley toward her. She stuffed the phone into her pocket and took off in the opposite direction.

She turned east onto Carnegie Street heading east. A cruiser passed her going the other way. When she looked in her rear-view mirror, his flashing lights went on and the car hastily make a U-turn. *Damn, they found me already.* She gripped the gas tank of her Triumph with her knees and opened the throttle.

The signs for I-90 flew toward her and she decided to get onto the interstate and out-race the police, get off their radar. In her panic she missed the ramp for I-90 and found herself on Route 77 South. She raced through all the gears until she reached 104 miles per hour. Her steel grip on the handlebars was the only thing that prevented the rushing wind from blowing her off the back of the bike as the telephone poles blurred by.

Knowing Route 490 would turn into I-90, she slowed to make the turn. She was beginning to think she might just pull this off, when she braked too hard and felt the dreaded wobble in the front end. It pulled her attention from the signs. She downshifted. Through sheer determination, she managed to re-gain control of the front end of her bike in time to get onto the ramp. Before she could take a silent sigh of relief, she realized she was on Route 490 East instead of West. She looked over her shoulder. There were now several cars with flashing lights be-hind her. *This is not good, but I can still pull this off. I can do this.*

She looked ahead. In disbelief she screamed to herself, *The highway* ends? *What highway ends in a T?*" There were flashing lights ahead where the road went left. A police cruiser blocked the north side of the intersection, preventing her from making a U-Turn and getting back onto 490 East. The only option was to go south. Escaping was still possible. All she had to do was find a way back to the highway.

She braked and downshifted hard, sliding her Triumph sideways to keep from going straight across the intersection. Through sheer muscle and grit, she maintained control as the bike spun around and she found herself inches from the grill of a Ford Taurus, staring into the wide eyes of a female driver stopped at the light. Desperate to get away, she finessed the bike around the front fender of the car and opened the throttle, shifting through all four gears, grating into third gear in her haste to get some distance between her and the cops.

Her only thought was to head west. The second right turn caught her eye, and she down shifted aggressively. It was a mistake. This road veered north and ended in another T-intersection. Her adrenaline was pumping and her head pounded in sync with the rumble of the bike beneath her. Downshifting as quickly as she dared, she leaned hard and, once again, muscled the bike to the left with the back tire sliding on the pavement. She recovered quickly, hit the throttle again, but the road ended in *another* T-intersection—one T-intersection too many. She slid diagonally across the pavement and when the back tire touched the grass on the other side of the intersection, she let go of the handlebars and slid across the grass beside her bike, slamming against a chain link fence with a thud that shook her whole body. A searing pain wrapped itself around her left ankle.

She got to her hands and knees, trying to get her wits about her. "Get face down on the ground. Let me see your hands," several cops repeated many times.

It was over. Out-manned, out-gunned, and physically exhausted from the chase, she complied with their orders. Four cops piled onto her and put handcuffs on her wrists. Before they got up one asked her, "Are you going to be calm or do we have to get the shackles?"

"No. I'll be calm," she muttered.

One cop deftly lifted her to her feet. Another cop quickly patted her down finding the gun, her knives and throwing stars. He asked the inevitable, "Is this why you ran?"

"No. Well, yes partly, I was told I had an outstanding warrant."

"Do you know what it was for? Outstanding parking tickets. You would have been out in a couple hours. Now you have two counts of felony assault on a police officer, felony eluding, resisting arrest, various weapons charges. You just screwed up your life."

"I wasn't thinking."

"I guess not." He gave her arm a tug and supported her as she limped toward the flashing lights of the ambulance that had just arrived on the scene.

Other than a few bruises and a sprained ankle, Joan escaped any serious injury. While EMS cleaned and bandaged her bruises and wrapped her ankle, she sat quietly on the bumper of the ambulance contemplating her fate with the Legion. With closed eyes and a shake of her head she thought, *Shit! Traffic tickets? Dammit, Duncan's going to rip off my head, and throw it into the fires of hell.*

She was not afraid of Duncan per se. He had never given any indication of getting physical with her, but she dreaded his reaction. It would be intense to the extreme. There was no doubt about that. Facing Duncan after this would be like basic training—you only remember the good parts, but you never want to go through it again. She seriously doubted if there were going to be any good parts. Maybe jail would be the lesser of the two evils. Dealing with convicted felons, confinement, and loss of her freedom would be a sunny day compared to facing Duncan's wrath.

Duncan would also be disappointed. She would have to start all over again rebuilding the Legion's faith in her and her abilities—if she was given another chance. And if she wasn't given another chance that would mean certain death. No one got out of the Legion alive. She gave a wry smile thinking of their motto, "Death is not the worst of evils." How true that was turning out to be. Death might be preferable to facing Duncan's anger. Jail time wasn't looking so bad after all.

And Duncan. He had been instrumental in training her to be successful at her jobs for the Legion. This was a betrayal of his trust and belief in her. This was an important assignment, and she had wanted to show him what she could do. She had let him down. Her future with the Legion was in serious jeopardy.

She was still vacillating between Duncan, jail, and death when the EMT finished patching up her injuries and handed her over to the waiting policeman, who helped into the back seat of his car.

The driver glanced over his shoulder. "Do you have anything to say for yourself?"

Joan responded from her heart. "I have dishonored all my martial arts teachers and all my fellow students. Worst of all I have dishonored my art. I didn't train all these years for this—an attack on a person in authority. I attacked a representative of duly appointed authority, which is indefensible. This is a dark day—" Joan swallowed the lump in her throat and hung her head as her eyes stung from the unwept tears.

The officer turned to face forward and pulled onto the road. "You are looking at some serious jail time. You have more to worry about than dishonoring your *art*."

"No. My art is everything." *I do have something more to worry about.* She was painfully aware that Duncan held her future with the Legion, and possibly her life, in his hands.

The officer shook his head and headed to the station.

CHAPTER 13

Two long weeks later, Joan stood on the walkway in front of Duncan's motel room. The lawyer, who had secured her release from jail, backed out of the parking space. Joan watched him pull out of the motel parking lot. She was on her own. Hoping against all odds that maybe two weeks behind bars was long enough for Duncan's anger to subside, she ran her fingers through her long brown hair and straightened her shirt. About to find out what this imminent meeting would mean for her life and career with the Legion, she never felt so alone, so helpless, so doomed.

She jumped at the harsh voice behind her. "Get in here," Duncan growled from the doorway of his room.

He stood in the doorway. Joan had to squeeze past him into the room. As she passed by him she took one look at his cold, glaring eyes and tense shoulders. Nothing had prepared her for the intensity. His anger made him appear taller and broader than he was. She quickly sat on the edge of the bed not daring to look at him again. "Sit on the desk chair. You don't deserve anything comfortable."

Joan darted to the chair. "Duncan, I—"

"Shut up. You don't have anything to say that I want to hear."

He stood with feet apart and his arms folded on his chest. His wrath filled the room and sucked out all the oxygen. It made Joan feel very small and weak, like a bug he was about to squash. She had never seen him like this and it became clear as glass why so many people were afraid of him. Then the pacing and fuming started. A knot formed in the pit of her stomach. She wiped her damp palms on her jeans.

"I put my integrity and reputation on the line for you time and time again," Duncan said. "When others wanted to dismiss you, I fought for you—for them to respect you and your abilities." He stopped pacing and approached her. "But this is not about me. This is about you and your poor judgment under pressure." He leaned on the desk with his face inches from Joan's, poking her chest with two fingers. "You're better than this. You have excelled in more tense situations—life and death situations. Where was your head at?"

He poked her forehead when he said the last five words. She resisted the urge to rub her chest where he had poked her, wondering if he purposefully had poked her where her Legion tattoo was inked into her skin.

He walked back across the room, running his fingers through his hair, stopping with a hand on each side of his head. "You jeopardized the operation and the Legion—hey, look at me when I'm talking to you."

Did he just say "hey" to me? Joan swallowed her pride and hesitantly looked up at Duncan. Her heart was about to break over betraying him and botching the biggest opportunity she had with the Legion. Did he see the remorse she felt? If he did, he was not ready to let go of his anger, or let her off the hook. She could see he was consumed with rage and wanted her to feel it. She swallowed the lump in her throat, ready to endure the full force of his wrath, like anyone else in the same situation.

"And the bike—the mother fucking bike. Didn't I tell you to leave it? But, no, you had to stay on your precious bike. Where's your bike now, smart ass?"

Joan opened her mouth to speak.

"In the impound lot," he said, cutting her off. "That's right. And why? Because you wouldn't listen to me. You called me for help and I told you to leave the bike and get on a friggin' bus and get out of that area. How hard was that? But oh no, you can't listen to what anyone else has to say." He stood again with his arms crossed. "You jeopardized everything for parking tickets?"

"I didn't know—"

"Shut up." He lunged toward her and Joan reflexively flinched. "For *parking tickets*, Joan. Jesus Christ, you would have been released within hours, but now you're going to have to hightail it back to Pennsylvania and stay out of Ohio. That's going to limit what we can do with you, that is, if you still have a future with the Legion. You put two cops in the hospital. If you get caught in Ohio after the court date, which you *are* going to miss by the way, they will not treat you with any kindness or leniency. You are about to find out what it's like to be a fugitive. You think what you've done so far is nerve wracking? Wait until your blood goes cold every time you hear a police siren."

"Shouldn't Kearney share some blame in this? After all—"

"What did I tell you? You have nothing to say here. And never mind about Kearney. This discussion is between you and me, here and now." He was in her face again, pounding his fist on the desk. "You have more at stake here than whether Kearney is going to share some of the blame."

"If he had given me a clean ID—"

"See? This is what I'm talking about. You don't listen. Didn't I say to shut up? Shut the fuck up." He slapped the back of her head for emphasis and started pacing again. He was getting physical with her and her dread multiplied. If he grabbed or hit her, she would not cower.

It wasn't in her to back down from a fight, and the ensuing battle would not be pretty—one, or more likely both of them, would get badly hurt.

He was back in front of her, standing over her, glaring into her eyes. "And what if the cops figure out who you are and your association with the Legion? I don't have to remind you that you were across the street from the fusion center. You better hope the locals don't share any information with the feds in the building—*across the fucking street*!"

He started pacing again. "I have to answer to Pallaton. This is his area, and I have to explain to him why you blew the whole operation. And then there's the boss. Kempton wants a pound of flesh for this. And believe me, it isn't going to be *my* pound of flesh. And that's not all. You've put me in a very precarious position here. My credibility is going to be questioned from now on. Do you know how long it took to build up my rep? Years, Joan—years."

He was approaching her again, and she braced herself for the possibility of more physical contact. He stopped inches away and stood there towering over her, boring into her sad eyes. She had to look away. He was breathing hard—she hoped in an attempt to gain some control of himself. He finally turned and started pacing again.

There was a long, uncomfortable silence. Memories flooded into Joan's consciousness. The helplessness she had felt in the nightclub during the attack many years ago. The realization that things were out of her control and getting worse by the minute. But now she was trained. Now she could keep herself safe in any situation.

She may be in a situation that she couldn't control but it wouldn't get worse. She would bet her life on it.

It was a long minute before Duncan spoke again. Odd how a minute could rush by during a happy event, but be interminable when in a bad place. "You know what I think?" he said, crossing his arms. "I think you don't have what it takes to be an operative. Oh, you can do the easy stuff, but as soon as it gets complicated, you panic. I think maybe we gave you too much too soon, and the fast track to more responsibility was too much for you. Maybe it's time for you and the Legion to part company."

Duncan leaned against the bureau and scrutinized Joan's eyes, face, and body language. He relaxed. "Your motivation is the same as everybody else. Fear." Joan started to speak, but he put up a hand to silence her. "Not fear of bodily harm for you, Joan. No, your fear is firmly planted in being rejected or incompetent. Over this past year, you got attached to the Legion. You eat, breathe, and live the Legion. But the question remains, what do you want?"

"I just want another chance," Joan said.

"Do you really think you deserve another chance?"

"Yes."

"Why? Why should we give *you* another chance?"

"I made a mistake, but I can learn from my mistakes."

"And?"

"And I want to see the Legion succeed in its mission to bring down the regime in Washington."

"And?"

Biting her lower lip, Joan struggled to come up with an answer. She thoughtfully continued, "And I want to be a part of that by doing whatever the Legion asks me to do."

Duncan opened his mouth to speak.

Joan spoke first. "And do it in a way that doesn't compromise the mission or the Legion."

"And?"

"And, what, you fuck?" She was at the end of her rope.

Duncan was stunned. No one had talked to him in that tone for a long time—not even Kearney. "Tell me you're going to get the job back at the store."

"I can't—"

"You *can't*? So, you want me to tell Kempton you can't do what the Legion is asking you to do?"

"I'll try." It sounded empty, so she added, "No, I *will* get the job back at the store. I'm sure Chuck will rehire me after I broke his jaw."

Duncan ignored the sarcasm. "Sit down and be quiet, if that's within your realm of possibilities. I have to call Kempton."

CHAPTER 14

Since the big blowout with Duncan, Joan had trouble sleeping. After a week of light, restless sleep, she had fallen into her first deep slumber.

She was awakened with a wildly beating heart and a sense of dread. No—danger.

"How many guns do you have?"

Joan was so startled that she took a loud gasp in, but nothing came out. Wide-eyed and gasping for air, she tried to think, but adrenaline was already creating a pounding headache. She reached for the knife under her pillow, never taking her eyes off the male silhouette standing over her bed. "Too slow. If I was an assassin, you'd be dead already."

"Damn, Duncan, you almost gave me a heart attack. Did you ever hear of knocking?"

"Not my style. How many guns do you have?"

"One. A .38, why?"

"You'll need more. I'll loan you one of mine."

Joan sat up, holding her head, trying to get the pounding to stop. "For what?"

"Get dressed. You have three minutes."

Duncan tossed onto the bed a set of camouflage shirt and pants still on the hangar that he got from her closet. Joan stopped short and stared at the clothes on her bed. *How long has he been in my room while I was sleeping? Better yet, how often has he done this?*

"How did you—" She stopped when she grabbed the clock

on the bedside table and was stunned. It was only 2:00. She'd only gotten two hours sleep. "What are we doing?" she asked, but she was talking to herself.

Duncan had vanished as if into thin air. Jason called him a shape shifter. Maybe he wasn't so far off the mark. For a big man, Duncan sure was light on his feet.

Joan quickly pulled on the clothes Duncan had thrown on the bed, ran a comb through her hair, grabbed her usual array of weapons, and ran out the door, quietly closing it behind her to avoid waking up her nosey neighbors. She slid into the passenger seat of Duncan's van, with one boot on and the other in her hand, three and a half minutes after Duncan disappeared from her room.

"You're late."

"It takes me a little longer to get down the stairs with this ankle," she said with the clip for the ace bandage in her mouth. She lifted the leg of her jeans and started wrapping her ankle. "What's so important?"

"We're about to find out if your driving skills are as good as you say they are." He glanced over at her. "You know they make bandages that stick to themselves, now."

"I know, but I can always use the clip as a weapon."

"Mighty small weapon."

"Some of the best weapons are small."

"Yeah? What weapons would that be?"

Joan thought for a moment. Duncan always managed to get her to talk herself into a corner. "Throwing stars, my fists—"

"Your fists are a little bigger than that clip."

"Fuck you."

Duncan chuckled and checked his mirrors.

Joan turned her attention to securing the bandage. She reached for her boot to put it on. "What are we doing driving around on two lane roads in excess of—" She leaned over to check the speedometer. "—sixty miles per hour at two o'clock in the morning?" Even after the barrage of wrath he had bestowed upon her, she persisted in treating him like she would anyone else. She refused to show him the fearful deference others bestowed on him. It wasn't her style.

"You'll see in time. There's a cup of coffee for you." He

gave a short nod toward the cup holder in the console. "You're gonna need it."

"I have to be at work this morning at eleven."

After a lengthy, and at times loud, discussion with Chuck, Joan had managed to get her job back at the deli—Duncan said she won him a lot of money from Kempton and a free dinner from Kearney. She pointed out to Chuck that he wouldn't have to be afraid of being robbed again as long as she was there. She offered herself as a kind of insurance policy, even promising to cover any lost money if any robbery attempt on her shift was successful. Nothing was working until she reminded him that if he had waited just another day or two her Social Security problem would have been straightened out. His impatience brought about her whole ordeal with the cops, courts and bail.

It struck a chord with Chuck. He liked Joan, and he felt guilty for getting her into this mess. Although, he reminded her, she did overreact and bring the most serious charges on herself. In the end, he agreed to take her back, emphasizing that it was on a probationary basis. One wrong move and she was gone for good this time. He moved her to the late shift when most of the robberies took place. It meant she would be closing up, but he knew she was volatile, not dishonest—no money had ever come up missing on any shift when Joan had worked.

"Worried about your job, are you?" Duncan was saying. "You weren't so worried when you socked those cops."

"I'm just sayin' I have to work in the morning."

"You'll be back in time."

Joan sipped the coffee, marveling at Duncan's keen cognizance of everything around him. She'd ordered coffee when they met in a diner to pass along intel but had never thought much of it. It was a small thing, preparing coffee, but he knew exactly how she liked it and he had brought her a cup prepared perfectly. She thought of saying something, but decided he would just brush it off. They rode in silence for an hour.

When they reached the rest area before the junction of I-79 and I-80, Duncan pulled off and parked beside a black SUV with darkened windows. The passenger window of the SUV rolled down and Duncan leaned over to talk to the driver. Joan couldn't hear exactly what they were saying, but Duncan pointed his thumb in her direction during the conversation. The windows went back up and Duncan turned in his seat to reach into a canvas bag on the floor behind his seat. "Here, take my Sig. You might need some extra fire power." He pulled out a well-oiled Sig Sauer semi-automatic handgun and held it out to Joan.

What is he getting me into? More fire power? For what? She took the gun he offered her. "This is a 9mm?"

"Yes, why?"

"Do you have a .45?"

"You always know better than everyone else, don't you?" He shook his head and exhaled loudly. "The Sig has plenty of firepower. It has an eighteen round magazine."

"The .45 has better knock down power—" She stopped in mid-sentence. He was right. She always seemed to think contrary to everyone else. "I'm just saying. I know what I like. Is that so bad?" She turned the gun over in her hand, feeling its weight and balance. Her adrenaline started pumping. "Duncan, I don't know about this—"

"About what? You'll be fine."" He leaned in toward her. "You'll be with pros, just do what they tell you. This is just in case things go to hell."

"What things?"

Joan never got an answer. Her head snapped back to her right when she heard a loud tap on her window. She rolled it down to find a 60-something year old man with an angular face and silver, bushy eyebrows over gray eyes that gave him the look of a bird of prey. He looked like he ate nails for breakfast.

"Good morning, St. Joan. I'm Gunther, come with me."

Joan anxiously looked back at Duncan. "*St.* Joan?"

He growled, "Go!" and indicated for her to leave with this stranger. Duncan had his game face on, which wasn't particularly encouraging. This was serious business.

"If you have to use the restroom, better do it now," this stranger named Gunther said.

Joan slid out through the door that Gunther held opened for her. She hesitated, not sure of where to put the Sig Sauer, then slipped it in the small of her back. As she stepped up onto the curb and headed toward the building with the restrooms she overheard Gunther say, "Don't worry, D., I'll get her back to you in one piece. See you at the other end."

She heard the door to the van slam shut and, as she opened the door to the lobby of the building, she glanced over her shoulder. Gunther stood leaning his arms against the open driver's side window of the SUV talking to someone inside. For an instant, she wanted to run through the lobby, out the back door, and slip into the woods to get away from whatever mysterious mission they had planned. She shrugged it off. They'd only hunt her down, and surely they were as heavily armed as she, maybe more so.

In one of the stalls, Joan fumbled with the Sig not sure what to do with it. She removed it from her waistband and placed it precariously on the toilet paper holder. As she pulled down her pants, she bumped it and it fell to the floor with a metallic rattle. She snatched it up and looked both ways up and down the row of stalls. No legs. Joan gave a sigh of relief. That would have been a tragic start to this whole event—whatever it was.

She finished up and walked toward the exit, where she stopped to take in a deep breath and put on an air of confidence. When she pushed the slam bar to open the door she noticed that Duncan's van was gone which left her committed to working with this stranger.

She strode toward Gunther, who was now casually leaning with his back on the driver's door of the SUV, patiently waiting for her. She hoped he wouldn't notice her shaking hands. He pushed off the door when he saw her approaching, narrowed his eyes, and nodded in slow motion. Her bluster was not fooling him.

As she got within earshot he put out his hand. "Piece of gum?" Joan started to wave him off, and he added, "It'll help calm your nerves."

She rethought it and took the gum from him. As she fumbled with the wrapper, she noticed the corners of his eyes crease ever so slightly. She put the wrapper in her pocket.

Chewing a piece of gum with a slow, thoughtful movement, he pointedly looked at the pocket where she had just placed the gum wrapper. His eyes then looked over her athletic build and posture, making their way up to her face. They locked eyes. He reached and opened the door behind her.

"Where are we going?" Joan started to get into the car, but abruptly turned and stood between the open door and the SUV. Gunther's eyes creased a little more—and was that a hint of sparkle in those cold gray eyes? "Do you find me amusing?"

Gunther didn't reply so she turned and slid into the back seat. Before he shut the door he said, "Nice to see you're living up to your legend, SJ"

Legend? SJ? And who were these other three guys in the car?

Joan had learned from Duncan that beating around the bush was a useless exercise. "What is going on?"

"You get right to the point. You are definitely D's protégé."

"Protégé? I don't really think—"

"Let's get started. Everyone, this is SJ" Gunther pointed to each of the men in turn. "This is T, K, and TJ." Joan looked at each man. This was becoming more bazaar by the minute. "This is SJ's first hijacking so stay alert. She has a rep of not listening to instructions, so keep an eye on her."

"I'm in the car. I can hear you—"

T, the guy next to her, elbowed her and shook his head then nodded toward Gunther.

"Yes, I can see that." His voice was sharp and now *he* had his game face on.

Joan felt the shaking stop as she looked from one man to the other. Each man was slowly chewing gum or sitting quietly. No nervous fidgeting or sweating. She had experienced this before—in Iraq. Her breathing settled into a comforting rhythm. She was still nervous, of course. Anyone who said they were not nervous in the face of a potentially dangerous mission was lying—or dead. Her inner strength surfaced and she thought to herself, *Okay, I can do this.* She put *her* game face on.

"From now on you refer to me as 'G,'" Gunther told her. "You see the pattern?"

Joan nodded.

"Let's go over the plan," he continued. "We've all done this before, but there's going to be one more truck in this convoy than we usually encounter, so that's why SJ is here. The hijack team stops the trucks and detains the drivers while we wait in this vehicle. They signal when the driving team—that's us—is needed, and you will, at that time, exit the vehicle and go to your assigned truck. There will be four trucks. SJ, I want you in the third truck, so you have trucks in front and behind you. You've been in Iraq—"

Joan nodded.

"—so you know that with the first shot the whole plan could become an audible."

Joan nodded again.

"So stay alert," Gunther ordered. "If you're not sure what to do, look to these guys. You probably won't be able to find me."

"Shot? Who's doing the shooting?"

"Hopefully, nobody. Nowadays all truckers are armed, and every once in a while one of them tries to be a hero." G looked at TJ, who was riding shotgun, as if they had an inside joke. "But most of them realize it's not worth it to defend a cargo that has more value to us than to them. When you get in the truck, get it ready to move out as quickly as possible, and just follow the truck in front of you."

"What if I get separated from the convoy?"

"You won't."

"Yeah, but what if—"

"D was right, you *are* a pain in the ass."

Joan looked to her fellow drivers for moral support, but they were looking at each other in disbelief. Joan was beginning to wonder if she was the only person in the Legion who questioned authority.

"Okay, if you get separated, and you won't, stop where you are and wait. Someone will notice your absence and come and find you. There'll be more men there than just us guys."

"I'm sorry, but it's the details that'll kill you."

"*You're* a detail that's killing me. You stop. And wait. Got it?"

"Roger that." Joan knew she had been duly put into her place. She turned her head to look out the window and didn't see the long, hard look he gave her in the rear view mirror.

They rode in silence until G drove into a gravel pull off. It was heavily rutted and they rocked against each other until he brought the SUV to a stop. After putting the vehicle in park, G put an earpiece in his ear and made contact with someone. Joan assumed it was the hijack team. She went over the sparse instructions in her head as she waited and swallowed the gum G had given her. She didn't want to choke on it at an inopportune time.

"We're on. Go hot," G said as he put the van in gear and pulled out onto the road. Each member grabbed their weapon of choice. The sound of slides being cocked and clips being checked filled the interior. Familiar sounds that Joan had buried in the back of her memory, but that now came back to the forefront, sending a reflexive signal to her body to pump up the adrenaline. Her head started pounding again.

T leaned close to her ear and whispered, "It's going to be okay. We've done this dozens of times. Most times it goes off like clockwork."

Joan struggled to hear what he was saying because her heartbeat was filling her ears. She guessed he was trying to say something supportive. "I'm good."

They drove up on a scene out of a movie. Four trucks lined the side of the road. Joan put her eyes on the third truck. It was an older Peterbuilt. *Please let it be an air-thirteen,* she repeated to herself several times. It was then, in the dim lighting of the headlights, she saw men dressed in black with body armor holding several men on their knees at gunpoint.

"When we get the word, approach your assigned truck on the passenger side. Climb in and slide over. Stay out of the hijack team's way." He looked in the rearview mirror. "Got that, SJ?"

"Got it." Her mouth had gone dry, and she barely got the words out. She wasn't so fearful that she was out of control. It was just enough fear to sharpen her senses. She watched the hijack team bind the hands and feet of the drivers. Then, as if by some unseen signal, two of the truckers jumped up and made a beeline under one of the trailers to get to the relative safety of the woods. Two Legs followed right behind them hot on their heels.

After several seconds there was a gunshot, and without

thinking, Joan jumped out of the SUV crouching and moving along the trailer of the nearest truck, stealthily approaching the spot she estimated they'd be.

"*God damn it*! TJ, get her six," Gunther yelled. TJ flew out of the vehicle to catch up to Joan. "The rest of you, take positions to support the hijack team so no more truckers get stupid." He bailed out to follow Joan and TJ.

Joan stopped at the tree line only long enough to get a sense of the location of the men. She saw TJ four feet behind her and to her right. Together they darted into the woods. When they were under the cover of the shrubs, TJ touched Joan on the arm and put his finger to his lips. They listened for voices, determined the direction, then crept toward the sound of men talking.

The voices got louder as they approached, and they stopped at the edge of a small clearing about twenty-five feet from a trucker with his back to them and holding the MAC-10 he had wrested from one of the members of the hijack team. He held it to the head of one of the Legion members, who was on his knees. Joan saw the other Legion member on the ground clutching his lower abdomen. She whispered to TJ, who was now four feet from her, "That explains the gunshot, but where's the other trucker?"

TJ shrugged.

Damn, he could be anywhere, Joan thought as she scanned the dark woods, trying to find a sign of the missing trucker—a moving branch, a twig snap, anything to give her a sense of direction and distance. When she shifted her weight because her knee was on something sharp, she saw something come down and hit TJ in the head. He fell to the ground. A blur came out of the woods.

Joan didn't wait to see Gunther expertly hit the trucker on the back of the head. She flew across the small opening toward the trucker standing over her fellow Legion member. By the time the trucker heard her coming, it was too late. He turned and brought the Mac-10 around to fire at her, but she was already too close. In one movement, she grabbed the arm holding the automatic weapon and smashed him in the jaw with the butt of her Sig Sauer. She recoiled and brought butt of the gun against the soft tissue behind his right ear. He wobbled, but remained on his feet. After a perfectly placed upper cut with the palm heel of her hand, he fell backward—down for the count. By this time the Legion member, who had been on his knees, was attending to the guy who had taken one in the abdomen. Joan picked up the Mac-10 and approached them. "Sorry I didn't get here sooner."

The kneeling man looked up at her, but didn't say anything. She placed his weapon by his knee, and turned to see G and TJ dragging the other unconscious trucker toward them. They placed him next to the one Joan had knocked out.

"Why didn't you shoot him?" Gunther asked.

"If the plan was to shoot them, the hijack team would have already shot the ones they had in custody. It's too messy, anyway."

"He was about to shoot one of our guys."

"If he was going to shoot him, he would have done it. He was just exerting his power. So I exerted some of my own. Besides this is Duncan's gun. If the shooting was traced back to this gun, it would implicate him."

"Are you always so protective of Duncan?"

"He protects me."

Gunther squinted at Joan, trying to determine if this was normal camaraderie between colleagues—or something else. Joan didn't flinch under his gaze. Gunther turned and walked over to the man she had just knocked unconscious and stopped six feet from him. He pointed his 9mm at the man's head and turned to look at Joan. They locked eyes and, without taking his eyes off Joan, Gunther fired his gun and put a bullet into the man's head. Other than a reflexive flinch at the sound of the shot, she allowed no other emotion to show on her face. There was a fleeting tightening of her jaw, but it disappeared as quickly as it had come.

"Well, he's dead now." Gunther gave a short nod and turned to see two more colleagues coming up through the woods toward them.

While he gave orders, Joan assessed her thoughts and feelings about what had just happened before her eyes. She was appalled that a man who was just trying to support his family was shot and killed for no reason. Death was not a stranger to her.

She had felt the sting of senseless loss in Iraq when friends had been killed in the midst of a firefight, but she had never seen anyone killed in cold blood for...for what? Her reaction? *What does it take to do that? What kind of man is Gunther who could walk up to an unconscious man and shoot him in the head? Were Duncan and Kearney as heartless?* She shook her shoulders, as if to throw off the revulsion building inside her, and turned to see if Gunther had anything for her to do.

One of their colleagues was binding the hands and feet of the unconscious trucker. The others were dragging the body into the woods.

With everything under control, Gunther said, "We have some trucks to drive, guys. Let's do what we came to do."

Gunther, TJ, and Joan headed back through the trees to the road.

୧୬୧୬

While the hijacked trucks were being unloaded, Joan dozed at the edge of the loading dock of an obscure warehouse. The rough edge of the wall scratched her back through her shirt. The whine of the fork lift motor and its squeaking tires filtered through the thin veil that separated dream from reality.

"I hear you didn't follow instructions." Duncan's voice pierced her drowsiness.

Her eyes popped open, and she inhaled deeply as she stretched and looked down into Duncan's eyes. "Yeah, I'm nothing but a pain in the ass," she said echoing Gunther. "What time is it?"

"Time to get you to work. Let's go."

Joan placed her hand on his offered shoulder and grabbed his arm with her other hand on the way down. When her feet crunched onto the gravel of the parking lot, she jerked her hands away, as if the familiarity of the contact burned her skin. As if the contact would relay her growing closeness to Duncan. Other than the normal musings about what he would be like as a partner, she hadn't had time to explore the deeper feelings that tugged at her at times like this.

Duncan had never indicated having any feelings for her.

And as he walked ahead of her toward his van, he seemed unaware of her uneasiness or that the touch meant anything more than an offered shoulder.

Gunther casually leaned against the grill of Duncan's van. "Hey, Saint Joan, thanks for everything tonight. I'll put in a word. Maybe we can get you on the hijack team."

The vision of the unconscious man he'd shot in cold blood flashed past her mind's eye. She forced a smile. "No thanks. Hijacking trucks isn't something I want to do again anytime soon."

Gunther chuckled and walked off.

"No word, Gunther, got it?" Joan yelled after him.

He turned and nodded his head then continued walking toward the warehouse.

❧❦❧

"St. Joan? What was that all about?" Joan said as soon as Duncan pulled out of the parking lot.

"You said you wanted a nickname like everyone else."

"I hate to state the obvious, Duncan, but my nickname has my *actual* name in it."

"Others don't have to know that. I think it's appropriate. Don't you? St. Joan is the patron saint of soldiers. She led men into battle. When she was captured, she didn't cave in, even under tough questioning. You don't like it?" He glanced over at her. "What would be your choice of a nickname for you?"

"I don't know." She stifled a yawn. "Xena the Warrior Princess or Iron Angel."

Duncan smiled. "Hmm, you're tough as nails but good and kind like an angel. Iron Angel it is."

They traveled in silence for a half hour before Joan spoke again. "I know you don't like a lot of questions, but, why does the Legion hijack trucks?"

"You're right. Usually, I do hate a lot of questions, but after the past several hours, I think you deserve an answer." He checked his rearview mirror and continued, "Ever notice that there's plenty of food at The Woods?"

Joan nodded. She hadn't really thought about how they always had plenty of food at The Woods, while the food supply in the rest of the state was spotty.

"Ever wonder why we only eat in certain restaurants or diners, and there's always plenty of food there, too? Well, the Legion supports them, and they support us."

"One hand washes the other," Joan muttered. Her eyelids were getting heavy.

She put her feet on the dashboard and leaned back into the seat. Sleep. She wanted quiet, beautiful sleep. As her muscles relaxed and her breathing slowed, she calculated she would arrive at her apartment just in time to shower, change, and catch the bus to work. Her bike was still in impound, so she was dependent on the local mass transit—Duncan's penance for not listening to his advice. *Lesson learned.* She yawned again and rested her chin on her chest.

"Yes, exactly," Duncan was saying through the drowsiness that was now only a snail's breath from pure, recuperative sleep. "And whatever we can't eat, we sell, and it helps to finance the Legion."

"Damn, I'm tired, and I have a twelve hour shift ahead of me," she mumbled.

The rocking motion of the van lulled her closer to the drop off into sweet slumber. Her eyelids opened and closed—the open phase getting smaller, the closed phase getting longer with each beat of the rhythm.

"Your life is *so* tough," Duncan said.

"Mock me if you must, but when I get off at eleven, don't expect a de-brief from me. I'm going straight home to bed." Joan opened one eye and looked at him. "And don't think of sneaking into my apartment and waking me up. I'm going to nail the door shut."

"What about the windows?"

"Them, too." Joan nestled her head into her hands as she leaned against the window. She said through a yawn, "And what are you doing today?"

"Me? I'm tired. I'm going straight to bed and get some sleep."

"You bastard."

CHAPTER 15

It was three weeks later, the job in Cleveland had wrapped up a week ago, and Joan went home to rest up. It was good to be back among her familiar things, but the house seemed empty without Jason and Vaida. Once a retreat from the world, the house had become an anvil, rather than the anchor it had always been. She decided to sell it.

Joan moved a slat in the blinds on the front window and peered out into her front yard. She thought she heard a rustling, but her front lawn was empty and quiet in the moonlight. Every familiar shrub and ornamental grass stood still and untouched. The grass was overgrown, and that, too, was untouched—no telltale track of someone treading over it.

Fresh after showering, she still felt the glow of endorphins. The gym was now the object of the task force's interest, so she exercised at home. The workout in her basement hadn't been as thorough as it would have been at the gym, but it had been sufficient. Her muscles were pumped. Her abs were tight. Her reflexes sharp.

Then she heard the sound again. As she tried to shake the sensation creeping into her bones that undercover work had jangled her nerves, she grabbed her Go-Bag with essentials for being on the lam. Vaida had insisted she prepare it, and Joan silently thanked her for the advice.

The endorphin high now tamped down by adrenaline, her heart pounded against the lump in her throat as she headed for the back door. It was not the smartest move, but maybe if she was quick enough she could get up the back bank to the paper alley that ran behind her house. A remnant of an earlier period when the city picked up the trash behind the houses, the paper alley hadn't been used in decades. It was overgrown, but it still had value as an escape route.

She yanked the back door open, and almost ran into Duncan standing on her deck.

"Hello, my Iron Angel," he said.

Her nickname seemed to be a source of amusement for him. If she had a time machine, she'd go back three weeks to erase the suggestion and embrace being called St. Joan.

"You gonna let me in?" he asked. "You look a little panicky," he said as he slipped by her into the dim light of the small kitchen. "You don't mind being called Iron Angel, do you? It fits you." The corners of his mouth twitched upward, but drooped before becoming a full-fledged smile—as if fun was a strange concept for him.

Joan shook her head. Her hands fidgeted around the collar of her tee shirt, screaming that her nerves were on edge. She crossed her arms to silence them.

Duncan gave her a long look. "No more undercover assignments for you."

"I'm fine. I'm okay, really."

"It takes time for frazzled nerves to toughen up and become steady and reliable again." His eyes searched her face, coming to rest on the newly formed creases around her eyes and mouth.

"I'm good. Fit as a fiddle. Undercover is a piece of cake."

After convincing Chuck to rehire her, the Cleveland job had gone off without a hitch. The intensity of the surveillance, and the fact that she had to succeed with a margin that could not be doubted or trivialized, had notched up her anxiety level. The accomplishment was her own, with no assistance from Duncan. He made her pay for her mistake, not to be mean, but to build up her self-confidence and re-establish his trust in her. She earned an A+. But it came at a cost.

His eyes were pinned on her. "Did the arrest get to you?"

"No."

"Because Lothar is on it, trying to take care of—"

"Who's Lothar?"

"Never mind." The coffee pot caught his attention. The scrutiny ended as he helped himself to a cup. "I think the lady doth protest too much," he said, raising the pot to offer her some.

She dropped her backpack next to the kitchen door and reached for a mug. He gave the backpack a long hard look before he poured coffee into her mug and replaced the pot. The coffee pot! She was about to run out of the house without a thought about anything but running. When did running become an option for her? She rubbed the back of her neck. *Get your shit together.*

Duncan headed toward the small dining room. Joan slid into the chair at the opposite end of the table from where he settled in. She fidgeted while he read and sent text messages. He was notorious for getting down to business—no fussing around, no small talk. Being so laid back was out of character for him.

His attention to his phone set off alarm bells in her head. The Cleveland operation had gone well. She had returned to her house in Pittsburgh to find that the task force surveillance had been removed due to lack of activity. Everything in her life seemed to be getting back to normal. So, why was Duncan piddling around on his phone? In her house?

To quell her rising anxiety, Joan thought about the real estate agent she had called earlier in the day to put her house on the market. The task force knew about the house. If she continued to do undercover work, she would never be here anyway. It was a liability.

Duncan was stalling. Joan decided to take the reins and find out what was going on. "To what do I owe the pleasure of this visit?"

He looked up with a brief smile. He was a hardened soldier who wore his scars in his demeanor as well as on his body. "I like humor when anxiety is high. It shows—" His phone rang.

"Talk to me." His smile faded. He glanced up at Joan. "Yes, she is…no they're not—a couple hours—good. Out."

He disconnected the phone and stood up. "Pack a duffle. Get your guns and ammo. We gotta go."

Her stomach flipped. Not stopping to ask any questions, Joan started packing immediately. She didn't stop to think whether it was excitement or dread. Whether it was at the thought of going undercover again so soon or Duncan's strange demeanor. She threw clothes into her duffle bag without thought. In time he would tell her what she needed to know. She could sort it out later.

She zipped her duffle bag. "Where are we going?" The question slipped out before she could stop it.

Duncan grabbed her duffle bag and walked out of the bedroom. "Someone wants to talk to you. Where are your guns and ammo?"

"In my backpack." She headed toward the kitchen. After turning off the coffee pot and locking the backdoor, she asked, "Who wants to talk to me?"

"You don't know him." Her blood turned to ice and she froze at the edge of her deck. How could she be so stupid? Her clothes were packed. Personal hygiene items—packed. Weapons—packed. The leadership could make her disappear, and no one would suspect foul play.

Duncan yanked her to get her moving across the backyard and up the bank.

She turned when she reached the gate in the chain link fence that bordered her yard. "What does this person want?"

"I'm not privy to that information."

"Bullshit," she hissed. "You're in on everything. Look, I'm not in the mood for games. I took one to the throat for the Legion, I've fought off punks in jail, spent two weeks in jail in Cleveland, I've..." The thought of fighting off Duncan, fighting for her life, flickered through her mind and she added quickly, "I've done everything the Legion has asked of me."

He pushed her through the gate in the fence, guided her to the right, and up the paper alley. "Good, then you have nothing to worry about."

She tripped over a downed sapling, but Duncan's strong grip kept her upright. "Why are we going this way?" she asked.

"The cops might be watching your house."

"I thought they were watching the gym."

Duncan glared her into silence. She shrugged and they walked in silence the rest of the short distance to the cross street. With his grasp of her arm, Duncan guided her to the left and up the short hill. At the next intersection, he pointed to his van parked two cars in from the corner.

They drove in silence while he made quick turns and U-turns to see if they were being followed. Then he pulled into a cul-de-sac, parked, and turned out the headlights.

"To the throat, huh?" he said, keeping his eyes moving from mirror to mirror then looked at Joan.

"Yeah, that Woyzeck—if I ever catch him anywhere where there aren't any cameras, he's going down."

"You're pretty sure of yourself."

Joan looked out the window. "I don't have to defend my skills to anyone."

"Spoken like a true martial artist." Another check of the mirrors. "Woyzeck, huh? What's his partner's name?"

"Massa."

"Woyzeck and Massa," he repeated quietly then said, "Keep your eyes peeled."

"For what?"

"Anything that seems out of place."

After thirty minutes, he broke the silence that had fallen between them. "You're the one with driving skills. You drive."

He got out of the van before Joan could say anything. She got out and went around the front of the van. They did a little shuffle as they each stepped to the same side to pass each other, then did it again to the other side. He grabbed her shoulders and moved her to his left, and they went around to the doors to get back in.

Joan adjusted the mirrors. "Where are we going?"

"To The Woods." He settled back and crossed his arms, chin to chest, to relax for the rest of the ride.

Joan started the engine. "I don't know where it is. I always fall asleep when Travis takes me up there."

Duncan broke out in a loud laugh.

"What's so funny?" The little smile at the house had been a surprise. Duncan laughing outright unsettled her.

"You," he said. "You're like a lost lamb—with a killer instinct."

"I've never killed anyone," she said.

He chuckled and shook his head. "Go to I-79, and wake me

when we get to I-80." He settled back in the seat and closed his eyes.

ᴄ⁄ᴐᴄ⁄ᴐ

Pallaton leaned forward and rubbed his hands to warm them. The campfire was burning down which allowed the evening chill to return to the four men sitting around it. It was early June and although the days were getting warmer, the evenings were still chilly in the mountains of Upstate Pennsylvania. He stood and motioned for Kearney to follow him inside into the makeshift office.

Kempton remained by the fading fire with Lothar, his new advisor.

After the screen door slammed behind him, Pallaton said, "So Kearney, what do you think of Lothar?"

Kearney shrugged and started stacking kindling in the fireplace.

Pallaton handed Kearney a box of matches. "He made a name for himself for being able to resolve differences between cells and between individual soldiers within the Legion," Pallaton continued. "I hear he's a real whip at smoothing relations with the police. He seems level-headed and by virtue of being new he'll be unaffected by old rivalries."

"I'm not impressed," Kearney said and jumped back when the fire roared to life.

Pallaton tightened the elastic band that tamed his wavy, dark brown hair. "I trust Kempton's decision. I'll withhold judgment on the new member. If there's a reason to object later on, I'll do so at that time."

Kearney was quick to temper and quicker to judgment—simply his full-blooded Irish way. "The addition of Lothar is barely tolerable, but I can see Kempton's reasoning." He lifted his ball cap, smoothed his thinning, sandy-colored hair, and repositioned the cap. "But now he's bringing in someone else. I don't like it." He smiled his big, toothy smile, but his eyes remained harsh. "But that's just me."

ᴄ⁄ᴐᴄ⁄ᴐ

The screen door slammed as Kempton and Lothar joined the group inside.

They slid their chairs closer to the flickering, orange heat. After everyone was seated, Kempton explained to his captains that things were getting too widespread. Although they were doing an excellent job, the Legion could expand operations faster with another captain on board.

"I'm not going to turn anything over to anyone," Kearney grumbled. "I have a lot of irons in the fire and after all the work I put into them, I'm not going to hand over any of my projects for someone else to reap the rewards."

"No one's asking you to give up any of your projects. This is new territory. We're expanding—"

Movement on one of the monitors caught their attention. It was from the surveillance camera at the front gate. There were four more camera shots on the other monitor which were from cameras in the woods surrounding the office. There were twelve cameras in all, and they switched automatically every three seconds from camera to camera. Electronic surveillance was new. It provided twelve extra eyes around the cabin. Kempton hoped it would alleviate the growing paranoia among members of the leadership.

They watched as Duncan got out of the passenger side of the van and unlocked the lock on the chain around the gate. After he pushed open the gate, the van pulled through and waited while he locked the gate and returned to the van. The van bounced and rocked into sight of the camera halfway up the rutted road.

They lost sight of it for several seconds until it reappeared on the camera covering the clearing in front of the office.

When Joan got out of the van, Kearny muttered, "Who's that?"

"Joan," Kempton answered

"Oh, no, not her. I hope she's not staying. We don't need her here."

"Zip it," Kempton growled as he brushed past him and walked toward the door.

Pallaton followed Kempton. Lothar stayed by the monitors with Kearney.

CRC

The men greeted each other like the old friends they were. Joan hung back. She wasn't part of this group and wasn't even sure why she was here. Kempton finally acknowledged her, put out his hand, and introduced himself.

So, this is Kempton.

Pallaton seemed genuinely pleased to see her. They all went inside where she was introduced to Lothar. When she was introduced to Kearney, he didn't even acknowledge her presence. He kept his attention on the monitors. A chill went down her spine, and she made a mental note to keep her distance from him until she figured him out.

Duncan put a hand on Joan's shoulder and pointed through a window to a cabin beyond. "Why don't you grab your gear out of the van and get settled in that cabin with the porch light on."

Joan was glad to get out of there and quickly gathered up her duffle bag and backpack. With every step toward the cabin, she mentally thanked Vaida for her sage advice about the Go-Bag. She opened the door and her mouth fell open. "Vaida! What the hell are you doing here?!"

Joan saw Vaida move her hand from under the pillow, but chose to overlook it.

"You are the *last* person I would expect at The Woods," Vaida said. She pointed behind her. "Put your things over here next to my cot."

Joan looked around the bunkhouse. There was a cast iron stove in the center of the left wall. The floors were rough-hewn wood like all the other buildings. There were no curtains on the windows emphasizing that this was a man's world. Vaida had pulled her cot to the center of the room so it was at a right angle to all the other cots and directly in front of the stove.

"This is the best advice you ever gave me," Joan said, indicating the Go-Bag, "except for going to the bathroom before going out on recon, of course. *That* has proved invaluable."

They both laughed as Joan reached into her duffel bag and started putting things away in the locker next to her cot. The new Glock went into the locker first. Then thinking better of the placement, she stuffed it under her pillow.

"Is that a Glock19? When did you get it? Let me see," Vaida said, taking it and pretending to aim and fire.

"After the thing in Cleveland I thought I'd bump up my fire power."

She handed the gun back to Joan. "Good choice."

Joan sat on the edge of her cot. "Do you know why I'm here?"

Vaida shook her head. "I didn't even know you were coming. These guys are like spooks. They're really good at letting you know only what they want you to know. They probably have a secret handshake and everything."

Joan smiled. She had never heard Vaida put so many words together at one time.

"I'm here for the electronics, and that's where I keep my nose," Vaida said.

"Where did you and Jason go after I got questioned by the feds?"

"The team was disbanded. I'm not sure where Jason went. I think maybe Buffalo. I haven't heard anything about him lately, though. Alice is everywhere with his bombs. I think Murphy is in Greensburg or Johnstown or someplace like that."

"What about you? You haven't been here all this time, have you?"

"I was in Erie for a while, then I was brought here to oversee the installation of the electronic equipment. So, I guess, yeah, I've been here most of the time since, you know, that day."

"I saw the monitors in the office. Quite a set up."

"That's not all. They have the capability to scan for unauthorized transmissions."

"You mean bugs."

Vaida nodded.

"Why can't you just say that?"

Vaida shrugged. "They can also check vehicles for GPS tracking devices. I'm surprised they haven't checked the van yet."

"Duncan's pretty careful. Besides, if they did it now, it would be too late." There was a brief silence before Joan added, "I saw Duncan laugh tonight."

"Duncan…laughing? No *friggin' way*. What was he laughing at?"

"Me. He says I'm like a lost little lamb with a killer instinct, or something like that."

Vaida smiled broadly. "That sounds like something Duncan would say. But he's right. You have this feminine way about you, but you can turn into a killing machine in an instant."

"I've never killed anybody," Joan was quick to correct.

"No, you only make them wish they were dead."

They both nodded and smiled.

"What about you?" Vaida asked. "I heard stories—"

Joan shrugged. "Nothing exciting." She told Vaida about losing her job and not really having anything to do. She just touched on undercover work, not knowing how much information the leadership wanted anyone else to know. Vaida's eyes widened at the recounting of the motorcycle chase and arrest, and nodded when Joan told her she couldn't be used in Pittsburgh anymore because she was too high profile.

The discussion turned to politics and the state of the current government which reinforced each other's hatred for it.

After forty-five minutes footsteps sounded on the porch. Joan reached for her gun.

There was a knock followed by Lothar's voice. "Are you decent?"

"Are you *serious*?" Vaida countered. "What—are we in high school?"

Lothar came into the room. "I'm just trying to be respectful."

"Thank you, Lothar, we appreciate it. Don't we, Vaida?"

"Yes, of course," Vaida said, rolling her eyes before she replaced her gun under her pillow.

"We're done with our meeting, and the leadership would like to speak to you," he said, looking at Joan.

"Me? What's up?" Joan asked. Her heartbeat quickened. This was it. The end.

"I'll let them tell you."

On the way over to the office Joan said to Lothar, "I have to go to the latrine first." She headed off into the darkness.

While she was still in one of the stalls, Kearney brazenly

walked up to the stall and said through the door, "You better not
be up to anything. I might as well just come out and say it, I
don't fucking trust you, you cunt."

Joan zipped up her jeans. "Well, I don't fucking trust you,
you dick. So we're even." She came out of the stall, gave him a
long hard look, washed her hands, and walked out the door.

Kearney followed her up the light grade to the office, har-
assing her all the way. "I'm going to make it my number one
duty to get rid of you. You are history. First Lothar joins the
leadership. Now you show up. We don't need either of you." He
walked ahead of Joan. "Especially you."

Joan had seen this kind of man before. He could be dangerous, but if he had the power to send her away from here, she'd
be gone. Besides, anything would be better than being at The
Woods with this acrimonious misogynist.

Kearney reached the office first and slammed the door behind him. She let him have his entrance and calmly waited at the
bottom of the stairs.

A few seconds later, Lothar opened the door, gave a bow
and a sweep of his arm. "Would you care to join us?".

"I thought you'd never ask," Joan replied as she bounded
up the stairs and into the room. She had upstaged Kearny—
beaten him at his own game. It felt good, but this one upsman-
ship would have to end before something bad happened.

After a stern look at Kearney, Duncan announced he was
being bumped up to captain and that would leave his job open.
After a great deal of deliberation, the leadership had agreed to
offer his position as Chief of Security and Operations to Joan.

She was speechless. Head of operations and security? She
thought she had royally screwed up the assignment in Cleveland. But she was being asked to join the inner circle. The Leadership. A brief discussion of what her job would entail ensued
and, once she was comfortable with the explanation of the responsibilities, she accepted. It was an honor to be trusted with so
much responsibility. Her mind swam with the depth of their confidence in her.

Lothar brought Vaida over to join them, and they all toasted
Duncan and Joan's promotions. When the serious drinking began, Joan settled down in an Adirondack chair on the far left

side of the hearth. The others pulled up chairs and sat with the soles of their feet warmed by the fire. Alone, she watched the dynamics of the leadership.

Cautious about her new colleagues and Kearney's antagonism, Joan just sipped the whiskey in her clear plastic cup.

Duncan pulled up a creaky, wooden chair next to her. "Why are you sitting over here all alone? You're among friends," he said. "Drink up. It'll help you unwind."

She glanced at Kearney. When her eyes returned to Duncan she saw that he was studying her.

"Don't worry about him," he said. "He'll get over it."

"Frankly, I prefer to let Jose have his way with me."

Duncan stared into her eyes. "I vetted you every which way I knew, and I kept a close eye on you these last few months. There was never any evidence of a boyfriend." He leaned forward with his elbows on his knees. "Who's Jose?" he whispered.

"You know, Jose Cuervo," she said, referring to her liquor of choice.

"*Pues, tu quieres mucho a este hombre*, Jose?" (*Well, you really like this guy, Jose?*) Duncan asked in perfect Spanish.

"*Si, el es mi corazon.*" (*Yes, he is my true love.*)

Duncan leaned back in his chair and rubbed his day old stubble with the back of his fingers. "Now here's something else I didn't know about you."

"What?" Joan asked.

Duncan chuckled. "I didn't know you speak such good Spanish. All the vetting that I did, and all these months we've worked together, I can't help but wonder what else there is to learn about you."

"Yeah, I'm a walkin' talkin' mystery."

Duncan snorted.

She avoided his eyes and looked at the other men sharing stories and laughing. His interest made her a little uncomfortable, and she tried to decipher the source of the uneasiness. He was good looking and he had the body of a god. More than that, he had mentored her, giving her insight into working undercover, what to look for, how to act, how to discern nuances in people's voices.

And although no one had said it openly, she knew he was the reason she was given this opportunity.

All those pluses were jaded by the repeated warning of others about his temperament. She had seen, and felt, the heat of his anger—scary, intimidating, and consuming. Dangerous? Even she could be dangerous under the right circumstances. What was it about Duncan that scared people?

"I'm just relieved there wasn't some guy in your life who might start nosing around and be a risk to the Legion," Duncan continued.

"Oh," Joan said. Duncan guarded his emotions, but she thought she saw a flicker of something more than concern. Personal interest? Maybe. She added, "I thought you might be making a pass at me."

"Would that be so bad?"

Joan rolled her shoulders to relieve the tension spreading across her back. "I know it's a corny saying, but I don't shit where I eat."

Duncan leaned back in his chair. "Well, *chica*, I'll see if I can find this *Jose* guy for you. Now, drink up."

They clinked their plastic cups and Joan took big mouthful of whiskey. They sat in silence for a while, part of the group yet detached, and listened to Pallaton's war stories and Kearney's jokes.

"So, Duncan," Joan said, "tell me something. Why are you here, you know, in the Legion?"

"I'm a soldier and I don't know anything else but soldiering. I'm getting too old to slog around the jungles and bake in the deserts anymore. So I joined the CDL. But you—you had so much else going for you—"

"So, why am *I* here?" She finished his question as he reached for the bottle to refill her cup. "You've already asked me this a couple times. Do you think you'll get a different answer after I've had a couple whiskeys?"

"Yeah, something like that."

"I took a vow to defend the Constitution. I can't defend it by doing nothing."

"Someday you'll tell me the real reason."

Joan ignored his comment. "Besides it's in my blood to do

something. You saw what a wreck I was when I lost my job—like a loose end with no purpose. Thank God the Legion came to my rescue."

Duncan raised his plastic cup in salute. "Thank God you came to the Legion's rescue. You were the deciding factor in Ohio. A real asset."

"An asset? Is that the new PC term for screw-up?"

"Stop belittling what you've done. When I say asset I mean asset."

I'm an asset. Joan reveled at the rare compliment from Duncan while she took a sip of whiskey. "It always seemed like a struggle. You know, every day, day in and day out. I never thought of myself that way."

"It's about to get worse."

"You have such a way with words," Joan muttered, making another visual sweep of the room. When Duncan didn't respond, she continued, "I like that—being straightforward, to the point, no room for misunderstandings. Minced words are a waste of time." She took another sip of whiskey and placed the half-empty cup on the corner of the hearth.

Duncan leaned forward with the whiskey bottle to refill Joan's cup, even though she had not finished what she had. She didn't stop him.

Joan looked around the room and noticed everyone talking and joking with each other except with Duncan. She looked at Duncan and studied his face.

"You're wondering why no one is talking to me, right? They don't interact with me when I'm drinking."

"Why not?"

"They're leery of me when I'm sober, and when I drink, they are terrified."

Joan looked into his eyes and squinted as if looking for some sign of danger. "Drink up. I want to see what's so scary about you."

"You're not afraid of me."

Unsure of whether he realized she was joking, she said, "No, I am not."

"I thought that day in the motel room would have changed your mind."

Her mind flashed back to that day, after her release from jail. She had a momentary glimpse at how scary Duncan could be and pushed it from her mind.

"Well," Duncan said to fill the silence that had fallen between them. "Let's hope nothing happens to change your opinion of me." He gulped the remainder of the whiskey in his cup.

As the evening passed, the familiar numbness enveloped her. Duncan was right. It was good to let go and relax for a few hours. She didn't see anything particularly terrifying about him after many drinks—not sure if he was simply on his best behavior or not—and at some point after midnight she and Vaida excused themselves to leave the guys to their man talk. They staggered through the darkened forest to their bunkhouse leaving Kearney and his antipathy behind.

CHAPTER 16

Joan woke with a start in strange surroundings. The motion of turning her head started the drumbeat in her brain. Firewater Indians were drumming a message to her—cut back on the whiskey.

Through squinting eyes, she focused in on Vaida, who was snoring on her cot, oblivious to the cold that had crept into the room as the fire in the stove had died. Joan looked down and saw she was still wearing the clothes from the night before. A bout of nausea hit her and, wrapped in a brown wool blanket, she raced outside.

But when she got to the side of the building, nothing would come up. She stood there for several minutes, bile in the back of her throat, hands on knees, praying her stomach would empty out the alcohol that had soured in her gut, her body having refused to absorb it.

When her prayers were not answered, she looked at her watch. It was only four-thirty, which explained the chill in the air. There was a brief internal debate whether she should go back to sleep or take a shower. At this hour, she was assured of privacy in the co-ed facility. And the shower might be the anecdote to the pounding in her head. She went back inside the bunkhouse, grabbed her shower paraphernalia, and headed down the slope to the latrine.

The latrine was a crude cinder block building with five urinals, three stalls, and two shower cubicles. Obviously built by men for men. But it was coed—no separate facilities for women.

Women were an afterthought. When did women become an *afterthought* for men?

She hung her towel on the hook in the farthest shower cubicle and turned on the hot water. Alone with her thoughts, she recalled the solitary life she had left behind when she joined the Legion. It explained her affinity for undercover work. On a mission, she was in society but not part of society. Before joining the Legion, she had worked, but they paid her to be there. She had gone to the gym, but she paid them to be there. They had been in her life, but not part of her life. The only thing she had ever felt a part of was her martial arts classes. Yes, she paid them, but they shared their self-defense knowledge with her. And they shared a common love of the art, the common desire to do well and to see others do well.

Had that been her whole life? Martial arts? She wasn't sure if that was a good thing, but it wasn't a bad thing. It must have been time to do more, because she had set off on a path to fight for something greater than herself. This was her life now.

She touched the water spray with her fingers and realized there was no hot water. She shook her head. *Men.* Steeling herself with all the fortitude as she could muster, she stepped into the cold water. Turning her head so the icy water sprayed on all the pounding areas, which was most of her head, it turned out to be what she needed. *Okay, maybe they got this right.* She soaped up and rinsed off quickly while she was still alone.

Just as she was putting on her deodorant someone walked into the latrine. It was Kearney. *Jeez, of all people.* Shivering and teeth chattering, she threw her clothes over her still-damp skin.

The sound of urine flow echoed in the sparse, cinder block building. When he finished urinating, he stuck his head around the edge of the shower divider. "Well, look who's here."

"Can't a woman have any privacy around here?"

"If you haven't noticed there aren't any facilities for women in The Woods. You know why that is?" Joan didn't answer. She started combing her wet hair. "It's because women aren't wanted here."

"What about Vaida?"

"She's not a woman, she's a soldier. Tried and true."

"And I'm not? After all I've done?"

"Like getting arrested?"

"Fuck you, Kearney."

Kearney leaned toward Joan and pointed his finger in her face. "No. Fuck *you*." He spun on his heel to walk away.

"What are you—fifteen years old?" The best thing to do would have been to stay quiet and let the immature lout go, but the words had a life of their own.

Kearney turned. "I'll show you how old I am."

"Not now. Let me put some make-up on first."

"You'll need more than make-up when I'm done with you. Your time is coming, so watch your back, bitch." He stomped out of the building.

Joan shook her head. Where did all this anger toward her come from? She had never had trouble getting along with people, so this was new to her, and she wasn't quite sure how to defuse it. Maybe Lothar could help. Content that she had a plan, she finished dressing, pulled her damp hair into a low ponytail and went back to the bunkhouse. It was almost five-thirty so she decided to lie down and see if she could get a little more sleep.

Just as she was drifting off, a loud banging on the bunkhouse door woke her.

"Breakfast in fifteen minutes." Pallaton's voice was muffled as much from the door as from the pounding in her head.

Vaida started moaning, smacking her lips, and grimacing.

Joan was relieved to know she wasn't the only one suffering from too much whiskey the night before. "Go take a quick shower. You'll feel better. I'll make sure there's some food for you."

"I don't eat breakfast, you know that. Go ahead without me," Vaida said with her face planted in her pillow.

"I'll save you something," Joan said, grabbing her denim jacket and heading for the door.

One step into the office and a knot torqued her already dicey stomach. Kearney was the cook. Joan pulled out a chair and sat down, thinking that if he poisoned her, it would be a step up from how she felt now. Maybe she should skip breakfast. Too late. Her stomach growled, begging for food.

They all greeted each other and made small talk, but mostly

they stuffed forkfuls of scrambled eggs into their mouths. While Joan nibbled on scrambled eggs and reveled in the aromatic, black coffee, she watched them shovel the food into their mouths and wondered how they could eat so much. They drank way more than she did the night before. She was silently questioning whether they had headaches, when Pallaton picked up a bottle of aspirin and passed it around the table.

Kearney took two and offered it to Joan. "Aspirin?" He smiled and looked toward Duncan like they had an inside joke.

Joan nodded. Kearney tossed the bottle at her. She caught in her left hand without even looking up from the coffee mug at her lips. She put down her mug of coffee, popped open the bottle with her thumb, and plopped a couple pills into the palm of her hand. She knew Kearney intended for the bottle to bounce on the table or for her to spill her coffee—anything to make her look bad. Her lightning reflexes foiled his plan. *Underestimating me is your first mistake,* Joan thought as she popped two aspirin into her mouth and took a swig of coffee.

Pallaton and Duncan exchanged glances and went back to eating. Kearney frowned. "What's your problem, Kearney?" Pallaton asked.

"There's no room for gatecrashers in the inner circle. We're a tight group. Joan is an outsider. She doesn't belong here."

"The decision has been made. Live with it," Kempton said before shoveling another forkful of eggs into his mouth.

Kearney leaned his elbows on the table across from Joan. "Who did you screw to get into the inner circle?"

"Kearney, zip it," Kempton commanded.

"No, let him get it out. Something's been bothering him since I got here last night," Joan said, placing her fork beside her plate in a slow deliberate motion.

"You've managed to get noticed by the task force and arrested in Cleveland. Not great additions to your resume," Kearney said.

"I've been out in the streets, in the middle of active operations. Where have you been? In your cushy apartment watching sports? Whole lot that can go wrong there, huh, big shot."

"You're too green for this position. You won't be able to handle it."

"Why because I have boobs and a vagina?"

"Yeah, something like that."

"I'm a soldier first and foremost. Being female doesn't have any bearing on what I do or how I do it."

He put down his cup of coffee and stared at her. "Then why have you done nothing but screw up since you joined the Legion? I don't know why you're still here, much less promoted to a leadership position. It must be true what they say: screw up, move up. Or maybe it's just screw and move up."

Joan stood up and leaned across the table toward Kearney. "If you're implying that I slept with—"

"That's enough. Both of you pack it. Joan, sit down," Lothar said, inserting himself into the pending argument. "You won't be able to overcome your differences by yelling at each other and calling each other names."

A smile curled one corner of Kempton's mouth. He looked at Lothar and gave him a quick nod.

Duncan stood up. "Well, Lothar and I have that job to do this morning."

He gathered his paper plate and plastic utensils and dropped them into the trash pail. Without a word, he headed toward the door.

Lothar took the last few sips of his coffee before following Duncan out. Everyone except Joan seemed to know what the job was, but she had learned over the past year that if she was meant to know something someone would tell her.

"Be back by one," Kempton said to Lothar as the door closed behind him. "Joan, we're going to the urban center mockup to do some shooting. Want to join us?"

"Wow! Yeah, I'd love to." She got up and helped clean up the table.

"Meet us outside in thirty minutes."

Before leaving to gather up her guns and ammo, Joan spread two biscuits with jelly and put them by the monitors for Vaida. Ready for a day of target shooting, Joan settled down on the steps of the bunkhouse waiting for the others. When the guys came out of the office, Kearney was with them.

She tried to allay her fears with a little humor. "Oh, no, Kearney is going to be there with a loaded gun?"

"Don't worry," Kempton said. "If he shoots you, we'll shoot him back."

"Can't you just shoot him *now* and save everybody a lot of trouble?"

They all chuckled, got into the Kempton's SUV, and bounced up the rutted road past the office until they came to a crude mockup of a city. It was merely sheets of plywood on small framed out houses. For all its crudity, they had pop-up targets. She had to hand it to them, they had their shit together.

Having never done anything like this before, Joan was not good at first. She repeatedly shot the good guys and hesitated on the bad guys, which was a source of good natured amusement for Kempton and Pallaton. Kearney's humor had a sharp edge to it, but firing guns and sharing pointers on shooting accurately seemed to soften him. In the exhilaration of target shooting, Kearney was demanding and tough, but patient as well. The urban mock-up was his area of expertise, and being in his element made him more congenial. He even let Joan fire his Desert Eagle 50cal handgun when she burned through her ammo.

Three hours zoomed by and they reluctantly returned to the office. Not knowing what was next on the agenda, Joan sat down with Vaida to watch the monitors. The combination of lack of sleep the night before and the morning activity in the fresh air made her sleepy. She nodded off, relaxed in dreamland, until Duncan returned from his errand and tapped her on the shoulder. She rubbed the gritty sleepiness from her eyes.

"Come outside," he said in a lowered voice. "There's something I want you to see."

As soon as she opened the door and stepped outside, she saw it. "Old Lady!" She ran to her Triumph motorcycle. Her leather jacket was draped over the seat.

She grabbed the jacket, ran to Duncan, and gave him a big hug. "I thought I would never see her again. Thank you, Duncan."

Caught by surprise, Duncan raised his hands to hug her back, but hesitated. He whispered, "You're welcome, *chica*."

But Joan was already on her way back to her bike to check it out.

He stood motionless, arms across his chest, watching her

childlike joy as she sat on her bike, relishing the familiarity of the seat and the handlebars, grabbing and releasing the levers as if pretending to be driving it. For the first time, he was painfully aware of the joy of life that had been robbed from him that fateful mission in the jungles of El Salvador and wondered if he would ever get it back.

Behind him, Kempton called everyone to the meeting. Duncan watched Joan for a few more seconds before calling to her and telling her about the meeting. He turned and went inside.

ৎওৎও

The meeting had been a brief exchange of information on everyone's projects. When it broke up, Kempton said good-bye to the guys and told Joan they'd be in touch—which she doubted. Duncan was her mentor in her new responsibilities. Everything would go through him until he took on his new job full time.

Much to her dismay, Lothar left with Kempton. She should have said something about Kearney earlier in the day, but things had been improving then. Kempton's SUV started up and she watched the monitors as he headed down the rutted driveway a few minutes later.

Pallaton clapped his hands together. "Let's get this party started."

Joan had never been a fan of the hair of the dog, but when Duncan said, "Can I pour you a drink?" and she saw the bottle of Jose Cuervo in his hand, she was in.

"I never could resist José," she said.

Duncan poured two shots and offered her salt and lemon. She declined them—they just hid the taste of the tequila.

He smiled and gave a little nod as he raised his shot glass. Before she tapped his glass with hers, he gave the Legion toast: "Live free or die."

"Death is not the worst of all evils," they all responded, raising their glasses in salute before chugging their shots.

He poured two more shots, one for each of them, but she sipped the second one.

"Slowing down already?"

"You can't rush José. He likes it slow."

Everyone drank freely. Joan was the only one who held back because every time she looked up, Kearney was watching her. As he drank his eyes became more harsh, his words more biting, his boldness more threatening.

While pouring her fourth shot glass of tequila, Joan was grabbed from behind and spun around. The alcohol slowed her reflexes, and she was angry with herself for letting her guard down, knowing Kearney's obvious ill will toward her. Because of her lapse of situational awareness, he was now directly behind her with his left arm around her throat. With his right hand, he held a gun to her temple.

In unison, Duncan and Pallaton drew their guns on Kearney.

"Hey, Duncan, here's your security expert," Kearney said. "Not so brave now with a gun to her head, is she? Her Kung Fu Chinese bullshit isn't going to save her now."

Duncan was directly in front of Kearney and Joan. Vaida, who had been checking the monitors, was to the left of Kearney, Pallaton had moved away from Duncan and to Kearney's right.

"Kearney, put the gun down, buddy. We can talk this through," Duncan said.

"She's been weaseling her way through the ranks. She has you all under her spell, but it doesn't work on me. I tried to tell you that she's weak, but no one took me seriously. You're taking me seriously now." While he stared them down, he said to Joan, "Where's your Kung Fu shit now, bitch?"

"She was promoted because she has proven herself," Pallaton said.

"Yeah, proven she can get herself arrested. And Lothar has to waste precious time cleaning up her mess in Cleveland."

"She made a mistake," Duncan said. "You've made your share. We've all made mistakes at one time or another, but she learned from it, and it made her stronger. All her jobs were successful."

"What about Cleveland?"

"She cleaned up the mess herself. Once it was trackin', it was the most successful operation so far."

"Yeah, sure, it was successful only because you knew your

rep was on the line. She couldn't have done it without your help."

"That's where you're wrong. I purposely stepped back and let her handle it to prove to everyone that she's good at what she does."

"Yeah, good at getting arrested."

"Kearney, we go way back, and sometimes I let things slide. But this time, buddy, you've gone too far. Let her go and we'll talk this through."

"There's been enough talk."

"She is good at undercover work and she's going to be even better as Chief of Security and Operations. Give her a chance to prove herself. If she fails, we'll pull the plug."

"You'll never let that happen."

"I will push for it myself."

The bantering was getting tedious to Joan. While in the Army, the male soldiers around her were asked to do the dog-and-pony shows for visiting dignitaries, while the female soldiers kept the units going.

She'd developed a motto: "If you want something said, give it to a man. If you want something done, give it to a woman." Enough talk. Something had to be done before Kearney accidentally blew her head off.

With both hands on the arm around her throat, she wanted him to bring the gun arm down closer so she could more easily grab it. "Hey, Kearney if you fire the gun the blast is going to sear your ugly face."

Kearney moved the gun so his hand was on her chest and the barrel of the gun was pointing at her throat. Joan couldn't believe the guy actually listened to her. He was a former CIA interrogator. Evidently, he was used to dealing with people after they were already restrained.

She winked at Duncan. Duncan glanced to his left to see if Pallaton had seen it. Pallaton glanced at Duncan and the look on his face confirmed he had seen it, too. Joan mouthed the words, "Make him say something."

"You're scaring Joan for no reason, put the gun down," Duncan said.

"See? Her Kung Fu is for shit—" Kearney replied, but he never got to finish his sentence.

Joan grabbed the arm with the gun with her left hand and, at the same time, thrust three powerful elbow strikes in quick succession. With each jab his gripped weakened a little more. She turned to face Kearney, reached up with her left arm and locked it around his gun hand. The gun was out of the mix. He punched her several times with his left fist. She blocked one. Took a left hook to the upper jaw. Another to her right eye. As she grabbed his left shoulder and pulled him into a sharp knee to the groin.

His legs turned to water and a groan escaped his throat. Holding him up by his arm still locked in hers, she executed three quick palm-heel strikes—one to the nose and two to his chin.

She pushed him away from her and he crumpled to the floor. Before the others could respond, she put her boot on his forearm just forward of the elbow, grabbed his wrist, and snapped the arm bone upward like a twig. "That's for putting a gun to my head!"

With the snap of the ulna, Duncan, Pallaton, and Vaida flew into action. Pallaton grabbed Joan in a bear hug that pinned down her arms as he swung her away. Duncan went to Kearney to administer first aid. Vaida approached Joan to calm her down, which was unnecessary. The fight was over.

"Let go of me, Pallaton. He's down. I'm done," Joan said struggling to free herself from his grasp. "Why didn't you guys come to my aid?" she said, finally breaking free and rubbing the side of her face.

"It was like poetry in motion," Pallaton said.

"It was so fast." Vaida looked at Joan's face and headed to the refrigerator at the other end of the room. "Let me get you some ice for that."

When Vaida handed the ice pack to Joan, she asked, "Did you have to hit him so many times?"

"Yes," Duncan, Pallaton and Joan said in unison.

"Did you have to break his arm?"

This time Duncan and Pallaton said, "No" and Joan said, "Yes."

Duncan looked over his shoulder and frowned at Joan. She reluctantly changed her answer to no.

"How's he doing?" Joan asked, approaching Duncan and Kearney slowly.

"Obviously, his arm is broken, maybe a couple ribs, too. I was a Special Forces medic, so I can set his arm, but the ribs will be trickier. Joan, Vaida, why don't you go to your bunkhouse and wait?"

As soon as they closed the door of the bunkhouse behind them, Vaida said, "Wow! You are fast and dangerous! Now I know why Alice was so pumped up that time in Pittsburgh. You know, your first time out with him and—"

"I remember it, Vaida."

"Could you show me some moves? I learned a little Tae-Kwon-Do years ago, but nothing like that!"

"I can show you a few moves to use in a pinch, but you really have to train regularly to get really good."

"Great. Thanks," she said, getting ready for a lesson.

"Not right now, if that's okay. I want to keep ice on my face. Why is it always the side of my face that gets hit?"

"Maybe your head is so big it has its own gravitational field."

About a half hour later, Duncan came into the bunkhouse and tossed his van keys to Vaida "You two are going out to pick up supper. We called in an order for pizza at that place in Tidioute."

Vaida acted surprised. "We never got take-out before."

Duncan scowled at Joan as he answered Vaida. "Yeah, well someone took out the cook."

"Oh, yeah," Joan joked. "Darn, I should have broken his leg instead."

His scowl darkened, deepening the lines between his brows. "You're still here?"

He crossed his arms and glowered at them as they rushed past him.

❧❧❧

Duncan watched while Vaida made a three point turn to get

the van headed down the drive toward the road. As he turned and headed back to the office, he wondered what it was about Joan that he liked so much. Was it her sharp discernment of security risks? Was it her fearlessness? Did she remind him of himself before his joy of life had been sucked out of him? Somehow she was cracking his hard shell and shedding light on a dark world, on his demons. For the first time in decades, he started thinking about the way things used to be. Happiness. Contentment. A woman in his life. This woman was pulling at memories he thought he tucked away. Pulling at him not by doing anything, but by being herself.

For the first time in decades, he was scared.

CHAPTER 17

The Constitution Defense Legion had inflicted enough damage to come to the attention of the FBI, and a task force was established to oversee the investigation. Their best source of information about the group came from Agent Cleary, known in the Legion as Murphy. He had spent the previous year working his way up through the ranks until he was positive he was next in line for promotion into the leadership of the CDL.

Agent Cleary stopped by the CDL Task Force office to debrief and catch up. He perched on the corner of Agent Woyzeck's desk. "Didn't you get rough with Joan Bowman?"

"Yeah, so?" Agent Woyzeck asked.

"You should count your lucky stars, man. You should see what she did to Kearney when he put a gun to her head. He has a broken nose, two cracked ribs, a strained neck, and his balls are the size of coconuts. Oh, yeah, and when he was a quivering mass of flesh on the floor, she stepped on his elbow and broke his arm—just for fun."

"And you thought you got rough with her. You had no idea what her idea of rough is." Agent Massa crossed his arms. "You know that look on her face after you let go of her? You know, that look on the tape you play over and over."

Agent Woyzeck snapped around to look at Agent Massa. "I'm not replaying that tape. It doesn't mean anything to me."

Agent Massa smiled broadly. "That was the look of revenge. You better watch your back, my friend. If she did this to a *fellow* Legion member, imagine what she'd do to a federal agent who made her feel powerless."

୧৲৩৲৩

Duncan returned to the van. Dangling from his hand was the key to the only motel room in a twenty mile radius. There was a regional classic car rally going on, and a flood of participants and car-lovers made rooms scarce. This was an older motel where the doors opened directly to the outside. Duncan parked directly in front of a room that was three-quarters of the way down the line of identical green doors. He unlocked the door to Room 110 and held it open for Joan. It was plain, and the furnishings were worn, but it was clean. There were two beds. And no surveillance.

Over the past month, they had shared a room a few times. Duncan had always been respectful of her privacy. He never made a move on her. She wasn't sure if she liked that or not. She idolized Duncan, but a part of her was relieved that he never made overtures. If they started a relationship and then it fell apart, things could go into the weeds in a hurry. And it never ended well when a scorned lover was armed and dangerous. Safety first.

They were just settling into the room when her cell phone rang. She connected the call. "Hi, Murphy. What's up?...Dinner?" She looked at Duncan to see what he wanted to do.

He nodded.

"We'd love to...Who's 'we'? Duncan is with me, of course...Where's that?...corner of Union and Main..." She raised her brows at Duncan.

He gave her the thumbs up.

"Seven-thirty?...You're on. Bye." She hung up. "Is it me or was that a little unusual?"

Duncan plopped onto the bed closest to the door. "How so?"

"Murphy hasn't contacted me at all since my interrogation by the task force."

Duncan laid on his back, hands behind his head. "You're in the leadership. The job he wanted. He's sucking up, that's all."

"Well, I'm not comfortable with sucking up."

"Get used to it."

"I can't picture anyone sucking up to *you*."

"Murphy tried with me. Once."

"So, this is just business. I shouldn't take this as something personal."

"Nothing in the Legion is personal."

"What kind of place are we going to? Do I have to change?" She looked down at her faded jeans and tank top.

"If you wear what you have on, you'll be overdressed. You might want to wear something that covers your tatt, though." He closed his eyes. "Wake me at six-forty-five."

With an hour to kill, Joan fluffed up the pillows on the other bed and turned on the television. Flipping through the channels, she settled on a cooking show.

She looked over at Duncan. His breathing was slow and even. She picked up her cell phone and hit speed dial. It went directly to voice mail.

"Hi, Travis," she said after the beep. "Just checking in to see how you're doing. I'll call you when I'm done in—" She hesitated to tell anyone where she was. "When I'm done here. Talk to you later. Bye."

She put down the phone and settled into the pillows. The TV chef was demonstrating her version of paella.

As requested, she woke Duncan precisely at quarter to seven. While she changed into a blue tee shirt with "Discover Pennsylvania" emblazoned across the front, Duncan splashed water on his face and ran an electric razor over his stubble. After grabbing his holster off the nightstand, he slid out the .38caliber revolver and checked the cylinder. He replaced the revolver and slid the holster onto his belt.

When he looked up at her, Joan looked away. She was surprised at herself for watching him do something so mundane. The loosened belt at his waist. His large masculine hands. The temperature in the room seemed to hike up five degrees. She busied herself with her hair.

If Duncan noticed, he didn't let on. "I'm impressed. You

didn't spill the beans to Travis about where you are." He picked up a comb. "Almost ready?"

"But you were sleeping."

He winked at her. "Was I?"

Duncan could be spooky at times. And manly. Her gaze fell to his biceps that strained the sleeve of the polo shirt as he ran the comb through his hair. She changed the subject. "You aren't going to blend into the crowd with a gun on your hip."

"In Johnstown? If I didn't have a gun on my hip, I'd stand out. You aren't taking yours?"

"My hands and feet are my weapons."

"Yeah. Good luck with that in a gun fight."

"Besides, I have you to defend my honor."

He just shook his head as he gently shoved her toward the door.

When they arrived at the bar and grille, Duncan opened the door for Joan. "Before you start any trouble in here, remember I only have six rounds to defend your honor."

She laughed and gave his arm a light slap on the way through the doorway.

c/ɔc/ɔ

Murphy waved them over to the booth he had secured halfway down the bar on their right. Duncan led Joan through an obstacle course of shoulders and elbows. When they reached the booth, he motioned for her to sit in the booth next to Murphy. Duncan slid across the bench seat opposite them. She locked eyes with him. He never sat with his back to the door. Evidently, he trusted her to notice anything unusual. He winked. She fingered the silverware wrapped in a paper napkin. A smile curled one corner of her mouth.

Duncan had his eyes on Murphy through dinner, but Murphy didn't seem to notice. His eyes were on Joan.

The country western band started to play. Duncan slid out of the booth and put his hand out to Joan. "Do you know the Texas Two-Step?" When they were on the dance floor, he said, "I know why Murphy called you."

"Why's that?"

"He's hitting on you."

"No way. Why would you say that?"

"I've hit on women before."

Joan half-smiled. "*You?*"

"Yes, me. But more importantly, I know it when I see it."

"You said it yourself," she said as Duncan swept her out of the way of a more energetic couple. "He's sucking up."

"This is not sucking, this is hitting."

"Well, it's lost on me."

"I know, *chica*. That's what makes it so much fun to watch." He smiled and pulled her in a little closer. They finished the dance without any more conversation. When the music ended they headed back to the booth. "Why don't you flirt back a little and see where it goes?"

"That would be teasing. I couldn't do that."

"It's harmless fun. Just don't leave with him."

"Why not?"

"It might be an ambush." Duncan made a sweeping gesture with his arm. "Hey, Murphy, good choice. The band is really good."

Joan's flirting boosted Murphy's confidence. His overtures toward her were more obvious, less subtle.

An hour later, Duncan looked at his watch and announced it was time for him and Joan to leave because they had an early day the next day.

On the ride home, Joan said, "Was that as painful for you as it was for me?"

Duncan smiled. The rest of the ride home was quiet.

As soon as she was in the room, Joan asked, "What did you mean by 'ambush' back there in the bar?"

"A man like Murphy doesn't call a woman out of the blue and start hitting on her for nothing. He didn't get your job, so he wants the next best thing."

"What's that?"

"You."

"Are you saying a man wouldn't be interested in me for me? He would have to have an ulterior motive? Do you think I'm that unattractive?"

"No, it's Murphy that worries me." With thumbs in his belt,

Duncan tucked his chin and looked at her through his eyelashes. "You, *chica*, are *hot*."

Duncan thinks I'm hot? Joan shook off the thought. "What did you mean by 'ambush'?"

"He could have had someone else back at his room."

"What do you mean? Like who?"

"I don't know. Forget I said it."

Joan squared off with Duncan and folded her arms across her chest. "Is there something I should know?"

"Not yet. And that's all I'm going to say about this." He started getting undressed for bed so Joan went into the bathroom and put on the shorts and a tee shirt she slept in.

෭ඁ෬

Duncan lay on his back, listening to Joan brush her teeth. Eyes closed, the music playing in his head, his thoughts savored the sensation of her body in his arms while they danced. It had been a long time since he enjoyed dancing with a woman. Usually dancing was just a means to an end, but tonight with Joan it hadn't been anything but what it was—a dance with a beautiful woman in his arms.

Her idealism, that had been corny and irritating in the beginning, became endearing. Conversations were comfortable, as were the silences in between. One more week and he would be busy working in his new area as captain. She would be busy doing what he used to do. They would only be able to get together when she was doing something in his area. He would have to make sure that happened on a regular basis.

His battle scars were too deep to think of a relationship, but it was pleasurable thinking about her. A woman like her wouldn't be interested in a broken-down old warhorse. He shook off the thought, turned on his side, and fell asleep.

Later that night, he dreamed that he was hiding in a house in the woods. As he pulled back the curtain to check the yard, a bullet whizzed by his head.

He dove to the floor and edged up the left side of the window. Inching one eye around the edge of the window to protect as much of his body as possible, he looked for who just shot at him. The shooter ducked. The movement caught his eye. The shooter brought the stock up to his shoulder and looked through the scope.

Duncan pulled back from the window opening in time to dodge another bullet.

After low-crawling across the small room, he slowly opened the door to the front porch. The yard was empty. He slipped through the open door and softly closed it behind him. He crouched and stayed in the shadows until he reached the tree line. After waiting and listening, sure no one else was moving in the darkness, he headed toward the location of the shooter.

Without a sound, he wended through the underbrush and around boulders until he was directly behind the shooter. The shooter wore camouflage head to toe but Duncan saw him, raised his handgun, and pointed it at the shooter's head. He told the shooter to turn around slowly, with hands where he could see them. The shooter raised his hands. They were small and delicate. The shooter turned around. It was Joan.

Duncan woke with a start, heart racing, breathing hard and fast. His wild eyes looked around the room and, in the dim light, he saw Joan's form in the next bed and heard her rhythmic breathing. He lay back down, arm over his head, and stared at the ceiling.

CHAPTER 18

A week later, Joan leaned her elbows on the shiny mahogany bar in the Black Bridge Restaurant waiting for Travis. Each time the door opened she looked up from her tequila and Coke. He had been so elusive lately. They had talked every other day or so from the beginning of her participation in the Legion, but lately all calls to him went directly to voice mail. He was out of the loop, but why? It was her responsibility to know everything about everyone, and yet, she didn't know what *his* problem was. *Did he have a problem? Could* he *be a problem? No, not Travis...and yet...*If she didn't get an acceptable answer tonight, she was going to make it her priority to hunt him down and stalk him, if necessary. She had to find out what was going on. It was her job. He was her friend.

When he finally answered Joan's voice mail, they agreed to get together for dinner, choosing the Black Bridge Restaurant because it was far enough out of Pittsburgh for Joan to relax. The intensity of undercover work had taken its toll on her, frazzling her nerves and intensifying her growing loneliness. Paranoia peeked at her from eye contact with any stranger, the sound of footsteps behind her, the silence in the dark. Her laser-like discernment of security risks was suffering. Talking with Travis would help her get back her edge.

As the bartender brought Joan her third tequila and coke she swiveled on the stool. With elbows propped against the cool bar behind her, she looked around the restaurant. The Black Bridge was dark and cozy with a fire pit in the center. It had interesting but meaningless portraits and other framed prints on the walls, adding interest to the room. There were several couples scattered about the dining room sitting at tables and in booths and a group of six at two tables pushed together in front of the fire. Nothing looked out of order and the quiet hum of talking and the occasional burst of laughter only served to increase Joan's loneliness.

"You look awful," Travis said in her ear.

She hadn't seen or heard him enter the restaurant. Her situational awareness was for shit.

She smiled at Travis and stood up to hug him. "You sure know how to flatter a girl."

The relief at seeing a familiar face was almost overwhelming. Traveling from cell to cell, meeting and working with fellow members, with whom she could not connect on a personal level, was draining and isolating. The need to remain objective, observant, and alert had created a loneliness deeper than anything she had ever previously experienced.

She motioned to the hostess that they were ready for a table and turned to the bartender, who had already reached under the bar to retrieve the helmet he had set aside upon her arrival. She grabbed her helmet and her drink and followed the hostess to a raised booth in the center of the far wall. Travis followed her. They both pushed their helmets to the far side of their seats and slid into the booth, facing each other. He looked well and relaxed. And alive.

A middle-aged couple entered the restaurant and sat at a table only five feet from the booth Joan and Travis shared. She watched them deliberate over what to order from the bar, lost interest in them, and turned her attention back to Travis.

After placing their orders, Joan good-naturedly chastised Travis for not answering her voice mails and giving her a scare. He was evasive about where he had been, apologizing for any anxiety he had caused her. Caught up in the joy of seeing him again, she ignored the evasiveness and was oblivious of the couple at the next table who were sitting quietly, no discernable conversation.

Over dinner they chatted about mutual friends in the Legion. She was careful to avoid giving out details. Even in her vulnerable state of mind, she could not let down her guard. Not even to Travis. Something was different about him, he was still being evasive, and until she knew what was going on with him, she could not, and would not, reveal anything that could compromise the Legion. Besides, he did not have a "need to know" the details of the operations or the leadership. His questions should have set off alarm bells, but she wanted one happy moment amid the sea of risk and isolation that was now her life.

While sitting over a cup of coffee ordered in lieu of dessert, Joan decided to prod him about his behavior. "Travis, I like to think that we're good friends."

"The best."

"We can tell each other anything, right?"

"I'd like to think so." He took a sip of his coffee and set the mug down on the table with great attention then flicked a wayward breadcrumb off the tablecloth.

"Lately you've been cagey and distant. In the spirit of being good friends, I have to ask. What is going on? Maybe I can help."

"Nothing's going on." Travis rubbed his thumb on the rim of the cup. "I've just been busy, that's all."

Joan scrutinized his facial expression, his movements. His body language virtually screamed that he was hiding something.

"That's a nice vanilla answer, Travis, but it doesn't cut it. Remember, my job is to know everything about everybody. I know a lot about you, but I cannot for the life of me find out what's going on with you. Hell, I can't even *find* you most of the time. Talk to me, Travis."

He looked quickly over his shoulder and around the room before answering her. His eyes fell on the couple at the closest table. "Let's finish up here and go outside."

A change swept over his face when he looked at the couple nearest to them. She now looked at them closely, but they were busy in their own conversation. She didn't see anything out of place.

After a brief scuffle over who would pay the bill, it was finally taken care of. They left the cozy atmosphere of the restaurant and walked out into the cool November air.

Travis had parked his bike next to hers. While the engines

warmed up, they sat next to each other, hands jammed into the pockets of their leather jackets.

There was a cool breeze, and Travis took his hands out of his pockets long enough to put up his collar. "Did the leadership send you here to shake me out of the bushes?"

"I'm your friend and I'm concerned about you," Joan said. "When I needed some moral support after the now-infamous task force interrogation, you were there for me. I want to be there for you."

"You didn't answer my question."

Joan put a hand on his arm and looked directly into his eyes. "The short answer is 'no.' I am not here at the behest of the leadership. I am here as your friend."

Travis hesitated. He looked past her at nothing in particular, as if searching for words, or making a decision. She wasn't sure what caused the uncertainty. They'd been friends from the beginning. There was something that he felt uncomfortable sharing with her. She had to find out what it was.

He finally looked directly at her. "I've wanted to say something to somebody. It's been eating me up inside, but I didn't know who I could trust."

"You didn't feel you could trust me?"

"You're one of *them* now. The inner circle. I wasn't sure I could trust you with this, but I have to tell someone, and—" Travis gave a short exhale. He shook his head and looked past Joan as if he couldn't believe what he was about to say. "You are the person I distrust the least."

Joan bit her tongue. He was on the verge of opening up and she didn't want to blow it.

"I've started questioning the motives of the leadership. Don't misunderstand me, the operatives in the cells, for the most part, are loyal. Like you were, maybe still are, I don't know, but the leadership has taken a disturbing turn to…to the dark side, for want of a better phrase."

"What do you mean exactly?" Joan asked.

"I think the Legion is starting to eat its own."

"What does *that* mean?" Joan knew what it meant. She wanted there to be no misunderstanding.

"Several members have disappeared. Poof—gone. I ask

about them, but nobody knows where they've gone, or at least nobody's talking. I think they've been executed."

"Executed? Isn't that a little overly dramatic? What makes you jump to execution rather than, oh, they decided to leave the Legion?"

"There's a rumor of someone being an enforcer who removes weak links, if you know what I mean."

"You said it yourself. It's a rumor, nothing else." *Am I off the net about this? Wouldn't it be my job to know about an enforcer and possibly feed information to him? If I'm being kept in the dark, why?* If she humored Travis, maybe he would tell her more. "Now that you mention it, there are some members I haven't seen in a while. Who have you noticed missing?"

Travis listed several names who Joan had believed to be some of the most loyal members, but one name stood out. Jason. She thought back to her conversation with Vaida who said she had lost contact with him. What Travis was suggesting might be true. But these guys were not members whose loyalty she would have questioned. Something was going on, but what? Why was she out of the loop? Did that mean she could be next?

"Why would they execute Jason? He was one of the most loyal members I know."

"I heard he was becoming a loose cannon," Travis said.

"Since when did that become a liability?"

"There's a general consensus that the leadership is changing."

"I'm at the meetings. There are some things I can't relate to you, but none of them involve dissatisfaction with any members to the extent of killing them." She would make it a point to ask Duncan about this. This was serious.

The question of why Travis had been hard to reach hung in the air. "What does this have to do with you being off the grid?"

"I just had to get away for a while to think this through, that's why I haven't been answering my phone. I needed time to decide what I was going to do."

Joan jerked her chin back in confusion. "What you're going to *do*?"

"I think maybe I'm next," Travis said.

"What makes you think they'd come after you?"

"I haven't been recruiting with the same enthusiasm."

"Everyone gets burned out at some time or another. Just tell them. They'll understand."

"I tried, and it was right after that I kept thinking I was being followed."

"It's just paranoia." Joan snorted. "Join the club."

"Just because a person is paranoid it doesn't mean there isn't someone actually following him." His weak smile faded. "Did you notice that couple that was seated at the table next to us?"

"I checked them out. Nothing out of place."

"I've seen the guy before. I think he's one of the people following me."

Joan pictured the couple in her head. "It's a coincidence, or you're mistaken. What kind of tail sits right *next* to the person he's following?"

"Too much is happening."

"Like what?"

"I think someone has been in my apartment when I was out of town. Nothing missing. But I find small, insignificant things out of place like someone was going through my stuff." He hesitated before adding, "I was riding my bike and I was run off the road."

"That happens sometimes. Drivers are oblivious to motorcyclists."

"Twice in two weeks? I get hang up calls—"

"I think you have a string of coincidences and you're jumping to conclusions. The mind tries to make sense out of chaos. It's normal."

"Perception is reality, and my reality is someone is after me." Travis changed the subject. "Are you still close to Duncan?"

Joan bristled. Prickles zinged across her shoulders. "Not as much as before. He's busy with his new job, and I'm busy with mine. Why?"

"As your friend I have to tell you. He's a very dangerous man."

"He's just menacing looking. He's not really—"

"Joan," Travis put a hand on her arm. "He's amoral. He has

no ability to be empathetic. He has a mean streak that probably hasn't cropped up in your presence yet. But believe me, it's coming. A leopard never changes its spots."

"So, now, you're a psychoanalyst?"

"Someone is behind these disappearances, someone in the inner circle, and my money is on Duncan. He was an assassin when he was a mercenary, did you know that?"

"Jason disappeared before Duncan was promoted to captain." Joan felt compelled to come to Duncan's defense. When he was Special Forces, he had been a medic. She saw his medical abilities first hand. This assassin label was just a rumor. Someone trying to make sense out of nothing. Or someone trying to bring down Duncan.

"When he had your job, he was still in the inner circle. And think about it. He gave up the powerful head of security and operations position to be a captain in a small territory in Western Ohio. Would you do that?"

"Maybe, if—"

"No, Joan, you wouldn't. Be honest with me—and yourself. There are red flags flappin' everywhere, right in your face, and you don't see them. Or won't."

Joan brushed away the memory of his temper after her incarceration. He was angry then. And rightfully so. "I think all that talk of being mean and dangerous is a reputation that has followed him from his past. He has moved beyond that and simply hasn't done anything to clean up his rep. I haven't seen anything that would substantiate your claims."

"Okay, maybe you know him better than anybody, except maybe Kearney. All I'm saying is be alert. Be very careful around him. And remember if you stay too closely tied to him, you could be taken down by the task force just by your association with him."

"As soon as the task force gets wind of my promotion to head of security, I'll be a big enough target in my own right. I'm already on their radar, remember?"

"Roger that."

"Besides, Duncan is not the only person in the inner circle. Frankly, if I had to put money on anyone, it'd be Kearney. He was quick to put a gun to my head."

"Did he pull the trigger?"

"Obviously not, but he had no qualms of endangering me, a member of the leadership."

"You know why he doesn't like you, don't you? No? He was there to pick up the pieces when Duncan came out of the jungle in Central America alone, plagued by PTSD. They've developed a strong bond over the years, and now he thinks you're pulling Duncan away from him."

"Bullshit."

"Open your eyes, lady." He tapped her forehead. "Do your job. Check everyone out. Everyone."

Joan thought for a couple seconds. "Let me ask you something. I've felt an increased intensity in his demeanor around me. What do you think that is?"

"I couldn't say for sure, but possibly the leadership has made you his personal responsibility and he's feeling that pressure."

"Damn it. Cleveland—" She put the back of her index finger to her lower lip, and seemed lost in thought.

"What?"

After a curt wave of her fingers, Joan put her hand on her bike's throttle. "Never mind. It's nothing." A short silence fell between them. "When you have any facts about the enforcer, get back to me. And if I hear anything, I'll let you know. Until then I'm not jumping to any conclusions." She dismissed the idea of an enforcer as gossip and innuendo.

She still wanted to get to the bottom of Travis' situation. "But you haven't answered my question—what are you going to do?"

The space between Travis' brows filled with furrows. He pursed his lips.

Joan stiffened.

"So...I'm...I decided to..."

"Just say it, Travis. We'll worry about the words later."

Travis hesitated then blurted out, "I'm working on a way to get out of the Legion."

"Like what?" Joan needed a solid answer from him.

"I can't say right now. If I get out alive, I'll let you know how I did it."

Joan's stomach tightened. *Oh no, please don't lay this on me.*

"You know you can't get out of the Legion alive, right?" Travis said.

Joan wasn't sure what to say to that. She suspected as much, but to actually hear the words put a knot in her stomach.

"The sooner you accept it the better," Travis said. "Maybe you should start thinking about how you can protect yourself if this whole thing goes into a death spiral. Develop an exit plan."

"Sure, the leadership and I have operational differences," Joan said, ignoring the burning in her stomach. "There are some things I don't agree with—for instance, not having a plan for the post-government victory. I think if we're responsible for bringing it down, it's up to us to make things right. They feel their job is to bring about change. It's up to the people and the politicians to restore the Constitution and Bill of Rights. What comes after might not be better. As bad as things are, they could always get worse."

"Do I detect a chink in the armor of your loyalty? I always expected you to become a hardcore revolutionary. That's why I hesitated to open up to you, but it's a relief that I'm not alone." He looked at her with a serious look in his eyes. "Please, Joan, just consider the possibility of getting out so you won't spend the rest of your life in jail."

"Don't misunderstand me, Travis. I'm still loyal to the Legion 110%. We're going to win this fight. We have momentum on our side."

"I hope so for your sake." He put on his helmet, signaling the conversation was over. He leaned over to give her a one-arm good-bye hug. "Just think about it."

He pulled out of the parking lot first and turned left, heading north.

As Joan tugged her helmet over her head, she saw a car pull out behind Travis and follow after him. It looked like the couple at the next table, but she wasn't sure. She pulled up to the edge of the parking lot and watched the tail lights disappear into the darkness. She started to turn north to follow them to see if Travis was in danger. Instead, she swerved and sped off to the south.

I'm not letting Travis pull me into his paranoia. I have enough of my own to deal with.

℘↷℘↷

The next leadership meeting was only a week later.

During the meeting, Kearney was quiet and brooding. His mood didn't improve as time went by. He didn't explain what was bothering him. Joan could only assume it was because she, the newcomer to the leadership, had the power to nix any of his projects. She had no intention of meddling in his plans and she had to find a way to let him know that. Maybe Lothar could help.

When operational business was completed, they moved on to a subject that Kempton said he'd been mulling over for a few months. Joan sat silently as he told the group the Legion wasn't getting the press they should.

They had to make a big splash, and he felt the only way to get the attention of the press was to increase their profile by racking up body count. There was silence as each member considered the proposal.

The ensuing discussion involved listing groups to be considered—military, political or civilian. This was followed by a heated debate of how many was enough for a big enough splash.

The discussion quickly spiraled out of control.

"Joan," Kempton said, "you've been quiet. What's your opinion?"

She looked around the table and, for the first time, saw a hardness in the men's eyes that she had not noticed before. If she was going to give her opinion, it had to be an honest one. "I don't agree with killing innocent Americans in order to *help* Americans. Is that what we're about, really?"

"We can't help Americans if nobody knows about our cause," Duncan answered.

"They know about us."

"Do they? Do they really know about us, or are we just something they hear about occasionally?" he asked.

"I agree with Duncan," Pallaton added, "we're just something to fill space on a slow news day."

"See, I told you," Kearney scoffed. "She's going to break and run the first time things get down and dirty. She doesn't have the heart for this."

Kempton scowled at Kearney. "Statements like that aren't helpful." He turned to Joan. "I'd like to hear your suggestion for upping our profile."

She looked around the table. "Don't get me wrong. I'll go along with whatever we decide to do."

"She's lying," Kearney mumbled loud enough for everyone to hear.

Kempton raised a palm toward Kearney. "Let her finish. We need everyone's input." He looked back at Joan. "That's a tidy, evasive answer. I say again, I'd like to hear your suggestion."

"Well—" Joan cleared her throat. "—although I'm against killing *innocent* Americans, there are *un-American* leaders who are destroying the country and are roadblocks to our success. High-profile, specific targets could yield the same press. And would we have to *kill* them? What about threats, letter bombs, physical attacks, things like that?"

They all looked at her with expressionless faces, and she continued, "Kempton, you're a smart man. A yes-man is no good to you. You need to hear all sides, right? You asked my opinion and I gave it to you."

"And what if we decide to attack people in a shopping mall? Where would you stand on that?"

"I'll do whatever is asked of me." She looked at Kearney and sneered back at him. "And I won't go running to the task force." She hesitated for emphasis before adding, "I trust your wisdom and that whatever you decide to do will be the right thing. Whatever that turns out to be."

Kempton closed the subject saying, "This was just a trial balloon. We'll discuss this again."

Joan's thoughts went back to her conversation with Travis a week earlier. Was this really a suggestion, or was it already being implemented *inside* the Legion, and now it was just starting to be projected outward? Or was it set up as a test of her loyalty?

Don't make this about me. That's the first step to full-blown paranoia.

CHAPTER 19

A few days later, Joan dialed Duncan's cell. It went straight to voice mail. She frowned and took a sip of her tequila and coke. Motels were lonely places. Just her and her paddle-wheel life, dragging her mind in circles—in the water, out of the water. Moving the heavy, cumbersome steamboat along. Moving her farther from the shore. Snapping the lines that connected her to the pier.

Her mind returned to the last meeting with the leadership that accentuated her distance from the group—of which she was supposed to be an integral part. A group she was different from in many ways. She started pacing with a bottle of tequila in her right hand.

Killing Americans to save Americans. How could they think that was a good idea? It would bump up the Constitution Defense Legion's publicity, but also intensify their charges, which would put a hot flame under the manhunt for them.

She turned at the door to the bathroom. The amber liquid sloshed in the bottle.

Except for Duncan, none of the other leaders were friends. Associates, yes. Colleagues, maybe. Friends who would respond in a pinch, doubtful at best. And Duncan. Was he a friend or just another CDL member climbing the ladder on someone else's back?

She stopped halfway to the door, set the bottle on the laminated top of the bureau, and looked in the mirror.

The hard eyes and set jaws she'd seen at that last meeting

were signs of an inner callousness in battle-hardened men. The only action she saw during her tour in Iraq was a poorly executed ambush on a convoy in which she was the driver of a truck somewhere in the middle. She had fired her weapon, but did she hit any enemy soldiers? Only the other side knew, and they weren't talking. No. The last thing she would be deemed is battle-hardened.

She took a swig, grimaced as the alcohol burned her throat, then paced toward the door.

The thought of Travis filled her with dread that snaked through her stomach, up her spine, around her heart. Since her dinner with him, he was out of the net. Could he have been right about the existence of an enforcer? An enforcer who got rid of weak links, who no one was willing to talk about, who the head of security should know about, but didn't. Keeping her out of the loop? That spoke volumes about her position with the Legion. She was on the chopping block. The last thought stopped the pacing.

She checked the locks on the door. After a long pull of tequila, she retraced her steps toward the bathroom.

Was the enforcer just a phantom produced by a man diving into the depths of paranoia? Travis was paranoid. No doubt about that. Paranoia was becoming a constant companion for her, too. But her job required her to find faults, to find leaks in security, to find the weakness in an operation. That was all fodder for paranoia. Yet, her mind had not produced this phantom. She had been blissfully unaware of an enforcer until just under two weeks ago, when she had dismissed the idea. A few days ago, the leadership gave the indistinct phantom substance.

A familiar voice would calm her jitters. She dialed Murphy's cell, hesitating before hitting the Send button. It was Duncan's voice she wanted to hear. Duncan was the only person who had taken time to get to know her. But he was out of the net—probably with some stripper. She flopped backward, spread-eagle on the bed, the tequila sloshing around inside the bottle.

She hit the Send button. There was ringing, then straight to voice mail. *Where was everybody? Was something going on she didn't know about? Was she a pariah?* After another long pull of tequila she told herself to snap out of it. Loneliness and paranoia were eating her alive.

Her cell phone rang and she jumped at the unexpected sound. Her heart sank when she saw the Caller ID. "Hi, Murph."

"Hi, you called. What's up?"

"Just sitting around this motel room. You're always calling me and I thought I'd call you for a change."

"So, this isn't business? Want some company?"

"I just needed to hear a familiar voice."

"I have a bottle of tequila with your name on it," he teased.

"You've stooped to bribery?"

"Guilty as charged. What do you say? We'll just talk. I'll come there. You won't even have to leave your room."

"You'll come here. You don't know where *here* is." *Shit, I don't even know where I am—in the grand scheme of things.*

"I'd go to the ends of the Earth to spend a few hours with you."

"You are so full of shit, Murphy." She wavered for a moment then continued, "I'm at the Palomino Motel on Route 119. Room 108."

"I'll be there in an hour."

While Joan waited, she made some instant coffee in the motel-provided coffee maker. She mused about Murphy's persistence in chasing her and how, over time, she started to accept his casual invitations to coffee or dinner. Duncan's warning in the bar in Altoona popped into her head. But Duncan interacted with her less as he put more energy into his new job. The power of his warning faded.

Although Duncan had never gone beyond being professional, his male, powerful presence had been reassuring. And welcome. It wasn't the presence of a man in her life that she avoided. It was the strings that inevitably developed. Maybe it was time for her to resolve her problem and move past it, but was Murphy the right man?

Fifty-five minutes later, Murphy arrived with the promised bottle of tequila. They drank tequila and talked for a couple hours. He was good at telling jokes, and the more he drank the raunchier the jokes got, but Joan loved them anyway—or maybe it was the tequila that liked them. It didn't matter. As the evening wore on, the familiar numbness relaxed her mind and her body. Murphy started moving in on her, slowly but deliberately. At first she wasn't interested but eventually loneliness broke the dam holding back her passion. She boldly ripped open his shirt, buttons popping across the room. Her brazenness seemed to turn him on. He lifted her tee shirt over her head and caressed her bare skin.

She started to feel the hair on his chest and stopped cold. He tried to get her interested again, but she hit him in the sternum with the heels of both her hands, followed by a chop to the throat and a right cross. Grasping his throat, Murphy stumbled backward onto the edge of the bureau and then sideways onto the floor.

He sat there for a moment, shaking his head, but when she stalked toward him, he struggled to his feet. "What's wrong?" He held his hands in front of him to fend off another attack.

"Where's your tattoo?" she asked, backing him against the wall.

"Let me explain—"

"No. Get out."

"I can't leave without explaining."

"You can walk out or I'll drag you out after I beat the shit out of you. Your choice." She turned to pick up her tee shirt lying on the floor next to the bed. When she turned around, she was looking down the muzzle of his .38 Special.

"I can't leave without talking to you first."

She started walking toward him. "You're pulling a gun on *me*?"

"Joan, let me explain. Stop right there. Do it now."

The authority in his voice stopped her in her tracks. She sat down on the edge of the bed, eyes staring him down, hands rubbing the tops of her thighs. Before he even told her, she knew what he was.

"Joan, I don't have a tattoo for a reason. I'm a federal agent, but I'm not your enemy. I know that doesn't sound right, so give me a chance to explain. I don't want to shoot you. I'm putting the gun down, see? I just want to talk to you and explain something to you—okay? See? It's down." He stood with both hands out, showing her he was unarmed, but he was still prepared to defend himself against a physical assault. When it didn't come, he slid gently onto the edge of the other bed facing her. This couldn't be happening to her. If she got arrested again, Kearney would have won. Everyone would question her abilities. Even Duncan.

He reached for her hands, but she yanked them away from him. "Like I said, I'm a federal agent so I can't have a CDL tattoo, do you understand?"

She looked him straight in the eyes. "I understand you're a traitor."

"No. No, Joan, I'm not. I should have told you before tonight."

"You think?"

"I was wrong. I know you must feel betrayed. I understand. I really do, but I can't walk out that door until we understand each other, right?"

She leaned forward and said in an ominous whisper, "You understand you won't be *walking* out that door, right?"

Murphy softened his voice and leaned toward her. "I deserve that. I've been a heel, and I deserve your anger. I'll take it. I just want to talk to you for a few minutes. Kearney knows about me."

"Bullshit!"

"Kempton knows, too. And Duncan."

Joan's eyes flashed and they bored into Murphy's. In a distracted voice she said, "So you have back up outside and you're here to arrest me. You were good. Real good. I didn't even see this coming." She shook her head slowly. "Duncan warned me about you."

"Warned you about what?"

Joan stood up. "You have to leave."

Murphy grabbed her arm. "Not yet. I can't leave until you understand everything."

She looked at his hand on her arm then directly into his eyes and growled, "Take your hand off me before I take off your arm."

He immediately let go and put both hands up in a sign of submission. "I'm sorry, Joan, please sit down for just another couple minutes. You can give me that much, can't you?"

She remained standing.

"Okay. Just hear me out, and if you still want me to leave, I'll walk out the door. Hopefully, I'll be *able* to walk out the door."

Joan didn't smile. She was hurt and confused. The last thing she wanted to do was show this cad any emotion. Mostly, she didn't smile because she was numb.

"I'm actually doing undercover work for the Legion," Murphy said. "I give task force information to Kearney and he passes it along to Kempton." Joan leaned back on the bureau and crossed her arms. "Think about it." Murphy continued. "How did everyone know you didn't give up any information when you were interrogated by the task force? I'll tell you—it was me. They wouldn't have trusted you after that if I hadn't verified that you were telling the truth."

"So you're a kind of double-agent."

"Yes! That's it. A double agent." Relief showed in his face. "But I have a problem, Joan. I have to give the task force something from time to time so they still think I'm on their team. Can you help me with that?"

She crossed her legs at the ankles. The relaxed posture belied the churning in her stomach. "No. I don't ask you to do my job."

"I'm not asking you to do my job. I'm just asking for a little help. Look, when you were undercover for the Legion there were people helping you, right? Getting you inside, finding you a place to live, helping you when you got into trouble." Joan glared at him. He quickly continued, "You weren't alone."

"It felt like I was alone."

"Sure, that's the nature of undercover work. You think I don't get lonely at times, too?" He stood up and leaned his right hip on the bureau next to her, careful to keep his distance. "But the fact remains you weren't alone. And I'm just asking for your support, just like you received support when you needed it."

"It's not the same."

He folded his arms across his chest. "How so?"

"The people who were supporting me were on the same team. I trusted them. In this case, I'd be helping the task force. What makes you think—"

"That's just it. You wouldn't be helping the task force. You'd actually be helping me stay employed by them so I could continue to help the Legion. Don't you see?"

Joan pushed off the bureau and stood facing him. "I'm not going to help you. Now get out."

"Fair enough. You know I can arrest you right now."

"I'd like to see you try."

Murphy absentmindedly rubbed his jaw then his sternum.

"You would need a squad of officers to take me down," she said. "So if you don't have that, you better start for the door."

Murphy didn't move.

"Duncan was right. He said you weren't interested in me, that you were chasing me for my position. Silly me to think a younger man like you would be interested in me for me."

His eyes snapped to hers. "Joan, I admit at first I had ulterior motives, but the more time I spent with you the more I became genuinely attracted to you."

Joan smirked. "And another time under other circumstances we could have been a great couple. Blah, blah, blah." She turned, picked up the half-empty bottle of tequila, and held it out to him. "I've heard you out. Now it's time for you to leave."

"You aren't angry anymore? I won't leave if you're still angry."

"I'm not angry. I just need some time to think about this. I'll call you in a couple days. Please, don't—call—me."

Murphy gave her a crooked smile. "Don't call me, I'll call you?"

She pushed the tequila bottle into his chest. "Yeah, something like that."

Murphy picked up his revolver from the bureau. "Listen, call Kearny. Call Kempton. Call whoever you like. They'll verify what I just said."

"That's exactly what I'm going to do. Now, if you don't mind—"

Murphy holstered his gun and walked toward the door. He turned to look at her, but she didn't look up until he softly closed the door behind him.

CHAPTER 20

Joan pulled back the curtain and watched as Murphy's car pulled out of the parking lot. Alone. Reeling from the near-miss of another arrest, she was not quite sure who to call first, or if she should make a phone call at all. It would advertise her lapse in judgment.

Kearney was too close to Murphy. He would tell her whatever Murphy wanted her to know. Besides, he would be elated at having another shortcoming to rub in her face. Giving him ammunition to shoot her down was not an option. She didn't know Kempton or Lothar well enough. Was the omission of Duncan's name in the list of people to call some kind of weird reverse psychology? He would be pissed at her for ignoring his warning. She didn't look forward to that call.

Dropping the edge of the curtain, Joan decided to sleep on it. Let the tequila clear out of her head. She turned on the television and opted for the National Geographic Channel. Lying in the flickering of the television, the tequila and the soft narrator's voice calmed her churning brain, and she fell into a fitful sleep.

At 9:12 a.m. she was awakened by the sound of a key in the lock on her door. She reached for her .38 revolver, but it wasn't under her pillow. Between the tequila and Murphy's revelation the night before, she had forgotten to put it there. Relieved it was housekeeping, she sent them away, and chastised herself for the sloppy security—a harsh reminder to pay attention to details. Details that could mean her demise if she didn't get her act together.

As she turned on the shower, she reminded herself she had to get on top of things.

By the time she was ready to leave it was ten o'clock and already the day was warming up a little, but it was still chilly. The time was quickly approaching when she would have to buy a car. Her job required extensive traveling and buses and bumming rides was not going to cut it.

She didn't have a specific task to do for the Legion that day, and she planned on going on a long bike ride after breakfast to relax and think about the phone call she had to make. Maybe she'd stop at a used car lot and see what was available.

There was a little town less than a mile from the motel, and she headed toward it. Riding down the almost deserted main street, she located a hole-in-the-wall, storefront luncheonette to have breakfast.

She was surprised to learn this particular place was experiencing a food shortage. All the places Duncan had showed her never seemed to have a problem getting food. She had almost forgotten about the shortages caused by the government's policies.

The pancakes and sausage patty, instead of the bacon she would have liked, were placed in front of her and, as she munched the homemade biscuit—a replacement for whole wheat toast that wasn't available—she went over every word and action of the night before. She looked for clues that might indicate it was anything other than what it seemed to be—a fed that got snagged. The waitress had just removed her plates and put down the check when Joan decided she was thinking about it too much. She picked up her cell phone and dialed.

"Talk to me."

"Duncan, I have to—"

"We have to talk," he said right away. "Meet me at the restaurant where you had dinner—the last time you were with Travis."

Joan's blood went cold. *How did he know about that dinner? The last time she had seen Travis.* Travis's warning to be careful of Duncan crashed into her thoughts. She was out of the loop. She was being stonewalled. She was being watched. Something was going on, and she'd better get her head screwed on straight before anyone else found out she was losing it. She finally said, "I'm not anywhere near there."

"Neither am I. Out." The line went dead.

She paid her bill and went out to start her bike. While the engine warmed up she tried to put herself in Duncan's place. If Duncan was the enforcer, it was his perception that mattered. He could be luring her to her death. Maybe she had taken too long to call someone, and Murphy had jumped on the chance to spread poison about her. Maybe Duncan was upset because she didn't call him sooner. Or maybe he was going to warn her about a plan against her. Maybe, maybe, maybe. She put her bike in gear, made a U-turn, and headed out of town.

It took her an hour to get to the restaurant. When she arrived, she didn't see Duncan's van, but checked inside anyway. He was not there, so she went back outside to wait. She was sitting on a picnic table at the edge of the parking lot, watching two squirrels chasing each other around a tree, when her phone rang.

In a flat voice Duncan told her to turn left out of the parking lot and look for a blue motel about two miles on the right. It was nothing unusual for Duncan to tell her to meet him in one place then call with a change. It was simply Duncan being careful.

As she pulled into the motel parking lot, he opened a door and waved her over. The room was small with one queen-size bed on the right. There was a television on the corner of the bureau opposite the bed. Duncan turned and walked to the far end of the bureau past the television.

She got right down to business, "Why didn't you tell me Murphy was a fed?"

"No pleasantries?"

"I learned it from you." The tone was harsh. Harsher than she would have liked.

"Tequila?" he asked, pouring some in a shot glass and offering it to her. She shook her head. He downed it and filled it again. Other than one time at The Woods, Joan had never seen Duncan drink in the middle of the day. She wondered why he needed liquid courage. Cautiously stepping toward him, she thought of the famous quote by Sun-Tzu: "Keep your friends close and your enemies closer." Not sure which Duncan was yet, she closed in on him.

"I have never lied to you," he continued. "There are things I have not told you, but whatever I have told you was the truth. Do you believe me?"

"Of course, I believe you. You've never let me down, but one of the things you should have told me was that Murphy was a fed."

"Roger that." He downed the second shot and hesitated, fingering the empty glass. "I guessed he would tell you before you found out the wrong way."

"That night in Johnstown—you knew he was a fed then?"

"I wasn't sure and I didn't want to say anything until I was sure. By the time I was sure, I figured he had already told you."

"So, everyone knows he's a fed, except me—the *security* chief—and everyone's okay with that?"

"We thought you knew. He gives us good intel. It's how we stay one step ahead of the task force. We'd be operating in the dark if it weren't for him." He leaned back on the bureau with both hands on the edge, eyes pinned on the wall across the room. "I never imagined that he didn't tell you. If it were me, *I* would have told you something like that early in the relationship."

Joan eyed his crushing grip on the edge of the bureau. "Relationship? What kind of relationship do you think I have with him?"

"Why don't you tell me?"

"I will, but first you tell me what you think it is. You opened the subject."

"Let's put it this way, I think you're more than friends."

"Really? Why's that? And are you going to look at me any time during this discussion?"

Duncan stood and looked directly into her eyes. "For one thing, he was in your motel room, and he must have had his shirt off for you to see that he didn't have a tatt."

"A man has his shirt off and that automatically means I slept with him?"

Duncan shrugged and crossed his arms across his chest. "I only know what he told me."

Joan tried to speak, but swear words and insults sputtered out incoherently. She finally stopped with her mouth open. Murphy had lied about their relationship—and to Duncan, of all people. *Who else has he told?* "We never—"

"Obviously I was misled," Duncan interrupted. "Is there anything you want to ask *me*? Anything you want to know?"

Joan was relieved at the diversion from her personal life. "Did you have anything to do with Travis' disappearance?"

"No."

"So he has disappeared."

"Yes."

"We're still being honest?"

"Yes and the answer is still 'no.'"

"Are you the enforcer for the Legion?"

"No. How do you know about that?" His response was too severe.

Something was going on.

Joan squinted at Duncan. "*You* are no longer the security chief and *you* know about this, yet I am *currently* the security chief and no one thought to…oh, you know…*inform* me?"

He grabbed her, but she pulled away. "Dammit, I'm the security chief. Like it or not. Whose decision was it to leave me in the dark? And why? I've been loyal, hard-working, forthright, and damn good at my job. Why am I being ostracized?"

"Plausible deniability."

"Plausible bullshit. It's you, isn't it? You are the enforcer."

Duncan's jaw tightened. "I said I wasn't the enforcer, and I meant it."

She had just accused him of lying. Not a good start. Her voice softened. "Then tell me who is."

"I can't."

She turned to leave the room.

"Wait, Joan. I don't know what others have told you about me to make you think I'm the enforcer." He grabbed both her hands and pulled her back into the center of the room. She didn't resist. "I'm a tough guy, yes, and I've done a lot of bad things, it's true, but I've never killed anybody in cold blood." He looked straight into her eyes.

"Then, who is the enforcer?"

"I can't tell you. I don't know what you heard. Trust me on this. You can do that, right?"

Something in his eyes telegraphed sincerity. And concern. She relaxed. "Yes."

Duncan put her hands on his hips and moved his hands to her throat then slid his right hand to the back of her neck right behind her left ear. "Your skin is so soft."

Joan braced for the snap. Kill her by breaking her neck. "You've touched my skin before."

"No, *chica*, I would have remembered."

She could smell the tequila on his breath.

"Be honest with me, *chica*. Whatever you say won't make any difference. I just have to know. Did you sleep with Murphy?"

"You said to tease him," she whispered. "You didn't say anything about going to bed with him."

Duncan chuckled. "You do everything I tell you?"

"Yes, of course, I trust you." *Do I? Aren't I afraid he's going to kill me, even though he said he's not the enforcer?*

"If I had told you to go to bed with him, you would have done it?"

"No. I couldn't have done that even on your order. I have a strong braking system."

"What's that?"

"You."

Duncan smiled and leaned in to kiss her.

"Wait," she said. "I have one more question."

He moved in a little closer. "Later."

She held him back. "Answer me first." When he hesitated, she said, "What's your real name?"

He studied her face, looking deep into her eyes, as if trying to find a glimmer of ulterior motive, and finally whispered, "Dennis."

"Dennis," she repeated, looking into his eyes.

"I haven't heard a woman utter my real name in a decade, maybe more." He sucked in a breath then leaned in to kiss her. His cell phone rang. His shoulders dropped.

"I'm sorry, that's Kempton's ring. I have to take it." He moved one hand to her arm and reached for his phone.

Joan was vaguely aware of what he said. She wondered what was going on. Was he really going to kiss her? Or was he going to kill her? Was he going to seduce her then kill her? She just couldn't shake what others had told her, but then Duncan had never lied to her, at least, not that she knew of.

He was saying, "Where is he?...We'll get right on it..." He looked at Joan. "She's here asking about Murphy...Yes, sir...You're right, there is bad blood between them, but she's a pro...Yes, sir. Out." When Duncan scanned Joan's face, the corners of his eyes hardened, but there was something else. Anxiety. Or fear. Or both.

The intimate moment had passed, replaced by a heavy feeling in Joan's chest.

The next time he spoke to her, Duncan had his game face on. "Where's the nearest safe house?"

"Youngstown."

"Kearney got mixed up in something. What's the address?" As she told him, he reached into his pocket and pulled out a wad of money. Peeling off several large bills, he said, "Get it ready. I'll meet you there with Kearney in about three hours."

Joan spun around, threw the strap of her backpack over one shoulder, and headed for the door. Duncan grabbed her arm to stop her from leaving. He stared into her eyes.

She waited expectantly.

"Be careful," he said. "Ohio isn't the friendliest place for you."

CHAPTER 21

The safe house wasn't anything fancy. It was a small apartment located in the basement of a big old Victorian house. The best feature was the rear entrance off an alley. Joan dropped three days' worth of groceries on the stained Formica counter next to the crescent-shaped burn mark. The safe house had essentials already there—a full-sized mattress with a frame, two sets of linens, coffee pot, toilet paper, and basic kitchen utensils bought at the local Good Will. Each safe house had basic personal hygiene items, five gallons of water, and freeze-dried camping meals so there would be something to eat if there wasn't time to get to the store before occupying the place. This one had a couch and a kitchen table with two wooden chairs that were thankfully left behind by the previous renters.

After putting the groceries away and getting the sheets on the bed, she did some calisthenics to pass the time. A few minutes into the workout, she received a call on a throw away. Duncan had picked up Kearney and they were ten minutes out. She gave them the final directions to the alley.

Luckily when they arrived, there were no kids playing in the alley to see Duncan half-carry the barely conscious Kearney from the van to the house. Kearney was dragging one leg and he winced every time he took a step with the other leg. His left arm dangled at his side. Duncan spanned the distance in mere seconds. As he squeezed the two of them through the kitchen door, he explained that Kearney had been caught in an altercation that had turned to gun play. The bullets had gone straight through the flesh on the outside of his thigh and through his deltoid at the tip of his shoulder.

Duncan took him straight to the bedroom and told Joan to start cutting off Kearney's clothes and cleaning the dried blood. Pulling out packages of gauze, scissors, clamps, needles and vials from his medical supplies backpack, Duncan feverishly cleaned the wounds and sewed them up. Helping wherever she could, Joan was mesmerized by Duncan's skill. In spite of the morphine Duncan had given him, Kearney still writhed in pain and Joan let him hold her hand and squeeze as hard as he needed to. With her other hand, she gently wiped the sweat from his face with a dampened washcloth.

Twenty minutes later, Duncan was done. Without the poking and prodding, the morphine took over and Kearney fell into a fitful sleep. Joan looked up at the tight-lipped frown on Duncan's face. It was an unabashed expression of worry for the welfare of his best friend. In that moment, in that overt sentiment, Joan saw the depth of the friendship between these two battle-hardened men. It answered one question but raised another. If Duncan could be empathetic, what other preconceived notions were wrong?

She took the bloodstained clothes and towels with her as she quietly left Duncan at the bedside of his injured comrade.

∽∾∽∾

The aroma of the meal Joan prepared drew Duncan into the kitchen. He saw the coffee, fixed himself a cup, and looked sideways at her as she stirred the cooked spaghetti into the pot of sauce.

The vision of her doing this simple task warmed his heart that had been cold for decades. Being beside her in a domestic setting tamed the wildness that flowed through his veins.

He wanted to say something about what happened at the motel earlier, but didn't know how to approach it. Being at a loss for words was unfamiliar to him. "Smells good," he said to break the ice.

"It's just spaghetti," she said without looking up. She

placed the tongs on a paper towel and looked at him. "You were great with Kearney."

"It's not over yet. We'll know in twenty-four hours how well I did." His arms ached to pull her in close to him, but if he did, he'd never get on the road. Duty called. "Do you feel comfortable watching him? I have something to do I can't get out of."

"You have to leave tonight?" she asked.

He sensed her discomfort with the responsibility of taking care of a seriously injured person. A person she'd rather hurt than tend to. "He'll sleep for the next several hours."

"I know basic first aid, but this isn't basic."

"I'll leave some pain meds with you."

Joan crossed her arms and looked at her feet.

"Call me if anything seems wrong. I'll be back some time tomorrow." Rubbing her arms, he continued in a soft, intimate tone, "And I'll finish what I started at the motel." He watched her eyes, trying to assess her mood, but Joan was being guarded. "You'll be all right here with Kearney, right?"

"As long as he doesn't pull a gun on me."

"He won't be doing much of anything for a while. Just in case, hide all the guns." He smiled and gave her a hug but she did not respond. Things had changed. He let go. "Let's eat. The sooner I leave, the sooner I can get back."

❦❦❦

After Duncan left, other than the occasional footsteps from the place above, the apartment fell silent and darkened as the day turned into evening. Joan fell asleep on the couch, the magazine she had been reading on the floor where it had fallen. She woke with a start when a voice pierced the darkness.

"How is your hand? I squeezed it pretty hard before when—"

"Kearney, you shouldn't be up. Go back to bed. If you feel like eating, I'll bring a bowl of spaghetti in to you." She sat up, rubbing the sleep from her eyes. When she opened them there was Kearney, his pale skin glowing through the darkness—all of it, head to toe. She put her hand over her eyes. "Cover up."

Kearney laughed. "I have to take a piss. If I can get up to do that, I can eat sitting on the couch." He limped into the bathroom and raised his voice over the sound of the urine stream. "Where's Duncan?"

Joan got up and started toward the kitchen. "Said he had something to do that he couldn't get out of. He'll be back tomorrow."

Kearney limped into the kitchen still naked.

When Joan turned from filling a bowl with spaghetti, she stopped short. Kearney had not covered up. "Put a towel on or I'll shoot you in the other leg."

"Stop being so coy, you little minx," he teased.

Joan glared at him, but the pain medication must have put a Happy Filter on everything.

"You saw everything I have to offer while Duncan was working on me."

"That was necessary. This—" she said, pointing up and down his body, "—is not. Sit. I'll get a towel." On her way to the bathroom, Joan mused that Kearney was almost charming. *Maybe he should be on morphine all the time.*

He ate only a small amount of spaghetti, apologizing to Joan that it wasn't her cooking. He asked if Duncan had left any painkillers. After a brief verbal disagreement, he gave in and Joan gave him what Duncan said he should get, not what he wanted. She helped him back into bed and gave him a gentle back rub. It seemed to help with the pain and by the time she was done, he was asleep.

In the morning he was looking much better. The color had returned to his face, and his appetite was improving. She made him stay in bed except for eating, just to be sure—and to keep him covered up. He made a comment about how well she was treating him in spite of the bad blood between them, and she sat down at the foot of the bed. "Why *do* you hate me?"

"I don't hate you. I just don't think you're right for the job."

"What do I have to do to convince you that I am?"

"Never mind. Forget I said it."

"You wanted your good ol' boy, Murphy, to get the job, didn't you?"

"He would be better at it."

"Even though he's a fed?"

"He's with us now."

"How can you be sure? How do you know he's not giving the Legion just enough intel so you don't suspect him anymore?"

"Forget I said anything. Actually, I have a confession to make. I think you're doing a good job as security chief." As if he couldn't let his words stand without a barb, he added, "Not great, mind you, but a good job just the same. What are you going to do now that you know Murphy's a federal agent?"

"There isn't much I can do. If it's okay with you, Duncan, Pallaton, and Kempton, then it's okay with me."

"I meant, what are you going to do about his advances? He really likes you. I can't for the life of me figure out why."

Joan playfully twisted his foot.

"Ow! So are you two going to hook up?"

"I doubt it. He's too light in the ass for me."

"Roger that."

"While we're speaking of hooking up, does Duncan tell you everything?"

Kearney responded with hesitation, knowing where this was going. "Sort of, we're best buds, why?"

"He made a pass at me yesterday. He did, right? I'm not imagining things."

"I don't know what he did yesterday, so I don't know if you're on target or not, but it sounds right. He has the hots for you—big time."

"How long? He never showed any signs of wanting more than a professional relationship."

"He didn't want to do or say anything that would possibly ruin his chances."

"Ruin his chances? Why would he feel that way?"

"You intimidate him."

"Yeah, right," she snorted. "Nobody intimidates Duncan."

"Let me rephrase that. The thought of a relationship intimidates him. He feels you look up to him. He doesn't want anything to change your opinion of him."

"But why would anything change?"

"I don't know. It's Duncan being Duncan."

"Okay, I can sort of buy that, but why now?"

"The story is that Murphy was undressed in your motel room—"

"With his shirt off," Joan said through clenched teeth.

"Yup, and Duncan's imagination took off at warp speed."

"But nothing happened." Joan's voice relayed the tension in her body.

"I know. Murphy was being a guy, you know, exaggerating his exploits. I tried to tell Duncan that, but he thinks he has to get to you away from Murphy. I tried to tell him that Murphy was finding it impossible to make headway with you, but the image of Murphy in your room undressed—"

"Shirt off," Joan corrected.

"Yeah, shirt off, was too much for him. He felt he had to act, and I guess he didn't waste any time."

"So, he's not trying to kill me?"

"Kill you?" Kearney's voice was raised and sharp. He cleared his throat. "Whatever gave you that idea? Why would he want to kill you?"

"Don't mind me, I'm not thinking clearly."

"I guess not."

Before Joan knew what she was doing. She heard herself asking, "Where's Travis? Nobody seems to know."

Kearney's eyebrows dropped to form a straight line across his brow. "Forget him, Joan. He's not with us anymore."

"Not with the Legion?"

"Forget him, he's gone."

"What happened?"

"He was going to leave the Legion. He knew too much. I'm sorry."

"What do you have to be sorry about?"

"I know how close you two were. It had to be difficult for you to turn him in." He studied Joan's reaction.

"Who told you that I turned him in?"

"It doesn't matter. It was a good thing you did. It showed where your loyalties lie."

"Who—"

"Who killed him? I can't tell you. Don't ask. You don't need to know."

"I'm head of security. I have a need to know."

"No, you don't." He hesitated. "Joan, it's not you or anything you have or have not done. Kempton is the only one who knows...and the enforcer himself, of course."

You just said you couldn't tell me, not that you didn't know. Duncan said the same thing. I now know of three people who know: Kempton, Duncan, and you. "You know. You just don't want to tell me." No answer. For Kearney the subject was closed. "You have to tell me. Is it someone I know?"

Kearney hesitated. "Yes, and that's all I'm going to tell you." He turned on his side, facing away from her.

CHAPTER 22

Joan's daily martial arts training had always been a form of relaxation. It was all consuming, and the concentration on her technique blocked outside thoughts. But today, it was anything but relaxing. It could not overcome the persistent thoughts of the Legion and where she stood within it. Thoughts of who might have killed Travis were too powerful, and the distraction led to poor technique, which only served to exasperate her further. Each thought affected the techniques. Each poorly executed technique opened a window to another disrupting thought. She was in a downward spiral.

She tried to increase the intensity of her training, thinking the exertion would clear her head. But she only became breathless and physically spent. The thoughts were still there as well as the questions they raised. She finally gave up.

While the water for a shower ran, she gave in to the insistent thoughts and questions that had plagued her workout. She climbed into the shower and, as the warm water ran over her body and massaged her shoulders, she wondered if Duncan was the enforcer. Her gut told her he was not, but she had to consider the idea. There was good cause to set up Duncan as the bad guy in this whole wretched affair. He was the driving force for Joan getting her current position at the expense of Murphy, who also had a friend in the leadership. Kearney, she was sure, had wanted his good old boy, Murphy, to get the job, but the one person he disliked the most got it instead, and the person who had made that possible was Duncan.

Kearney had the disposition and the ability to be cold-blooded. Would Kempton have tapped him for this sinister job? Kearney couldn't fight, or at least she hadn't seen any indication of it. If a confrontation turned physical, he could not handle himself as well as Duncan could.

Gunther was definitely cold-blooded, but he was a minor player. He was busy with his own hijacking operations. Although he had the predilection for murder, finding the time to do it would be harder than for Duncan, who was starting up a new area and didn't have a lot of men under him or operations in the pipeline.

Everything came back to Duncan.

Kearney said that it was someone she knew, so then who could it be? She knew everybody from the leadership down to the new recruit in an obscure cell. It could be anybody. And if it wasn't Duncan or Kearney, then her position was being undermined. Why? Had they noticed her diminished enthusiasm for her job? Was she in danger?

Joan made a mental note to watch her back around everyone—even Duncan. His actions toward her over the last twenty-four hours had been out of character for him. She wanted desperately to believe he was being honest with her. Correction—she *needed* for him to be honest with her. He had never given any indication that his interest was anything more than professional. If he was trying to seduce her, why now? If he was, in fact, the enforcer was he trying to distract her so he could kill her, but again the question arose, why now?

It came to her as a distant vague sensation and increased in intensity like thunder in an approaching storm. Duncan thought Murphy had finally seduced her and he was making his bid for her attention before it was too late.

Joan looked back upon their relationship, the way he watched her, protected her, supported her. She felt a nagging sensation that she had always considered Duncan as more than a friend, but had taken the safe route and defaulted to being professional, assuming it was the same with him. *Why didn't I see it and take the initiative?* Men's advances made Joan apprehensive, preferring to be the one who made the move.

Joan leaned against the tile wall of the shower and let the

water, now turning cold, run across her shoulders and down her back. Were his actions a diversion so he could kill her while she was distracted with the possibility of his feelings for her? Yesterday's act was without the opening lines men use to soften up the woman, but it didn't alter the fact that take-charge Duncan stumbled into his seduction. Like anything else, if his thoughts advanced too far ahead to the next step, he might fumble through the current actions. *So, maybe it's what I thought before—seduction before he goes in for the kill.* Kearney said I wasn't on the chopping block. Had that been a cover-up for the Legion?

Stop it, it's not Duncan. Until she knew for a fact who the enforcer was, for self-preservation, she had to keep her eyes open, her mouth shut, and her mind alert.

She shook her head, got out of the shower, and dried off. When she was dressed, she paced around the living room and wondered why she was thinking that the enforcer would be coming for her. *Admit it. Your resolve and loyalty to the Legion are eroding. Others have to see it. You're edgy, evasive, and aloof. Just like Travis was.* One wrong word and she could be meeting the same fate as Travis.

Instead of thinking the situation through and finding peace, her paranoia shifted into high gear. Packing up her few belongings, she made the decision to leave as soon as Duncan returned. Getting out of that apartment and to a safe place to think this through was paramount. She debated about going to the safe house she had set up under a secret alias that even the Legion didn't know about. She had set it up just in case she had to get away from the Legion, but the number one rule of safe houses was to never, never go to it until absolutely necessary. But was this instance serious enough? If she went there, she could never use it again when she may need it for something more serious.

"Goin' somewhere?" Kearney said.

Joan hadn't heard him get up or walk to the doorway to the bedroom. "I cleaned your guns for you."

"You are the master at evasive answers. I say again, you goin' somewhere?"

"I have things to do other than nurse you back to health. As soon as Duncan returns I'm going to leave."

"What's so important? You aren't running out on Duncan, are you?"

"No. It's work, and I don't have to justify my work to you."

"That's true, you don't, but Duncan may want to know." He was looking at something over her left shoulder. It was an old trick. She was not falling for it.

On the way to the bathroom to get her personal hygiene items she said, "He'll understand." She gathered her things and turned toward the door and almost bumped into Kearney leaning on the doorjamb blocking her exit. Damn he was quiet for an injured man.

"I've known Duncan for a very long time and I've warned him about you, but where you're concerned he seems to have lost his objectivity." He leaned in toward Joan and almost whispered, "I don't know what you're up to, but you'll go down before Duncan goes down. I'll make sure of that." He turned and limped toward the bedroom door.

Joan followed after him. "I thought we were starting to get along. You're turning on me because I have work to do and I have to leave? You'd think you'd be happy to see me go so you can poison Duncan's mind about me." He shut the door to the bedroom. Joan put the last of her things in her bag.

"Having a bad day?" Duncan said.

Two quiet men. She should put jingle bells on their shoe-laces. "I just went through this with your long-time friend and I'm not in the mood for a lot of questions."

"Whoa. What's going on here?"

"You're here. You can take care of Kearney. I have to leave."

"Now?"

"Yes. I have things to do."

"Nothing that can't wait."

Joan spun her head to look at Duncan. The sternness in his voice got her attention.

He approached her and softened his tone. "You're just up-tight from spending too much time cooped up in this apartment."

"Don't patronize me." She zipped up her duffle and turned to her backpack to finish packing it.

Duncan looked at the bedroom door, thought a second, then

said, "Stay right here. Don't move." He walked to the bedroom door, opened it, and said, "Hey, buddy, how are you doing? Joan needs to get out for a few minutes. Will you be okay by yourself?" Joan could not see or hear Kearney, but Duncan waved and told him they wouldn't be long. Duncan grabbed her bags. "Let's go." Joan didn't move. He grabbed her arm. "*Vamos.*"

Duncan slid her bags behind the seats while Joan slid into the passenger seat. Joan reached for the seatbelt and struggled to click it. *Great, he has all my things. He can dump my body and my bags and, poof, I just disappear.* She looked up at Duncan. "Why did you bring my bags? Aren't you going to try to talk me into staying?"

Duncan half turned toward Joan his left arm on the steering wheel and the other on the back of the seat. "I want you to stay more than anything in the world, but I know I can't talk you into doing anything you don't want to do. If we talk and you still want to go today, I'll bring you back to your bike and you can go." He turned to start the engine and slowly drove down the alley. "I understand that you have work to do. It's not your job to support and stay with people in a safe house. I was just hoping we could spend some time together." Silence filled the van as he maneuvered through the traffic. It lasted until he parked next to a small park. They sat for a moment watching a middle-aged woman walk her golden retriever and a father and his young son kicking a soccer ball back and forth.

He turned in his seat to face her. "Do you want to tell me why you have to leave?" Joan opened her mouth to speak but he quickly added, "Other than you have a job to do. Did Kearney say or do anything to you?"

"No. As a matter of fact, we were starting to get along."

Duncan snorted. "Yeah, like a mongoose and a cobra."

"As crazy as it sounds, we talked out some of our issues. Then when he saw me packing my stuff, he did a one-eighty. I know you don't want to hear it, but it's my work, Duncan. Kempton is expecting a report on three new targets, and there's a new recruit in Kittanning who—"

"Kempton can wait another day. He knows where you are. Is it because of the things I said at the motel yesterday?"

She shook her head.

"Joan, we agreed we were going to be honest with each other. Tell me what's going on."

She laid it on the line. "It's partly what you did and said at the motel yesterday, but it's also more than that. This whole enforcer thing is putting my paranoia through the roof. Killing our own...*really,* Duncan?"

"It's not what you think."

"Yeah? Then what is it?"

"I can't tell you, but trust me when I say no one is after you. You are a much appreciated and valuable asset to the Legion."

"An asset? Is that how you think of me?"

"I don't think of you that way, but the Legion does. Hell, *I'm* just an asset to them."

"Just so we're clear. How *do* you think of me?"

"It's hard to put into words. I haven't put words to the feelings in my own mind so how can I explain them to you?"

There was a silence while Joan patiently waited.

"Duncan..."

"Okay. Here goes—when I first met you I was emotionally shut down and, except for a few very close friends, I did not interact with anyone else socially. Having said that, in the beginning, I, too, thought of you as an asset, nothing more. But over the past several months, working closely with you and watching you, I began to miss the happiness that you seem to exhibit so easily. Wanting that happiness makes me want you in my life."

"I am in your life."

"I don't mean in my 'Legion' life. I mean...uh, in my..." Duncan's eyes studied her face, his mouth was open, but no words came out to finish his sentence.

"In your personal life." How was she going to explain this without alienating him? "Duncan, I love being around you. Your strength. Your take no prisoners attitude, but—"

"But you don't look at me that way."

"I didn't say that. I know it sounds corny, but it's not you. It's me. If we get serious, I'll become a different person. I'll become obstinate and unpredictable, you know, hard to deal with."

"And that's different from the way you are now?"

Joan smiled. "It's a matter of degrees. Believe me, you

don't want to see me that way. My sense of humor disappears and I would blame you for sucking the joy out of my life. It wouldn't be pretty."

"What if we got together but we made no demands on each other?"

"Like friends with benefits?"

"No." Duncan's eyes pinned themselves on Joan's eyes. "It would have to be more than that. I want more than that with you."

"How would that work without strings?"

"I don't know. This is new territory for me. All I know is I want to see you more…as more than just a colleague."

"It won't work. Maybe this is just that psychological thing where two people are attracted to each other as a result of working together during stressful situations. Let's just stay friends."

Duncan hesitated before answering. "Okay, but I'm warning you, when I know what I want I go after it. I won't give up until I figure how to make this work."

"Just don't become a pain in the ass about it."

"I won't stalk you, if that's what you mean." Shaking a finger at her, he added, "You've been warned."

They smiled.

She saw him lean over as if to kiss her, but she turned her head to look out the side window at a car that just pulled into the adjacent parking space.

The moment evaporated. "So are you going to stay at the apartment or are you still going to leave?" he asked.

"I get antsy staying in one place too long."

"I didn't mean to make you feel uncomfortable." Duncan reached across the console and put a hand on her shoulder. "You can tell me anything, you know that, right?"

Joan turned to face him, pulling her shoulder away from his hand. She could see the quizzical look in his eyes, and her resolve almost broke down. She reached out to touch his face, but instead she touched his arm on the back of the seat. She wanted to open up to him, and she knew her body language told him that. She moved away from him.

They just looked at each other for what seemed like minutes, then Duncan turned to start the van's engine. "Okay,

I'll take you back to your bike and you can go do your work, but only if you promise to stay in touch. Okay?"

She nodded.

"I'm serious. Okay?"

"Yes. I'll stay in touch."

"One more question, chica."

"What's that?" She watched the father pick up the soccer ball and walk toward the edge of the park with his hand on his son's shoulder.

"Yesterday when I asked if you had any questions for me, you could have asked *any* question. Why didn't you ask me how I felt about you?"

"I was afraid of the answer."

"Which answer would that have been?"

"It doesn't matter anymore. I know the answer." The phone call from Kempton had told her all she needed to know—the Legion would always come first. They drove back to the safe house in silence.

Rather than do the work her job required, she went to her safe house in Eldersville. It was actually a small camper trailer in a campground. It would be the perfect place to get her thoughts together. Pulling into the campground at six-thirty, she immediately opened up the camper and hooked up the electricity. With lights on and windows open, she started putting away the groceries she had bought along the way. Neighboring campers knocked on her door to introduce themselves and invite her to sit by their fire, but she begged off, saying she was tired from the long drive. She suggested that maybe the next night she might be interested if the invitation was still open. They assured her it would be, and they left her alone with her thoughts in her tiny, stuffy camper.

She ate a salad for dinner and washed it down with tequila and diet cola. When she was done eating, she turned out the lights and sat in the dark. The only light was the glow from the campfire three camper trailers down the lane and strings of lights outside the neighboring trailers. She could hear country music playing and bursts of laughter from the people gathered around the fire.

She watched the small oscillating fan blow warm, humid

air around the inside of her camper. It would go to the right then come back and blow a warm breeze on her then continue to her left until it would go back to the right again, washing her with the same warm breeze on its way by. She watched it go back and forth as her thoughts oscillated about the Legion. It was the right way to defend the constitution then back again, thinking it was the wrong way to go. Each time her thoughts switched direction, she was washed with a feeling of despair. She tried to decide what she could do that would actually be effective.

She ached for Travis's common sense. He had always been able to cut through the fog and discern what was right and what was wrong. She had never realized how much she depended on him, but now that he was gone, it was abundantly clear that he was the one who had kept her focused over the past year. The fact that the Legion would kill him because he had doubts about the effectiveness of their activities was chilling. Her thoughts kept swirling around her—if they would get rid of him, why not her? After all, she spoke up when she saw the lethal operations the leadership was planning. Kearney had always doubted her loyalty. Maybe he knew more about her than she did herself. If he doubted her, what would prevent the rest of the leadership believing the same thing? If not now, in time he would bring them around to his way of thinking. After several more tequila and diet colas, her thinking became cloudy and barely coherent.

෬෬෬

Joan's odd behavior prompted an emergency meeting of the leadership. Since Kearney could not travel they all met at the safe house in Youngstown.

Once everyone had arrived, Kempton got right down to business. "Joan's behavior in the past month or so is becoming a concern. The work she does is impeccable, but her attitude is troubling. Her objection to the new direction of operations is of utmost concern. She is integral in ensuring high profile targets are effectively attacked, but if she doesn't agree with the reason for choosing the target or the means of attack, will she would subconsciously, or even consciously, undermine its effectiveness?"

Kearney cleared his throat. "I'm not going to repeat my concerns. I think everyone here knows where I stand as far as Joan is concerned." He winced as he changed his position on the couch. "Duncan, you know I love you like a brother and we go way back but I feel you've lost your objectivity where Joan's concerned."

"You haven't liked her from day one," Duncan said, pointing his finger for emphasis. "I think it *your* objectivity that's questionable."

"I'm objective because I'm thinking with the right head."

Duncan moved to the edge of his chair. "What's that supposed to mean?"

"Listen, guys," Lothar interject, putting a hand on Duncan's arm to prevent him from moving any farther forward. "Hurling insults at each other isn't going to help us find some common ground. Correct me if I'm wrong, Kempton, but we have to hash out where Joan stands in the organization and what action, if any, we're going to take."

"If I may interject some objectivity," Pallaton said. "My opinion isn't colored by too much connection or—" He looked at Kearney. "—disconnection. All of Joan's work in my area has been more than satisfactory. And that's been *since* the meeting where she disagreed with the new operational direction. I don't see where her disagreement with operational policy has affected her attitude or behavior."

Kempton turned to Duncan. Duncan had worked very closely with Joan over the past year, and it was he who had recommended her for her present position. He would be biased to a certain extent, but Kempton still felt Duncan could be objective in order to best serve the Legion. "Duncan, what is your honest assessment of this Joan situation?"

Duncan leaned back in his chair and crossed his arms. "To be honest, sir, I have noticed a slight diminishing of passion for her job. There is something bothering her. I don't know if it's Travis's disappearance or what. We have to remember, we've all been soldiers for hire, sometimes on foreign soil. We expect the unrelenting stress. This is new to her."

"I thought she did a tour in Iraq," Kempton said. "What did she do there?"

"She was in a transportation company. I don't think she saw any real fighting."

Kempton nodded, the frown deepening on his face. "I think she's experiencing the paranoia we're all experiencing—"

"I'm not paranoid," Kearney said.

Kempton shook his head at Kearney in an attempt to let him know his comment wasn't helping.

"Sir, I think this might be short-lived," Duncan said. "She's strong. She'll bounce back."

Kempton looked around the room. "So, it comes down to what we do from here. I think we should give her an opportunity to prove herself—some act that would demonstrate her loyalty and willingness to be a part of the Legion. Any ideas?"

Several ideas were put forth and, after a great deal of discussion, it was decided that she would take part in the bombing of the Fort Pitt Tunnel. Duncan objected to the location because she was a high profile target for the feds in Pittsburgh and she could compromise the ability to successfully carry out this operation. It was argued that it was the ultimate test of her loyalty to put herself into such a dangerous position. If successful, she would cement her place in the inner circle.

The meeting broke up and, because Pittsburgh was in Kearney's area, he was the overseer of the operation from beginning to end. Duncan objected on the grounds of bad blood between Kearney and Joan. To Kearney's surprise, he suggested that Murphy could step in and supervise the operation. Kempton remained unmoved and Duncan acquiesced. If Joan could overcome the odds against her, she would not be doubted again. He wanted that for her.

CHAPTER 23

Joan woke up at seven in the morning with a headache and a sour stomach. Last night, the fact that no one would find her was comforting as well as cathartic. In spite of the pounding head and churning stomach, she felt more relaxed than she could remember over the past several weeks. The new day held the possibility of a new perspective.

After showering in the communal, cinderblock latrine, she made a cup of instant coffee. She sat on the metal step of her camper, drinking the awful coffee and nibbling at a peanut butter sandwich, and made small talk with neighbors who passed by—and came to a decision.

She locked up the camper and packed up her bike. While the engine warmed up, her neighbor came over and asked if she was leaving already. She assured him she had some errands to run but she would be back the following day. She wasn't sure if he believed her, but it didn't really matter. She would not be back.

Unaware of the leadership's meeting the night before, she decided to go to the leadership and plead her case. The first step was to make sure they were confident in her loyalty, so the danger of being eliminated would cease.

It would be one less thing on her mind. The constant distrust was draining, and that preoccupation could cause her to make a mistake.

She had important work to do for the Legion, and she didn't need that distraction. With all the things that increased her paranoia off the table, she could concentrate on trying to determine where her future with the Legion lay.

Halfway between Steubenville and Pittsburgh she pulled into a small country-style restaurant and turned her phone on. She checked her messages and, as she expected, there were two messages from Duncan. After finishing the coffee and bagel she had ordered for breakfast, she took a deep breath and dialed Duncan's number.

Her stomach jumped at the familiar, "Talk to me, *chica*."

"I'm checking in like you asked."

"Why didn't you call sooner? I left two messages."

"I saw them. I just needed some time to unwind, but I am back." She took a sip of her coffee and cursed because she burnt her lip on it. "I am 110% and eager to get back to work."

"Good. I can hear it in your voice. What are your plans for today?"

"I'm on my way to Kittanning to check out that new recruit for one of Pallaton's cells."

"There's a change in plans. I'm not supposed to break the news to you, but, uh, Kempton wants you to do an operation in Pittsburgh."

"In Pittsburgh? Isn't that dangerous for me? You know, with me being on the task force's radar?"

"You'll be okay. Just keep a low profile. I know that's hard for you, but give it a shot, okay? This is an important assignment for you."

"This is great!" There was silence at the other end. "Really. It's exactly what I was going to suggest to redeem myself with the leadership."

"Joan, there's something else you need to know. It's in Kearney's area and he has been tasked to closely oversee the operation."

"Oh." The downcast tone got out before she could stop it. *Put a positive spin on this.* "Well, we had a good conversation the other day. I think he might be coming around."

"Just watch your back, okay, Iron Angel. By the way, I wasn't supposed to break the news to you, so when Kearney calls you with the details, act like you don't know anything."

"Got it. Oh, and Duncan, thank you for giving me a heads up."

"Anything for you, *chica*. I'm concerned about your welfare. I guess you know that." He rubbed his day-old stubble. "I'm out of this one. You're on your own. If I get involved, it could blow your chance at regaining the leadership's confidence in you."

"I understand." *So, the leadership* has *lost confidence in me.*

"I better go before I say too much. Out." The line went dead.

CHAPTER 24

Joan had barely placed her phone back on the table when it rang. The caller ID indicated it was Kearney. "Hi, Kearney."

"Hey, Joan, where are you? We were worried about you last night."

"I'm at a restaurant west of Pittsburgh. I feel much better today. I just had to tie one on, you know."

"Don't I know it? I could stand the same thing myself." Joan waited for the news. "Listen, Kempton thought we should do an operation together," he continued. "He thinks by us working together, we'll settle our differences, and there'll be less tension in the leadership."

"Together? You and me? What did you have in mind?"

"I don't want to talk over the phone. Can you come up to Youngstown?"

"I'll have to cancel my plans for today, but, yeah, I can do that. I can be there in a couple hours. Is that okay?"

"Great. Can you pick up some Chinese food on the way?"

"Will do. Bye."

Kearney seemed to be overly solicitous. Was he really trying to make amends? Duncan's warning to watch her back echoed in her head.

She arrived at the safe house in Youngstown at five-past-one, Chinese food in hand. Kearney dove right into the food and did not say much, except how good the food was, until he was cracking open the fortune cookie.

Joan smiled at his energy and high spirits.

"About this operation…" He picked some food out of his teeth with his fingernail. "We have to put our differences aside and make this work. Can you do that?"

"Whatever I have to do, I'll do it." She watched him guzzle down a bottle of cola and wondered, *Why do men have to eat like hungry wolves*? This was not going to be easy. "But what about you?"

He belched. "These past few days were good for us, you know, getting to know each other and all and, though we don't fully trust each other yet, I think we're both professional enough that we can pull this off."

"What about your little tirade in the bathroom before I left yesterday."

"When?"

She noted his puzzled look. "You know the threats about taking me down."

"Oh, that. Don't mind me. Morphine does that to me. Ignore me when I get like that." He looked around. "Any more soda?"

"No. Here take some of mine, if you don't mind my germs."

He winked and reached for her soda bottle. "Your germs are my germs."

Joan fought to keep the corners of her mouth from turning up. "Take a few extra meds today?" She gathered up the empty take-out boxes. "We can't show anything other than solidarity around cell members, agreed?"

"That goes without saying. We'll air any differences in private." He offered his hand across the table, still trying to get food out of his teeth with his tongue. "Deal?"

Joan hesitated then reached out and took his hand in hers. "Deal. So what did you have in mind?"

He watched her closely. "Bomb the Fort Pitt Tunnel."

"Tell me about it," she heard herself saying as she leaned forward. Her stomach went into a knot. The tunnel was busy all hours of the day, and at rush hour it could mean the loss of hundreds of lives. Joan put up her emotion shields.

He explained his view of what had to be done regarding

recon and the choice of explosives. Joan was relieved she would be working with Alice again—at least there'd be one person on the team she felt she could trust. There was one nagging question and, when Kearney was finished, she just had to ask, "Why are you honchoing this operation?"

"Remember? We have to work together to work out our differences. Kempton thinks it's a good idea."

Nice touch—dropping Kempton's name like that. Joan went over the details to make sure she understood them, and Kearney seemed happy to explain each one to her. She sat back and thought about it for a minute. Though Kearney's gaze was steady, she sensed his anticipation of resistance.

"May I make a suggestion?" she finally asked.

"Hear it comes," he said, crossing his arms. "You understand I'm the boss on this project and I don't have to make any changes." At her tightened lips and glare, he ended with, "Sure, let me hear your ideas."

"If the authorities get wind of a bomb in the tunnel they'll close them."

"They won't—"

"Hear me out."

Kearney nodded and motioned for her to continue.

"What if we put the explosives on the Fort Pitt *Bridge*, and call in a bomb scare for the tunnel?"

Kearney leaned forward.

"They'll close the tunnel, but the traffic will be backed up on the bridge," Joan continued. "*And* they won't be looking for explosives on the bridge."

Kearney finished the last part together with Joan. "They'll be searching the tunnel."

"I'll call Alice and get him up here so he can re-calculate the explosives for the bridge."

He picked up his phone and started dialing.

"Wait." Joan stood up and started pacing around the kitchen. "We need to be closer to Pittsburgh to plan this." She was talking to herself as much as to Kearney.

"Go on," Kearney said.

The pacing stopped. She looked directly at Kearney. "What if we keep the original plan for the bomb in the tunnel and just *add* the bomb on the bridge? If the feds find one, there's still another one."

Kearney jumped up in excitement, but grabbed his leg and winced. "That's ingenious!" He made an exaggerated gesture of pointing at her. "You are good. You are really good."

"It's what I do." Joan was not sure what she was feeling. Did she just make the plan even more lethal? What was going on in her head?

"Can I call Alice now?" Kearney said, oblivious to the subtle shift in the leadership of the operation.

"Wait, Kearney."

Kearney looked up at her expectantly.

"How many phone calls have you made with your cell since you've been here?"

"I don't know," he said. "More than five, less than twenty. Why?"

She looked around the room. "Did the leadership meet here last night?"

"Yeah. Why?" Kearney dragged out the words.

"Any phone calls?

"Yes. You wanna tell me where this is going?"

He'd mentioned Youngstown in his call to her earlier in the day. A flurry of phone calls from that area. Joan's stomach clenched. "Are you well enough to ride on my motorcycle?"

"I'm not sure, why?"

Joan's gut was telling her to get out of Dodge. "Maybe it's nothing, but pack your shit. We have to go."

"I don't have any 'shit.' The only thing I brought here was a couple bullets, remember?"

"Then let's do a complete wipe down and get out of here."

Kearney hesitated. "Why this one-eighty degree turn around from planning an operation to leaving the safe house in a hurry?"

"I don't have time to explain. Do it now!" Joan knew a wipe down would get rid of fingerprints but some DNA would still remain. The feds would have to find it though. The apartment was small, and she was done in ten minutes. Kearney's energy was fading, but he did what he could with his one good arm.

When she was satisfied, she gave him an extra pain pill. They hopped onto her bike and headed for Eldersville. Though unwise to return to her safe house, they would only stay for one night.

They stopped for gas just outside of East Liverpool. Kearney tried to hide his fatigue and pain, but Joan noticed it. He had been heavily leaning on her the last ten miles. He didn't complain, and she respected him for that. This stop gave him an opportunity to sit back on a bench by the front window of the gas station and give his shoulder a rest. She told him they only had about thirty miles to go and asked if he could make it, knowing he didn't have a choice. They stopped once more to buy some groceries and, by five o'clock, they pulled into the campgrounds.

As she pulled up to her camper he said, "This is it? The two of us in this tiny thing?"

"A jail cell would be smaller."

"And my roommate wouldn't be as pretty," Kearney added.

"Maybe, maybe not. Just remember that when you get claustrophobic. Here's the key. Take the food inside, and I'll hook up the electricity. If anyone asks, you're my brother," she said as she placed the key to the door in his hand. "Hey, what's 'my brother's' name?"

He smiled. "I have ID for a Joseph Clanahan. What about you?"

"This is rented under Donna Congemi."

She helped him inside then went around back to hook up the electric. By the time she got inside Kearney had stripped to the waist. He limped as he put groceries in the fridge and the cabinets. She eyed the small, pudgy spare tire emerging around his waist. He needed to get into a gym, that's for sure. There was a dot of blood on the bandage over his shoulder wound.

He saw her eying him and grabbed the flab at his waist and, with his big, toothy grin, said, "Hey, it's more to love."

"Having more to love doesn't make you more loveable."

Kearney pretended to be hurt.

She pulled a bottle of Port from her backpack. "You said you needed to tie one on, so here, put this in the fridge to cool off a little. We'll break it open after dinner."

"Is it a good idea to mix it with the pain meds?"

"You're right. Nix the wine."

In less than five minutes, her neighbor stopped by to remind her about the open invitation to sit around the campfire. When he saw Kearney, he introduced himself and a dinner invitation for her boyfriend. She corrected him and told him Kearney was her brother, Joe, who had been a victim of an assault. She just got him out of the hospital. That was why she left in such a hurry the day before. He seemed satisfied and said supper would be ready in about thirty minutes.

Joan saw the humor in Kearney's eyes and gestured with both palms up to indicate "What?"

He shook his head and grabbed a throw away cell to set up a meeting for the next evening at a strip joint in Weirton called The Glass Slipper.

Dinner consisted of grilled chicken filets, an excellent macaroni salad, fruit salad, and lots of beer. Joan brought their bottle of Port as a "hostess gift" which was gratefully accepted. When they finished eating, people from a couple of nearby trailers joined the group. They moved to the campfire area and sat on folding chairs or the ground. Kearney sat in a chair because of his leg and she sat on the ground about five feet away so she could keep her eye on him.

As the night wore on Joan became more animated and talkative with the group. They listened to country and western music on someone's radio. Joan did a two-step around the fire a couple of times with a couple of the guys. Kearney kept an eye out for jealous wives or girlfriends, but everyone was there to have a good time.

The mood changed when the news came on the radio. The announcer related details about a raid on a suspected safe house for the Constitution Defense Legion in Youngstown. A brief summary of who the CDL was and what they wanted. It faded into the background as Kearney and Joan locked eyes. The world around them became a blur, sounds were muffled. The only things in focus were their eyes on each other. She tried to close the distance between them, but before she could get to Kearney's side, one of their fellow partiers grabbed Joan's arm. Joan prepared to fight, to get Kearney to safety, but realized the woman was just trying to get her attention. Suddenly the rest of the world came back into focus and she became aware of the animated conversations around her.

The conversation turned from boisterous, alcohol-fueled fun to the current political oppression. They were all supportive of the things the Legion was doing. *They are aware of the Legion and what it's doing! We don't have to step up operations to a murderous level.* They talked for two hours about what the government should and should not be doing and what they'd love to see the Legion do.

Kearney watched Joan interact and connect with the people around the fire, and saw a person he had no idea existed. She was good at what she did for the Legion and she was tough, but at the same time she was a down-to-earth person who could interact with people on their level. People liked her, and he could see why Duncan had always championed her, why he had a soft spot for her. Kearney wondered why Murphy failed to close the deal with this talented and likeable woman.

ᗣᗧᗣ

Around midnight, Joan stood up to go to the latrine and found out she had had too much to drink. She lost her balance and Kearney grabbed her arm to steady her. He struggled to his feet and said good night to everyone, telling them it was time for "Donna" to go to bed and sleep off the booze. He thanked the hosts for the dinner and they lumbered off to the latrine. When they returned to the trailer, he stood back and watched as she converted the kitchen table into a bed for him. She then headed to the back to go to sleep.

He needed an extra cushion to get comfortable. The only extra cushion was at Joan's end of the trailer so he headed back to get it. He picked it up and stood there for a while watching Joan, who had fallen asleep the second her head hit the pillow. This physically dangerous woman was laying there in total vulnerability and trusting him completely. He shook his head. Twenty-four hours earlier he would have taken advantage of this opportunity and eliminated her and all the problems she had caused him. But that day and evening he had seen a different

woman, a woman who was dedicated to the Legion and enchant-
ing with the local people in the camp ground—a woman who
saved him from being arrested.

◡◠◡◠

When Joan woke up the sun was streaming through the
dusty windows of the camper. She wiped the sleep from her
eyes and looked up at Kearney, who had brought her a cup of
instant coffee.

She thanked him for the coffee. "Hey, where are my
clothes?"

"I don't know. You had them on when you went to bed.
You must have gotten hot and took them off."

"And you've been awake for who knows how long watching me in my underwear?" She found her sweatshirt and jeans in
the corner of the bed and handed the cup back to Kearney so she
could pull them on.

"You saw my junk, now I've seen your treasure—"

"You're a pig." As soon as she was dressed, she took the
cup from Kearney sipped the coffee. "I've never been this hung
over after a few beers and wine—"

"I don't think it was the few beers. Maybe it was that clear
stuff in the mason jar that put you over the edge."

"What clear—oh, no." Joan groaned and pulled her fingers
through her tousled hair. "What did I say last night? I didn't give
us away or anything, did I?"

"On the contrary. I think you doubled the number of people
in the Legion all by yourself in one night." He sat down on the
edge of her bed. "You had everyone ready to drop everything
and join up."

"But they don't think—"

"No." He chuckled. "They're just all fired up."

"Great, I'm like the friggin' Pied Piper."

"Pied all right."

Joan gave him a smirk and sipped her coffee. "Hand me my
bag. I need some aspirin."

There was a knock on the camper door. "I'm not interrupt-
ing, am I?" It was their nosy neighbor.

"No, not at all. Donna's just trying to decide whether to throw up in the trailer or outside."

"Man, she did get trashed last night."

"What can we do for you this morning?" Kearney asked.

The man told them he had a television and the raid on the CDL safe house was all over the news. Kearney asked if he could come and look and, on his way out the door, he turned to Joan and mouthed the words "You are good."

She just shrugged her shoulders.

When Kearney returned, he was composed, almost nonchalant, but they both knew the seriousness of this. The news did not say anything about the police looking beyond the house— only that there had been no one there at the time. They both knew the police controlled the information the television stations could report, and there could be a manhunt going on behind the scenes. It was a dilemma. If they panicked and fled, it would alert the people in the campground. If they stayed too long, they could get caught. They finally settled on a compromise between the two options, and decided to wait until it was time to leave to meet up with Alice. Kearney could travel in Alice's car and find a place to lay low. Although he didn't show it, Kearney's energy was draining fast. The ride to Weirton would have to be the last one on a motorcycle.

CHAPTER 25

They could hear the thumping bass of the music and feel the vibration under their feet even before they reached the strip club. When Kearney swung the door open, it blasted their ears. The bouncer had to repeat what he said to them. After checking their weapons at the door, they headed toward the bar area on their way to the backroom. They stopped while Kearney ordered a drink for him and a diet cola for Joan.

The club was dimly lit with the only light coming from the stage. Men sat singly and in groups, many not even paying attention to the dancers. While they waited for their drinks, Joan watched the dancer, unaware that Kearney was studying her. He leaned over and said, "I knew it—you're 'bi.'"

"Yeah, and you're gay. You haven't looked at the dancer once."

Kearny looked directly at Joan as he handed her the diet cola. He smiled, his lips parting to flash his teeth, but they didn't turn up at the corners. In the dim light of the club, his teeth seemed larger than before. The dark circles under his eyes gave him the look of a character out of a black-and-white Bela Lugosi film.

"I was just wondering how she got her stomach so flat." Joan had to raise her voice to be heard over the music. "Even when I worked out in a gym two hours a day, six days a week, my belly wasn't that flat." She thought a moment then added, "My abs were stronger, but I always had that little flabby belly thing going on."

"Your abs are great. Take it from one who—"

"Shut up, you fucking pig. Just forget that ever happened. Wipe it from your memory."

Kearney smiled again and pointed toward the back room. Joan turned and led the way. Pallaton and Alice were already seated at a table in the far corner. The loud music would be a good foil to prevent anyone from overhearing their conversation. She surveyed the adjacent pool room, looking for anything out of order. Confident the place was safe, she headed for the table where the others were already gathered. When she saw Murphy approaching her, her shoulders tensed. She turned to ask Kearney what Murphy doing there, but he slipped past her, heading for the table.

"You look great tonight," Murphy said.

"I don't feel great. Why are you here? This isn't your operation." Joan still hadn't made up her mind about Murphy being a cop *and* a member of the Legion. The fact that she was the last to know only intensified her misgivings.

"Kearney asked me to help out."

"With what? Annoying me?" The music couldn't drown out the irritation in her voice.

He moved a little closer and lowered his voice, "Why didn't you call me?" His arm slipped around her waist. "I've missed seeing you." He reached out his free hand for hers but she immediately pulled away and wriggled out of his embrace.

"Get your hands off me."

"Give me a chance, Joan. Being separated from you made me realize that I really care for you—for you—no ulterior motives. Everyone else be damned." He reached out again and put his hand on her elbow. She yanked it away. She was surprised to see his bravado deflate.

He looked over her left shoulder and muttered, "Shit."

"What's going on here?" Duncan asked from behind her. "It looks like this woman doesn't want you to touch her." He put his arm around Joan's waist and continued, "A woman will let you know when she wants you to touch her."

"You're not supposed to be here," Murphy warned.

"It's a public place. Don't worry. I won't crash your meeting."

Murphy spun on his heel and strode across the room to the table. Duncan turned Joan to face him so her back was to the group waiting for her at the table. He shot her a cocky half-smile. "Wow, he really likes you. What did you do to him?"

"Nothing. And don't stand there like the cat that just ate the canary. You got me into this. 'Flirt with him a little' you said. Now I can't get rid of him."

Duncan's smile faded. "You look like shit."

"If you're trying to flatter me so you can get in my pants, it's not working."

"What's going on with Kearney? He's not giving you a hard time, is he?"

Joan's tone changed. "No, actually things are going well—especially since I saved him from being arrested yesterday."

"I saw that. How did you know—"

"Just a gut feeling. Too many phone calls from one cell from one place, that kind of thing."

"I knew you were perfect for this job." He looked over her shoulder at the meeting that was about to get started. When he looked back at Joan, his gaze was direct. Moving his hand to her shoulder, he brushed a strand of hair behind her ear. "We have unfinished business," he said, his voice taking on a softer tone.

"Exactly what is this business?"

"We aren't teenagers, *chica*. You know what I'm talking about."

"Tell me anyway."

"All right, I'll say it. We have a date with destiny looming over us."

Duncan, poetic? This is new.

"It's going to happen sooner or later."

"What's going to happen?" Joan asked. "Say the words."

"You're pushing it, *chica*." He shook his head with his lips tight together, looking across the room at nothing in particular. "But, okay, I'll say the words. We are going to have sex. Wild, passionate sex—unlike anything you've ever had before. You can't run away from it—from me—forever."

A wave of heat flowed from her head to her feet. "Dun-can—" Joan felt flushed as she looked over her shoulder at the corner table. She took a half step closer to him. "Dennis, I promise, the first time we are alone in a room with a bed, we'll turn off our phones and we'll—"

"You aren't acting coy with me, are you? 'Cos if this opportunity arises, you'll put out. You'll put out till it hurts, *chica*."

Joan tucked her chin and looked up at him through her lashes. "Duncan, you won't be hard on me, will you?"

There was a slight hesitation before he got it. He threw his head back and laughed. "This is exactly why I want you." He leaned in to kiss her then, as if thinking better of it, pulled away. He looked over her shoulder at the group gathering in the corner. "They're waiting for you so they can start the meeting." He turned her away from him so she was facing the table in the corner. "Go do what you do best."

Joan turned back to him. "No strings." It was a statement more than a question.

"What?" Duncan was at a loss.

"If we ever get together—no strings. Strings ruin everything."

He looked over her face from her hairline down to her mouth. "No strings, *chica*."

She pointed a thumb over her shoulder. "By the way, that isn't what I do best."

"Go." He pointed to the corner and Joan dutifully went to the meeting, feeling his eyes on her as she walked away from him.

She joined the group and got involved in the meeting. It was imperative that he stay out of this operation. There was nothing she could do about it. This was her ticket to being fully accepted into the leadership and he wanted that more than anything else she could think of—*except time in bed alone with her.*

The meeting went just as Joan had anticipated. Everyone was excited about the escalation of the potential damage, especially Alice. He had already reconfigured the explosives and was eagerly making plans to check out the bridge the next day. No street cams viewed the structure of the bridge. They would have to find a way to install their own so Vaida could keep an eye on things before, during, and after the operation. Murphy would pick the place to meet again in three days. They started talking about other topics and operations and Joan's mind started to wander.

She was jolted back to reality when the waitress placed a shot of Jack Daniels in front of her.

"To a better future," Kearney said.

Joan dutifully chugged her shot and looked around the table at this group of men she had come to know very well over the past year. What the hell she was doing with this group of misfits? *Misfits?* Where did that come from? Did that make her a misfit? Funny, she didn't feel like a misfit.

"Joan, do you play pool?" Kearney was heading for the nearest pool table.

"No. Shouldn't you be resting? Aren't you tired? " she said, wondering how he was going to rack the balls with one hand.

Kearney shook his head. "Better living through chemistry."

Pallaton joined Kearney. Alice disappeared into the other room to watch the dancers. That left her alone at the table with Murphy. He slid over to the chair between them and motioned to the waitress. After ordering two tequila shots he turned and tried to start a conversation. She got up to go to the bathroom and left him alone at the table.

Joan was tired from the past few days of driving and drinking hard. The shot of J.D. had done nothing to enhance her mood. On the way to the bathroom she searched the club for Duncan. He was gone. She continued on to the ladies bathroom and looked at her image in the mirror.

Duncan was right. She did look like shit. Huge bags under her eyes gave her a general tired look. Her hair was unkempt and hanging limp. *It's a wonder anyone takes me seriously.* She leaned over the sink and peered into her eyes. *Who are you?* she asked the reflection in the mirror, and she realized she really did not know who she had become.

Murphy stood as she approached the table. Joan told him to sit down in the most sarcastic way she could. While she had been gone the waitress had brought the two tequila shots to the table. He almost begged Joan to drink the shot, using every tactic he could think of. She eventually capitulated. Why not? Duncan was gone. Murphy was so pathetic, and besides, she really had nowhere else to go, nothing else to do.

After a few more drinks and a couple hours, the craziness of the previous few days caught up with Joan and she left the club to go to her room—before going to the Glass Slipper, she and Kearney had rented motel rooms that were within walking distance of the club. Joan picked up her revolver at the door, stepped out onto the sidewalk, and walked the short distance to the motel. Murphy insisted on walking her to her room, which only made her bad mood worse. When she reached her door she threatened him with bodily harm if he tried anything, and he dutifully backed away. She unlocked her door and went inside.

The dancing light of the television caught her attention. The alcohol fog made it hard to remember if she had left the television on when she had left hours before.

A man's voice pierced the fluttering cobwebs in her brain. "You're getting a little slow, *chica.*"

She jumped and pulled her .38 out of its holster. As soon as she aimed it she recognized Duncan sitting on her bed, barely visible in the flickering glow from the television. He was leaning against the headboard legs straight out in front of him. He looked like the picture of relaxation with his shirt and shoes off, belt unbuckled.

"You bastard, I almost shot you. How did you get in here?"

"How do you think?"

She thought back to Duncan's lessons on how to pick locks. No lock was too tricky for him. She holstered her revolver then unclipped it from her waistband and put it on the bureau. Reaching into her pocket, she pulled out her phone and turned it off. "Where are your phones?"

Watching her with mild amusement, Duncan nodded toward the table in front of the window.

She picked up the phone and turned it off. "For someone who is notorious for getting right down to business, you waste an inordinate amount of time when it comes to getting in my pants." She picked up his second phone from the nightstand and turned it off. "There won't be any wasted time tonight, right, Dennis?"

"No, ma'am." His eyes didn't leave her as she started walking toward him. "You know what using my given names does to me, don't ya?"

She heard his breath quicken as she approached him. "What's that, Dennis?" She smiled as she picked up the phone on the nightstand, called the front desk, and directed them to hold all calls.

"You know."

"No strings?" she asked.

"No strings."

Joan kneeled on the bed, straddled him, and removed her shirt. "Is there anything I'm saying or doing that appears coy to you?"

He reached up and put his hands on the soft skin of her waist, not taking his eyes off her. "No, ma'am." He moved his hands to her back and brought her forward to kiss her. Then he quickly pulled her to the side and turned so that he was partially on top of her. "Nena—"

She stopped him with a hand on his chest. "Who's Nena?"

Duncan chuckled. "It's a Spanish word of endearment. You never heard it before?"

"No, but I like it."

"A word of warning, *nena*," He put the slightest emphasis on nena. "I've been known to get rough during sex."

"I can take anything you can dish out."

"You've been warned."

And before they knew it, they were one explosive mass of passion.

After the second round of lovemaking, the stresses of the past few days caught up to Joan and she fell asleep with her head on Duncan's shoulder.

He liked seeing her relaxed for a change. In less than a minute, his eyelids quietly slid closed, his breathing evened out, and he fell asleep with the head of the woman of his dreams on his shoulder.

❧❧❧

After four hours, Duncan awoke with a start, drenched in sweat, and gasping for air in a panic. It was the nightmares again. Joan was awake instantly and tried to calm him. When he saw her beside him, the wildness left his eyes and the panic dissipated. He clutched her to him. "Sorry, nena. I still have nightmares—"

She gave him a light kiss on his lips. "No need to explain. Sometimes our past just won't stay there." She nodded toward the bathroom. "Let's take a shower."

He playfully chased her to the bathroom and the warm water splashing over their bodies led to another round of lovemaking. After they were dry, they returned to the bed and lay in each other's arms. Joan let out a big sigh. Her body finally relaxed from head to toe. After a few minutes of silence, she asked, "Where do you see all the Legion's efforts heading?"

"What do you mean?"

"Are we going to ultimately be successful?"

"Of course. With people like us it can't fail." He kissed her on the forehead, but he saw the serious look on her face and knew there was something bothering her. "Why? What do you see?"

"Sometimes, I think all that's going to happen is we're going to spend the rest of our lives in jail, and the government will go on like we were just a speed bump on their way to total domination."

"Don't think like that, nena. You have to believe we'll succeed."

"Duncan, I don't think I'd mind going to jail if, in the end, the Legion succeeded, but I don't want to spend the rest of my life locked up for nothing."

He felt the ever so slight shift from intimacy to professionalism. '*No strings*,' he reminded himself. "Are you having second thoughts about being a part of the Legion?" He wasn't sure he wanted the answer, but the question was already out there.

"I can't lie to you—" She sat up and pulled the sheet around her. "—sometimes I can't see where we're heading. There are times when I feel like everything is stacked against us. We'll never succeed."

"That's because your job entails *looking* for everything that can go wrong. It's your job to see *every weakness* and possible danger. That's your job, and a job you are good at, by the way." He reached up and pulled her down beside him. "Don't let the details blur the big picture."

She touched his cheek. "I don't know. Maybe in the short term you're right, but in the long term, I'm not so sure."

"Are you regretting joining the Legion?"

"Sometimes when I watch people who are not part of the Legion, people going about their lives unaware of the dangers we face every day—yes, sometimes."

Her eyes held his, her mouth slightly open. Under other circumstances, it would have been a match to tinder, but her hesitancy doused any desire before it burst into flame.

Finally she went for it, "Duncan, let's just walk away from all this. You have some money stashed away and so do I. We could go somewhere and never be found—start over. Turn over a new leaf."

"I can't do that."

"Why not?"

"I believe in the Legion and I have to finish what I start. Besides, no strings, remember?"

"We could start something new."

"Joan!" She was set back by the voracity of his tone. "I can't leave the Legion." He sat up. "And neither can you." He swung his legs over the side of the bed, his back to her. "No one leaves the Legion—alive." Glancing over his shoulder, he saw that this concept was foreign to Joan's free spirit. "I strongly suggest you get your head screwed on straight."

"Do you think less of me because I have some doubts?"

"No. We wouldn't be human if we never had doubts."

"Have you ever had doubts?"

"No, but I'm not human. Ask anybody." He kissed her and held her tightly. Eventually he released her. "You should get some more sleep. You'll need it to stay sharp."

She smiled, put her head on his shoulder, and closed her eyes. It took a few minutes, but eventually she fell back to sleep. Duncan, on the other hand, could not stop his mind from racing. Could he have been wrong all this time? Could Joan be a weak link in the Legion? If she was, he knew what he had to do, but it was not an easy decision.

She was the first person he had opened up to since his last mission to El Salvador when his whole team was killed, and he was spared—like some kind of sick joke.

It had left him with nightmares and an inability to connect with others.

Joan was the first person who gave him the hope that his situation could change. He had spent many hours trying to determine what it was about her that was different. At times he thought it was her sense of humor, especially under stress. Other times it was her inner strength. Mostly, he thought it was her fearlessness. Unlike most people he came in contact with, Joan was not afraid of him, and she treated him like she treated everyone else. He hadn't been treated like anyone else in decades, which intensified his sense of isolation. But now, when she had given herself to him and she was at her most vulnerable, she had reason to fear him. His allegiance to the Legion was unshakeable, and tantamount to everything else—even her. How could this be happening? Just when he was turning the corner to a better life, the catalyst of that paradigm shift was the one thing he had to destroy. He thought his survival in the El Salvadoran jungle was a cruel joke, but it was child's play compared to this position he now found himself in.

He slipped from beneath her head and gently placed it on a pillow. Pulling on his jeans, he picked up his .38 Special. He opened the cylinder and checked the bullets, although he knew it was fully loaded. With a flick of the wrist, the cylinder clicked back into place. He stood there, looking at the revolver in his hand. After an unknown number of minutes passed, he looked at Joan, peacefully sleeping on her side where he had left her. Tears slid silently down his cheeks. He wiped them from his face with the back of his hand, thinking of the last time he had cried—Andrews Air Force Base when his teammates were offloaded from the C-130. That was the day he psychologically closed down and never cried again—until now.

Picking up the extra pillow, he put it on the side of Joan's head. He pulled back the hammer with his thumb and pressed the muzzle of the .38 deep into the pillow, pointed at Joan's temple. He gripped the gun and put his finger on the trigger. After what seemed like eternity, he began releasing his fingers and re-gripping the gun. *Finish it,* kept going through his head. Torment hardened the lines on his face. His finger was a mere millimeter from plummeting him back into the darkness of the last

few years. Tears were streaming down his cheeks when he grimaced, removed the muzzle from the pillow, and put the pillow
back on the bed. He paced the small room for a minute then sat
down in the chair beside the table and put the muzzle in his
mouth. If he could not kill Joan and remove the weak link in the
Legion, then *he* was the weak link and he'd have to take himself
out of the equation. He was a slave to his honor, yet he could not
kill Joan to save it. He was weak, yet he could not kill himself to
save the Legion. After two quick inhales, he gently replaced the
hammer and put the gun on the table.

He sat there for the next two hours, trying to understand
what was happening to him, and what he was going to do about
this situation.

૯∙૭૯∙૭

There was a knock on the door. Joan stirred. "Who's that?"

A muffled voice made its way through the heavy door.
"Joan, are you up? You want to go for breakfast?" It was Murphy.

"Go away." Joan was awake now and looking at Duncan.
The revolver on the table beside him.

"Can I bring you something? A cup of coffee?"

"No. Go away."

His shadow glided past the window.

Her eyes looked from the revolver to Duncan's face. "Are
you okay?"

His red-rimmed eyes gazed back at her. There was something there she had never seen before. Hardness or sadness,
maybe hopelessness. She wasn't sure.

"I'm fine. Just another nightmare." His shoulders slumped.
He braced his forearms on his knees and stared at the floor. His
whole life was a living nightmare.

Joan stretched. "I feel great. Thank you for letting me
sleep." She sat up and turned up the television. They sat there in
silence for several minutes watching the news and weather.

There was another knock on the door. "*Go away.*" Joan
yelled.

"Are you okay? You aren't answering your phone." This

time it was Kearney. Joan braced her elbows on her knees and dropped her head into her hands.

"I got this." Duncan opened the door and Kearney stepped back in surprise. The last thing he expected was to see Duncan stripped to the waist. "Joan doesn't want to be bothered." Kearney glanced over Duncan's shoulder at Joan sitting cross-legged on the bed, hair tousled.

Duncan saw the glance and moved to block the door a little more. "It's her day off."

"We're going to have another meeting—"

"What part of 'day off' don't you understand? Besides, you need to rest your leg and shoulder."

Kearney sneered. "She's my subordinate now."

Duncan stepped outside the door, holding it open a crack so it wouldn't latch and lock him out. She could hear the two men in an animated conversation in lowered voices. She could not make out what they were saying, but it was getting heated. Finally, Duncan stepped backward into the room. "Fuck off!"

He slammed the door and turned to her. "Let's go get something to eat. There won't be any peace with these jokers around."

CHAPTER 26

Duncan's words, 'No one leaves the Legion alive,' echoed in her head for the next week. *What had happened to her resolve to not share her inner thoughts with anyone?* In a weak moment, she'd blurted out her insecurities about the Legion—and to Duncan, of all people. Travis had told her he wanted to get out, and she had turned him in—her friend. Her friend had trusted her and now he was dead. *His blood is on my hands.* She stared at her hands before shoving them in her pockets. She had too much going on in her own life to think about it now, and she exiled the thought to the dark, distant part of her mind.

She reached for the bottle of tequila, screwed off the cap, and glanced at the clock on the bedside table. Two o'clock in the afternoon. She hesitated with the mouth of the bottle at her lips. If Travis couldn't trust her, what made her think she could trust Duncan? Just because they had spent the evening having passionate sex? She took a long pull. As the liquor burned her throat, she wiped her lips with the back of her hand.

Duncan 'was the Legion.' He and the Legion were one and inseparable. If the Legion would not let her out alive, Duncan would not let her out alive. *Damn my big mouth.* She took another long pull of tequila. And another.

Over the next five days, she went to meetings and on recon like a robot, trying to show enthusiasm, always sure the others picked up on her change in attitude. As each day passed, her paranoia increased exponentially, certain the group was on to her, and more certain she had to get out. She bit her tongue. It was difficult to control her thoughts. Killing innocent Americans who were just trying to make a life for themselves and their families—a life that was hard enough for families since the economic collapse—was wrong and she could not be part of a group that condoned such evil.

Evil. There was no other word for it. Her heart, hell her very fiber, rebelled at the potential outcome of this operation, but she clamped her mouth shut. She couldn't afford another mistake.

As the operation seemed to take on a life of its own, the possibility of sabotage came to be untenable. The way out became crystal clear. Notify the authorities. Prevent it. But time was of the essence and every day that passed only made it more difficult and risky. She finally boiled it down to two tasks: get out of the Legion and prevent the operation.

Turning herself in was terrifying. Would they be willing to make a deal? Or would they thank her for saving them time, money, and effort—and, without a second thought, throw her in prison? And, more importantly, who were 'they'? She guessed it would be the District Attorney. Would the task force have input? There was only one person she could trust, and he was gone, his valuable advice gone with him. She paced the room each night. If Jose Cuervo knew the answers to her questions, he wasn't talking. His only contribution was keeping her demons at bay so she could develop her exit strategy.

While on recon one afternoon, Murphy kept shooting looks out of the corner of his eye at her. She was biting her thumbnail and hunched against the door of his blue Altima. The sound of his voice hung in the air, but she didn't catch his words. Until this moment, her predicament had consumed her, but the solution now filled her with confidence. She sat up, looked directly at him, and smiled.

Attorney-client privilege would ensure fair treatment. Maybe she could avoid a lifetime in prison. But, more importantly, by telling the authorities what she knew, she could prevent the wholesale slaughter and destruction planned for the Fort Pitt Bridge and Tunnel. There was one big problem. Never having needed legal advice before, she didn't know any lawyers, and asking around would increase the chance that word would get back to the Legion.

That evening, when the guys headed out for a night of carousing, she begged off. Finally free from their incessant presence, she went to the library and, after asking the librarian for the yellow pages, she went to the farthest unused computer and jumped online. Lacking any other method of choosing a lawyer, she decided to turn to her longtime hobby of learning the meaning of names. Her fingers raced down the columns of listings under Attorneys and checked names of lawyers in the downtown area. She finally settled on Ira Levine, because Ira meant "watchful" and Levine meant "friend." Watchful friend— exactly what she would need to get out of this alive. She memorized his number and left the library to return to her room.

At eighty-thirty the next morning, while the guys were still recovering from their hangovers, she dialed the number for Ira Levine, Esquire and, as expected, the secretary was already at work. She made an appointment for the next afternoon at three, hoping she could break away from the prying eyes of Kearney and Murphy.

Recon was notoriously slow and boring, so she called Kempton to see if there was something he wanted her to do that did not involve the current operation. Though impressed with her work ethic and zeal for her work, he hesitated to remove her from Kearney's oversight. With a little sweet-talking and a lot of rationalization, he capitulated and gave her the name of a new recruit to be vetted. *Perfect, I have an escape.* But it was in Duncan's area—not so perfect. He had been avoiding her since they hooked up a week ago, which suggested she could avoid him for the next thirty hours until the appointment with Mr. Ira Levine, Esquire. This was "eyes only" work and it gave her an excuse to get out from under Kearney's overbearing and watchful eye. After disconnecting the call with Kempton, she took a long inhale and smiled.

Over the usual breakfast meeting, Joan broke the news to Kearney that she would be out of the loop for a couple days starting the next day. She scheduled a meeting for that night to go over the plans before she left town, hoping it would cover her tracks.

He made a half-hearted objection. There were no indica-
tions that anything was wrong. Her distracted demeanor was
boredom. And who wasn't bored during the recon phase? She
was thorough and, as far as he could tell, enthusiastic about the
operation. Recon could be mind-numbing, and he was almost
jealous that she would be escaping the monotony for a few days.
Besides, he was getting tired of being a babysitter.

Murphy put up the most resistance. If she went on the road,
the distance between them would work against him. To placate
him, Joan asked if he would go with her to get her car out of
storage. With her new responsibilities that required continual
travel, Joan had purchased a ten-year old Toyota Corolla during
the summer. With cold weather around the corner, the motorcycle would hamper her ability to get around. Taking buses or
begging rides during the winter months was out of the question.
She smiled inwardly. When making arrangements for winter
transportation during the summer, she could not have known
that, at this dangerous turning point, it would give the impression of a long-term commitment. Murphy eagerly agreed to help
her.

They spent the morning at the storage area. Two tires had
gone flat, and she let Murphy use his AAA membership to get
them road worthy. She also massaged his ego by letting him
help her prepare her bike for winter storage and putting a couple
boxes of winter clothes into the trunk of her Corolla. He insisted
that she needed two new tires, so they spent the afternoon at the
tire shop where she let him "be the man," pick out the tires, and
deal with the service representative. He seemed to enjoy helping
her—anything to keep him distracted. It was easy to be solicitous toward him, knowing she would not see him again—except
maybe in court.

When they returned to the motel, Murphy wandered off to
find Kearney. She took the time to make a courtesy call to Duncan to inform him she would be vetting someone in his area.
Maybe she could do some damage control. Her call went to
voicemail, and she left a brief message about being in his area
the next day.

While busying herself with packing her backpack, she
hoped that she would be able to clear this up before betraying

the Legion—and Duncan. Betrayal. Her breath caught in her throat and she stopped with jeans in her hand in midair. The word hit her with the full impact of what she was about to do. It was like a tidal wave knocking her off her feet, leaving her desperately struggling to keep her head above water. The last thing she wanted to do was betray Duncan, but betraying one was betraying the other. He obviously had not betrayed *her*. She would be dead now if he had. Her resolve collapsed and she started to cry uncontrollably.

☾☽☾☽

With all emotion released, it no longer had impact on her actions. She was confident that the road she chose was the right one. She was resolute. She would attend the final meeting with the Legion with professionalism, directness, and calm. Once through it, she would be free.

On the way into Kearney's room, she bumped into the pizza delivery guy who was leaving. The realization hit her that she had not eaten since lunch that afternoon. After they had each finished a couple slices of pizza, Joan started going over the operation. The meeting was unnecessary, and she knew that the information exchanged was nothing new, but it was a gesture she had to make. Hoping for a negative answer, she asked if she could go on the recon that night. To her relief, Alice said they were skipping that night because they thought it needed a rest. They had been there too much lately. The rest of the evening turned into an eating and drinking fest.

Joan excused herself at eleven, citing a busy day the next day and, as usual, Murphy stood up to walk her to her room. Her shoulders curved in an over exaggerated slump. It was frustrating and insulting. What could happen to a woman proficient in three martial arts? She looked at Kearney who mouthed the words "Humor him." She rolled her eyes and walked to the door.

When they reached the door to Joan's room, he asked to come in and talk to her for a few minutes. She initially refused but hesitated. *I'm never going to see him again. Let me give him a taste of what he'll never enjoy. After all, Kearney said to hu-*

mor him. She put her arms around his neck and pressed her body against his and planted an open mouth kiss on his lips—pressing her tongue deep into his mouth. He responded by kissing her back and holding her tight. After the long passionate kiss, she ended with a little nip on the lower lip.

Murphy did not release his grip. "Let me in, Joan, please."

She broke free from his grasp. "Absolutely not. Thank you for all your help this afternoon. Good night, Murphy." She unlocked her door and went into her room, leaving Murphy stunned on the outside of her door.

CHAPTER 27

Her cell phone rang early the next morning, waking her to a sunlit room. She checked the Caller ID and smiled. She took in a deep breath to clear her head. As she stretched and exhaled she thumbed the Talk button. "Good morning, Duncan."

"I'm sorry about missing your call. My battery went dead," he lied. "How are things going?"

"As expected. We're just in the boring recon phase. You know how that goes."

"You want to get together tonight?"

"Yes." Suddenly, Joan realized what day it was. Her stomach knotted and a wave of nausea came over her.

"Joan? You still there?"

"I have to throw up. Call you back in a minute." She disconnected the call and ran to the bathroom. When she was in position and ready, the nausea passed. She waited a minute, but her stomach had settled down. She put some cold water on a washcloth and put it on her forehead. She lay down on the bed and dialed Duncan back.

He answered with, "I've never had that effect on a woman before."

"Sorry about that." She decided to not explain her nausea. "I'm vetting a new recruit in your area. You want to meet at that motel where…you got things started." Joan winced at the adolescent comment, but she could not think of any better way to put it without naming the town or motel.

"Okay. How about dinner?"

"I don't know how long this will take. Can we just make it late, like ten, or so?" She had no idea how turning herself in worked. She doubted if she'd be arrested because that would be too public, but she did not know how long the wheeling and dealing of the lawyers could take, or when her deposition, or whatever they do, would happen. "I'll call if I reach a stopping point early, okay?"

"You realize it's one of *my* new guys you're vetting, right?"

"Yes, of course."

"I can make it short and sweet for you."

"Let me do my job, Duncan." Her sternness ended the discussion about how she would vet the new recruit.

"Yes, ma'am." Duncan smiled.

Joan doing her job was as exciting as when she had climbed on top of him and took off her shirt that first night together. He'd played that evening over and over in his head so many times it had become more like a dream than a reality. He wanted to see Joan again. He told himself it was to clarify her position, but in his heart, he knew it was more than that.

"Okay, nena, I'll see you at ten—unless you surprise me." He disconnected the call and wondered what was going on with her.

Joan looked at her phone and wondered how she was going to pull this off.

❦❦❦

At two-forty-five Joan entered the professional building on Smithfield Street that held the office of Ira Levine. It was one of the beautiful older buildings in the downtown area that had avoided urban renewal and had retained its classic art deco charm. The lobby was small but still had its marble walls and floor and a staircase along the right wall. Joan jogged up the stairs to the second floor and found herself at the end of a long, well-lit hall with dark wood trim. The office doors still had the old-fashioned translucent glass that reminded Joan of a Sam Spade movie. When she reached the door that had *Ira Levine, Esquire* painted on it she took a deep breath, turned the knob, and opened the door to a new chapter in her life—maybe the final chapter. She shook her shoulders and forced herself to relax.

She walked into a small outer office with two wing chairs along one wall and a water cooler at one end with a couple more less comfortable chairs flanking it. Straight ahead was the secretary at a large wooden desk piled with file folders. It looked like pure chaos, but Joan knew from experience that the secretary knew exactly where each file was.

The secretary was on the phone taking notes. She looked up when Joan approached the desk and raised her index finger, indicating she would be with her in a moment. Waiting patiently waiting for the secretary's attention, Joan looked around. The secretary was about Joan's age with dyed, light brown hair. She was tastefully dressed in a teal suit with a few, well-chosen pieces of jewelry. It contrasted with Joan's tweed jacket and jeans tucked into knee-high, black boots.

She smiled inwardly. Mr. Levine's secretary probably wasn't armed to the teeth as Joan was. She thought wistfully of the days when being armed wasn't even a consideration.

After the secretary hung up the phone, and Joan introduced herself, she was informed that Mr. Levine was running a little late, but was on his way to the office from the courthouse. The secretary mentioned the water cooler and motioned toward one of the chairs across the room. Joan availed herself of the seat and used the time to organize her thoughts.

About twenty-five minutes later, a human ball of energy entered the office and asked if there were any messages, which the secretary handed over to him. She then pointed behind him toward Joan and told him that Joan Bowman was there for her three o'clock. The human ball of energy put out his right hand and introduced himself as Ira Levine. He had on a dark blue suit that he wore unbuttoned. Peeking between the lapels was a wrinkled white shirt. It did little to hide a pudgy belly that spoke of too many late night, fast food dinners at his desk. His neck protruded over his collar. He rubbed his finger between the collar and his chafed neck as he motioned for Joan to follow him into his office. Though he exuded a lot of energy, she noted the tiredness in his eyes and posture.

She followed him into an office that boasted more work than energy. More cases than time. He pointed to one of the chairs facing his desk while he hung up his trench coat and placed the messages next to the phone on his desk. Joan followed his direction and slid into the chair on her left, comfortably placing her arm on the arm rests. She glanced around his office, taking note of the framed photographs of family and friends, his graduation certificates, and finally her eyes fell on his desk that was piled even higher than the secretary's with file folders. Joan was sure he had no idea where anything was. But that's what secretaries were for.

He pulled out the iconic yellow legal pad and smiled. "I apologize for being late, mid-town traffic can be horrible this time of day." Joan raised her hand in understanding. "Now, Joan Bowman, what can I do for you?"

"I am a member of the Legion—"

"The Legion," he interrupted. "As in the Constitution Defense Legion?"

"Yes, and I want to turn myself in. And I'm hoping you can make some kind of deal for me so I don't spend the rest of my life in jail." *There. I said it.*

"Any outstanding warrants?"

"I assume so. The task force knows who I am, and I can only guess that they know what I've done."

He made a notation on his pad. "We'll get to that in a minute. What made you decide to turn yourself in?"

"There's an operation in the planning stage that is designed specifically to kill people, and I don't want to be part of it or an organization that purposely kills the very people it says it's fighting for."

"But the Legion is known for avoiding killing people."

"I know. This is a new avenue the Legion is taking to get better press coverage."

"Why not just leave? Get out of the organization?"

"It's like the Hotel California," she said, referring to the legendary Eagles' song. "You can check out, but you can never leave—alive." She thought for a minute then added, "But mostly it's because I feel that they have to be stopped, and I feel obligated to do something to make that happen."

"What exactly is it you want to do to stop them?"

"I want to give you, the DA, or whoever whatever information I can to catch them and bring them to justice. I know it sounds corny, but I've thought about this a lot for a long time, and..." Joan shrugged. "Well, that's it in a nutshell."

He raised his eyebrows and looked directly at her. "And to get out alive."

"If possible."

"I'm assuming you have information to offer to obtain immunity."

"Yes."

"In general, no specifics for now, what kind of information can you provide?"

"I know the location of every cell and safe house. I know who was involved in all operations since July of this year, and all operations currently in the works. I know how the organization is set up. I have cell phone numbers of the leadership and the team leaders. I know with probably 75% surety where the leadership is located at any point in time." She thought for a moment. Ira waited patiently. "I wish it was more accurate, but paranoia runs high, and these guys move around a lot. And I know where their training area is, and how the electronic surveillance is set up to protect it."

Ira feverishly scribbled notes. Finally finishing his note taking, he asked, "How do you know all this?"

"It's my job."

At this answer, Ira Levine looked up and raised his eyebrows. "Which is?"

"I'm head of security—*was* head of security." Joan closed her eyes. The corners of her mouth turned down and tightened. She swallowed hard. The seriousness of what she was doing was sinking in.

"You okay? Want some water?"

"I'm fine. This is so difficult—" She took a deep breath and exhaled slowly before continuing. "—because it's been my life for the past year or so."

"I understand." Ira tried to put his client at ease then added incredulously, "You made it to head of security in a year?"

"It's a long story."

"Can't be *too* long." He saw the harsh look in her eyes. Any doubts he had about the truthfulness of her story evaporated. "Anyway, why do you want to provide all this information? This could be very dangerous for you."

"I want to bring down the Legion. They are not only planning on killing innocent civilians, but they've started eating their own."

"Eating their own?" Ira asked to clarify the phrase.

"You know, murdering members of the group they think are weak links."

"Do you know personally of the murders within the organization?"

"No, will that be a problem?"

"Not necessarily. Is there anything else I should know?"

"Yes. There's one member I will not give any information on. The task force will have to gather information on him on their own or 'turn' someone else they pick up."

"We'll deal with that later. Let me get some information on you." He continued on getting contact information from Joan and explaining the retainer. He ended their meeting with, "I'll get started on this today. I have someone I work with closely in the DA's office and I'll get the ball rolling." He stood up and offered his right hand. "I'll call you when I have something, and we'll make an appointment for you to come in. I'll get more information from you at that time."

Joan shook his hand and reached into her backpack. She pulled out an envelope with the $1000 in cash for the retainer.

Ira counted the cash and placed the envelope on top of the yellow pad that held Joan's fate. "I have to warn you, this could take two hours, or it could take five days. Be patient, okay? My secretary will give you a receipt."

Joan thanked him and left his office.

ᘓᘐᘓ

Reality smacked Joan in the gut as she stepped onto the sidewalk in front of the building that housed Ira's office. A real punch directly in the stomach would have been easier to take. *I am a traitor*! Reflecting on her new status, she tried to decide if she was uncomfortable with it or if it would just take getting used to. She was jarred out of her soul searching when a casually dressed, stocky man bumped into her and passed on by with only a glance over his shoulder—a penetrating, cold look. The prickles hit her from her neck to her feet. Her spidey-senses were suddenly in high gear. Over the past month she had become so hardened by the constant paranoia that she hadn't felt the prickles in a while—instead opting for a general state of anxiety—but now they were back in spades.

Senses heightened, she scanned the sidewalk and the park across the street, looking for something out of place. The hair stood up on the back of her neck. If someone was watching her, there was no reason to move quickly to evade their observation. They already had her in their sights. Ignoring the tension building up in her spine, she casually leaned on the handrail and continued to scan every person, car, and window. Nothing was out of place, but she still couldn't shake the feeling of eyes on her.

With binoculars, they could watch her from across the park. A walk directly through the park, to check out the cars parked along the street on the opposite side, might answer the questions whirling around her head. As she walked along the leaf-strewn pathways, she scanned the cars on her left and right parked along Sixth Street and Oliver Avenue. After what seemed like eternity, she neared the opposite side of the park. Peering into all the cars parked along that street turned up nothing useful. None of those cars had occupants, and only a few of the cars along the sides of the park had people inside. None of those people were acting overly casual or trying to hide. Satisfied that no one in the cars was watching her, she shook off the spookiness and headed to the garage to pick up her car.

She entered the garage and walked up the ramp to the second level. As she turned the corner to head up the passageway where she had parked her car only a few hours earlier, she saw movement out of the corner of her eye. She snapped her head to the left and saw a man leaning back in the driver's seat of a van, hiding from view—or trying to. Throwing caution to the wind, she walked directly toward the van. She was leaving herself vulnerable to an ambush, she knew, but she had to put her unsettling feelings to rest. When she was in front of the car next to the van, she reached down and pulled her knife out of the sheath in her boot. Holding it in her right hand in a reverse grip, hidden by her forearm, she approached the driver of the van. He saw her coming and rolled down his window.

"You look familiar. Do I know you from somewhere?" She had never seen him before, but it gave her an opportunity to scan the front seats and get a glimpse into the back seats.

"I don't think so."

"Where'd you go to high school?"

"I'm not from Pittsburgh. I grew up in Chicago."

Nothing seemed out of place, but Joan decided to be direct. "Why are you following me?"

"I'm not following you. What makes you think—hey, I don't want any trouble. I'm just waiting for my girlfriend to come back."

"Why did you duck back and try to hide when I looked over at you?"

"I wasn't hiding. I just put my seat back to take a nap while I waited."

Joan checked everything in the van and took another look around the garage. She took a deep breath. "I'm sorry. I have a jealous boyfriend and sometimes I think he has people following me around to make sure I'm not...you know."

"It's not me. Like I said, I'm just waiting for my girl-friend."

"I apologize again. I'll leave you to your nap now." Joan took a last look around and backed away from the driver. Once she reached the rear bumper of the van, she turned and walked up the passageway to her car. When she got into driver's seat, she removed her .38 from the small of her back and put it on the passenger seat next to the knife. She paid for the parking and pulled out onto Liberty Avenue.

Earlier in the day before she had headed downtown to meet with Ira Levine, she had reserved a motel room under an alias in the North Hills, hoping to rule out the chance of crossing paths with Kearney or any of the other Legion members. As she maneuvered through downtown traffic, she decided to get there via Brighton Road, a back road out of town that would prevent any tail from paralleling her direction of travel.

She turned onto Sixth Street and headed for the North Shore.

Unable to shake the feeling of being followed, she kept her eyes on cars ahead of her and behind her as she crossed the Sixth Street Bridge and approached Allegheny Center. She followed the traffic counter-clockwise around Allegheny Center and, as she reached the turn off for West Ohio Street, she found herself in the wrong lane. Because of the crush of rush hour traffic she decided against causing a disturbance by changing lanes and circled the Center again. She followed the road around again, closely watching her mirrors. When she negotiated the last curve before the West Ohio Street turnoff, she purposefully got into the wrong lane again and at the last minute swerved, making a last-second turn off West Commons onto West Ohio, cutting off a silver Ford Focus in the process. No cars in front of her or behind her made any quick movements, which eased the tension that had been building all afternoon.

Joan fully realized that if there actually was a tail, and if they were professionals, they could be paralleling her movements on any number of other streets. There would be more of them than she could keep track of, and all her maneuvers designed to detect them were for nothing. She would be unable to throw professionals off her tail, no matter how well-rehearsed and complex her attempts at detecting or eluding them. Nothing she did would make much of a difference, but she couldn't let herself think about that. Maneuvering her car and staying alert to the cars around her kept her mentally occupied and prevented her from getting wrapped around the axles about a tail that was—or was not—tracking her. Her actions also kept at bay thoughts of the events she had set into motion less than an hour ago.

Once on Brighton Road she relaxed and turned her thoughts to Duncan and the evening that loomed ahead. She kept going back and forth about meeting with him. Ira did not say to stay away from the Legion, but she was out of the Legion now.

On the other hand, she wanted to see Duncan one more time because, in some kind of convoluted rationalization, she did not want to be on bad terms with him before she vicariously betrayed him. She also knew that if she stood him up he would hunt her down and find her no matter what she did to hide her tracks. She pulled into the parking lot of a fast food restaurant and dialed her phone.

"Talk to me." Duncan's casual tone greeted her.

"I decided to do all the electronic background stuff in Pittsburgh today and do all the hands-on checks tomorrow. Do you still want to feed me?"

"You have zero romance."

"I was taught by the best," she retorted. "So should I eat before I come or not?"

"I'll feed you," he said, mocking her. "Meet me here, then we'll decide where to go." Duncan looked at his watch. "So, you'll be here in about an hour?"

"Or so."

He was already waiting at the motel. It was a little exhilarating to think he was that anxious to be with her. Under other circumstances she would have felt special.

"Or so. Out. Hey, nena?" He hoped he had caught her before she hung up.

"Yes?"

"Wear something nice—you know what I mean."

"I know what you mean."

"Out." Duncan disconnected the call, wondering if he was doing the right thing.

He wanted to be with her, there was no doubt about that, but she was toxic. He could not hide his disappointment that she had not grown into being the full blown revolutionary he had thought she would become, to say nothing about his disappointment in his judgment. Maybe Kearney had been right all along.

He had a blind spot and lost all objectivity where Joan was concerned. At least he'd have a chance tonight to bring Joan back into the fold, and if he failed, this time he was psychologically prepared to make sure she was out—for good. He shrugged and chalked it up to his need to live on the edge.

Joan disconnected her phone and turned it off. She did not want to be tracked by the task force. She wanted one last night to...to what? She was closing this chapter in her life, and she should just let it go, but she couldn't.

She wanted to say it was one more time for old time's sake, but she and Duncan did not have any "old times." As she tossed the phone in her purse, she wrote it off as an innate desire to live on the edge.

CHAPTER 28

As she pulled into the mall parking lot and parked ten spaces away from the entrance to Macy's at the Ross Park Mall, Joan caught a glimpse of a white Ridgeline as it pulled into a space three rows over. She saw that same vehicle, or one that looked just like it, when she stopped at the fast food restaurant to call Duncan. She watched the driver as he got out of his truck and walked into Macy's, only looking up to check traffic before stepping into the crosswalk.

Joan admonished herself for being so edgy and got out of the car to find something "nice" to wear to dinner. As she stepped into the crosswalk, a woman sitting on the bench at the bus stop looked up from her paperback book. It set off alarm bells in Joan's head. She walked past the woman, hoping her casual stride belied her roiling insides. When she turned to check out the woman again, she just missed being hit by the door as someone was coming out of the store. She once again admonished herself for letting herself get distracted.

In less than thirty minutes, she found something "nice" and headed toward her car. The woman at the bus stop was gone and so was the Ridgeline, but she wasn't sure what it meant, if anything. She scanned the parking lot thoroughly on her way to her car, and saw a young man dressed in camouflage pants and a black hoodie walk past her car. Not sure if he cupped his hands to look into her car, or if her paranoia getting the best of her, she rushed toward him, but by the time she got there, the man was gone and had already gotten into a black SUV. She saw his backup lights go on. Too late. She wouldn't be able to reach him before he was gone.

She quickly got into her car, locked the doors, and stared at the passenger seat in disbelief. She had left her .38 and knife on the passenger seat. She gave a sigh of relief when she saw they were there undisturbed. The image of the guy looking into her car filled her mind's eye, and she backed out without checking her mirrors. She slammed on the brakes when she heard a honk, just missing the black SUV. She grabbed her .38 and jumped out of the car, but after the passenger flipped her the bird, the vehicle sped away. *Shit*! *I think I've seen that man before. Did I see him earlier? Is he a Leg? Shit, pull yourself together, girl.* She wondered how many black SUVs could there be, and when she looked around the parking lot, there were several.

After opening the driver side door of her car and tossing her revolver onto the passenger's seat, she took a minute to lean against her car to clear her head before getting in. She stood with her forearms on the edge of the roof, her head down, warning herself to pull herself together before driving up to Grove City or she could quite possibly not make it—or possibly kill someone by being so distracted. And she knew she had to pull herself together before meeting with Duncan. He would see through her and would be relentless in trying to find out what was going on.

She felt movement behind her. She spun around with lightning speed, grabbed a forearm, and kneed a man in the groin then in the abdomen. His legs got wobbly, so she grabbed him by the throat and slammed him against the side of the car in the adjacent parking space. She found herself looking into the eyes of middle-aged man. His eyes were filled with terror—and pain. It was then she heard a woman screaming for help, and she was on the phone. *Damn it*! *These aren't professionals. I am fucked!*

She had to think fast. "I'm so sorry." She let go of the man's throat and helped him remain standing, "I didn't take my medication today, and I'm not right. Please don't call the police. I'll leave peacefully."

"Damn straight, lady. You are not right."

His lady friend came over. "You better stay where you are. The police are on their way."

Joan jumped into her car and started it up. She backed out as fast as the little Toyota would go. As she pulled the shifter into Drive, she was surprised that they did nothing to hinder her escape. *Wusses*. She took one last look in her rearview mirror to see them calmly getting into their car, which had been parked in front of hers. Jumping into the lane to exit the mall, she realized that that whole incident had gone smoothly—almost too smoothly. He had been almost too calm, his wife, or whatever she was, had been almost too hysterical. But the terror in his eyes when she first grabbed his throat—that couldn't have been acting. Or could it?

Joan caught the red light at the end of the exit road and nervously waited for the light to change. She kept an eye on her rearview mirror, but the couple wasn't following her. The light seemed to take forever to change, and she heard distant sirens getting closer.

Well, it's done. I'm done. Maybe Ira can do something. She sat listening to the sirens getting louder until she caught sight of the flashing lights. An eerie calm came over her as the cruiser came into her sight and slowed down and, when the intersection was clear, it went straight through, picking up speed as it passed. *What the hell?* Her eyes snapped to her rearview mirror—no sight of the car the couple had gotten into. The light turned green and, as she pulled to the left to go to the Holiday Inn, out of the corner of her eye she caught a glimpse of a white pickup truck in the parking lot across the street. She turned sharply into the far exit to the parking lot and sped up the grade to where the white pickup truck was parked. It was the Ridgeline, and it was unoccupied. She parked a couple rows behind it to see who would come to it and if anything else would appear out of place.

When nothing happened for thirty minutes, she got out of her car and entered the restaurant in the strip mall—the most likely destination of someone parking in that part of the lot. Up- on walking through the front door she spotted the guy who had gotten out of the truck at the mall. He was seated at a table with his right side toward the door. He was eating dinner and reading a paperback. He didn't even glance up when she stepped through the door and started to walk toward him. *Well, he's not a professional. Hell, he may be just some guy who is coinci-*

dentally everywhere I happen to be. Remembering her mistake only a few minutes earlier—if it had been a mistake—she stopped halfway to him, pretended to be looking for someone. She feigned disappointment, left the restaurant, and returned to her car.

She put the window down and took deep breaths of fresh air, trying to clear her head. For several minutes, she went over everything that had happened since she left Ira's office. Turning in her seat to make sure the coast was clear, she started to back out. Out of nowhere, a black SUV zoomed into view and she backed into the running board below the driver's door with the agonizing *Ka-thunk* of metal on metal. *Damn it to hell! What did he do—drop in from a thousand feet?* She put her car in park and glanced in her side-view mirror. The young man from the mall parking lot, dressed in camouflage pants and black sweatshirt, hood up this time, approached her with something in his hand. She grabbed her revolver from the seat beside her and, in the second it took for her to turn back toward the window, she was face to face with a 9mm. She immediately cocked her .38 and shot twice. He returned fire, but she hit him both times. His bullets went wide and into her dashboard. The man struggled to return to the SUV and, when he was clear of her door, Joan got out and aimed alternately at him then at the driver. The heavily-tinted driver side window was going up, and a faintly familiar face disappeared from view. The opportunity to return fire gone, she backed to the driver side door of her car. It came to her who the driver looked like, but she didn't have time to think about that now. The SUV sped off.

Gunshots. The police are really coming this time. Time to go, girl. Joan jumped in her car and left at a reasonable speed—although her adrenaline was screaming at her to get out of there as fast as her little Corolla could take her. Driving parallel to the strip mall to avoid electronic surveillance identification, she made her way out of the parking lot. Her thoughts were only on getting away to the Holiday Inn so she could think through everything that had happened. She pulled into a parking space near the sidewalk to the door that had a sign over it that read "Door C." Sirens were screaming in the distance and closing in. Wild-eyed with adrenaline still pumping, she gripped the steering wheel and waited for the screech of tires as they closed in on her. But once again, the sirens went on past her, this time to the strip mall she had just left.

She got out of the vehicle and stood, one hand on the top of the door, the other on the roof of the car. Her mind was racing. Her breathing was more like gasping than inhaling and exhaling. She looked straight ahead, eyes focused on nothing. If someone was following her, they no longer wanted to remain undetected. But there was nothing that confirmed she was being followed. No. Those were coincidences. Someone just shot at her, though. Assassination, carjacking, or uncanny vortex of coincidences? She tried to overlook her paranoia and concentrate on the facts.

Fact: the black SUV had been in the mall parking lot. Fact: the same man who shot at her had looked into the window of her car. There was a possibility that he saw the gun and was after it. But he already had a gun. It could have been a carjacking. But why would someone want a ten-year-old Corolla? No answers came.

She shoved the gun and the knife into the Macy's bags, grabbed her backpack, and walked toward the door to the hotel. Better to get inside to think this through. Once inside her room, door closed securely behind her, she took a deep breath. *Dodged another bullet*—she ran her fingers through her hair then covered her mouth—*literally*.

CHAPTER 29

Duncan casually leaned on the round table and glanced out the window of his motel room. Joan was running over an hour late and it wasn't like her not to call, so he checked the parking lot again. This time he did a quick double take. A sexy woman stood next to a Toyota adjusting her skirt. For a moment he was frozen in place, watching the woman as she took out a compact and applied some lipstick.

☙❧☙

Joan wore a black skirt that hugged her thighs five inches above her knees—not too short, but short enough. She added an animal-print, long-sleeved top that hugged her torso and breasts, with a slim black belt to accentuate her waist. She could not conceal even a piece of paper under her clothes, which she hoped would distract as well as relax Duncan. She couldn't rule out the possibility the Legion had caught wind of her visit to a lawyer that afternoon, and acted swiftly to eliminate the threat like they did with Travis. Neither could she rule out that Duncan was involved in the events earlier in the evening.

Since she couldn't conceal a weapon in the usual places, she wore her knee-high-boots that had a sheath for a six-inch blade in the inside seam of each calf, and she had put a Dragon hilt-less throwing knife in each sheath. It would have to be enough, if it came to that.

e/œ/ɔ

Duncan finally jerked back to reality, opened the door to his room, and waved to get Joan's attention. She saw him and waved back. They locked eyes as she walked across the parking lot toward him with the slinky confidence that drove him crazy. As she got within arm's length he put his arm around her waist and ushered her into the room, never taking his eyes off her. This was a persona he had never seen before, and his passion was rapidly getting out of control. He had seen her in business clothes when she was undercover as a receptionist, and of course, the jeans and tee shirts—not that she did not fill them out well, but this was more than he could have hoped for. He asked for nice, he got *Nice*. The door had no more than shut and he pulled her tight against his body. Instantly, his hands were on her thighs and under the skirt.

She let him hold her buttocks for a few minutes, giving in to his long, passionate kiss. As she pulled her head back to end the kiss, he picked her up and placed her on the bed, falling on top of her, careful to hold most of his weight off her.

"Whoa, big guy, dinner first."

"Too late, nena. Dinner is going to be delayed." He kissed her so she couldn't object while he unbuckled his belt and loosened his pants. He felt her give in to the passion.

Less than five minutes later, he watched as she combed her hair and put herself back together. With both arms clutching her around the waist from behind he said, "Sorry about my…impetuousness, but you were so hot. I'll make it up to you later."

"Yes you will," she said, emphasizing each word. He smiled and kissed her on the shoulder. "Just remember one thing," she added.

His kissed her lightly on her neck. "What's that?"

"I am not one of the strippers who you pay by the hour for sex." His eyes snapped up to meet hers in the mirror. Before he could ask how she knew about that, she continued, "You were the one who told me that when things were slow to check up on what members were doing in their off time."

"I didn't mean the leadership."

"You didn't specify to *not* check up on the leadership."

"Okay." The pleasure of her work ethic and zeal for her job warmed him. He wanted to go another round, but said instead, "I'm curious, what does Kearney do in his spare time?" He turned her around to look her in the eyes.

She put her arms around his neck. "I don't talk about members to other members. It's a need to know thing. I wouldn't even tell Kempton unless he asked."

He smiled and slapped her butt. "Let's go."

℮౧℮౧

Duncan chose a piano bar that had just opened. The room was dark with the glow of candles on each table. The only other light was over the bar and on the piano. When they arrived the pianist was on break, so they could hear the low murmur of people talking quietly to each other. The hostess seated them at a table toward the back of the room where they would have a little privacy.

Duncan ordered a bottle of wine and, as the waiter poured the Cabernet into their glasses, Joan saw a man stand in the doorway and look around the room. Their eyes met and he quickly turned away and exited to the vestibule. She got the prickles. She couldn't stop herself before she said, "Fuck."

"Dinner conversation isn't your forte, is it?" Duncan teased.

"That guy—"

"What guy?" Duncan asked. "I only see a beautiful woman seated at my table."

"That guy who looked around the room then locked eyes with me."

"It's because you are so eye catching in that outfit. I know I can't take my eyes off you."

"Duncan, stop, I'm being serious. I can't help it. I just feel it. Do you have an alias or false ID?"

"You're wound too tight. Like I told you before, it comes with the job. Relax or you're going to become so paranoid, you'll lose your edge." He tried to sound supportive. As he scrutinized her face, he saw the tightness around her eyes, the dark shadows under them that she tried to hide with makeup. They were now darting around the room, checking the other patrons, rechecking the door. "I didn't see anything. What's going on?"

"I told you, that guy."

"No, I mean, what's *really* going on? Your nerves are getting the better of you. We're being honest with each other, remember?"

Joan hesitated. It was going to look like she was going crazy or worse, falling apart. Maybe she *was* falling apart, but she didn't want Duncan to know that. "Before—earlier today."

"Just spit it out. We'll worry about the words later." He leaned in closer. His bulk, his masculinity, his presence made her feel safe. Touching her hair lightly he coaxed, "C'mon, talk to me, nena."

Joan told him about what happened, starting with the events in the parking garage. As she was telling him, she began to think how ridiculous she sounded, turning coincidences into some kind of murder plot. "Sounds crazy, doesn't it?"

He gently kissed her on the temple. "I think you've been working too hard lately, and as soon as this operation is over, I will demand that Kempton give you a couple weeks to go somewhere where no one knows you and you can totally unwind."

"What about the guy with the gun?"

"It was a carjacking."

"For a ten-year-old Toyota Corolla?"

"Or a gang initiation. Who knows what goes on in these guys' heads? You simply had the bad timing of being the next person to drive into the parking lot. I don't know. What I do know is no one is out to get you."

"But the driver—" Joan inhaled with a sharpness that caught Duncan's full attention. "—the driver was Gunther."

"Gunther? Why would he be after you? He liked working with you."

"I know what I saw."

"Did you get a really good look at the driver?"

"Well, no, he was putting the window up."

"Well, see? Remember, nena, you were just shot at seconds before you saw the driver. Our minds try to make sense out of chaos. You wanted to know who the driver was, and your mind filled in the blank. That's all."

Duncan's breath on her neck was intoxicating. "Maybe you're right. I'm glad I told you. I feel better, but let's get back to that guy who just locked eyes with me." Duncan groaned and dropped his head in mock submission. "Just in case I'm not crazy. My alias is Donna Congemi. What's yours?"

He put his arm around her. "Listen to yourself. Rela-a-a-x."

"Humor me. When has my gut been wrong?"

"Other than earlier this evening?" Joan didn't smile, so he continued, "Okay. I'll humor you. My alias is Victor Mancuso."

"Victor. Okay. Our story will be we met a week ago in a bar in the Strip District and this is our first date."

Duncan smiled and leaned over to kiss her on the ear. "This *is* our first date, nena."

Joan smiled and put her hand on his thigh. The pianist had returned from his break and started playing "Moon River." The waiter came with their meals—prime rib for Joan and filet mignon and lobster tail for Duncan. The mellow music, soft candlelight and delicious food relaxed her.

She was halfway through her prime rib when two uniformed policemen walked up to their table and the closest one said, "Joan Bowman? Please come with me."

Joan looked up demurely. "I'm sorry. You have me confused with someone else." Outwardly she was calm, but her heart was racing.

"Please come with me so we can confirm your identity. If everything checks out, you'll be back to your dinner in a few minutes."

"Okay, officer, I guess I don't have much choice." She turned to Duncan. "This is some kind of mistake, Vic. I'll be back in a few minutes."

He whispered in her ear, "Does it ever stop with you?"

She smiled, got up, put her napkin on her chair, and picked up her purse. She walked to the front of the restaurant with both officers following her.

They motioned for her to go outside. One grabbed her elbow and guided her to the front of his cruiser so she stood in the headlights.

The other officer dumped her purse on the hood of the cruiser, picked up her wallet, looked through it.

"Don't you have to have probable cause to do that?"

"This is a simple identity check, but we can make it real serious in an instant, and you'll be spending the night downtown."

"Just asking."

The officer ignored her comment and pulled her driver's license out of her wallet. "You are Donna Congemi?"

"Yes." He took it to the front seat of the car and ran the information through the onboard computer. Joan leaned back on the hood of the car while his partner questioned her about her date and what her actions had been that evening. She gave him the story she had discussed with Duncan. She looked up and saw Duncan standing in the doorway of the restaurant.

☙☙☙

Duncan watched the scene unfolding in the parking lot. The flashing lights of the cruiser flashed on the officers and Joan, giving them an almost surrealistic appearance. One officer was questioning her and the other was checking her identification. Another police cruiser entered the parking lot. When the newly arrived officers approached the officer talking to Joan, he pointed at Duncan, who watched the officer walk toward him, presumably to check out his identity and story.

Every molecule in his body wanted to fight the officers and rescue Joan, but instead he stood calmly with his arms across his chest.

The officer asked Duncan for his identification and asked the usual questions to get his story so they could compare it with Joan's.

When he was done with his questions, Duncan asked, "Who is she? Should I be worried?"

"If she's who we think she is, you won't have any worries. She'll be taken away and you won't see her again tonight. If she's not, she'll be released and you can continue your date."

They both looked up as an unmarked car careened into the parking lot, stirring up a cloud of dust, stopping several yards from where Joan was leaning against the hood of a police car.

"Good luck, buddy," the officer said as he turned to walk toward the new arrivals.

A tall white man and a short African-American woman got out of the car. CDL Task Force agents—Duncan recognized Woyzeck instantly. He turned and went back into the lobby of the restaurant before the agents saw him, and dialed his phone.

"Kempton, Joan and I are at a restaurant in Grove City and she's being detained by the CDL Task Force. I recognize one of the agents, and he knows Joan. She's going downtown for sure." Kempton asked if there was anything Duncan could do to save her. "No, there's nothing I can do. There are too many of them. As soon as I know anything I'll call you back. Out."

He stepped closer to the doorway, looked through the glass in the door in time to see Agent Woyzeck stop short and put a cell phone to his ear.

Joan cringed inwardly—Woyzeck. The timing could not be a coincidence. Ira Levine or the DA must have leaked her visit that afternoon. Agent Woyzeck glanced over his shoulder at her and frowned. Her breathing got shallow and fast. She could only hear snippets of his phone conversation.

"Yes, sir...I understand...why?...Can you give me a reason? Something. Anything..." He pinned his eyes on Joan. "I need more...Yes, sir. Got it." He disconnected the call then said something Joan couldn't hear to the female agent standing next to him.

He slid his right hand over his short hair and down the back of his head until it cupped his neck. He remained like that for a minute to get his head into the new game.

He approached Joan and leaned on the hood of the cruiser next to her, legs outstretched in a gesture of informality. The female agent stood facing them, waiting for her partner to begin the interview. Agent Woyzeck crossed his arms and talked to Joan without looking at her.

"Well, Miss Bowman, that phone call was from my boss. I don't know what is going on. He wouldn't give me details." He looked at her out of the corner of his eye. "I'll bet you know what it's about."

Joan didn't respond. She could guess the topic of the phone call, but it could have been about anything.

The best plan would be to give him the least information possible.

"My boss says to handle you with kid gloves, so kid gloves it is." Agent Woyzeck let out a loud, deep breath. "Look, Bowman. Excuse me, *Miss* Bowman, I was out of line the last time we crossed paths. I assure you it won't happen again. I'm here to ask you a few questions, then I'll get out of your hair."

"My steak is already cold," Joan said. "So you might as well ask me whatever it is you want to know."

The police officer handed Joan's fake ID to the female agent. She looked at it and asked, "Donna Congemi?"

"Let me see that," Agent Woyzeck said as he pushed off the car hood and stood with a wide stance. He examined the license then flipped it over to check the back. "If I didn't know better, I'd be fooled by this. Want to tell me who made this for you?"

Joan wanted to give up Kearney to get him back for all the trouble he had caused her. She clamped her teeth together instead.

"No? I'll just hold onto this." He tucked the license into the inside pocket of his sport jacket. "So do you want to tell me about the planned bombing of the Fort Pitt Bridge and Tunnel?"

"You need to talk to my lawyer." *So someone flapped their gums. I have state's witness protection. I could be okay, but if this goes bad, it could be dreadful.*

"That's not how it works anymore, Miss Bowman. Nowadays you have to answer any question I ask you—whenever I ask you."

"Or what, you're going to beat me again?"

"I didn't beat you." Agent Woyzeck pressed his lips together and took a couple breaths. "I said I wouldn't get rough and I won't. I'm just asking a question."

"Whatever happened to lawyer-client privilege?"

"It went the way of the Constitution. In the event of knowledge of an event that will result in the loss of life, lawyers are now obligated to inform the authorities. So, the DA told our team leader about a possible lethal attack. When is it planned to happen?"

Joan bit her lip to keep from panicking. If Woyzeck knew,

did Murphy know? If Murphy knew then Kempton and Kearny knew and Duncan probably knew by now. She was dead. There was no getting around it. She stood up, grabbed her purse and stuffed her wallet, compact and lipstick into it. Her hands shook. The shaking spread to her legs. "Who knows?"

Woyzeck saw her shaking hands. "Relax," he said softly in an attempt to seem sympathetic. "We aren't taking you downtown. I'm just here to ask a couple questions, then we'll be on our way." He looked at his partner who nodded agreement. He looked back at Joan and saw her legs getting weak. "Here, sit in the back of this car." He guided her around the front fender of the cruiser, opened the rear passenger door and helped her sit on the edge of the seat, her legs still outside the car. "You look shook up. What's wrong?"

Joan took some deep breaths, trying to get the shaking to stop. Finally she said, "If the task force knows about that operation, then I'll be dead by morning."

"The only one who knows everything is our team leader. Me and my partner, we only know what we've been told, which isn't much. Don't worry. We aren't going to compromise you. If you're dead, you're no use to us. Sounds harsh, but I'm sure you're used to that, being in the Legion and all."

He didn't get it. He obviously didn't know who she was having dinner with, and she wasn't going to tell him. "Does Murphy know?"

"Murphy?" He leaned on the door and the roof of the car, effectively making their conversation private. "Why do you ask about him?"

"He'll tell the leadership, and they'll kill me. Well, that's not completely accurate. They'll torture me *then* kill me." Her voice cracked and she felt a tear roll down her cheek. The last thing she wanted to do was show weakness in front of this brutish agent. She pushed the side of her cheek against her upper arm just below her shoulder to sop up the tear, put her head down to hide her emotions, and tried to pull herself together.

"He won't tell the leadership. It would blow his cover."

"His *cover*?" Joan snorted. "He's not one of you anymore."

Agent Woyzeck looked over his shoulder at his partner then leaned in closer toward Joan. "What do you mean by that?"

"He tells the leadership everything the task force is doing—*everything*. He's working both sides."

"What makes you say that?"

"He told me." She gave him a brief recap of the night in her motel room when she discovered Murphy was a cop. "His exact words were, 'I give the task force just enough information so they won't suspect I've gone over to the other side.'" She looked Woyzeck straight in the eyes. "He's gone native on you."

Woyzeck turned to his partner, and Joan overheard him tell her to call the chief and make sure absolutely no one knew about the operation or this interview. He turned back to Joan. "That's all very nice, but you haven't answered my question. When is this bombing supposed to take place?"

Joan took some deep breaths to give her time before answering. "Three weeks." She licked her lips and took another deep breath. If she told them everything now, it could jeopardize her bargaining position. The operation was planned for Light Up Night—the Friday before Thanksgiving. "The exact day and time haven't been chosen yet," she lied.

"Who sets the day and time?"

"This time it's Kearney. You know him?"

The agent nodded. "I know of him." He pointed a finger at Joan. "You better be telling me the truth. If this thing goes off and people die, it'll be on your head." Agent Woyzeck's voice was stern. Accusatory.

"Three weeks for sure. You have time. Now take me downtown or I'll be compromised."

"No can do, Miss Bowman." He was under orders not to bring her down to the station for questioning. Against his better judgment, he turned to the police officers. "She's not the one we're looking for."

"No. Don't release me, please."

"Why not? Is your date a member of the Legion?"

Joan was over a barrel. "No," she replied weakly.

Woyzeck turned and walked away to join his partner. Joan stood up and stood next to the cruiser.

"Hey, Woyzeck."

He turned to look at her.

"Was that you guys following me earlier this evening?"

Joan saw the confusion in his face.

"Follow you? I don't know anything about anyone following you."

If it wasn't the feds, who was it? The Legion? "How did you find me?"

"We pinged your cell phone."

"But how did you know…" Her voice trailed off. *Murphy! It had to be.* "But I turned it off."

Agent Woyzeck flashed a gotcha smile. "We turned it back on."

"You can do that?" This bit of information was something the Legion needed to know. Joan bit the inside of her cheek. She wasn't one of them anymore, but she was still thinking like she was. *Get your head on straight. You can't have two masters, girl.*

Woyzeck gave her a mocking salute and went back to his car.

When Duncan saw Joan get out of the back seat of the car and Woyzeck return to his car, his heart sank. He called Kempton back and went to the far side of the lobby. When Kempton answered he told him. "Something's not right. Woyzeck let her go. I know he knows her."

"Why would they let her go? If she was working with them, they would take her in as a cover. To not do so would be a dead giveaway."

Duncan winced at Kempton's choice of words. "Maybe she felt it was safe to be released. She doesn't know I know what Woyzeck looks like."

"In that case, you have to question her tonight. You have to get it out of her—whatever it takes." Kempton paused and added for emphasis. "*Whatever* it takes."

Duncan's legs got weak and he leaned his arm against the wall. "Yes, sir."

"Are you okay with this? You know what, stall for time. I'm sending Kearney."

Duncan put his head on his arm. "No. I don't want anybody else touching her. I'll take care of it."

"Are you sure? I know what she means to you. I've noticed the change in you since you met her."

"I'll take care of it tonight. Out," Duncan said in a mono-
tone.

He disconnected the phone, took a deep breath, and shook
his shoulders to loosen them. He turned to see Joan standing
behind him. He did not know how much she had heard, but he
had to pull himself together to prevent her from becoming suspicious.

"What do you have to do tonight?"

He tried to look relieved. "Something's come up and I have
to take care of it tonight, but not for a while. I still have some
time I can spend with you."

Joan wanted to be fooled by his act, but she wasn't. "Dinner is ruined, but let's go sit at the bar and tie one on."

He turned and opened the inner door to the restaurant and
followed Joan in. When the dinner tab was taken care of and
they had settled at the bar Duncan asked her what had happened
in the parking lot.

"They got wind of something going down in Pittsburgh and
evidently I was the only Legionnaire they could locate."

"How did—"

"I asked. They pinged my cell phone. I know, it was off,"
she added before he could ask. "They said they can remotely
turn a cell phone on. I didn't know they could do that. We have
to tell everyone. This is potentially devastating."

"Who were the agents from the task force that showed up?"

"The man was Woyzeck—yes, the one who roughed me up
a year ago." Joan downed the shot of tequila in front of her.
"The woman—I don't recognize her."

"What was the name of Woyzeck's partner? Massa? That
wasn't her?" He was asking Joan questions he already knew the
answer to trying to test her honesty.

"No, Massa was a man. I thought I told you that. Anyway,
maybe she's a new partner or something."

"Yeah, maybe you're right." Duncan motioned to the bartender for two more shots then reached behind him for a bowl of
peanuts, taking the opportunity to check out the other patrons at
the bar. "If they knew who you are, I have to ask: why did they
let you go? There have to be outstanding warrants."

"They were checking some details on an ongoing investigation, or at least that's what they told me. I don't know why they let me go. I'm as surprised as you are." *Damn Woyzeck, he should have taken me in*!

"Why you? Why did they drive all the way up here to ask you a few questions?"

"I was the only one they could locate, I guess. Or maybe, like everyone else, they think I'm the weak link."

"Are you? Are you the weak link?" He put his hands on her thighs tucking his fingertips under the edge of her skirt. "I keep thinking back to the last time we were together. Do you still want to leave the Legion?"

"No. Not anymore." She could smell the tequila on his breath. She reached up and cupped the side of his face. "I guess I just had to hear the words out loud to realize how much I want to be a part of the Legion. I could never leave until our work is done. I mean totally done and the Constitution is restored." Duncan handed her a shot, which she raised. "Live free or die."

"Death is not the worst of all evils." he responded lamely.

Joan sensed the hesitation in Duncan. "Is there something I should know?"

"What do you mean?"

"Something isn't right. You're up to something. I can feel it."

Duncan stood up to get closer to her. He put one arm on the back of her stool the other on the bar. "I told you I would never lie to you." He nodded to the bartender for two more shots. "I'm getting the same feeling about you. Something's going on with you, too. We need to put everything out on the table. We have to clear this up tonight." He accented the word "tonight" by tapping his index finger on the bar.

Joan wanted to tell Duncan everything, but she knew she could tell him absolutely nothing. "You know me. I get overtired and stressed and I say stupid things, but when I get rested or the stress goes away, I'm with the Legion 110%. I've never acted on any of these stupid things I say when I'm venting. You know that."

"That's what gets everybody nervous about you. You pull back, and we get edgy."

"We? You don't believe in me?"

"You know me. I 'am the Legion.' I have trouble trusting someone who is not, and so does the rest of the leadership."

"I'm sorry, if I've caused everyone grief. I guess my relationship with the Legion is like my relationships with men— push/pull. When I feel like circumstances are closing in on me I push away. When I feel like I have too much space, I start pulling everything back. It's just the way I am." She hoped her explanation was believable. "I hoped that we were close enough that I could vent to you, and you would know enough to take it for what it is, venting."

Duncan moved his hand from the bar to her thigh. He was distracted. The tequila and the wine at dinner were making it hard to focus on the task at hand. "That's how you are with men, huh?"

"I pushed you away for months, then when I thought you were pulling away, I pulled you in."

"Yes, you did, nena." He thought back to the first time they were together. "And you think you can push me away now that we're...we've..."

"Think? I know I can. It's what I do."

He was distracted. Good. She just might get out of this evening alive.

oɔoɔ

Kempton called Kearney immediately after hanging up with Duncan. He knew Duncan could never do what it would take to get the truth out of Joan. He knew that Duncan had to be devastated, and he shuttered to think how Duncan would be after this.

CHAPTER 30

With a phone to his ear, Kearney stepped into the soft glow of the light from the walkway in front of the motel room doors. Two local cell members Joan vaguely recognized got out of a car parked in front of him. They positioned themselves between Kearney and Duncan's car as he parked in an empty space two doors down. Even through the alcohol buzz, Joan's gut told her something wasn't right.

As she and Duncan approached the group of men, Kearney handed his cell phone to Duncan. Kempton wanted to tell him something. Joan watched as Duncan's eyes darted to her then to Kearney.

"Why the muscle?" Joan asked, trying to shake the chills zipping up and down her spine. She looked to Duncan for a sign. Together they could take out the three guys.

"Just to make sure Kempton's orders are carried out."

"What orders?"

"I'll let Duncan tell you." They both looked at Duncan who was making an effort to look like everything was okay. She made a dash for her car. "Go get her," Kearney said in a tired voice.

The two thugs chased her down and caught up to her as she reached her car. The first one to reach her slammed her into the car, knocking the wind out of her. She struggled to breathe. When she was finally able to take in a breath, she kicked and managed to get in a head butt, but it was too late. He already had a good hold on her. The second guy pulled his pistol, put it to her ribs, and told her to calm down and comply or he would shoot her.

When Duncan saw the thug pull the gun and put it to Joan's ribs, he pulled his gun and pointed it at the thug. Instantly, Kearney pulled his gun and pointed it at Duncan.

Kearney yelled across the parking lot, "Now see what your unruliness has done? Everyone's going to get shot because you are out of control. Relax, and we'll all put our guns away."

Joan got in one more kick to the knee of the guy who held her, but she was off balance and it just grazed him. Finally, she relaxed. The thug released his bear hug and held her tightly with his arm around her shoulders, as if they were lovers having a spat. He walked her back toward Kearney. Duncan and Kearney holstered their handguns. Joan was hoping Duncan would give her a sign to fight.

"Kempton has decided that Kearney will..." Duncan did not want to use the word *interrogate* because it might panic her again, "...ask you a few questions to clear up what we were talking about tonight."

"But we already cleared it up." She wriggled in the grasp of the thug. "Let go of me." Kearney nodded to the guy to let go. "You told him that, right?"

"He just wants to be sure. Just answer Kearney's questions and everything will be okay. I'll be right next door."

"Why can't you be there during the questioning?"

Duncan's glance slid from her to Kearney. "It's just how Kempton wants it. He's the boss." He couldn't tell her that if Kearney got out of Joan that she was going to defect, he would have to eliminate the threat. Kempton feared Duncan would prevent that from happening.

"Fuck the boss," Joan yelled as she was half-dragged to Kearney's door by the thug who had tackled her.

She stopped and took one long pleading look at Duncan before she was manhandled through the doorway. Barely clearing the threshold, still trying to make sense of what was happening, and a small part of her believing a member of the leadership had a modicum of protection, she felt a *thunk* followed by lightning bolts of pain in her head that ended any thoughts of a positive outcome. Through the pain and the mental fog, anger boiled at being sucker punched. But the pain was greater and the fog thicker than the anger. On her knees, lacking basic muscle control and chin to her chest, she was barely aware of the strong hands under each armpit that dragged her across the room and unceremoniously dumped her into a chair.

Unable to resist, her arms were put over the outside of the arms of the chair, pulled back through, and tied together behind the chair. While one man wrapped a ligature from her wrists and around her throat, the other man was tied her ankles together then tied ligatures from each ankle around her neck. She was immobilized and could not move without choking herself. The three ligatures pulled her neck so that it was stretched backward leaving her with a restricted view of the wall where it met the ceiling.

Her adrenaline kicked in, clearing the fog and adding a throbbing to the piercing pain in her head. As her thoughts mucked through her head as if wading through hair gel, she tried to formulate a plan.

Physically escaping was not a possibility. She had to get her wits about her and talk her way out. She swallowed hard as Kearney came into her field of vision.

"I see you've become fully aware of the predicament you're in. Good." He took a pull of cold water from a water bottle. Beads of condensation clung to the plastic sides. "Ah, nice and cool and refreshing. Thank you," he said to the one thug that remained in the room.

"I'm going to dispense with the niceties and get right down to business. We need some information from you." He leaned on the arms of the chair. "Joan, all you have to do is tell the truth and we'll untie you and let you go back to Duncan. Do you understand?"

Joan wanted to release a litany of epithets, but she thought better of it. "Yes," she squeaked out. Her arms and legs were already deadened and heavily pulling on the ligatures.

"Good. We have received information that you want to leave the Legion. Is that true?"

"No. I said the words once, but as soon as I heard them aloud, I knew it was wrong. I'm here—" She tried to swallow. "—for the duration."

"Joan, our source does not make mistakes. Just tell the truth and you'll be free to go."

"What I told you *is* the truth."

"We'll come back to that later. We've also heard that you are working with the task force."

"No! That's not true." It felt like her stomach dropped, passed through her intestines, and turned to lead in her anus. Her eyes darted to the left and right trying to figure out where the other guy was. "I don't know why Woyzeck let me go. I—"

"I know it's true, Joan. I just need to hear you say it." He grabbed her face and leaned in toward her. She could feel his breath. "You know what they say?" he asked. She shook her head. "The truth will set you free."

His teeth looked larger than Joan remembered. *All the better to eat you with.* Joan clamped her eyes shut. Kearney's face was hard, his eyes like laser beams that seemed to cut through her skull, shredding her thoughts. She steeled herself for the worst.

An eerie calm came over her. The pain dulled and receded to the edges of her consciousness. "I'm not lying. I would never work with the task force against the Legion. Like I said—"

"I know what you said and I don't want to hear your lies anymore." He stood up and nodded to the thug who immediately put duct tape over Joan's mouth. "When you decide to change your story, I'll remove the tape."

He pulled his knife from its sheath. After making a show of checking its sharpness with his thumb, he made a shallow, wide cut on Joan's thigh and tore a swath of skin off. The tape kept Joan's scream inside, but her eyes flashed out everything. The pain. The horror. The—defiance.

"I'm going to ask you again," Kearney said,

ↄ৹ↄↄ

Duncan sat on the edge of his bed with his head in his hands. Every fiber of his being wanted to break down Kearney's door and pull Joan out of there. But Kempton had ordered him to stay out of it.

Being a member of the leadership afforded her some pro-

tection, some consideration in dealing with potential problems—
some self-control.

Having been his friend and brother-in-arms for over a decade, Kempton knew without Duncan telling him that Joan was
the cause of Duncan's opening up and stepping back from the
ledge. But if she was turning on the Legion, and something had
to be done about it, Kempton did not want Duncan to be a part
of it.

Duncan understood Kempton's reasoning, that if she was
cleared, she would feel comfortable, turning to Duncan for help
getting back on an even keel. But sitting on a bed with eight feet
and a wall between them didn't make it easy or acceptable. He
knew what Kearney was capable of.

Sometime during the twenty minutes of making small talk
with his guard, trying to get him to relax, it became obvious to
Duncan that at some point he would have to get Joan away from
Kearney. Twenty minutes was too long. Kearney was a first-rate
interrogator.

If he was going to get anything, he would have gotten it by
now. Duncan had to get into that room.

He calmly walked toward the door. "I'm going to check on
the progress next door."

The guard stood with his back to the door, arms crossed in
front of him, a picture of impassable defense. "I only take orders
from Kearney."

Undaunted, and vaguely amused at the man's bravado,
Duncan exhibited as much camaraderie as he could muster and
patted the clueless guard firmly on his right arm. "C'mon, that's
my lady with Kearney. I just want to check on her. You'd want
to check on her if she was your lady, right?"

As soon as the guard started to say, "Back up," Duncan
seized the man's right arm to secure it and landed a powerful
right hook. The guard staggered to Duncan's left. A blow behind
the guard's ear put him face down on the carpet, motionless.

Duncan yanked open the door. Joan was all he could think
about as he banged on Kearney's door demanding to be let in.
He kicked on the door, but it didn't budge. After the third flurry
of knocks and kicks, he stopped at the sound of the locks being
unlatched.

The door opened to reveal Kearney standing over Joan tied in a chair—limp with her head back.

Duncan's head swam. "Is she—"

"Dead? No, she's unconscious. I was just going to wake her up for another round of questioning."

His eyes on Joan, Duncan started across the room. "Did she admit to turning on the Legion?"

"No, but another half hour will confirm it."

Duncan pushed past Kearney's thug and walked up to Kearney until he stood nose to nose with him. "The interrogation is over."

Kearney didn't back down. "I'm in charge of this interrogation, and I'm done when I say I'm done."

"You're done." Duncan headed for Joan. He stopped in his tracks at the sight of her. And the blood. It was everywhere. "Jesus Christ, Kearney, what the *hell*?"

On the tops of Joan's thighs, where there once had been skin, there was bright red blood that flowed over and ran in rivulets down the sides of her legs onto the floor. The front of her abdomen was a red mass of blood that soaked into her lap and down the crease between her thigh and hip, adding to the pool on the floor. As a Special Forces medic in combat, Duncan had seen a lot of gruesome, gut-wrenching sights, but he stood in shock at what he saw in front of him.

"She's a tough one, but give me another thirty minutes, and I'll get her to break," Kearney persisted as he walked up behind Duncan.

Duncan grabbed the knife out of Kearney's hand. "If she hasn't changed her story after *this*, she isn't going to." He pulled the tape off her mouth then slit of the ligatures that were attached to her wrists. He knelt and sliced the ones that secured her ankles. "Did it ever occur to you she just might be telling the truth?"

"She could be telling the truth. Maybe not." Kearney put his hand on Duncan's arm then took a step back at the hard, menacing look in Duncan's eyes. "We have to be sure."

Joan started to moan. Duncan turned his attention back to her and pulled her arms from around the arms of the chair. She opened her eyes and saw Duncan with the knife in his hand.

He saw the terror in her eyes. "It's okay, Joan. It's over. I'm cutting you loose." He dropped the knife on the floor by his right knee.

"Like hell you are." Kearney stepped forward and reached for the knife. "I'm not done here."

In one move, Duncan snatched the knife, stood, and lunged at Kearney, slamming him against the wall, knife to his throat. "I say you're done."

Kearney's assistant came to his aid. Duncan turned and sent a straight punch into the thug's solar plexus. As the thug struggled to breathe, Duncan kicked him so hard he stumbled backward all the way to the door, bouncing off the edge of the bed as he flew by it.

Kearney tried to slip away, but Duncan pulled him back. "This interrogation is *over*." After a long two seconds, he took Kearney's silence as compliance. Duncan locked eyes with Kearney. "This—between you and me—isn't over," he growled with one last shove for emphasis.

Duncan turned his back on Kearney and went to Joan. He gently placed Joan's lifeless arms, deadened from lack of circulation, in her lap. He pulled her legs forward. They were swollen and turning blue from impaired blood flow. His movements were slow and methodical.

"Go get my medical bag out of my van," he said to no one in particular.

"Get it yourself. I'm going to be a little busy telling Kempton what you've done," Kearney replied, pressing numbers on his phone.

Duncan got up, backhanded the phone out of Kearney's hands, and hastily grabbed towels from the bathroom. On the way back into the room, jaw set, eyes hard, mouth pressed into a thin line, he approached Kearney, who recoiled. Duncan got right into his face. "You just tortured and mutilated a woman, a member of the inner circle, for nothing—*for nothing!*" He poked a finger into Kearney's chest. "Tell Kempton that." Duncan headed toward Joan. "The least you can do is show her some respect, and the best way you can do that is by doing everything you can to help me fix what you did to her."

Duncan tended to Joan, applying pressure with the towels

to stem the flow of blood. In his peripheral vision, he saw Kearney's goon approaching. With the speed and agility of a wild cat, Duncan grabbed the thug's collar and told him to get the medical bag out of his van. The thug looked to Kearney for direction. Kearney jerked his head toward the door, indicating to do as Duncan ordered.

Joan stirred. As her eyes focused she saw Duncan treating to her wounds. She raised her hand to touch him, but her arm acted like an unresponsive, alien appendage and her swollen hand felt like rubber when she finally touched his face.

He grabbed her hand, lightly kissed her fingers, and placed it in back her lap. "Just relax and let me take care of you."

"Duncan, the pain—" Her voice was raspy. She groaned.

"I know. I'll give you something for it as soon as my bag is brought in." He shot a look over his shoulder at Kearney. Kearney pretended not to notice.

"Hey, tough guy," she said to Duncan. She emitted a dry cough and licked her dry lips, "You said only a tough woman could last with you. Was I tough enough?"

Duncan stopped and looked up at her with his lips pressed into a thin line as if to keep his emotions from tumbling out. With the corners of his mouth turned down, he quietly said, "You were tough enough for the both of us."

"The pain—Duncan, please."

"It's coming." Duncan continued to clean, disinfect, bandage.

"Why did Kearney have to torture me?"

Duncan glared over his shoulder at Kearney. "There is no reason. He's an animal."

"He had to have a reason. I don't believe he would have done this for no reason. We could have just talked—person to person—like you and me."

Duncan stopped attending to her wounds and looked up at her in awe. She had just gone through an excruciating ordeal, and she was obviously in agony, yet she was willing to think the better of her torturer. Her *torturer*.

Duncan knew then, at that moment, she was not meant to be a part of the Legion, at least not what it had become. She was too good, too refined, too pure—so much so that even torture did not break her spirit.

Duncan snapped out of his reverie and continued her medical care. "We had to be sure you were still one of us."

"Well, are you sure?"

"Yes, we're sure," he said, looking at Kearney who noticed this time.

"That's all that matters."

Duncan shot a quick glance up at her, but she had passed out again and continued to go in and out of consciousness during Duncan's cleaning, patching, and stitching of her wounds. She would regain consciousness, and the pain would cause her to pass out again. During one of her alert phases he managed to get her to swallow a couple painkillers. Having finally cleaned her up, he wrapped her in a sheet, picked her up, carried her to his room, and put her on his bed. He handled her as though she was a precious work of art that would shatter at the merest touch.

While he was covering her with the blanket, his phone rang. Kempton's ring tone. He picked it up, "Yes, sir?"

"I hear you cut the interrogation short."

"Yes, sir. Before you judge, come down here and get a look at Joan. Anyone would have broken under this type of torture."

"Torture?"

"Yes, sir, there's no other word for it. *I* would have broken under this." He had to swallow to clear his throat. His training had taken over but now, with nothing left to do with his hands, the reality of what had just happened hit him—hard. The hand holding the phone shook.

"What are we talking about? Did he rough her up?"

"*Rough her up*?" Duncan was coming unglued. He pulled his arm back to throw his phone across the room but thought better of it and took a long breath before continuing. "It took over a hundred stitches to patch her up and there are wounds that I don't know how they're going to heal."

"A hundred stitches—what the hell did he do?"

"You'll have to ask him. I wasn't allowed to be present, remember?"

"I'll get back to you." The line went dead.

Duncan called Kearney's room. "Hey, when you send out

your thugs to clean the towels and sheets, have them pick up some clothes for Joan. We can't take her out of here wrapped in a sheet."

"We're a little busy here. You take care of it."

"If I come over there, you're going to find yourself tied to a chair and mutilated."

"Okay, if you think you can do it."

"I'm on my way."

"Hey, Duncan." Kearney caught him before he hung up the phone. "I don't want any trouble between us over a woman. I'll send one of these guys for some clothes for her. What size?"

"I don't know. Look at what's left of the clothes you shredded and ripped off her and see what sizes are on them."

Livid, Duncan got up to take out his emotions on Kearney. Give him a taste of his own medicine.

"Okay. I'm on it. No problem. You stay there with Joan. I'll take care of it."

CHAPTER 31

The second morning after her ordeal, Joan insisted she no longer needed someone watching over her twenty-four hours a day, telling Duncan she needed some time alone. In reality she wanted to call Ira Levine.

His secretary sounded relieved when she answered the phone. "We've been trying to reach you. Mr. Levine would like to meet with you tomorrow morning at ten."

"I'll be there, if I can."

"If you can? You're still turning yourself in?"

"Something's happened here, and I'm being watched like a hawk. I'll see if I can slip away." There was the metallic sound of a key sliding into the lock on her door. "Gotta go." She disconnected the call and threw the phone onto the nightstand. When Duncan walked through the door, she acted angry. "I thought I made it clear, I want to be alone."

"I'm not staying. I just wanted to bring you a cup of coffee." He placed the cup on the nightstand next to the bed. If he noticed the placement of the cell phone, he didn't show it. He sat on the bed next to her, "I understand you need time to sort things out. Please don't push me away. I want to help you."

Ignoring his pleading tone, she said, "Do you think I could take a shower the next time you change my dressings?"

"I don't know how. The places where the skin is missing will sting like a mother. If you can stand it, I think a quick one would be okay. I'll be right next door. Call me if you need anything."

CHAPTER 32

Joan arrived at vestibule of the building that held her law-yer's office the next morning at eight before anyone else had arrived. Five hours earlier she had slipped out of the motel room in Grove City and headed for the room she still held at the Holiday Inn in the North Hills.

Standing in front of the mirror, the jogging suit Kearney's thug had bought her at her feet, she surveyed her injuries. Purple bands marked her neck and wrists. Gauze covered her abdomen and thighs. The physical pain had eased to a point where she could stand it, but the mental anguish pierced her soul. The glint of the knife in Kearney's hand, the hard, unemotional look in his eyes, the pain on Duncan's face, flashed into her mind without anything seeming to trigger them.

"Well, I'll never wear a mini-skirt again," she said to her image in the mirror in a futile attempt at dismissing the intensity of her mental and physical injuries.

After digging through her boxes of winter clothes, she decided on a turtleneck sweater to hide the marks on her neck and wrists. She put on a blazer to hide the gun at the waist of a pair of dress pants. In a lucky move, Duncan had brought her boots from Kearney's room, so she had them to carry her knives as well. She debated about the throwing stars because her coordination was not at 100% yet, but in the end she put a half dozen stars into the pocket of the blazer. Confident that she could defend herself if necessary, she headed to downtown Pittsburgh—not that Pittsburgh was a dangerous place, downtown was very safe under normal circumstances. She simply felt more confident when she was armed, and confidence was all she had to get her through the day.

She entered the office with the secretary who arrived at eight-twenty-five. She showed Joan into the conference room and asked if she would like some coffee. Knowing the secretary had more to do than attend to her, Joan declined. While she waited, she looked out the window at the metro buses zipping through the traffic. People were walking along going about their business of the day without a care in the world. Joan envied their freedom—freedom she could have had, had she not joined this nefarious group. It certainly was not what she had signed on for.

While wondering where her idealism had ended and the shock of reality hit, the conference room door opened and Ira blew into the room—already a ball of energy at quarter past nine. He told her he had some things to take care of, but he'd be back in a few minutes to explain what was going to happen that morning. He left and Joan turned back to the window—alone with the pain that was growing more intense as the medication wore off.

Ten minutes later, while she still wistfully watched the parade of commuters, the conference room door opened and she turned to see Ira followed by a middle-aged man in a nice suit and colorful tie. He was the Assistant District Attorney. She shook his hand and Ira motioned for Joan to take a seat. They went over the terms of the deal as they waited for the stenographer and the members of the task force.

When the court recorder took her seat inconspicuously at the end of the table, the ADA explained what they were going to be doing that day and, just as he finished up, Agents Woyzeck and Tremaine came into the room. Woyzeck gave Joan a quizzical look at her raspy voice. Hunched in her chair, she wasn't showing the bravado she was known for. She saw the quizzical look on his face, but chose not to bring up the incident in the restaurant parking lot and how it had set into motion a line of dominoes that ended poorly for her. The time wasn't right.

Wondering where Agent Massa was, and recognizing Agent Tremaine from the restaurant parking lot, Joan took advantage of the light in the conference room to size her up. She had a milk chocolate skin coloring that accentuated gray eyes. Full lips painted red, just the right touch of blush, tasteful gray pantsuit—she looked both feminine and strong. When she greeted Joan her voice had the husky, African-American tone, and was firm. Not aggressive—firm and all business. Joan smiled at her and decided she would have liked her under other circumstances.

The ADA led off the discussion with the Fort Pitt Bridge and Fort Pitt Tunnel bomb threat, which Joan was sure was the task force's priority. She told them it was scheduled for Light Up Night and she could see Woyzeck relax a little. She explained how it was going to go down, how they did their surveillance, who was involved, and answered all the questions they had about it. When Woyzeck was satisfied, the ADA moved on to Joan's participation in the Legion, giving the instruction to give an overview for today. They would come back to the details in future sessions. Joan, struggling to keep from losing her voice, reached the explanation of her duties as chief of security when Ira suggested they break for lunch. A rest for her larynx would go a long way and, if she ate something, she could take several of the naproxen capsules she had purchased on her way into the city that morning. They might take enough of the edge off her pain to get through the afternoon.

Soup brought back to the office by the secretary and three naproxen capsules later, the deposition resumed, and it continued for another three hours. When the ADA was about to wrap up the day's session and make arrangements for the next session, Woyzeck piped up, saying there was something he had to ask.

"Who did you send to attack me and Massa?" He had returned from lunch edgy and short tempered, but now blood was turning his neck red, and it was creeping into his face. Agent Tremaine put a hand on his arm and whispered something to him. He shook her off.

"What? I didn't—" Joan started to respond

"You lying b—" he snarled. Agent Tremaine put her hand on his arm again, and he refrained from using foul language. "You're lying."

Joan looked at her attorney. She was blindsided by this accusation and she wasn't sure if this was a setup or a valid question.

Ira spoke up. "How do you know your assault involved the CDL?"

"One of the attackers said, and I quote, 'This is for Joan.'"

Ira turned to Joan. "Do you know anything about this?"

"No—"

Woyzeck started to say something, but Ira raised his hand, indicating for him to wait and listen.

"This is the first time I heard of it," she continued.

The ADA stepped in and reminded Joan if she lied about anything, the deal was off. Joan looked from Ira to the ADA to Woyzeck. Proving a negative was nearly impossible. She finally turned to Woyzeck. "I'm assuming you think this was a result of the interview where you grabbed me, among other things," she said, referring to the choking. She cleared her throat and continued. "But let me assure you that when I was released and the door of the fusion center closed behind me, it was history as far as I was concerned. I knew it wasn't personal. You were doing your job, and I was doing mine. It *wasn't* personal, right?"

"No, but you made it personal by having federal agents assaulted."

"What makes you think that if I thought it was personal, I wouldn't have taken care of it myself?"

"Who knows why you people do the things you do?"

Joan visibly winced. The words, "you people" stung. Stung as much as if he had slapped her in the face. She wasn't one of the CDL anymore. Being here, in Ira's office, with the ADA and a court stenographer should have been evidence enough. Her cooperation should have been proof of her change of loyalties. She gathered what strength she could manage and, hoping it was enough to make her point, asked, "Where did this supposed assault happen?"

"You're here to answer our questions, not the other way around."

She took a sip of water. "You brought it up."

Woyzeck looked at the ADA who agreed with Joan that Woyzeck had brought it up and made it clear he wanted to resolve this matter today so they could move forward tomorrow.

"All right, we were leaving Rosie's Tavern where we downed a few after a particularly hard day."

"Let me tell you this. If I thought for an instant your antics during that interview at the police station were personal, I would have attacked you in a personal way. For instance, I don't know anything about you, but if I found out you had a family, I would have waited until you were out, say, at a pizza parlor with them, and I'd beat the shit out of you in front of them and make sure your wife knew that you rough up female suspects and your children knew what a wuss you are."

"You would screw with my *family*?"

"Only if it was personal, but it wasn't personal, right?" Watching him over the edge of the glass, Joan took another sip of water.

"You fucking bitch—"

Everyone jumped in and told Woyzeck to calm down. He tried to protest, declaring it was low to screw with someone's family. They reminded him that her response was hypothetical, and didn't the agents deal with hypotheticals to get perps to talk to them?

Ira put a hand on Joan's arm. "Maybe Joan could identify the men if you describe them."

She nodded.

It took a few seconds for Woyzeck to calm down. "They had on ski masks, but one man was tall, maybe six or six one, blue eyes, well-built with long brown hair that hung in a pony-tail out of the mask in the back."

"It could be one of several guys, but my guess would be Pallaton. I told you about him earlier."

Ira nodded.

"The other was shorter, maybe five eleven, brown eyes and *very* well-built—"

Woyzeck went on saying some other things, but Joan didn't hear any of it. She started to hyper-ventilate. Ira suggested she put her head between her knees, but it was too late. The room was getting dark. Duncan must have recognized Woyzeck in the restaurant parking lot. That meant that when Woyzeck let her go—

She looked up directly into Woyzeck's eyes. He watched as her one-inch stare slowly focused and pinned on him.

Ira handed Joan a glass of water and encouraged her to tell them what was going on.

"The second guy was—" Joan took a few breaths. "—was—" The room was getting dark again, and everyone seemed far away. She put her head down between her knees. After a few deep breaths her head cleared. She wiped off the beads of sweat that had accumulated at her hairline and realized she had grabbed Ira's arm in a death grip. She let go quickly, thinking her grasp was going to leave a mark, and mouthed the word, "Sorry."

"Who was the second guy?" The ADA asked in a soothing voice.

"My date that night at the restaurant." Woyzeck had a puzzled look on his face. Joan saw he did not get it. "He had to have recognized you. He knew that you knew who I was. When you let me go—I begged you to take me in, remember? He—" Joan looked at Woyzeck then at Ira then back at Woyzeck. "Well, it explains this."

With that she pulled down the neck of her turtle neck sweater to reveal the three purple ligature marks. The ADA stared at them. Agent Tremaine half-stood to get a better look. Agent Woyzeck covered his mouth with the palm of his hand and slid it across his jaw.

"Who did this to you?" Ira asked in a quiet, distracted tone.

"I didn't know at the time that he knew who you were. I walked right into his ambush later that night."

"What happened?" Agent Woyzeck asked.

"You're the detective. You figure it out." She showed them her wrists then lifted one of the dressings on her abdomen.

It was Agent Tremaine's turn to blanch. "How did they— what did they do to make that?" She was referring to the wound under the dressing.

"He skinned off sections of me." There was horror in every one's eyes. "There are more on my legs."

"What were they trying to get from you?" Woyzeck was the first to snap back to reality and try to put the pieces together.

"They thought I might be working with the task force after you didn't take me in."

"What did you tell them?"

"Nothing. They think I'm still fully behind the Legion," Joan said as she pressed the tape on the dressing to adhere it to her skin.

"All that—" He glanced at her abdomen, referring to the worst wound he had seen in his fifteen years as an agent. "—and you didn't tell them about this deal? I don't believe you."

"I didn't tell them anything. My being here, alive, is testament to that. They trust me more than ever now. Ironic isn't it?"

"What's ironic?"

Joan shook her head. "When I was fully invested in the Legion, they never trusted me. Now that I'm turning state's evidence, they trust me like never before."

Woyzeck was the first to fully comprehend the impact of what had happened. "How will this affect the bridge and tunnel bombing?"

"I'm not sure. They must know I'm missing by now, but they probably think I walked off in a drug-induced haze."

The ADA grasped onto that. "Are you on any pain killers now? Drugs may affect the veracity of your testimony."

"No. I only took a couple naproxen caps this morning and a few more after lunch."

"The pain must be unbearable," Agent Tremaine said sympathetically.

"Not more than I can stand."

Woyzeck was like a terrier, still fixated on the potential bombing. "Let's get back to the bombing. How will this affect the bombing?"

Joan respected his tenacity for staying on target. "As long as they think I'm lost in Vicodin Land, nothing will change. Everything will stay on schedule. At this point, two weeks or so out, it's pretty much on auto-pilot. My absence won't change anything. However—" Joan's voice was fading fast. She cleared her throat and took another sip of water. "—if at any time they start to suspect that I've fooled them and am working with you guys—I'm not sure whether they would move it up or abort. They certainly wouldn't leave it the same."

"We need to know, Bowman. Can you find out?

"No. If I wandered back in now, I'll have a twenty-four hour escort, and probably not for twenty-four hours, if you know what I mean. The last thing they need is me out in the public on drugs. I know too much. It would be devastating for the Legion if I developed loose lips." Joan gave a wry smile—if only they knew. Well, she had to make sure they didn't find out. "I would never be able to get any information to you. Can't Murphy help you with that? He's helping out with the operation."

Woyzeck and Tremaine looked at each other and said in unison, "Murphy?" They turned and looked at Joan.

"Would you excuse us," Woyzeck said. "We need to talk something over with the ADA." He motioned to Tremaine and the ADA. They left the room.

Joan was left in the conference room alone with Ira. *Damn them. They mentioned the pain and now it's all I can think about.* She looked up and, through the glass wall of the conference room, she saw the two agents and the ADA in an animated conversation. Then they started nodding. Tremaine glanced through the glass into the conference room and motioned to Ira to join them in the hallway.

Woyzeck turned away slightly but Joan could see he was dialing his cell. *What the—*

Ira emphatically shook his head. More conversation with the two agents and the ADA talking at Ira. Ira looked over at Joan hunched over in pain. She sent a pleading look back at him. After another few minutes they all returned to their seats in the conference room.

Joan led off the conversation. "You know, of course, you can't really trust Murphy and what he tells you." She hesitated. Agents Woyzeck and Tremaine were looking straight at her "But maybe you can glean something from him…" Her voice trailed off. Something wasn't right.

Woyzeck cleared his throat. "When we get you and Murphy together, do you think you could get him to admit to turning on the task force? Once we get that, we can get the information we need from him."

"No. I told you. I can't go back in—wait, did you say 'when'?"

The ADA spoke up. "We decided that since you were being so cooperative, you could do this for the task force."

Joan looked at Ira. His face was emotionless. He chose his words carefully. "They've been very generous in their cooperation in helping my office forge this deal for you." He stopped talking when Joan stood up. He looked up at her. After a tricky moment, until she could feel her feet—her circulation was not fully up to par yet—she walked to the window to watch the "free" people one more time.

She was out. Out. She could not go back in. Tears rolled silently down her cheeks. Ira asked everyone to clear the room so he could talk to her in private.

"Joan, in the past I would be representing you on police brutality charges for Agent Woyzeck's handling of your interrogation. But these days, the police and courts are wielding tremendous power, and I'm afraid I have to advise you to go along with them."

"What kind of world is this? I have a choice of life in prison or death. Because if I don't do this, the deal is off, right?"

"Yes, but—"

Joan snorted and shook her head. "My choice is really no choice. They have me over a barrel, and they know it. If I wanted to die, I could have stayed in the Legion and died at their hands."

"They won't kill you. The task force will protect you."

Joan did not believe him. "Ira, death is not the worst of all evils, but torture has to be right up there." She leaned her head against the windowpane that felt cool from the fall breezes that blew outside.

"What?"

"I hate to burst your bubble, Ira, but the task force will not be able to protect me. They might as well try to light a penny candle with a star."

"Joan, they're good at what they do. Trust them."

"*Trust* them! In case you haven't noticed, trust is becoming a rare commodity around here. The Legion thinks they can trust me—now that they can't. And I'm now supposed to trust the task force because, why? Now they're trustworthy?" She turned to look at Ira. "They can't even trust their own agents, and they want *me* to trust *them*. This is becoming a morbid joke, a *lethal* joke."

"Look, you said yourself the Legion probably still thinks you're just wandering around in a drug-induced haze, and that they trust you now. If the task force can get you in and out before the Legion finds out or suspects you've turned on them, do you think you could pull this off?"

"I'm out and I'm alive. I can't go back." Pleading was a new emotion for Joan but that was exactly what she was doing. "Can't you come up with some other kind of deal?"

"You can do this. You can use your injuries to cover anything that might be suspect. Get the information the task force needs and they'll get you out." He stepped forward to look her in the eyes. "Joan, you're in, you get the information, and, boom, you're out. A few years ago we'd have some wiggle room, but today..." The unspoken words hung in the air. He put his hand on Joan's shoulder to comfort her. "Why don't we listen to what they have to say?"

"You're sending me to my death, you know."

"You'll be all right."

Ira motioned for the others to come back into the room. Joan took her seat at the table.

CHAPTER 33

The pain medication was kicking in. The throbbing, searing pain that had haunted her during the deposition was gone, but it was now replaced with a haze—a deliciously blissful haze.

Vaguely aware that she was in a cafe in downtown Pittsburgh, Joan knew she was supposed to call Murphy to come and get her. There was a phone number written on the palm of her hand. Not quite sure how the number got there, she tapped the numbers into her phone and absent-mindedly rubbed her hip.

When Murphy's familiar vice was on the line, she started to panic in a slow motion sort of way. The name of the café escaped her. Murphy's voice nagged her from the handset as she reached for a glossy advertisement at the end of the table. The tent-shaped advertisement proved too elusive for her drugged hands, so she gave up on it and talked to Murphy.

She told him she was messed up and she needed him to come and get her, but she did not know where she was. He said he knew where she was and he was already on his way. A bout of nausea passed over her as she tried to figure out how he knew which café she was in. And how could he already be on his way? He reminded her that she had just called two minutes before. She was beginning to think she should not have taken that extra pill.

The plan had been for her to take one Vicodin then act more doped up than she was. The first dose didn't seem to work, so she took another—or was it two? She rubbed her hip again.

The nurse for the task force had injected an RFID chip under the skin of her hip so they could track her. Woyzeck assured her the newest versions had a range of a half mile, and they could track her with a drone at twenty-six hundred feet, no one on the ground would be aware of the drone at that height. She toyed with her new earrings, which were tiny transmitters. As soon as they had what they needed, they would get her out of there. She was wired up, the bases all covered. *I'm wired, all right.* No one had planned on her taking a second Vicodin, or maybe a third. She couldn't really remember.

Murphy was babbling in her ear. "I'm worried about you, Joan. Stay there. Don't move. I'll be there in five minutes, tops." He waited for an answer that did not come. "Joan? Are you there? Did you hear me? Joan?"

"Hurry, Murphy. I don't—" She swallowed some hot coffee to lubricate her throat. "I don't know how long I can hold it together."

"I'm on my way. Stay right there."

"I'll stay here, okay?"

"That's right. Stay where you are and stay on the phone with me so I know you're still waiting for me, okay?"

Two uniformed police officers appeared through the haze. They stood at her table, saying something to her. The female café manager stood behind them with her arms crossed. The last thing she needed was someone overdosing in her cafe.

Joan licked her lips. "I have to go. The police are here."

"No! Joan, don't hang up. Let me talk to them. Joan, give them your pho—" the line went dead.

Joan was sure that something wasn't right. Woyzeck had not mentioned uniformed police officers. She shook her head in attempt to clear it, but it only brought on another bout of nausea—this time with a touch of vertigo. Where was Murphy?

The cop was telling her to stand up and turn around. Joan swallowed trying to clear her throat and quell the nausea. The chair scrapped across the checker-patterned tile floor as she staggered to her feet. The officer told her to turn around and put her hands behind her. The room was swaying. Dry throat, churning stomach, panic set in. But the panic was slow in working through her body. Moving too slowly for his liking, the police officer grabbed her wrists and held her hands together by her thumbs. As he clamped the handcuffs on the first wrist he saw the purple ligature marks on her wrists.

"What the—How did you get these marks?" the officer said.

Joan tried to answer, but her throat was dry and only a raspy cough came out. The cop asked again less patiently this time. Looking longingly at the coffee, desperately needing it to lubricate her throat, Joan swallowed and with a hoarse voice she replied, "Torture." She coughed again.

"Torture, huh?" He looked at his partner in disbelief. "Who tortured you?" He fastened the cuffs, locked them with his key. Grabbing her arm just above the elbow he guided her toward the door.

"The CDL."

"The CDL. And why would they torture you?"

"They thought I was a—" Joan had to cough and swallow again. "—a traitor to the cause."

Her legs buckled. The cop supported her and guided her across the sidewalk to the cruiser at the curb.

When they got to the car the officer said, "Do you have any weapons or sharp objects on you I should know about?"

"Stars in my blazer pocket, knives in my boots, a .38—"

Joan marveled at how good the cold metal of the hood of the car felt while her face was smashed against it. Pressing her roughly against the car, the police officer removed the .38 from its holster on her waistband. He did a quick pat down and found her two knives, the throwing stars, and a Zip Lock baggie with pills.

"What is this under your pant leg and on your torso?" The pat down had revealed the gauze bandages that Duncan had put over the larger wounds.

Joan looked down swaying trying to remember what could be on her legs. "Dressings."

"Dressings? From what? Did you have surgery?"

Joan looked at him and tried to focus. She thought she re-membered telling him about the torture. All she could get out was, "Torture—"

"They tortured you then dressed your wounds? You want to start telling me the truth?"

Her story didn't make sense even to her. "The CDL tortured me," she reiterated. "But it wasn't personal."

"There isn't too much in life that's more personal than torture, but, okay. What are you doing with all these weapons?"

"They're mine."

"Try to focus. I know they're yours. Why are you carrying them?"

"I never go anywhere unarmed. It's part of my job."

"And what job is that?"

"Head of security."

"Security? Where?"

Joan hesitated. Didn't she tell him about the CDL? He pushed her harder against the car and she said, "For the CDL."

His partner immediately got on the radio and called dispatch and explained their situation. To his surprise, dispatch immediately gave him a cell phone number to call, which turned out to be the CDL task force. They told him to hold her there. They were sending an agent to pick her up. The cop asked if he should call EMS, but was assured the agent would handle everything when he arrived.

Three minutes later, Murphy screeched to a halt beside the police car and saw Joan in the back seat with her head on her chest. He identified himself to the cops and asked what they had.

"We have a woman who is whacked out on drugs, probably these," he lifted the baggie to show Murphy. "She says she was tortured by the CDL, then they dressed her wounds—and that she's does security for them."

"Any signs of torture?" Murphy asked, thinking the drugs must have mixed her up.

"Her wrists are purple. Looks like from some kind of rope. And there are what feel like bandages on her torso and thighs. She says they're covering wounds from the torture."

Murphy opened the rear passenger door and leaned in to talk to her. "Joan?" She did not look up. He grabbed her chin and turned her head to look at him. "Joan, I'm going to help you get out of the car. I want to check your wrists, okay?"

"Murphy? You're here."

"Yes, I'm here. Now I'm going to bring your legs out of the car and help you stand up, okay?" After placing both her feet on the ground, he helped her stand up. "Turn around and lean against the car. Good."

Murphy checked out her wrists and was horrified. "Whose cuffs are these? Take them off."

The cop unlocked the cuffs. Murphy turned her around to face him and checked her pupils. They were dilated.

"Joan, what's wrong with your voice?" Murphy continued.

She pulled down the collar of the turtleneck sweater and all three of the men stared at the three purple ligature marks on her neck.

"Who did this to you?"

Knitting her brow in confusion she said in a slow and matter of fact way, "The Legion."

Murphy grabbed her chin to steady her head. "Who, Joan, what person?"

"Kearney."

"That fucking insensitive bastard."

"It wasn't personal."

"*What?*"

"They just wanted to be sure—" She had to swallow again.

"Sure about what?"

Joan's mind was fading again. There was something that Murphy couldn't know…and something else.

Murphy had an idea of what they wanted to be sure about. He still could not understand torture to get the information. "Joan, look at me. What are the dressings for?"

"To cover the big wounds."

"What wounds? What did they do to you?"

Joan tried to think. It was fading quickly like a dream you try to remember upon awakening. "Joan?" He grabbed both her upper arms and gave a slight shake to try to clear her head. "The wounds—what are they from?"

"Duncan." She had to clear her throat and wait for a wave of nausea to pass then continued. "He…uh…skinned me."

"I didn't think he would ever hurt *you*." Murphy knew what Duncan was capable of, and he had tried to warn her, but he never truly believed Duncan would ever hurt her. "I guess a leopard never changes his spots."

She saw the horror on Murphy's face, not realizing the mistake she had made, and added, "But Duncan took good care of me."

"He took care of you all right. Come on get in my car. I'm getting you some place safe."

After fastening her seatbelt in the front seat of his car, he took the weapons and pills that the officers had confiscated and bagged. Wondering what really happened, he slid into the driver's seat.

ᎿᎧᎿ

Duncan leaned over Vaida's shoulder, eyes on the monitor that showed Joan being questioned by the police officers. When they saw her swaying, semi-conscious state, it confirmed their suspicions that she had taken off after taking too many pills.

The street cam showed Murphy swoop in and take her away. It was a relief that she was back in the hands of a Leg. Everyone needed a break from the constant vigilance, and they all agreed to let Murphy take care of her for a while. Murphy's apartment would be a temporary safe haven. Duncan could continue to take care of her medical needs from a distance.

CHAPTER 34

With an arm tightly around Joan's shoulder, Murphy ushered her into his apartment and sat her down on his sofa. He took her blazer and put it on the back of one of the stools at the breakfast bar. After turning up the thermostat, he grabbed a blanket out of the hall closet. When he returned to the living room, she was lying down.

She looked up at him. "Murphy, you came to me when I called you."

"I always told you that all you ever had to do was call me and I'd come."

He gently covered her with the blanket, and she immediately relaxed and fell asleep in the middle of an incoherent sentence.

During the three hours while she slept off the drugs, Murphy called in to the task force and told them what was going on. He still owed them that much. The next call was to Kempton. He needed some answers, but Kempton was evasive when asked why things had gotten so out of hand. His orders were to keep his eye on her and to take care of her. Someone would stop by and bring him up to speed. All he had to do was wait.

Not realizing the task force was one step ahead of him, Murphy turned his attention to Joan's cell phone. Maybe there was some usable information in messages and phone book. But when the task force bugged her phone, they deleted all messages that might incriminate her—like the voicemails from Ira Levine. Joan memorized all numbers so there was not much in her phone book to be taken care of. Her phone was essentially sterile by the time Murphy had access to it.

He was working on his laptop when he heard Joan stir. Looking over his reading glasses, he asked if she would like a cup of coffee. She spun around to look over the back of the sofa toward the breakfast bar where Murphy was sitting.

Pushing her hair back from her face, she asked, "Where am I?"

"My apartment." Murphy refilled his cup while pouring some coffee for her. "How do you like your coffee?"

"Milk, one sugar, one packet of sweetener." Duncan would have known how she liked it. She frowned and pushed the thought away. After a big inhale and a big stretch, her head started to clear. She had work to do. "How long have I been here?"

"Three hours. You were in la-la land when I brought you here," Murphy answered while stirring her coffee. He set down the spoon and headed for the area that served as a living room. He offered the cup to Joan over the back of the couch. "Do you remember the café and the cops?"

"Vaguely." She carefully took the blue cup in both hands, still not confident in their dexterity. The warmth of the cup felt good. She took a sip of the hot cream-colored liquid. Too much milk. Not how Duncan would have prepared it. Taking another sip, her plan started to take shape. "I remember you appearing out of nowhere to save me."

"You called me twice. Don't you remember?"

"I called you? Wow, my subconscious reached out to you and not—"

"I'm the only one who has your best interests at heart. Duncan only thinks of himself."

Joan decided to ignore the slur against Duncan. She was on a mission and the sooner she got what the task force needed, the sooner she would be safe. "And the Legion."

"What?"

"The Legion. He only thinks of himself and the Legion."

"Yes, that's right. I tried to tell you he was dangerous, but you wouldn't listen."

Joan knitted her brow. Why was Murphy going on about

Duncan being dangerous? She thought she had told him that Duncan had saved her from Kearney and from a painful death, and he took care of her wounds.

She decided to let it go. There would be time to straighten it out later. First things first. She had to get the information the task force needed.

"By the way, what are these?" He held up the baggie with the pills.

"Vicodin. I took NSAIDs yesterday, but evidently they weren't strong enough so I took one."

"One?"

"Maybe more. I can't remember exactly." The coffee was clearing her head. The pain medication that remained in her system was making her sleepy, so she decided to get right to task. "I never really gave you a chance. I was always pushing you away and sometimes I was downright mean to you. And yet when I called for help, you came to me and saved me from the police. I'd be in jail now if it weren't—"

He sat down on the sofa beside her. "I'm a patient man."

"You are a wonderful man and I want to get to know you better. Tell me about yourself."

"There'll be time later for that."

"Maybe it will relax me and I can fall back to sleep."

"Thanks a lot."

Joan blinked at him, at a loss about what he meant.

Murphy continued. "You think my life is that boring?"

"No—I meant the sound of your voice—not—"

He brushed some strands of hair out of her face and smiled. "What do you want to know?"

"I don't know. Where you are from originally, why you became a cop, your first kiss—"

"My first kiss?"

"Just checking to see if you're paying attention."

"Well, my first kiss…" He started out lightly mocking Joan, but launched into telling her about his background. She listened attentively, asking questions at the right time, but mostly listening.

⌘

Meanwhile, Woyzeck was listening to the conversation. He turned to the audio tech. "She's working him already. She's good."

He half-listened through the conversation. Murphy offered to make Joan something to eat and Woyzeck continued listening through the small talk while Murphy cooked. Joan convinced Murphy that a couple drinks would not be bad, because the painkillers were working their way out of her system. He eventually capitulated and they a glass of wine with dinner. With the dinner dishes cleared away and stacked in the dishwasher, they sat on the sofa with another glass of wine.

There was the sound of movement—she and Murphy sitting on the sofa.

"But enough about me, what about you," Murphy said.

"What do you want to know?"

"Oh, I don't know. Where you're from originally, what you did before joining the Legion, your first kiss."

"I do believe, kind sir, you are mocking me," Joan said with a dramatic flourish. They heard Murphy chuckle as she continued. "Well, my first kiss was…"

The task force agents half-listened to her guarded and carefully narrated story.

After Murphy refilled her glass, she finally said, "So why did you join the Legion?"

Woyzeck sat up straight and motioned to Tremaine, who had just entered the van to relieve him, to pick up the spare headphones.

"I joined the Legion because of you," Murphy was saying.

"Bullshit. I'm not so wasted that I don't remember you were my team leader when I joined."

"Let me clarify. I was a member of the Legion, but I was still undercover at that time so I wasn't *really* a member, if you know what I mean."

"I don't understand. How could I have been the reason you joined the Legion when you were there already. I don't get it."

"Okay, I was undercover, like I told you before. So I wasn't really a member, but over the months I saw your fervor and dedication to the Legion and it inspired me to join for real."

"So I'm the vamp who stole you away from the police and turned you over to the Legion?"

"You aren't a vamp, you're a minx. There's a difference." There was the sound of movement and what sounded like a light kiss, then Murphy continued. "But, yes, your enthusiasm inspired me to give the Legion my all."

"What about the task force? Don't you have to give them information and maybe an arrest now and then?"

"I only give them enough to keep them from becoming suspicious. My allegiance is with the CDL."

"Says the man to the head of security," Joan interjected. "It would be a death knell to tell me anything else. How do I know you're telling me the truth?"

"I have no reason to lie to you." Murphy was close, caressing her cheek, Woyzeck guessed. "You already know I'm a federal agent, and Kempton, Kearney, Duncan are all good with it." More sounds of movement.

"But you don't have the tatt—" Joan whispered,

"Are you sure?" Sounds of movement, clothing rustling.

"You got the tattoo," Joan said. Then continued. "Hey, wonderful man, what's your real name?"

Without hesitation, he said, "Mike. Mike Clancy."

"Mike, I am beginning to like you more and more." He must have pulled her close to him, because she involuntarily cried, "Ouch."

"I'm sorry. I'm supposed to be taking care of you and instead I hurt you."

"*You*, my friend, have not hurt me. What Kearney did to me—"

Sounds of kissing and shuffling and rustling filled the headphones. After a minute of kissing, Joan must have spilled her wine on her pants, and the next five minutes were filled with signs of cleaning up the mess, finding something dry to wear, throwing her clothes in the washer.

There was a loud knock on the door.

❧❧❧

Duncan stood in the hallway outside Murphy's apartment

and watched him as he looked through the spy hole. When the door opened he saw Joan, wearing only a man's white shirt. She stood where she could see who was outside when Murphy opened the door.

"What do you want?" Murphy asked.

"I'm here to take care of Joan."

"You've done enough already. I can't believe you could do this to her."

"What? I didn't do that. I stopped it." He saw Joan through the opening in the door. He eyed her half-dressed state, but continued. "Joan, tell him I didn't do this. Tell him."

Joan stood frozen in place. He looked at her, pleading, but she just stood there—silent—numb from the events of the past few days and glassy-eyed from the wine and Vicodin.

"What is going on here?" Duncan was starting to lose control. "Let me in, just for a drink. We can talk this out." He was giving Joan the chance to tell him to save her—the code was the word "whiskey" said twice within a few words—but Joan remained silent. He slammed the doorjamb with his palm. "Murphy, I didn't do this to her. If it wasn't for me, she would have died a slow, painful death at Kearney's hands."

Duncan looked past Murphy again and pleaded, "Joan, say the word and I'll beat this door down. Joan?"

Murphy pulled his phone out of his pocket. "That's it. You're going down to the station tonight." He started dialing.

"Sure, you friggin' wimp. You can't face me like a man. You have to call in back up."

Duncan scrutinized Joan's actions. She seemed to have snapped out of whatever was going on with her. She now looked anxious. Her hands were shaking as she removed her earrings. Duncan squinted as she neared the door.

Joan put her hand on Murphy's. "Stop. Let me talk to Duncan for a minute."

"Are you sure?" She nodded. "Okay, but I'll be right here." Murphy was addressing Joan, but he said it for Duncan's benefit.

She looked over her shoulder at Murphy then talked to Duncan through the opening in the door. "I got this."

"What does that mean?" he demanded.

"I have everything under control. I'm doing what I have to do right now."

"You aren't making sense. Come out here." She hesitated. "I'm not going to kidnap you and take you against your will—although I should." He glanced past her into the apartment. "I respect your decision to stay here. Come here."

Once outside in the hallway she explained. "I spilled wine on my pants."

"I don't care about that." He put a hand on each side of her neck and gave her a gentle kiss. When he stopped, he asked, "How are you feeling?"

"Good."

"How's the pain?"

Joan shrugged. "Better, I guess."

He smelled the wine on her breath. "That fucking bastard gave you alcohol with the Vicodin?"

"I haven't taken anything for four or five hours. I thought it would be safe."

Duncan frowned and looked at the now closed door to the apartment.

"Don't be mad at Murphy. I insisted," she continued.

"What's going on here? Why won't he let me in?"

"He's being protective, I guess."

"Why is he protecting you from *me*?"

"I don't know." She shrugged again, still unaware of her slip up. "Some macho thing."

"Let me in, Joan. I need to take care of your wounds."

Joan fidgeted with the collar of the shirt—Murphy's, Duncan guessed. Her anxiety showed in the tension in her tone, "Duncan, please go."

"What's going on? Are you caught up in something?" He stood, cupping her shoulders in his hands. He leaned close and spoke softly. The pain had to be worse than she was letting on.

"We don't have much time," she said. "Did you assault Woyzeck and Massa?"

"How do you know about that?"

"Never mind that. They're out for blood. Watch your six when you leave here."

"Why?"

"They're watching this place. Don't come back here."

Duncan looked at Joan long and hard. "How could you know about that unless—" He pushed her away from him, grasping her upper arms. She winced, but he didn't loosen his grip. "Joan, what have you done? If staying here is making you nervous, why are you staying? Is it the result of what Kear—"

"No."

He looked into her eyes. They were darting and slightly unfocused, but he was sure she wasn't lying. If she was being truthful, then—He knew without her telling him. "You endured that torture and did not give it up?"

He pulled her to him and hugged her hard. He knew it had to hurt, even with the alcohol and drugs in her system, but she didn't pull away. This woman had grit, but he was stunned by the depth of her fortitude at having endured extreme torture and not giving it up. He closed his eyes and said silently, *What strength. What courage. What a great asset for the Legion—if only she were loyal.*

"Why did you turn your back on us?" he whispered in her ear. "Why?"

She pushed him away. "Stop it. I don't want to talk about it."

"Did Murphy turn you?"

"He doesn't know."

The look on her face revealed that she shouldn't have said that. She wanted to tell him, but couldn't. In a different time, in a different setting, he would have loved her for that.

"He doesn't know? What the *fuck*. Is. Going. On?" He emphasized each word, hoping the intensity would filter through the drugs and alcohol to the rational part of her brain.

"I'm doing what I have to do right now. That's all I'm going to say. Now, go."

"Talk to me, nena," he said.

She winced. He could see the endearment hurt her more than her injuries, but she would not answer him. No matter how hard he clung to her, he felt her drifting away.

Duncan pressed his lips together. "Tell Murphy to come out here so I can tell him how to tend to your injuries."

"Don't say anything to him, please."

The concern in her eyes forced him give in to her. "I should, but against my better judgment, I won't, but only because you've asked me not to. I just want to tell him how to take care of you."

Murphy went into the hallway and Duncan gave him the medical supplies he had brought with him. He explained about changing the dressings and massaging Joan's extremities to make sure the circulation returned. Murphy was attentive, but hostile, and was impatient for Duncan to leave.

ℰ∕ℐℰ∕ℐ

The surveillance team had a camera in the hallway covering Clancy's door, and they were hacked into the apartment complex's outside surveillance cameras. When Duncan appeared at Clancy's door, Tremaine said, "Where did he come from? Did he just materialize out of nowhere? I'll watch this, you replay the last few minutes of the outdoor feed." The audio tech played back the previous two minutes of the video from the outside cameras, but saw nothing. He shrugged his shoulders and shook his head at Tremaine.

Tremaine asked no one in particular, "What is she doing? She took off the earrings. Who is this guy?"

The audio tech started running pictures in their database of known Legion members. He stopped on Duncan's photo and nudged Tremaine to get her attention. She read over his profile and looked back up at the monitor. "He's a captain in the organization. I'll bet that's the guy who was her date the night we questioned her in the restaurant parking lot, and one of the guys who assaulted Woyzeck and Massa."

She immediately picked up the radio, gave the surveillance teams Duncan's description, and told them to pick him up when he came out of the apartment building. She knew Woyzeck wanted this guy, and maybe they could nab someone in addition to Murphy.

ℰ∕ℐℰ∕ℐ

Joan was standing at the window, trying to see Duncan one

more time, when Murphy returned inside, medical supplies in hand. He tried to console her, but she was devastated. Duncan was gone, and it would not be long before he figured out what was going on, if he hadn't already. Where was the task force? She'd gotten Murphy to say what they wanted to hear. It was imperative that the task force get her out of there before Duncan returned. Her life was in the balance, and she was painfully aware of it.

Murphy dutifully cleaned Joan's wounds following Duncan's instructions to the letter. He was aghast at some of the wounds and his hate for Kearney and Duncan intensified. It was getting late, so he suggested she lay down on his bed so he could massage her arms and legs, because if she fell asleep, she would be comfortable. He decided to sleep on the couch for the night just in case Duncan returned.

CHAPTER 35

Duncan paced behind Vaida and harangued her, not with words, but with the apprehension that radiated off him like hot air from an electric heater. She was working as fast as she could to hack into the surveillance cameras. It took time. Time Duncan didn't want to give her. The incessant pacing, the grunts that sounded dark and ominous, the occasional tapping on the desk was disrupting her concentration. She had already hacked the newly installed camera in the hallway because it belonged to the task force. She already knew how to get into their system. If the apartment complex had a closed system that did not transmit its video to an online site, she was helpless.

He hoped she understood that his agitation wasn't aimed at her—not directly anyway. Kempton finally called him to the other side of the front room to go over their plan again, and to get him off Vaida's back.

They had hastily set up shop in the front room of a farmhouse in Elk County about fourteen miles north of I-80—Duncan's personal safe house. It was in the middle of nowhere and a perfect place for what they had to do. The Woods was the preferred location to bring Joan, but if he was right about his assessment of the situation, every location of every cell, every safe house, every member's residence was compromised. This run down old house would have to do for now.

Vaida was the best at what she did, but she was overwhelmed by the requirements of setting up new surveillance systems outside to monitor the approaches to the house as well as trying to hack into the system at the apartment complex. As members of their Special Recovery Team arrived, it gave Vaida more assets to get the cameras up and running. Things were going as fast as could be expected. Duncan's pacing and disturbing behavior was not going to make everything come together any faster.

Like Joan, Duncan had set up a safe house for himself that was not part of the Legion's array of safe houses. He had chosen it purposefully because of its remote location and because it sat in the middle of rolling pastures that, though overgrown, provided great line of sight to deter a sneak attack. There was a barn and an equipment shed which provided great cover for their vehicles. With the video surveillance, the need for several squads of armed perimeter guards was greatly reduced. Yes, this had been an excellent choice.

Six months prior, the Legion had initiated training a Special Recovery Team, called the SRT, to extract members who were kidnapped or detained by the task force. Their job was to breach the defenses and get their member out. Each SRT member was specially chosen for what they could bring to the team. Some were explosives experts, others were experts at silently assassinations, picking locks, electronic communications, or interrogation techniques. This was the first live mission for the SRT—everything had been training up to now. The only team member who had taken part in a live mission was Kearney's assistant when he had interrogated Joan three days earlier.

Vaida had obtained a floor plan of Murphy's apartment off the internet and Duncan drew a map with the locations of the cameras and task force members who were watching the apartment. They were going over the plan for the sixth time, trying to iron out any wrinkles that could appear. Everything was falling into place except their control of the video.

Vaida raised her arms in triumph. "I'm in."

CHAPTER 36

Six dark figures clad in black, faces concealed, stealthily covered the distance from their van to the front door of the apartment building. They stood silently while one member picked the lock. When the door was unlocked they slid through the door one after the other. Two peeled off and remained in the living room and took silent, immediate control of Murphy. Four headed straight toward the bedroom. Outside, two teams of two were controlling the task force agents in the communications van and the two uniformed police officers assigned as protection.

The Legion's SRT had finally arrived at the apartment after leaving the farmhouse before midnight. Duncan thought he would relax once they were on their way, but remaining behind and not being a part of the operation was more agonizing. They were in radio contact the whole time, but it was nerve wracking as hell. He listened as the team reached the apartment complex and separated into separate, smaller teams. He watched helplessly as each task was completed, and waited impatiently as they picked the two locks on the apartment door. The worst part was the planned four-minute radio silence when the extraction team was inside the apartment. He would not hear from them again until they were back in the van and on their way to the farmhouse He had to remind himself to breathe.

The four-man team assigned to extract Joan approached her in the semi-lit bedroom. Duncan had hoped four would be enough to discourage her from fighting, and he prayed under his breath she would not resist. The team was authorized to use extreme force if necessary.

At any other time, she would have awakened immediately upon sensing a presence in the room, but the pain killer and alcohol in her system as well as being dead tired, deadened her senses. The intrusive presence in the room went undetected. On cue one man put one hand over Joan's mouth, one grabbed both her ankles and the other two each grabbed an arm. She woke with a start and was terrified at being completely immobilized. The man at Joan's head whispered in her ear to stay quiet and identified himself and his team as CDL SRT. He went on to explain that they were going to remove her from the apartment— one way or another. They were authorized to use whatever force was necessary to bring her in, and if she cooperated, everything would go easier on her. They did not want to hurt her, but they would if given no other choice. The choice was hers. Joan put up no resistance. Fighting was useless, she was out-manned and overpowered. Even if she were in optimum physical condition, this would be a no-win situation—she would have given them the fight of their lives, but they would have won in the end. In other circumstances, her training would have dictated waiting to see how the situation would play out, waiting for an opening to fight and escape, but she already knew the ending to this story. No help was coming from the task force. She could only guess what the SRT had done to them.

The man whispered in her ear and asked again if she was going to cooperate. Joan nodded her head. He slowly removed his hand from her mouth and when he was confident she was not going to yell or scream, he told her to get up and get dressed. Joan was fully aware of the MAC-10's and 9mms trained on her. She did as she was told.

Joan knew exactly why they were there, and she elected to face her death with dignity. In previous situations that were dire and possibly lethal, she was confident she would find a way out of it alive. Now she was painfully aware that her story was over—not at the hands of the extraction team. They were just here to capture her. Her end would come later when she finally came face to face with the enforcer.

When she was dressed, her hands were secured with plastic

zip ties and her ankles were shackled. Two of the team members grabbed her arms one on each side and escorted her into the living room where Murphy was similarly bound. They were half-carried, half-dragged as they all rushed out of the apartment and into the waiting van that took off out of the parking lot and onto the city streets. The whole incident had taken less than five minutes. Five minutes of silent, efficient teamwork.

Once inside the van, Joan and Murphy were separated and each surrounded by three of their six kidnappers—Murphy toward the front, she toward the back. Once she was seated, one of the men, still with mask on and still without a word spoken, put handcuffs on Joan hooking them through the shackles which kept her bent forward and effectively immobilized—perfect for a martial artist. He cut the zip ties off then sat back against the side of the van.

"Come on, why this?" She tried to get one of them to talk. She must know who they were because she knew every member of every cell, but the masks made identification impossible. She had vaguely recognized the voice of the sole person who had spoken to her, but she couldn't figure out who it was. He was most likely someone she had only met once or twice, which was probably why he had been chosen for that particular task.

"I've complied with everything so far," she continued.

Nothing. Not even a glance her way. In spite of the discomfort and the imminent doom that faced her, she was very impressed with their discipline. She could hear the driver talking quietly, and she assumed he was giving a situation report to whomever they were taking her to. She resigned herself to a lonely and possibly long ride to somewhere darker than the depths of hell. She laid her head on one of her knees. Closing her eyes, trying to refrain from thinking of what was ahead of her, she thought, *Death is* not *the worst of all evils.*

ℰᗏℰᗏ

The audio tech started to stir and slowly regained consciousness. He leaned over, trying to arouse the other agent in the communications van. He immediately hit the switch on the radio and tried to contact the uniformed officers, but there was no answer. Without hesitation he put out the "officer down" radio call then put out a 911 text message to Woyzeck and Tremaine.

While he waited for backup, he reversed the video to see what had happened while he was unconscious. To his dismay he saw six heavily armed men dressed in black pile out of a van and rush into the apartment building, then a few minutes later Murphy and Joan were hastily escorted toward the van by the six kidnappers. The clock on the video showed the whole incident had taken a little less than five minutes. The kidnappers were obviously well-trained professionals. None of the camera angles captured the license plate so he put out a BOLO for a dark-colored late model Ford Van.

Within minutes four cruisers screeched to a stop in front of the apartment complex and they approached the outside door to the apartment building. The door was open to Clancy's apartment and they entered and cleared it. There was no sign of Clancy or Joan, no sign of forced entry, no evidence left behind of who had taken them. This had been a clean extraction.

❧❧❧

When Woyzeck received the urgent text message, he turned to his wife. "Gotta go. My key witness has been kidnapped."

"Oh, no. Be careful," his wife mumbled.

After twenty-three years of marriage to a federal agent, she was used to middle-of-the-night calls that led to her husband rushing out of the house, donning clothes and equipment on the way to the garage. It was a rarer event than movies or television might have one think, but it was a reality she had lived through before.

While he was backing out of the driveway, he was already on the phone to the task force leader, demanding every drone be put into the air to try to find Joan and Clancy, and to execute every search warrant they had obtained over the past thirty-six hours. They had to start shaking the bushes right away. Time was his—and Joan's—worst enemy now. He had promised her safety in exchange for information against Clancy aka Murphy. He had to find her fast.

"And get the DA out of bed. We need the rest of those warrants now."

"He's not going to be happy."

"Do *I* sound happy?" The team leader did not offer a response. "If I'm unhappy, then I want the DA unhappy, too." Woyzeck slowed to check his mirrors then zoomed past a slow moving car. "And I don't think Bowman and Clancy are very happy right now either."

The task force leader wanted to catch this group as much as anyone. "Fuck it. We don't need no stinkin' warrants," he said, alluding to the famous line from *The Treasure of the Sierra Madre*. "We know where all these scumbags are. Let's fire up police departments all over western Pennsylvania and eastern Ohio, and get these rat bastards picked up."

"That's what I'm talking about!" Woyzeck disconnected his phone and stepped even harder on the gas pedal as he crossed the West End Bridge.

ᕤᕥᕤᕥ

Duncan could finally breathe. The driver was reporting that everything went even more smoothly than anticipated. The two targets had been in separate rooms and were secured without incident. There was a sense of satisfaction that Joan and Murphy were not found in bed together. He knew that certainly in a few hours Joan would be dead, and he asked himself why it should matter to him. He tried to shake it off, but there were still a couple hours before the team would arrive at the farmhouse with Joan in tow, and all he had to do was wait—and think.

The image of Joan, about to melt into his arms, saying, 'No strings' filled his head. The one thing she had asked of him, the only stipulation Joan had made for them to come together in bed. It had seemed an easy request to agree to at the time, but he should have known better. He finally found someone who could crack the shell he had built around himself. He had counted himself as fortunate that someone turned out to be this woman, someone he could share the rest of his life with. The rest of his life—another vision of Joan popped into his head. This time she was asking where this whole resistance movement was going.

What made him think he could spend the rest of his life with her when the possibility of getting arrested always loomed large in his life. If caught, he'd be looking at many, many years behind bars—effectively the rest of his life. He felt a hand clamp down on his shoulder.

"I'm sorry, man." Kempton had been watching Duncan standing motionless with his arms crossed, just watching the monitors that now showed swarms of police officers around the empty apartment. Radio traffic had slowed to nothing a half hour ago. Kempton saw that Vaida was shooting concerned looks at Duncan. Kempton decided to try to distract Duncan and give Vaida a little breathing room so she could do her job.

"You have nothing to be sorry about," Duncan said to Kempton.

Kempton replied, "Yes, I do. I should have seen this day coming a long time ago when it wouldn't have been so hard for you to break ties with her."

"No one saw it coming." Duncan wiped his mouth with his hand and looked at his long-time friend. They had slogged through the jungles of Central and South America together for years—sometimes under the auspices of the United State Military, sometimes as mercenaries when they didn't want the combat adrenaline to end. If there was anyone here at this time, he was glad it was Kempton.

"Except Kearney," Duncan continued. "He was the only one who called it." He looked across the room at Kearney dozing by the fire. How could he sleep knowing what he was about to do? How did he ever sleep after everything he'd done? Hundreds of people tortured over his career—many of them innocent, like Joan. Duncan wanted to cross the floor, grab Kearney, and shove him face-first into the fire. The vision of him doing it filled his eyes. He pressed his thumb and index finger to his eyes to push the vision from his mind—to prevent him from acting on it.

The debt he owed Kearney for saving his life was losing its power in light of the price he had to exact from Kearney for what he did to Joan. It wasn't over between them.

Yet, Kearney had been right about Joan.

"He was just being the misogynist that he is," Kempton replied. "He didn't see it coming any more than anyone else. He just happened to be right."

"I really thought she had it in her to become a real revolutionary. How could I have been so wrong?"

Kempton squeezed Duncan's shoulder and turned away. "Sometimes women do that to us, my friend."

Duncan gave a cursory look over his shoulder in the direction of Kempton, took one long look at the monitors, then walked out the front door and stepped into the overgrown front yard. He turned and gave a brief nod to Vaida through the camera on the corner of the porch and disappeared into the darkness.

Vaida knitted her brows and turned in her chair to look at Kempton. "Where's he going?"

"He just needs to be alone for a while. Get his head on straight. He'll be back in time."

Vaida turned back to her monitors. She didn't want to hear what it was that he was going to be back in time for.

❧❧❧

Joan heard the driver say, "Two minutes." She heard safeties being switched off on the weapons in the hands of CDL SRT members. They had only been driving for five minutes to the best of her estimation. *Now what?*

At the one minute warning the man who had cuffed her wrists to her shackles leaned over and said, "In one minute we're going to be changing vehicles. I'm going to unlock your shackles, and you'll go where you are directed. You've been cooperative up to now. Let's keep it that way."

She knew that voice. "Jason?" No response. Did she see a flicker in his eyes? It was Jason. She was sure of it. "I thought you were dead." Still no response. "How can you let them do this? You know they're going to kill me, right?" Still nothing. "I saved your butt that time at the federal building. You owe me."

"This isn't about owing anybody anything. Now shut up or you'll travel the rest of the way unconscious."

Joan was stung, but at last she had a glimmer of hope of getting out of this. The van she was riding in came to a halt. The metallic clanking of a commercial garage door opening followed. As soon as the van pulled forward and stopped, the door closed. The back door of the van opened and a guard pulled her out. She glanced over her shoulder to see what was happening to Murphy, but the guard jerked her so hard she lost her footing. She was dragged to a white sedan and pushed into the back seat. Before the door shut the shackles that had been removed from her ankles were used to secure her handcuffs to the driver's headrest in front of her.

The rough handling made the wounds on her thighs and abdomen throb. She gritted her teeth and said, "How long am I going to have to travel like this?"

The only response was the door being slammed in her face. Her glimmer of hope dimmed when she realized that Jason was not one of the men who got into the car with her.

Three vehicles left the old abandoned service station and went in different directions. Joan wanted to ask where they were taking Murphy, but knew she wouldn't get a response, and they certainly weren't going to tell her where they were taking her. She grabbed the chain of the shackles so the weight of her arms would not put pressure on her already bruised wrists. Her injuries from the torture a few days earlier were screaming for a painkiller that would not be coming. She put her head down on her arms wishing Jason's threat had come to fruition and she could make the remainder of the trip unconscious.

ぐぅぐぅ

At the fusion center, the senior technician turned to Woyzeck. "We have her! She's in a white sedan headed north on I-79 just south of the I-80 junction."

Woyzeck's heart leaped. "Re-route the other two drones to that area."

"I'm on it," the technician said, turning back to his console.

Woyzeck radioed dispatch. "Get our SWAT team on a helicopter and get them headed toward I-80. The exact final destination will be relayed en route. As soon as we know where she ends up, contact local police and get our team in there so we can set up, get some intel, and get her out. Get a helicopter over here to pick me up, too. I want to be there." He turned to Tremaine and fist-bumped her. "Good job putting that RFID chip in her hip."

"Do we know where Clancy is?"

"No. Our only hope is that they're together. He's one of them, and I think they took him along just to tie up loose ends. I think he'll be okay. Besides, it's not *them* he has to worry about."

❧❦❧

The road was getting bumpier and they were winding around corners on a country road somewhere in upstate Pennsylvania. They had to be getting close to their destination, wherever that was, but Joan could not find it in her to care. No one would ever find her body—or the crime scene for that matter. Her adrenaline started racing through her system and she could not get the lump out of her throat. Dread was like an anvil tied to her ankles, dragging her to the depths of Lake Erie.

She breathed through her mouth, gasping for air. Her head was pounding so hard she thought it was going to explode. She half-wished it would and put her out of her misery. She quietly said a brief prayer. "God, I know I only call on you when I need you, but I *really* need you now. If you can't prevent this, please make it quick."

❧❦❧

The dried grass swished against Duncan's pant legs as he crossed the open field that had once grown hay to feed farm animals. The air was crisp and clean. He took deep breaths to clear his head.

He kicked aside a rotting fence post and stepped between the strands of rusting barbed wire that threatened to snag the cuff of his pants. What kind of man was he? Letting this organization brutalize and kill the one person who had brought joy back into his life. She was all he could think about—all day, every day. But she had betrayed the Legion. The Legion was his life—he was the Legion. She betrayed *him*. And he hadn't even seen it coming.

With a look over his shoulder, he entered the tree line, climbed over a crumbling stone wall and melted into the woods. The musky smell of earth and trees filled his senses. He was able to walk at a good clip because there was enough moonlight to see tree roots and stones. He picked up a game trail and turned south.

Lost in thought he didn't hear the whop-whop of a helicopter until it was less than a kilometer away. He looked up to get a glimpse of it and didn't see the wispy end of a tree branch. It swatted him in the face and...

ℰↄℰↄ

He was in the hot, humid El Salvadoran jungle. He hid behind a fern with wide fronds, head on the swivel, looking for anything out of the ordinary. He was bloody, mud-covered and alone. His team had been picked off one by one, making everything seemed darker, deadlier, lonelier. The jungle was different without a team and the extra eyes they provided.

The sound of the helicopter's rotors got louder as it neared where he crouched behind the giant fern. The radio crackled in his ear bud for the first time in three days. The pilot was telling him where to go to be picked up. And something about being alone. Duncan's heart turned to stone. But the pilot meant no resistance fighters in the area. Duncan raced to the LZ, slashing vines and tropical plants that blocked his path and caught on his clothes as if they were trying to prevent him from leaving the jungle.

He found the clearing and waited just inside the tree line for the chopper to make a pass.

The engine sounds got louder. He saw it land and someone waving him forward. When he reached the open side door of the helicopter, a hand reached out and pulled him onto the deck of the chopper.

The man put out his hand. "I'm CIA. Welcome aboard, soldier." Kearney's youthful face smiled at him. The first time they had met...

ℰↄℰↄ

A loud metallic sound brought Duncan out of his flashback. *I haven't had one of those in a while—over a year. Must be the stress.* He shook his head to clear it as he squatted behind a white oak and scanned the area. A metallic sound in the woods was out of the ordinary. The woods were now quiet. Too quiet.

When nothing seemed out of place, Duncan stood and walked slowly along the game trail, ducking branches and avoiding sticks. Although everything seemed natural and safe, the hair on the back of his neck felt otherwise. He knew that when everything's okay, it's okay until it's not—then it could go to shit in a hurry.

He heard a sliding van door open and…

೮ઝ೮ઝ

He was lying in an alley, propped against a green dumpster that smelled of rotting food. Two little, beady rat's eyes peered at him from behind a meat packing crate. When he moved, every part of his body ached. His white tee shirt was bloody, and after checking his nose, he discovered the source. His wallet was gone. His watch was gone, too. Shit, even his shoes were gone. *Who takes a man's shoes?*

He tried to remember how he landed in a litter-strewn, urine-soaked alley, wearing clothes that smelled of sweat and stale beer. But the last three days of binge drinking turned them into a blur, or worse, blackness. Hell, the last two years of his life were an alcohol-induced blur—an attempt to block out the cries of his team as they died one at a time, the smells and sounds of the jungle. The unrelenting fear. The loneliness.

A hand reached out and tapped him on the shoulder. "Hey, buddy, let me help you up."

He swatted at the hand in a feeble attempt to defend himself.

"It's me, Kearney," the man said.

As Duncan's eyes focused, an adult Kearney came into view, hand outstretched to help Duncan to his feet. He struggled to get up and when he did, his head reeled. Kearney steadied him and supported him as they headed toward the van parked at the end of the alley.

"You are a hard man to find."

"You were looking for me? Why?"

Kearney ignored the question as he helped Duncan into the back seat of the van, climbed in beside him, and nodded to the driver to take off. "I can help you get a handle on your PTSD, if you'll let me."

He slid the door shut and...

෬ఎ෬ఎ

The finality of a door shutting brought Duncan back to reality. He was standing past the tree line at the edge of a parking lot of a small HVAC company. He stepped backward into the covering darkness of the forest and watched men dressed in black milling around a large, black straight truck with no lettering.

Damn, that was close. I almost walked right into the hands of a SWAT team. He shook his head to send the residual vision flashes scurrying to the darkest corners of his mind. The flashback almost got him arrested. *Why now? Why these flashbacks after a year of nothing. Not one. Not since...Joan.*

Not since he had shared his bed with Joan.

Duncan rubbed his forehead. She had brought him to a place where the past stayed in the past. It was she who had made his life worth living again. The power of the present kept the past at bay—and the powerhouse was Joan. She brought his life back. True, Kearney had saved his life—twice.

But Joan was his Life.

Duncan turned and ran through the woods, mindless of the tree branches. He knew what he had to do.

෬ఎ෬ఎ

At the farmhouse, Vaida turned and repeated the radio message, "Ten minutes out." Kearney got up and cracked his knuckles. Pallaton cleared his throat and sat as far as he could from the chair Kearney placed in the center of the room.

Since Joan was part of the inner circle, this task fell to the leadership. Kempton had disapproved of Kearney using an assistant for the unauthorized torture he had perpetuated on Joan.

This time Kempton made it clear that leadership was dealt with by only members of the leadership.

Murphy entered the room.

"Why is Murphy here?" Pallaton was on edge. "He's not part of the inner circle."

Kearney responded before Kempton could explain. "He will be after tonight."

The room fell silent, each man alone with his thoughts. The only sound was the popping of the fire. An ember jumped out of the fire. Kempton picked up a stick and pushed it back to the safety of the firebox.

Vaida broke the silence. "Two minutes out."

Kempton knew adrenaline was pumping and everyone was jumpy. He had to maintain order. "Let's stay focused on our mission. It's not to simply inflict pain." He gave Kearney a long hard stare. "Is anyone questioning whether she's talked?"

No answer.

"Then what we have to find out is how much she told the feds," Kempton continued. "We have to assume she knows what is about to take place here tonight. Maybe she'll be forthright and save us a lot of trouble." He looked around the room and repeated what was discussed at the meeting that set this whole scenario in motion, "No matter what. She has to be eliminated. We all agree to that, right?"

Nods all around.

"Murphy, you stay in the background on this one."

He nodded and leaned against the wall to the left of the monitors.

"They're turning in the drive," Vaida said.

"Okay, let's do what we—" Kempton was going to say "do what we do," but they were not about beating and killing women, or was that what they were becoming? He finished his statement with, "—came here to do."

CHAPTER 37

On the real time video from the drone Agent Tremaine saw three men get out of the white sedan. One man opened the driver side back door and, after reaching in, presumably to release any restraints, he extracted Joan from the car and pulled her toward the house. After a few minutes the three men got into the car and drove away. Tremaine told the drone operator to keep one of the drones on that car. She had the video relayed to each of the helicopters so the SWAT teams could see the house and the layout, identify a staging area, and find a way to get intel.

Woyzeck was in the second helicopter, and when he saw Joan being pulled toward the house he said under his breath, "Hang in there, Bowman. We'll be there as soon as we can."

When they landed, the teams went about establishing a staging area and setting up their gear. A small team was dispatched to get eyes on the house. After a few minutes that seemed like forever, the audio tech turned to Woyzeck. "We have audio."

"Okay."

"No, I mean we have audio from *inside* the house."

Woyzeck had only dared to hope that when the earrings with the transmitter in them were not found at the apartment that Joan had had the presence of mind to put them on. This was too good to be true. *That's my girl,* he thought as he motioned to the SWAT team leader to come over. "We have audio inside the house." He explained about the earrings.

When the recon team reached the house, they reported the through-wall radar system showed three people around another person in a chair. There was another person off to the side and one person in a room in the upstairs portion of the house.

After a final briefing, the teams in the staging area mounted the waiting vehicles.

ꕥꕥ

As soon as Joan came through the front door and turned into the front room where everyone was waiting, she couldn't stop herself from struggling. She caught her two guards by surprise and managed to get a backhand to the nose of the one on her left, but it was ineffective. He countered with a punch to her stomach. She doubled over when the skinned area sent waves of pain through her body. Her guards dragged her to the chair. They used duct tape to tie her wrists to the arms of the chair and her ankles to the chair legs. Blood oozed through her sweater just above her waist.

Kempton told Vaida to go upstairs, saying he would keep an eye on the monitors.

The room was dark and lit only by the fire in the fireplace, the security system monitors, and one lamp on a desk on the other side of the room. The monitors were diagonally to her left and someone was leaning against the wall to the side of them. She thought it was Murphy, but wasn't sure. Vaida gave her a worried, apologetic look on the way past her. Kearney was in front of her waiting for Kempton's cue to begin. He was somewhere behind her.

Getting the cue to start, Kearney said, "You know why you're here, and you're going to tell us what we need to know. But there is an order of business that has to be taken care of first." He ripped her sweater from the shoulder seam revealing her Live Free or Die tattoo. "You no longer can wear this, and we're going to take it from you."

"No, Kearney, please don't."

It was useless to plead with him, and she let out a blood curdling scream as he took his knife and pealed the top several layers of skin to remove the tattoo. It took five passes to get the whole tattoo and by that time the room and everything in it was starting to drift away. Smelling salts brought her back and she focused on Kearney right in front of her. She was panting, trying to keep from vomiting.

She looked up at Kearney and he said, "Okay. Now we can get down to business. Are you working for the feds?"

"Fuck you, Kearney."

He backhanded her across the temple and cheekbone. Her eye watered from the blow and started to swell immediately.

The pain from her stomach, her chest, and now her cheekbone and eye socket was proving to be almost too much for her. Tunnel vision was setting in. Kearney's voice sounded distant.

"Actually, we already know the answer to that question. I'll ask another question: how much did you tell the feds?"

"Why don't you just kill me, Kearney? It's what you really want. Just do it." She couldn't really see him, but she knew he was there. She was having a hard time holding her head steady.

He grabbed her hair to pull her head back. "Oh, that's going to happen. You are not getting out of here alive, but first we have to know what you told the feds."

"Your name is the only one I gave them."

He back fisted her and broke her nose. Now both eyes were watering and she could feel something warm on her upper lip. The raw-meat taste of blood coated her tongue.

She heard Kempton in her right ear. "We know you're working with the feds. Just tell us what they know, so we can do some damage control. Why make it hard on yourself? Just tell us, Joan."

She turned her head to look at Kempton. "And deprive Kearney of the pleasure of beating up a girl?"

Kearney reacted quickly by smashing the butt of his gun against her right hand. She yelled in pain and almost passed out, but through sheer will power managed to stay conscious.

"Did you tell them about the Fort Pitt Bridge and Tunnel operation?"

"Fuck you, Kearney. I won't tell you anything. You'll eventually beat me so bad I'll die, then you still won't know anything."

He smashed her left hand with the butt of his gun and this time she did pass out.

e⁄ɔe⁄ɔ

Agent Woyzeck flinched when Joan let out the heart-wrenching scream. He knew the SWAT team was doing everything it could to get into position to save her, but he demanded to know what was taking them so long anyway.

The team leader gave the command to move out, and the vans carrying the SWAT officers headed down the two-lane country road toward the farmhouse.

e⁄ɔe⁄ɔ

Smelling salts brought Joan back and as her eyes focused she saw Kearney leaning over her. She could not take the pain any longer. She gave up the fight and finally told Kearney that she had told the feds everything: names, locations, past operations, pending operations—anything so he would kill her, and the pain would stop.

Duncan slipped in through the backdoor of the farmhouse as the SWAT team headed up the gravel drive on foot. They were there to rescue Joan. There was no way he and the others would be able to fight their way out. It was over for them, but maybe he could save her—one last time. He owed it to her.

He pulled his Sig Sauer handgun from its holster, turned the corner into the front room, and stepped forward. Kearney had placed the muzzle of his 9mm against Joan's temple.

Duncan pointed his gun at Kearney. "Put the gun down."

Kearney turned and pointed his semi-automatic at Duncan. Duncan stepped into the room, looking down the barrel at the bastard who used to be his friend. "No one get stupid. This is between me and Kearney."

Murphy pulled his gun, but before he could aim and fire, Duncan shot him, then pointed his gun back at Kearney.

Murphy dropped to the floor. A dot of red grew and spread across his chest.

"Anyone else?" Duncan asked without taking his eyes off Kearney.

The others put up their hands and backed away—partly because they knew Duncan wouldn't hesitate to shoot them, but mostly because they knew Kearney deserved anything Duncan dished out.

"Pallaton, take Kearney's gun."

Kearney pointed the gun at Pallaton. He stopped.

Duncan fired. Kearney dropped his gun and grabbed his right shoulder.

Duncan strode across the floor, kicked the gun out of Kearney's reach, and hit him on the side of the head with the butt of his gun.

Kearney groaned, staggered sideways, and fell to one knee.

Duncan turned to Joan and cupped her head, covering both earrings. "You okay?"

Joan gave him a lopsided nod. "I'm tough, remember?"

He leaned in and whispered in her ear. "*Chica*, if you have a code word, now's the time to use it."

Code word? Joan searched through the dull heaviness in her head. Code word. Duncan had stopped calling her *chica* and switched to *nena* after they had slept together. *Chica* became their code word for the feds. The only other code word she knew was for the feds to storm in and get her out of a bad situation. He couldn't possibly mean that. Or could he? Nothing was making sense. She looked into Duncan's eyes, hoping for clarity, but found none.

She closed her eyes and groaned silently. Goodbye. Goodbye was the code word for the feds to rescue her. That's why they never came to get her out of Murphy's apartment. Duncan was trying to tell her something. Before she could ask him, he let go of her and stood up straight.

He turned to Kempton. "Cut her loose. I have something I have to take care of."

He walked over to where Kearney still knelt, moaning, and supporting his arm. The shoulder and sleeve of his shirt were bright red with blood. He looked up when he saw Duncan standing next to him and mustered a half-smile. "You're going to let a woman come between—"

Duncan kicked him in the temple, sending him sprawling onto his back, and pointed his gun at his forehead. "Yes, I am."

"Duncan, wait."

He looked toward the voice and did a double-take.

Joan stood, wobbling but resolute, on the other side of Kearney. "You said you had never killed anyone in cold blood. But if you kill Kearney now, that's exactly what you'll be doing."

Duncan loosened and tightened his grip on his gun. He looked from Joan to Kearney. Back to Joan. Then settled on Kearney, taking aim with his finger pressing on the trigger. "I have to do this. For you. For us."

"Please don't do this, Duncan," she said. "I have more reasons than anyone else to want this no-good-piece-of-shit dead. But killing him is not the right thing to do. Let him live with the memories of all the evil things he's done. Death is not the worst of all evils."

Duncan pinned his gaze on her. His eyes stung. She was better than any person in the room. His Iron Angel. He dropped the gun to his side.

Joan winked at him, smiled, and said, "Good-bye, Kearney." Without breaking eye contact with Duncan, she threw herself elbow first onto the moaning wretch on the floor.

There was a crack as Kearney's jaw broke, followed by a white flash, and a loud bang.

Duncan dove to cover Joan, to protect her, as armor-clad, heavily-armed men swarmed the room, shouting orders to get on the floor and to keep hands where they could see them.

She succumbed to pain-free darkness in the safety of Duncan's arms.

CHAPTER 38

The beeping was the first thing she heard before she even opened her eyes. Slowly the room around her came into focus. She was alive—in a hospital. She looked around the dimly lit room and licked her dry lips. She quietly moaned and lifted a hand to her head.

A man got up from a chair at the foot of her bed and limped toward her. It was Agent Massa.

Her mouth was dry and she managed a raspy, "Agent Massa, I'm so sorry for—"

"You have nothing to be sorry about. All you have to do now is rest and get better."

"You were nice to me and—" In spite of the pain killers, her emotions welled up from inside of her. "—because of me you were beaten up. And now you're on medical leave and can't work."

"I'll be fine. Don't worry about me."

She smiled, but it was weak and faded quickly. "Actually, I'm worried about Woyzeck. Without your influence, he could spin out of control."

"Agent Tremaine will keep him in line."

"Duncan. Is he—"

"He's alive. He's under arrest and is cooperating with us." He rubbed her fingers sticking out of the cast covering her left hand. "You should know that the last thing he did as a free man was to protect you."

Joan smiled, smacked her dry lips, and fell back to sleep.

The SWAT team had ordered everybody on the floor, secured them, and brought Vaida downstairs. The first fed into the house, once it was secure, was Agent Woyzeck who went directly to Joan. At first he groaned, thinking he had arrived too late and she was dead. There was blood on the side of her head and blood flowed from her nose. Her eyes were swollen shut and both her hands were swollen and purple. If he had not known where she was in the house, he would not have recognized her. He called for the paramedics right away and stepped aside while they assessed her injuries and stabilized her. He was genuinely relieved when they said she was would be okay. They removed her from the house and waited by the ambulance for the Life Flight helicopter to arrive to take her to Allegheny General Hospital in Pittsburgh. Agent Woyzeck waited by her side.

It was quite a night for the task force. They managed to take down the whole leadership of the CDL without firing a shot. The agent who had turned on the task force and betrayed them was dead. The only casualty was Joan, who had taken the beating of her life.

Woyzeck knew what she had been through over the past forty-eight hours and he had a newfound respect for her tenacity and fortitude. He knew the physical injuries would heal over time. He just hoped she had enough strength left to endure the next several years as she dealt with the psychological trauma she was yet to realize. Even with excellent counseling, it could take years to resume the life she used to know—if ever. She would wind up wearing scars on her psyche as well as her body.

He made a promise to himself that he would make sure she received the counseling she needed while she was in prison as part of her deal agreement. Prison.

He shook his head. She shouldn't do any time for what she did for the task force and for the lives she saved by informing them of the planned bombing of the Fort Pitt Bridge and Tunnel. He made a mental note to talk to the DA, but he knew the police department was adamant that she should do time for the assault on the two police officers in Cleveland.

Federal time was hard time, but maybe they could see their

way clear to offer her time off for good behavior like the state penal systems did.

ᏌᎾᏨ

Joan woke up again six hours later, needing some pain medication. This time Agent Woyzeck was waiting in the room with her. "Hey, Woyzeck, thanks for finding me."

He got up, walked to the side of the bed, and looked down at her. "You are one tough lady."

"Yeah, real tough. Look at me—no, don't look at me. I must look terrible."

"You look fine," he lied.

"If you're married, your wife must be a happy woman."

"Why's that?"

"If you tell me, someone you hardly know that I look fine after a brutal beating, you must tell her she is the most beautiful woman in the world."

"Really, you don't look that bad."

"Well, it feels really bad from this side. How long was I out?"

"Two days."

"I need some pain medication, but—"

"No 'buts.' I'll ring the nurse's station."

"Before they come is there anything you want to ask me before the meds put me back to sleep?"

Woyzeck couldn't believe his ears. They were negligent about getting her out of the apartment on time, but Joan was not holding a grudge. She still wanted to give them information.

"I do have a few questions. Do you want some water or anything?"

"I'd love some water. What do you want to know?"

"Those guys who kidnapped you. Who were they? Kempton, Pallaton, Duncan, they're not talking."

Joan took a long sip of water through the straw in the cup Woyzeck held for her. "I vaguely remember at a meeting about six or seven months ago a discussion about developing a special extraction team for special operations—kinda like what they did to get me. I never heard about it again, and I was so busy that I didn't think about it."

"Did you recognize any of them?"

She took another sip of water. "They all had masks. Only two ever spoke."

"Did you recognize the voices?"

She heard Jason saying, '*It isn't about owing anybody anything.*' She clamped her eyes shut, hoping to keep the wetness inside her lids. "They were vaguely familiar, but I couldn't place them." There was no need to turn in Jason now. "They were probably guys I had only met once or twice. Sorry."

The nurse came in and gave Joan an injection. Woyzeck waited until she was out of the room to say, "Don't be sorry, Joan."

"Anything else before I doze off again?"

"No, just rest up and get better."

CHAPTER 39

Joan hoped she was wrong. She was out in the open with only two federal agents, one of them a rookie, between her and the endless possibilities of things that could go wrong. She looked out the car window, hoping she was mistaken in her belief that the Legion would never let her go. She could not fathom the agents' complete lack of understanding of the CDL, or maybe it was she who did not understand the extent of the dragnet that had spread across western Pennsylvania and eastern Ohio, bringing almost a hundred members, including the whole leadership, to justice. The task force was adamant that they had broken the back of the CDL and, at the very least, had cut off the head of the snake.

It had been her job to pick apart operations to find any detail that could go wrong. Was that what she was doing now? Old habits die hard, she told herself. It was the first time she was not under intense security so maybe it was just different—not dangerous. Maybe.

They were one hour into the three-and-one-half hour trip to the Allenwood Federal Correctional Institution. The federal agents escorting Joan had settled into sporadic conversation mixed with taking in the scenic beauty of central Pennsylvania. They were relaxed and confident that it would be a routine, uneventful trip, which was the reason for having chosen to take Route 22 to Route 99 rather than taking I-80 for the major part of the trip. Joan would have preferred I-80 because it was a controlled access, six-lane highway that would have provided fewer chances for any attempts on her life or safety. As long as any Legion members remained at large, she could not relax. For obvious reasons, which she could understand, she was not allowed to be armed so she would not be able to defend herself. It was a new concept for her to place her personal safety in the hands of someone else, and she was completely dependent on these agents. She wished they would take her security more seriously. At one time this trip would have entailed a fully armed team of agents to protect her as well as to keep her under control, but now she was considered a compliant, doped up, female felon, and there was no viable threat. This was going to be a quick trip, a pleasant day out of the office. Joan shook her head—and kept her eyes open.

She felt the car slow down and she looked out the front window to see what was going on. There was a flagman up ahead and the northbound traffic was stopped to allow southbound traffic to pass through the one open lane. The electric company was trimming trees that were interfering with the power lines, and the road was reduced to one lane of traffic for public safety. Her heart started pounding and before she could stop herself she heard herself saying, "Woyzeck, this could be a ruse."

She thought her heart was going to beat right through her chest wall. Her mouth got dry and her head was on the swivel checking every window, every angle.

He looked in the rear view mirror. "Relax, Bowman. You're not going to flip out on us are you?"

Joan gritted her teeth. "Stop looking at *me*. The threat will come from out *there*." She emphasized the last word by jerking her eyes and head toward the outside of the car.

Fraser, the rookie federal agent, turned in her seat to face Joan. "It's going to be okay. We'll be moving in a minute."

"Stop it. Stop looking at *me*. Look out *there*."

Fraser turned in her seat and met Woyzeck's eyes.

"Look, Bowman, we're being waved through. We're moving. See, everything's going to be okay." He checked her in the mirror. "Take some deep breaths. Relax."

"I know what you're thinking. You think I've gone off the deep end. Maybe I have—" Joan turned to look behind the car.

The tree trimmers were continuing to do their jobs unaware of her momentary panic attack. "—but do you think you could at least be aware of the *possibility* of something happening on the way to Allenwood?"

"I've made arrangements for counseling for your PTSD, and I assure you I will make it my personal mission to make sure it happens."

"Please—" Head pounding, tightness in her chest and throat—the panic attack was returning. "—tell me you'll stay alert and open to the possibility. If anything happens, you're in as much danger as me." She looked behind them again.

Woyzeck looked at Fraser. "Okay. We'll stay alert."

"That's right. Relax and let us do our jobs." Fraser was trying to sound as calm as possible.

"*Then do your fucking jobs,*" Joan yelled.

"Hey!" Woyzeck pulled the car over to the side of the road. He turned in his seat and locked eyes with Joan. He was losing his patience. "Calm down back there. Don't give us any trouble, or we can make the rest of this trip very uncomfortable for you."

When the car stopped moving, Joan's whole body became a ball of anxiety, but she knew she had to get a hold of herself. "I'll calm down. I promise." She looked behind them. "Please, please keep driving." She put her head back and took some deep breaths. "Look I'm calming down, please keep moving."

Woyzeck waited a few seconds, staring at Joan to impose his authority, but he also wanted to make sure she was starting to calm down, then he turned and pulled back out onto the road glancing in the mirror every few seconds. After a few minutes he asked, "Is there something you need to tell us?"

"No." She took a few deep breaths. "What do you mean?"

"You are too panicked for something that may or may not happen. Do you have any information on anything that's going to go down? If you do, we need to know. We need to know now."

"No." Joan didn't open her eyes. She was breathing hard and making her best effort at maintaining her composure. "It's me, not you. I'm just ultra-paranoid right now. I apologize for making you deal with my panic and paranoia." Several minutes passed. She was still breathing hard and she was starting to sweat. Out of the blue she said, "Woyzeck?"

"What?"

"How many Legion members did the task force convict and send to prison?"

"Eighty-seven, why?"

"Were any of them the guys who kidnapped me that time?"

"No one confessed to it."

"So, as far as you know, none of the people arrested were members of the Special Recovery Team?"

"That doesn't mean we didn't get them. They just didn't own up to it."

"So they could still be out there."

"Is that what's bothering you? Even if we didn't get them, and I'm sure we picked up most of them in the general round up, they're scattered and on the run." He glanced at her in the mirror again. "I wouldn't worry about them. They aren't a threat anymore."

"Yeah, maybe you're right. I just can't shake the feeling that they're out there waiting for the opportunity to finish the job—and what better time than when I'm in the middle of nowhere, shackled and unable to defend myself, and with only two agents to protect me." She leaned forward a little. "You can see my position, right? I'm not being crazy, right?"

"You're not being crazy. You've been through a lot and everything will seem like a bigger threat than it actually is. It's normal, and you'll get over it in time."

Agent Fraser turned in her seat to look directly at Joan. "I'll grant you that it is a real possibility, but it's just that—a possibility. Let's not worry about it unless it becomes a reality. And if it does become a reality, and I'm not saying it will, we are highly trained agents and we'll be able to defend you."

"Thank you, Agent Fraser." Joan leaned back in the seat, but could not help thinking, *Don't patronize me you naïve, half-trained, useless bitch. If anything happens—and I'm not saying it will—I'm fucking dead.*

Woyzeck's phone rang. The second after he answered it seemed like the air in the car became dark and heavy. Joan's panic returned.

After only a few words, he said to Fraser, "The van taking eight Legion members to prison was attacked. The guards were killed. The eight prisoners escaped."

Joan was going to say something like "I told you so" but thought better of it. She did not want to give them any reason to turn on her. "Will you now get additional assistance to protect me?"

"They're contacting the police in Altoona to send a couple cars. When we reach I-80 we'll have the interstate police escort us the rest of the way to Allenwood." He glanced at Joan in the mirror. "Happy?"

"It won't be enough." Without looking around she said, "There's a van behind us. It's been there for the last several miles."

"I saw it. It's just someone else on the road. Don't get hinked-up on us again, Bowman."

"Where did the attack happen?"

"Near Ebensburg."

"We just went past there."

"Bowman, I'm not going to warn you again. Zip it."

Before anyone knew what was happening, a van in the left passing lane drifted right. It forced Woyzeck to slam on the brakes and swerve onto the shoulder to avoid hitting it. The vehicle stopped in front of the car, forcing Woyzeck to slam on the brakes again. The van that had been following behind slammed into the back of the car. They were sandwiched between the two vans and, before the agents could draw their guns, eight armor-clad, masked men in black uniforms had assault weapons aimed at the occupants of the car. Woyzeck and Fraser knew they were outmanned and outgunned. They put their hands up.

Joan started yelling. "Do something, Woyzeck. Fraser draw your gun. Help me." The door next to Joan was yanked open and she screamed, "Don't let them take me. Do something. Help me."

The masked man reached into the car and released Joan's seatbelt. He grabbed her arm and said, "Get out."

Joan grabbed onto the headrest begging for the agents to help her. The man pulled her legs out of the car and Joan lashed out and kicked him in the jaw. Without so much as a flinch, he reached in, grabbed her by the hair, and jerked her out of the car. He dragged her by the hair toward the van in front.

As soon as she was inside, two other men jumped into the van leaving five men behind with the agents. In the van, she pleaded with her kidnappers to let her go. She tried everything to convince them they did not want to turn her over to the Legion. The van was speeding and it was hard to maintain her balance, but she begged for her release the entire ten minutes until the van screeched to a halt. She would have cracked her head against the back of the driver's seat if one of her kidnappers hadn't grabbed her. The man who had dragged her into the van reached over and unlocked her handcuffs. He opened the door and pushed her out. "Wait here. Your ride will be here in a few minutes."

Joan she scrambled to her knees and rubbed her wrists.

"And Joan."

She looked up at the sound of the familiar voice. "Jason?"

"We're even." He looked over his shoulder, at the other men in the van, then looked back at her. "I'm sorry for not helping you before. I hope we cross paths again."

He slid the door shut and the van sped away kicking up small bits of gravel.

She watched it disappear from sight.

The silence and the isolation were overpowering. For the first time in months, she was alone. Alone at a crossroads near a ramshackle building that looked like it might have been a roadside vegetable stand a half century ago. She kicked at the usual human trash found anywhere on the roadsides in America as she searched her mind for clues as to why she was here and who might be picking her up. The bazaar nature of the situation was slowly becoming overwhelming when there were sounds of a vehicle approaching.

She ducked behind the vegetable stand. A pick-up truck hauling a horse trailer drove by. She watched the black horse tail outside the back of the trailer until it was too small to see.

Well, she was free. Maybe nobody was coming for her. She leaned against the south side of the building and rested her head on a faded, red-and-white Coca Cola sign. *A Coke would be good right about now.*

She waited by the quiet, country roadside, and tried to figure out who was coming. A plane burred in the distance. She could hear a motorcycle long before it reached her. It was coming from the opposite side of the building, so the driver didn't see her as it whizzed by and disappeared in the distance like the truck and horse trailer before it.

Another vehicle approached. Slower than the ones before it, as if it had purpose. Joan's heart slammed against the inside of her chest. Her first instinct was to run, hide, regroup. But instead she stepped from behind the building and walked through the short expanse of weeds toward the vehicle, a white, circa 1970 Blazer. It inched toward her as she rubbed her wrists and faced her fate—freedom or death.

The Blazer rattled and squeaked to a stop right in front of her. The blacked out passenger window rolled down. Duncan leaned across the bench seat toward her. "Waiting for a ride?"

Joan checked the front seat—no weapon. No holster on his belt. She checked the back seat, relaxed, and crossed her arms on the door. "Very funny. Where are you going?"

"Some place hot."

She snorted. "Aren't we all?"

Duncan looked through the windshield, at nothing in particular, then back at her. "Look, Joan, I don't know how long we'll be free—five minutes or five years. All I know is that I want to spend every second of that time with you. How about it?"

"Why?" *Be careful.* "I mean, I betrayed you."

Duncan shook his head slowly. "You did what you thought was the right thing to do. You didn't second guess yourself or anyone else. When you decided on a course of action, you acted on it. I love that in a woman." He pinned her with his gaze. "I love that about you."

She sucked in a breath and waited until she was sure her voice would be steady. "But aren't you afraid I'd do it again? How can you trust me?"

"I can trust that you'll do the right thing." A half-smile graced his lips. "I just have to make sure I'm part of that right thing from now on." He gave a nod with his head, indicating for her to get into his SUV. "What do you say?"

Joan opened the door and climbed in. "Well, we're already free. The only thing better than that is to be free together."

No one was there to see them drive out of sight.

About the Author

After 22 years in the Army, Janet McClintock exhaled and settled down in Pittsburgh with her aging Pit Bull. She has completed two novels of her four-part Iron Angel action series, the first of which is *Worst of All Evils*. While she edits the second book in the series, she is trying her hand at a paranormal novel before returning to her passion—action.

Action comes easy to McClintock. Over the years, she has owned motorcycles and horses and driven a tractor trailer across the country. She has trained in various martial arts over the past 38 years and is currently training in Kali and Jeet Kun Do. She is also a certified Edged Weapons Combatives Instructor.

16764085R00179

Made in the USA
Middletown, DE
25 November 2018